# DISNEY MASTERS

## DONALD DUCK: THE FORGETFUL HERO

*by Giorgio Cavazzano*

Publisher: GARY GROTH
Editor: J. MICHAEL CATRON
Archival Editor: DAVID GERSTEIN
Designer: KEELI McCARTHY
Production: PAUL BARESH and CHRISTINA HWANG
Associate Publisher: ERIC REYNOLDS

Disney Masters showcases the work of internationally acclaimed Disney artists. Many of the stories presented in the Disney Masters series appear in English for the first time. This is Disney Masters Volume 12. Permission to quote or reproduce material for reviews must be obtained from the publisher.

Fantagraphics Books, Inc.
7563 Lake City Way NE
Seattle WA 98115
(800) 657-1100

Visit us at fantagraphics.com. Follow us on Twitter at @fantagraphics and on Facebook at facebook.com/fantagraphics.

Cover and title page art by Giorgio Cavazzano, color by Max Monteduro
Thanks to Paolo Castagno, Christos Kentrotis, Anne Marie Mersing, and Solveig Thime

First printing: October 2020
ISBN 978-1-68396-312-7
Printed in China
Library of Congress Control Number: 2017956971

The stories in this volume were originally published in Italy and appear here in English for the first time.
"Plantastic Voyage" ("Zio Paperone e l'operazione foglia") in *Topolino* #1455, October 16, 1983 (I TL 1455-BP)
"The Dazzling Duck She-Venger" ("Paperinika e il filo di Arianna") in *Topolino* #906, April 8, 1973 (I TL 906-C)
"The Case of the Cut-Off Calls" ("Topolino e il mistero della voce spezzata") in *Topolino* #1834, January 20, 1991 (I TL 1834-AP)
"The Forgetful Hero" ("Paperino e l'eroico smemorato") in *Topolino* #1059, March 14, 1976 (I TL 1059-A)

# Walt Disney
# Donald Duck
# The Forgetful Hero

FANTAGRAPHICS BOOKS

SEATTLE

# CONTENTS

*The stories in this volume are presented here in their entirety as first created in 1973–1991.*

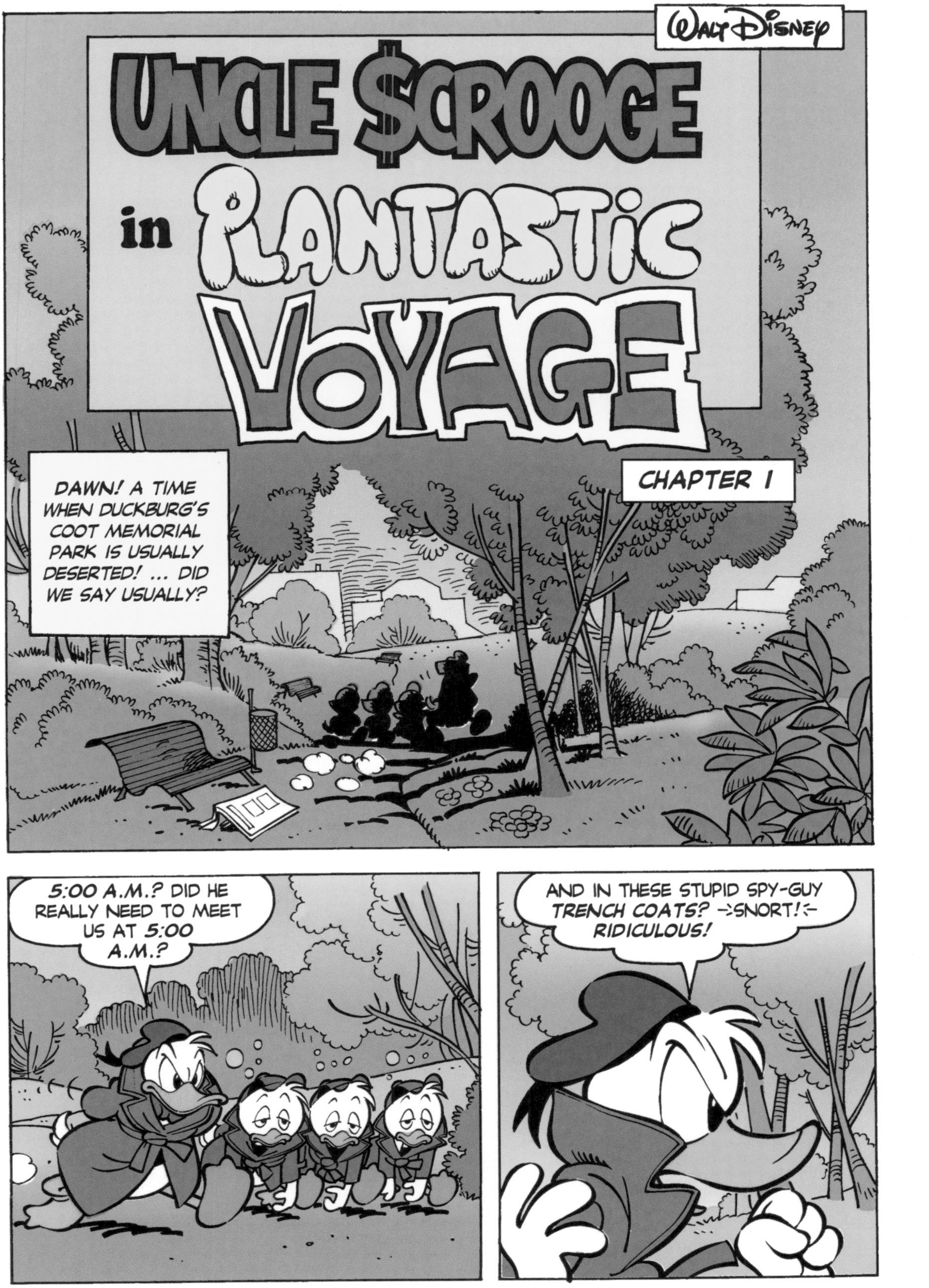
WALT DISNEY
UNCLE $CROOGE
in PLANTASTIC VOYAGE
CHAPTER 1
DAWN! A TIME WHEN DUCKBURG'S COOT MEMORIAL PARK IS USUALLY DESERTED! ... DID WE SAY USUALLY?
5:00 A.M.? DID HE REALLY NEED TO MEET US AT 5:00 A.M.?
AND IN THESE STUPID SPY-GUY TRENCH COATS? -SNORT!- RIDICULOUS!

STORY BY FABIO MICHELINI • ART BY GIORGIO CAVAZZANO • TRANSLATION AND DIALOGUE BY JOE TORCIVIA
EDITING BY J. MICHAEL CATRON AND DAVID GERSTEIN

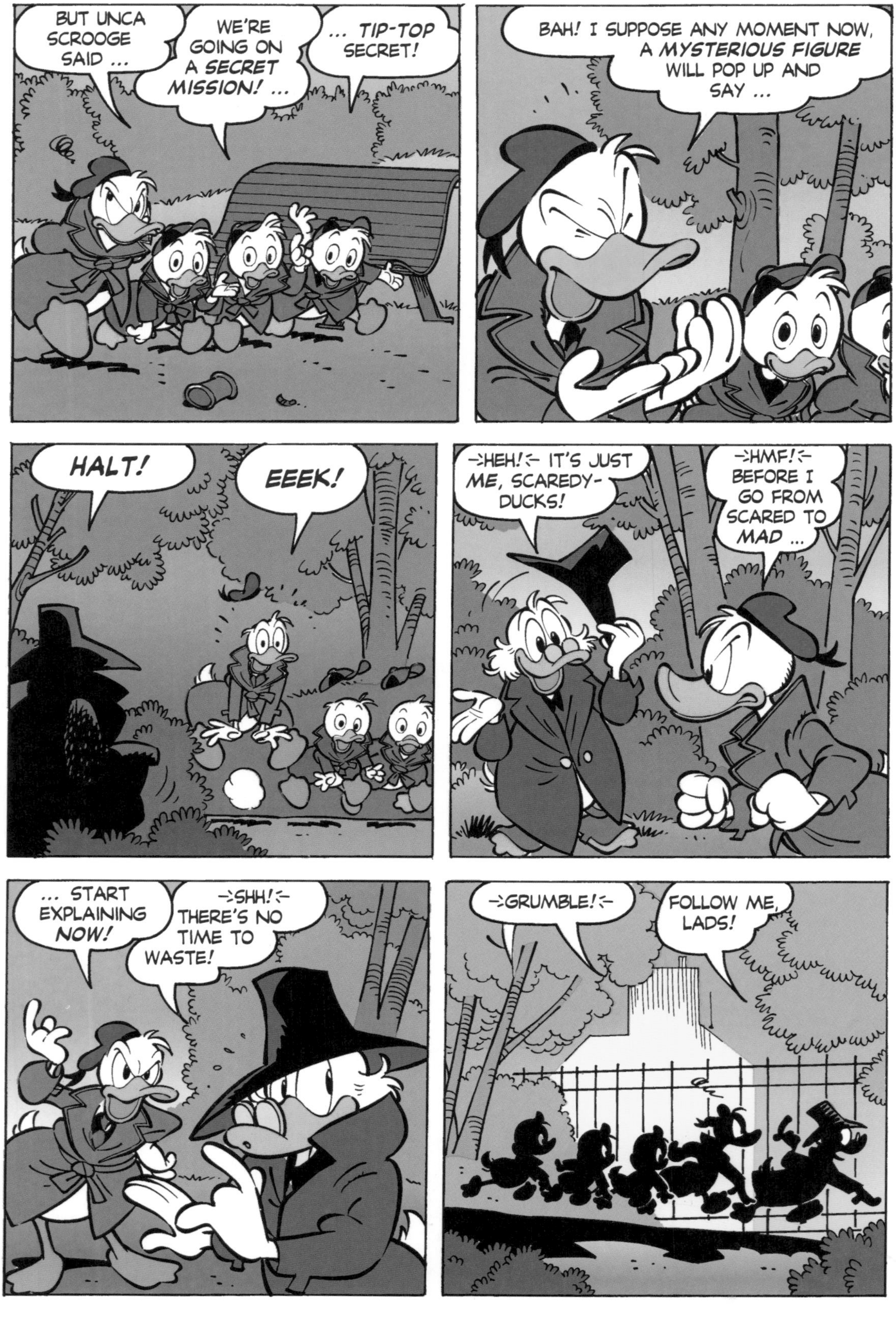
BUT UNCA SCROOGE SAID ...
WE'RE GOING ON A *SECRET MISSION!* ...
... *TIP-TOP* SECRET!
BAH! I SUPPOSE ANY MOMENT NOW, A *MYSTERIOUS FIGURE* WILL POP UP AND SAY ...
*HALT!*
*EEEK!*
-HEH!- IT'S JUST *ME*, SCAREDY-DUCKS!
-HMF!- BEFORE I GO FROM SCARED TO *MAD* ...
... START EXPLAINING *NOW!*
-SHH!- THERE'S NO TIME TO WASTE!
-GRUMBLE!-
FOLLOW ME, LADS!

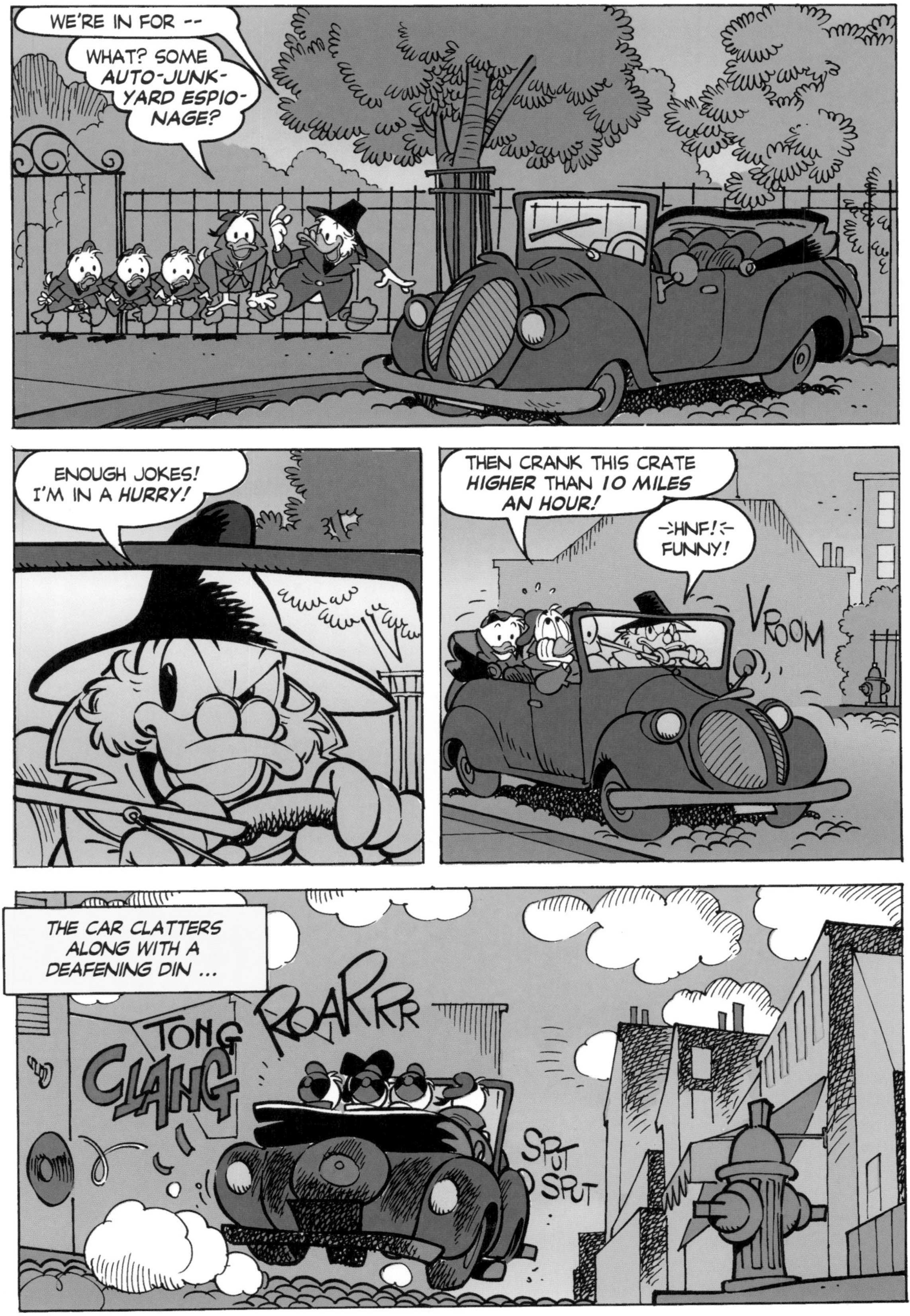
WE'RE IN FOR --
WHAT? SOME AUTO-JUNK-YARD ESPIONAGE?
ENOUGH JOKES! I'M IN A HURRY!
THEN CRANK THIS CRATE HIGHER THAN 10 MILES AN HOUR!
HNF! FUNNY!
VROOM
THE CAR CLATTERS ALONG WITH A DEAFENING DIN ...
ROARRRR
TONG
CLANG
SPUT SPUT

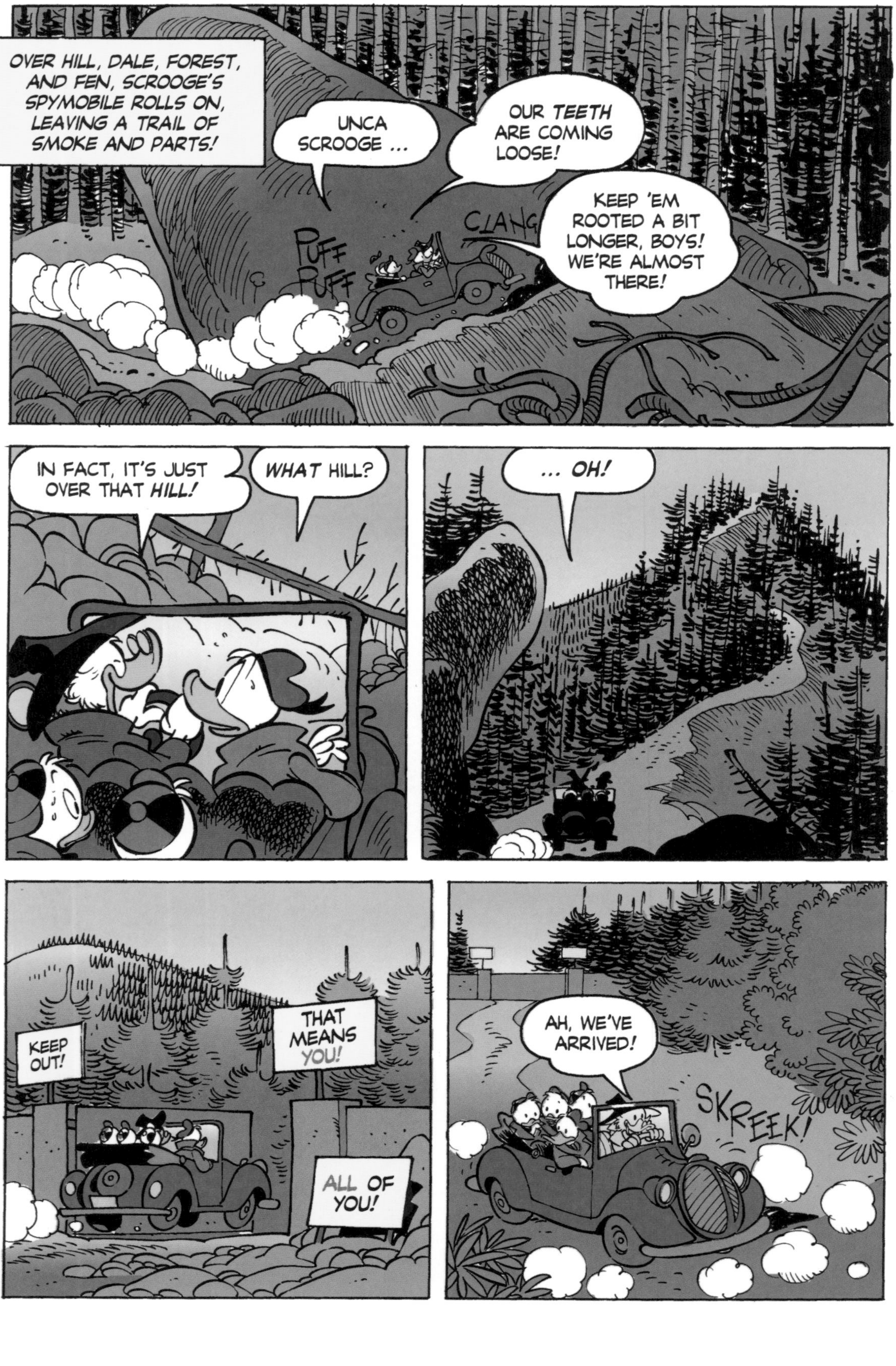
OVER HILL, DALE, FOREST, AND FEN, SCROOGE'S SPYMOBILE ROLLS ON, LEAVING A TRAIL OF SMOKE AND PARTS!
UNCA SCROOGE ...
OUR TEETH ARE COMING LOOSE!
PUFF PUFF
CLANG
KEEP 'EM ROOTED A BIT LONGER, BOYS! WE'RE ALMOST THERE!
IN FACT, IT'S JUST OVER THAT HILL!
WHAT HILL?
... OH!
KEEP OUT!
THAT MEANS YOU!
ALL OF YOU!
AH, WE'VE ARRIVED!
SKREEK!

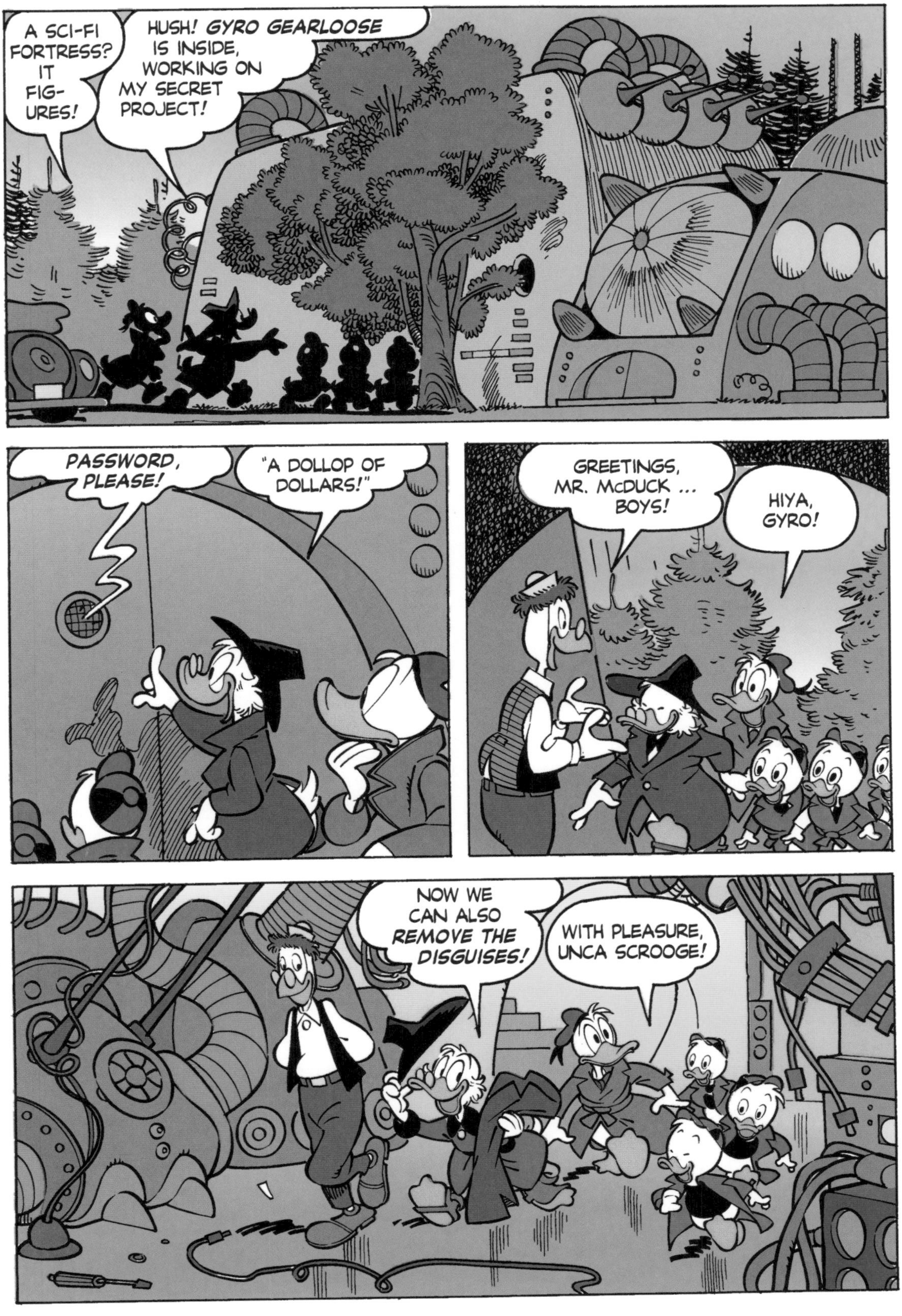
A SCI-FI FORTRESS? IT FIG-URES!
HUSH! GYRO GEARLOOSE IS INSIDE, WORKING ON MY SECRET PROJECT!
PASSWORD, PLEASE!
"A DOLLOP OF DOLLARS!"
GREETINGS, MR. McDUCK ... BOYS!
HIYA, GYRO!
NOW WE CAN ALSO REMOVE THE DISGUISES!
WITH PLEASURE, UNCA SCROOGE!

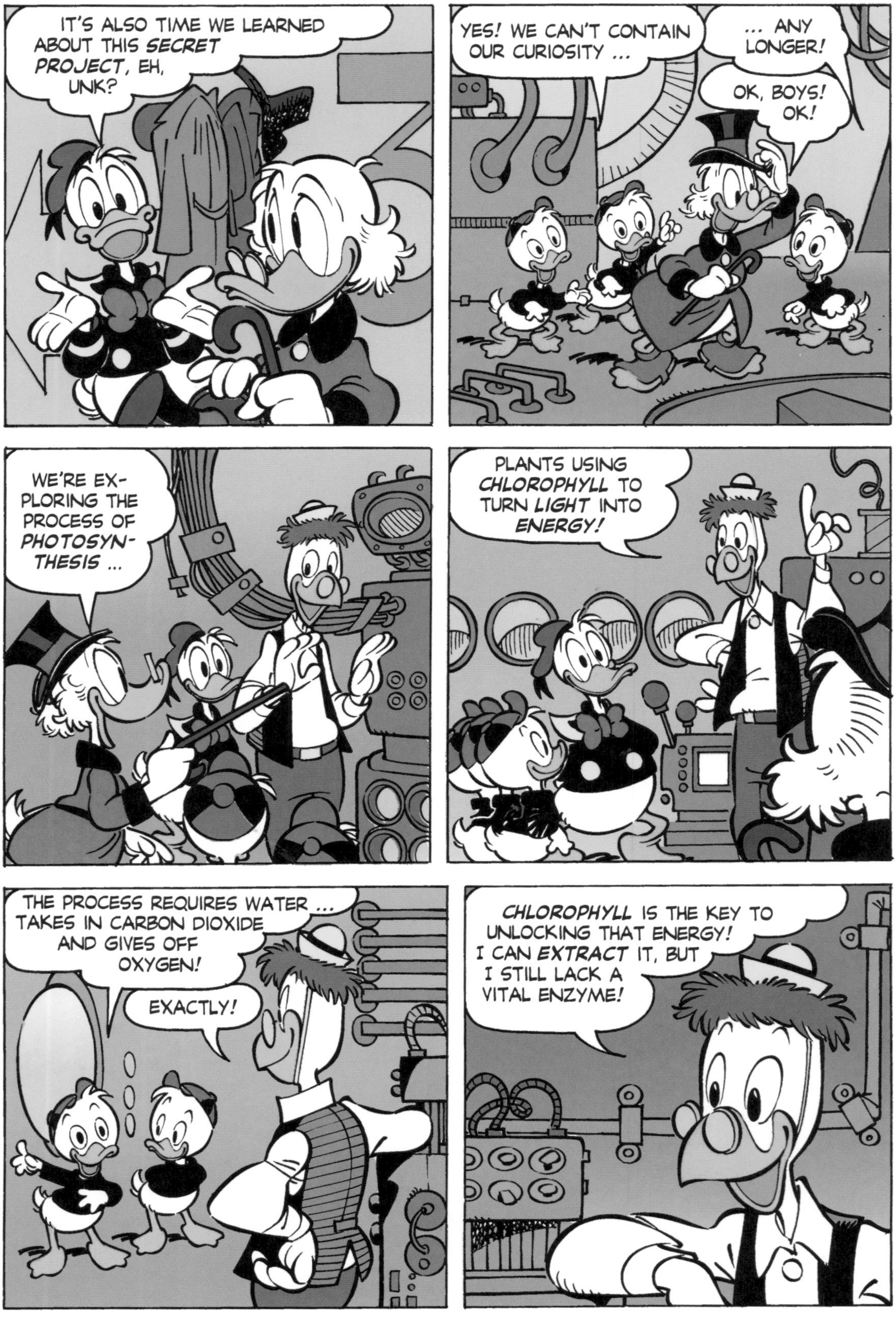
IT'S ALSO TIME WE LEARNED ABOUT THIS *SECRET PROJECT*, EH, UNK?
YES! WE CAN'T CONTAIN OUR CURIOSITY ...
... ANY LONGER!
OK, BOYS! OK!
WE'RE EXPLORING THE PROCESS OF *PHOTOSYNTHESIS* ...
PLANTS USING *CHLOROPHYLL* TO TURN *LIGHT* INTO *ENERGY!*
THE PROCESS REQUIRES WATER ... TAKES IN CARBON DIOXIDE AND GIVES OFF OXYGEN!
EXACTLY!
*CHLOROPHYLL* IS THE KEY TO UNLOCKING THAT ENERGY! I CAN *EXTRACT* IT, BUT I STILL LACK A VITAL ENZYME!

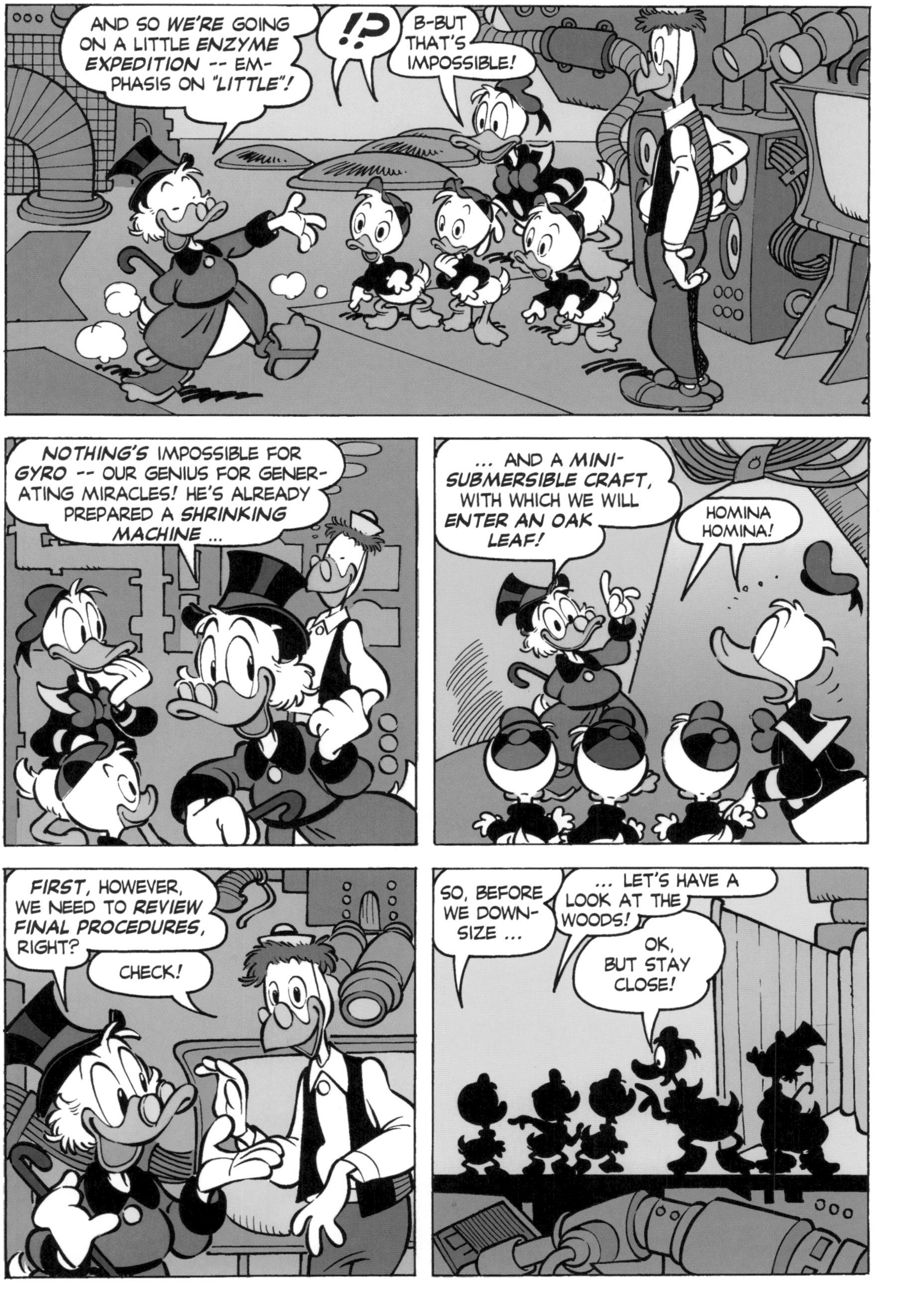
AND SO WE'RE GOING ON A LITTLE ENZYME EXPEDITION -- EMPHASIS ON "LITTLE"!
!?
B-BUT THAT'S IMPOSSIBLE!
NOTHING'S IMPOSSIBLE FOR GYRO -- OUR GENIUS FOR GENERATING MIRACLES! HE'S ALREADY PREPARED A SHRINKING MACHINE ...
... AND A MINI-SUBMERSIBLE CRAFT, WITH WHICH WE WILL ENTER AN OAK LEAF!
HOMINA HOMINA!
FIRST, HOWEVER, WE NEED TO REVIEW FINAL PROCEDURES, RIGHT?
CHECK!
SO, BEFORE WE DOWNSIZE ...
... LET'S HAVE A LOOK AT THE WOODS!
OK, BUT STAY CLOSE!

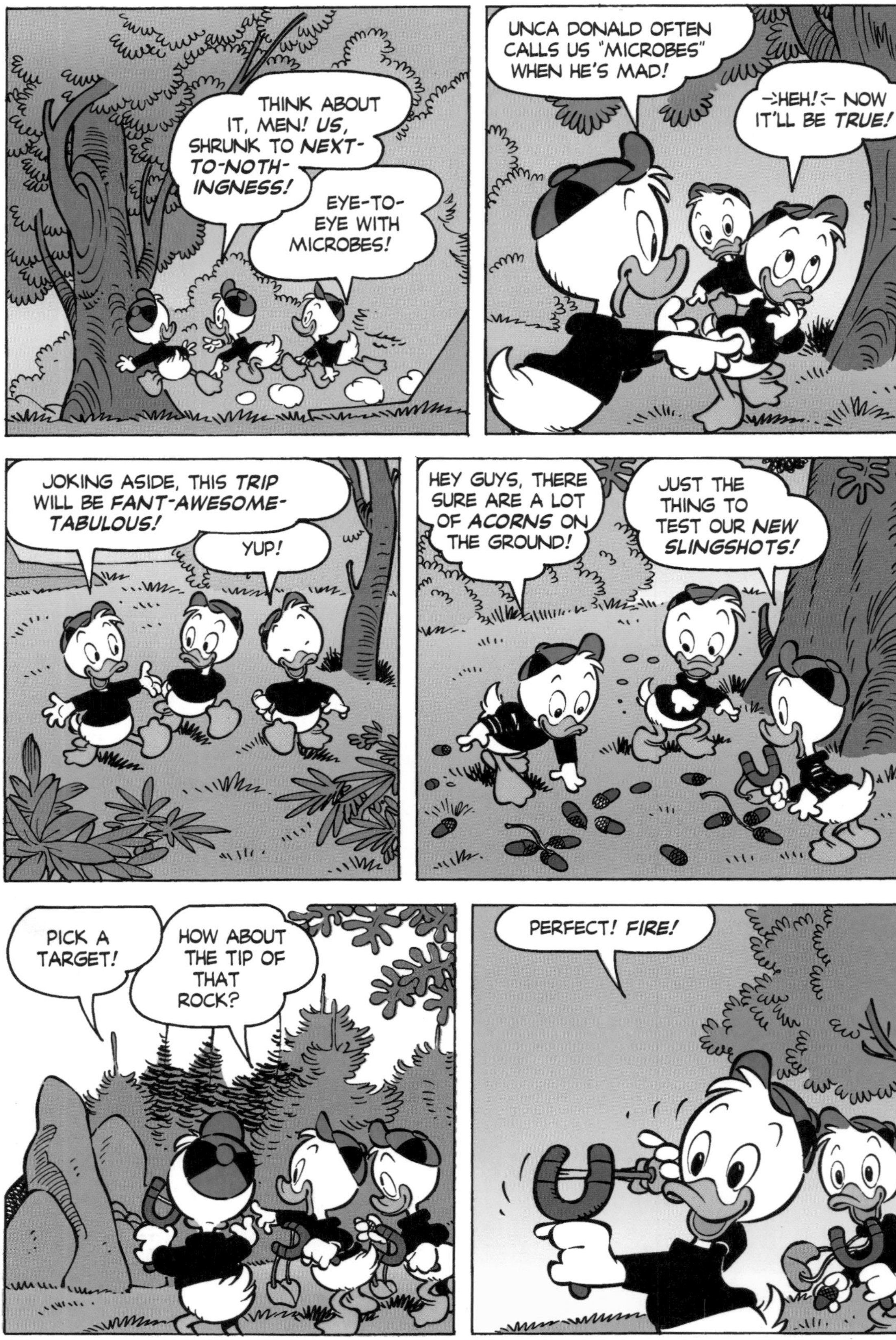
THINK ABOUT IT, MEN! US, SHRUNK TO NEXT-TO-NOTHINGNESS!
EYE-TO-EYE WITH MICROBES!
UNCA DONALD OFTEN CALLS US "MICROBES" WHEN HE'S MAD!
HEH! NOW IT'LL BE TRUE!
JOKING ASIDE, THIS TRIP WILL BE FANT-AWESOME-TABULOUS!
YUP!
HEY GUYS, THERE SURE ARE A LOT OF ACORNS ON THE GROUND!
JUST THE THING TO TEST OUR NEW SLINGSHOTS!
PICK A TARGET!
HOW ABOUT THE TIP OF THAT ROCK?
PERFECT! FIRE!

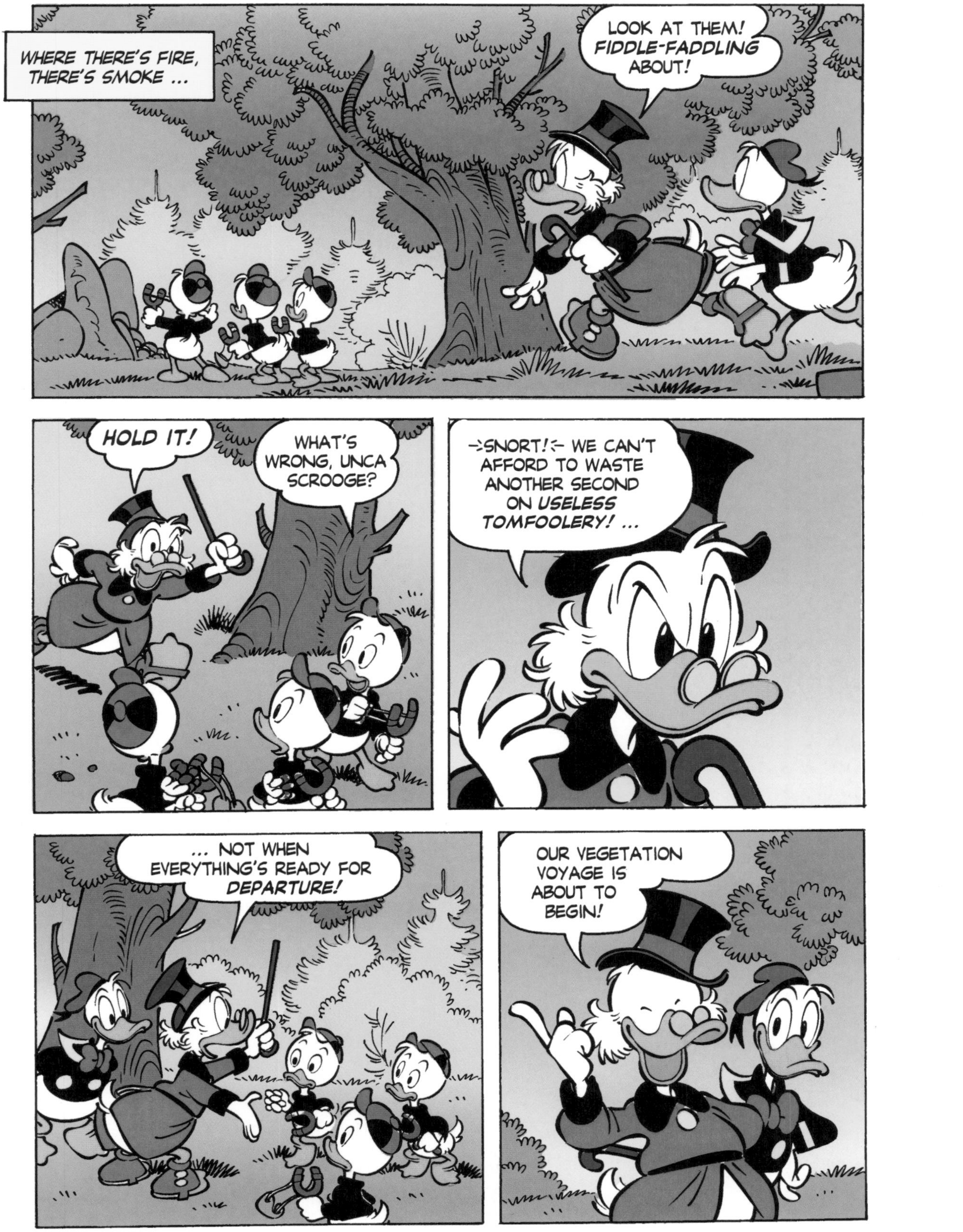
WHERE THERE'S FIRE, THERE'S SMOKE ...
LOOK AT THEM! FIDDLE-FADDLING ABOUT!
HOLD IT!
WHAT'S WRONG, UNCA SCROOGE?
-SNORT!- WE CAN'T AFFORD TO WASTE ANOTHER SECOND ON USELESS TOMFOOLERY! ...
... NOT WHEN EVERYTHING'S READY FOR DEPARTURE!
OUR VEGETATION VOYAGE IS ABOUT TO BEGIN!

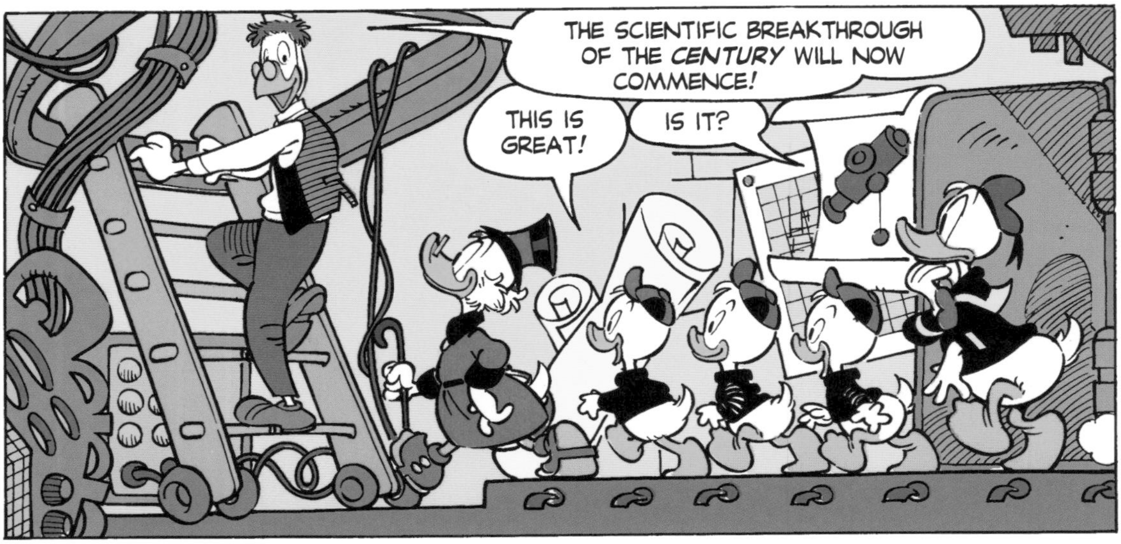
THE SCIENTIFIC BREAKTHROUGH OF THE *CENTURY* WILL NOW COMMENCE!
THIS IS GREAT!
IS IT?

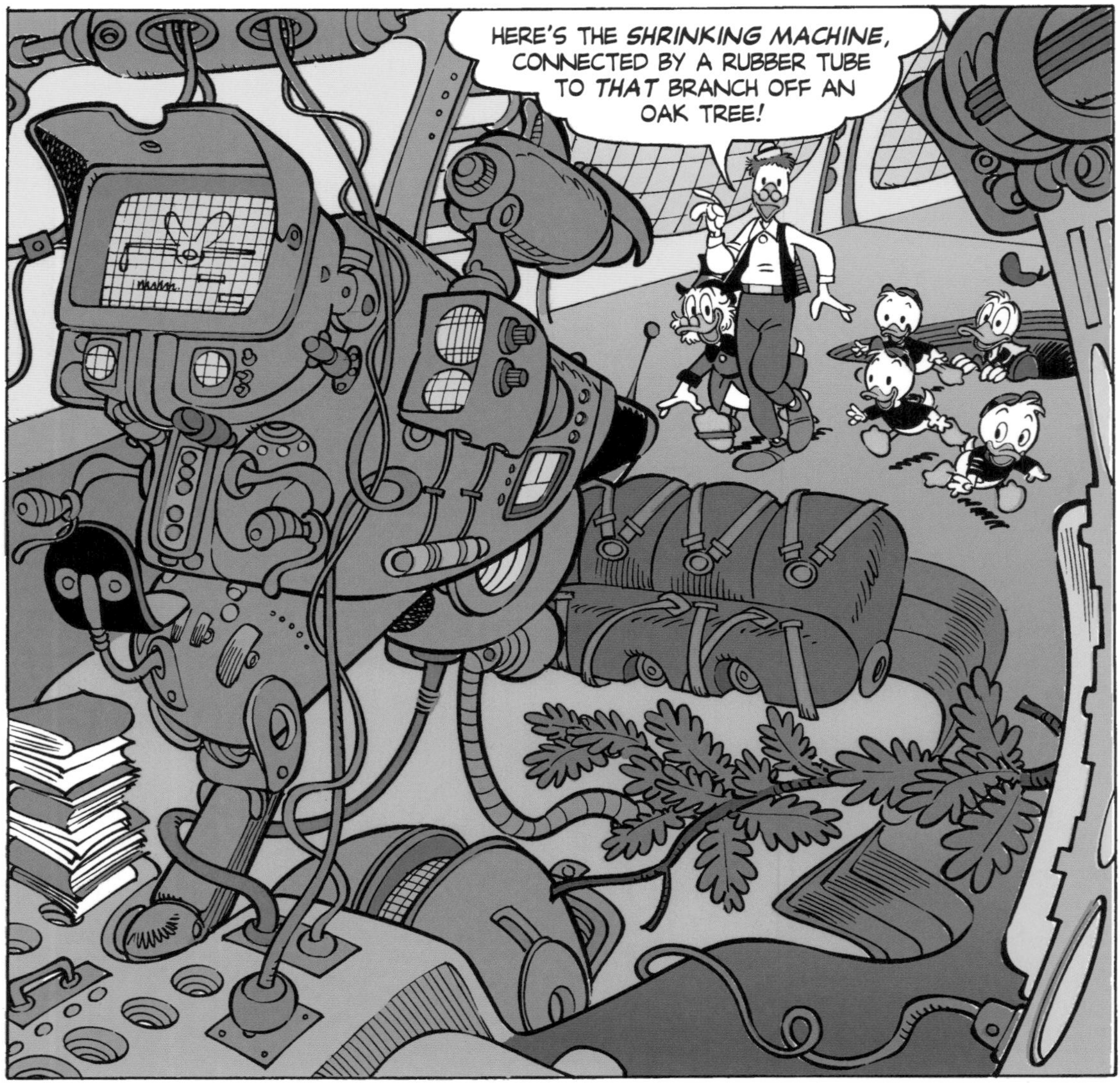
HERE'S THE *SHRINKING MACHINE*, CONNECTED BY A RUBBER TUBE TO *THAT* BRANCH OFF AN OAK TREE!

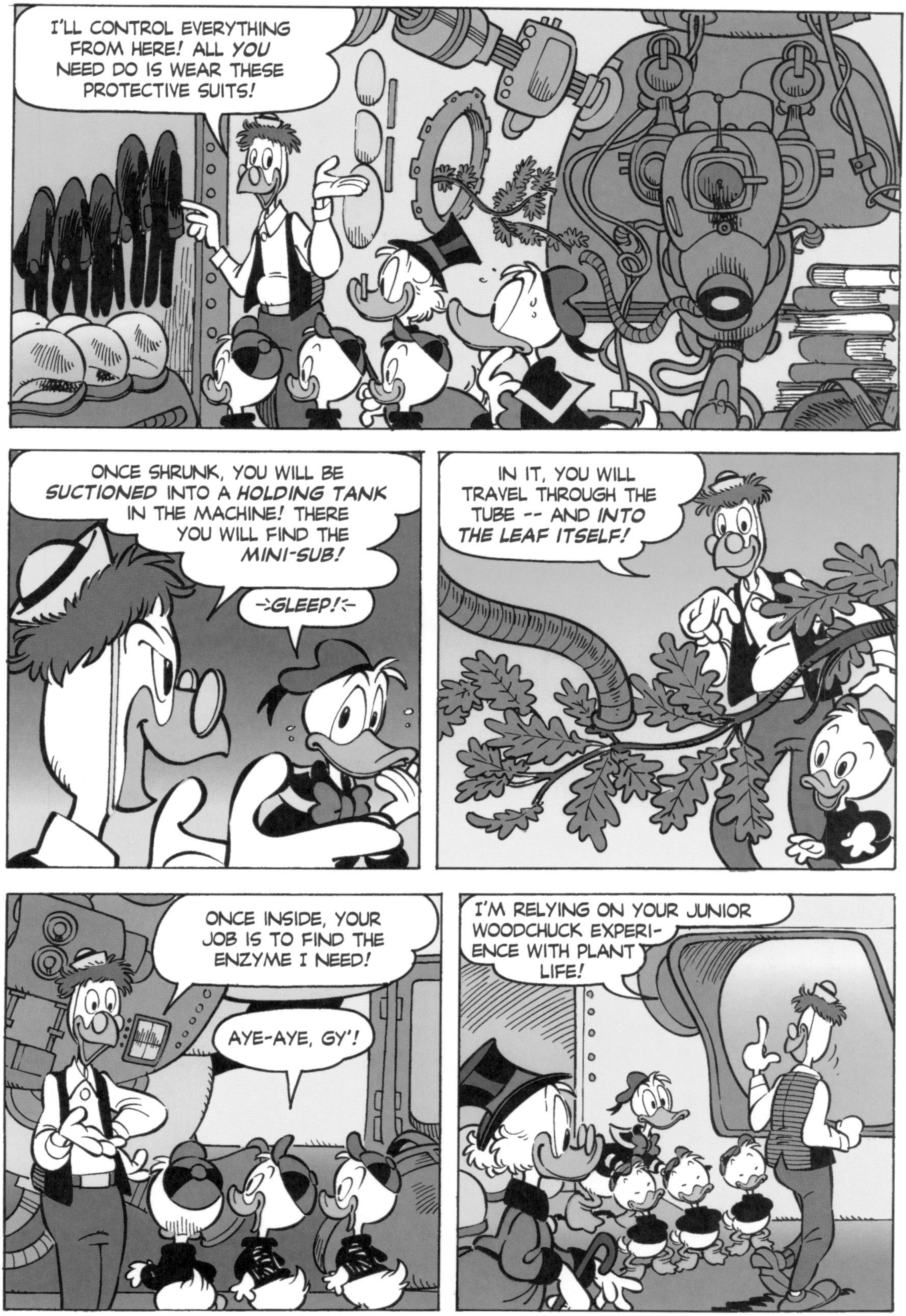
I'LL CONTROL EVERYTHING FROM HERE! ALL YOU NEED DO IS WEAR THESE PROTECTIVE SUITS!
ONCE SHRUNK, YOU WILL BE SUCTIONED INTO A HOLDING TANK IN THE MACHINE! THERE YOU WILL FIND THE MINI-SUB!
-GLEEP!-
IN IT, YOU WILL TRAVEL THROUGH THE TUBE -- AND INTO THE LEAF ITSELF!
ONCE INSIDE, YOUR JOB IS TO FIND THE ENZYME I NEED!
AYE-AYE, GY'!
I'M RELYING ON YOUR JUNIOR WOODCHUCK EXPERI-ENCE WITH PLANT LIFE!

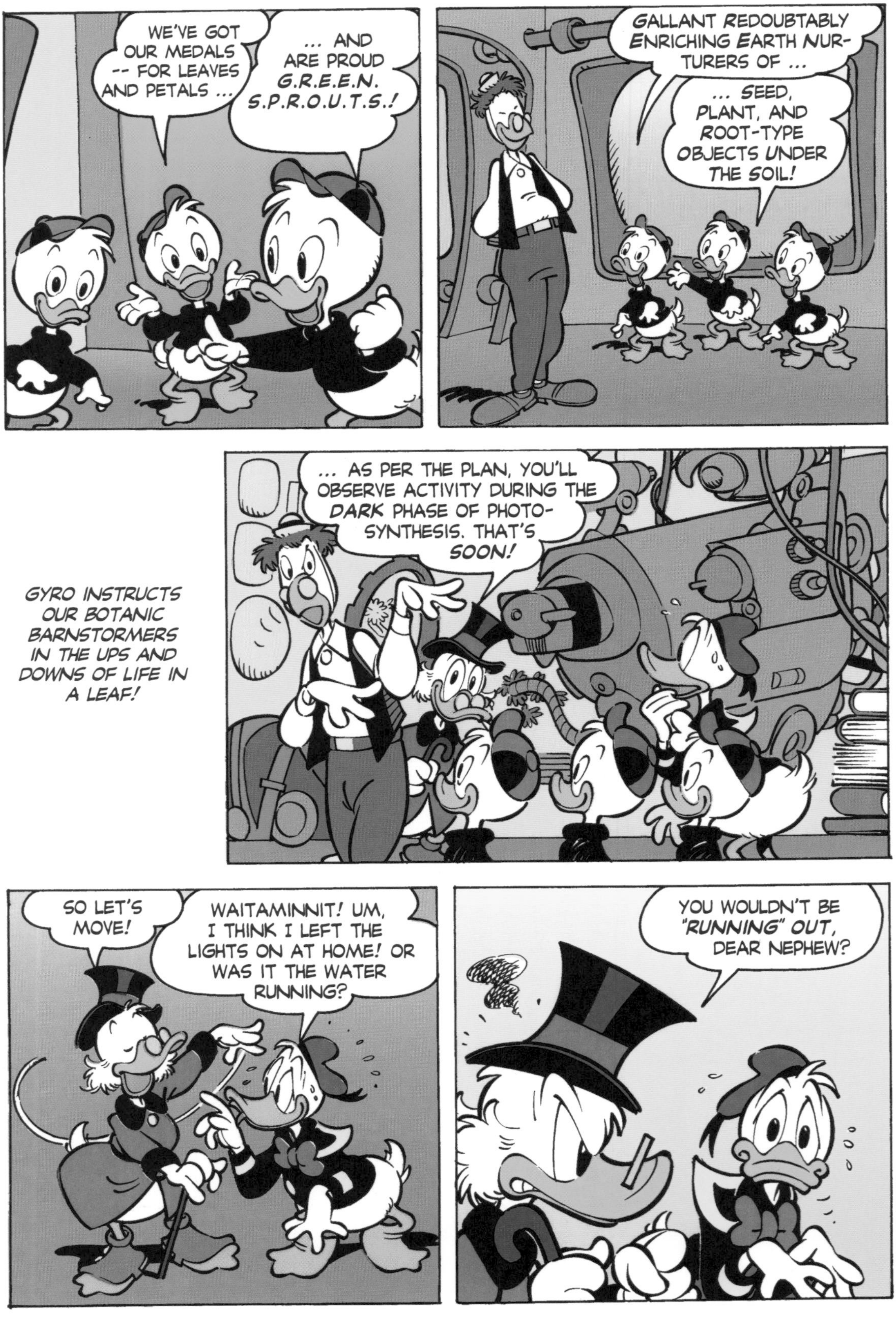
WE'VE GOT OUR MEDALS -- FOR LEAVES AND PETALS ...
... AND ARE PROUD G.R.E.E.N. S.P.R.O.U.T.S.!
GALLANT REDOUBTABLY ENRICHING EARTH NURTURERS OF ...
... SEED, PLANT, AND ROOT-TYPE OBJECTS UNDER THE SOIL!
GYRO INSTRUCTS OUR BOTANIC BARNSTORMERS IN THE UPS AND DOWNS OF LIFE IN A LEAF!
... AS PER THE PLAN, YOU'LL OBSERVE ACTIVITY DURING THE DARK PHASE OF PHOTOSYNTHESIS. THAT'S SOON!
SO LET'S MOVE!
WAITAMINNIT! UM, I THINK I LEFT THE LIGHTS ON AT HOME! OR WAS IT THE WATER RUNNING?
YOU WOULDN'T BE "RUNNING" OUT, DEAR NEPHEW?

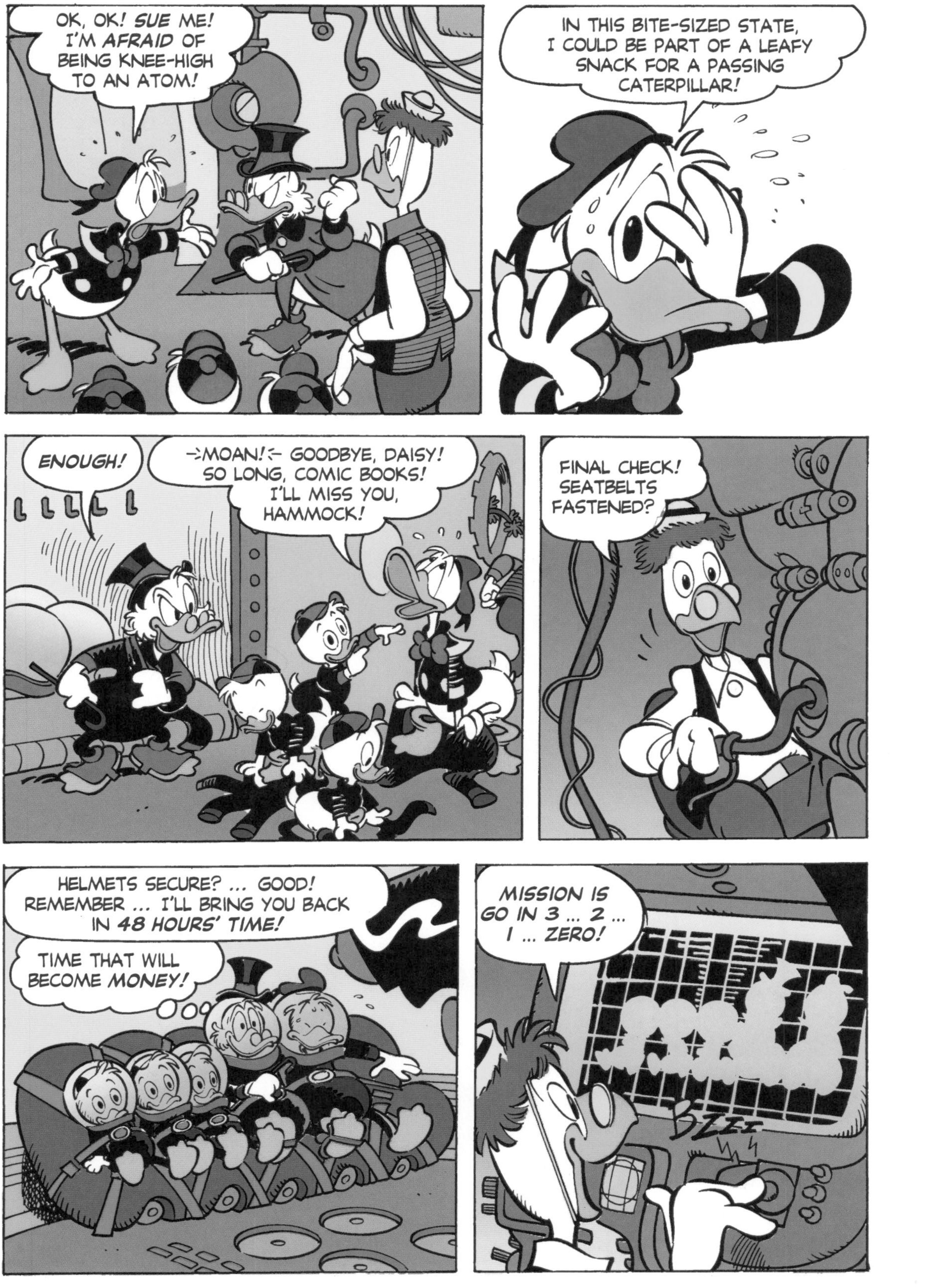
OK, OK! SUE ME! I'M AFRAID OF BEING KNEE-HIGH TO AN ATOM!
IN THIS BITE-SIZED STATE, I COULD BE PART OF A LEAFY SNACK FOR A PASSING CATERPILLAR!
ENOUGH!
→MOAN!← GOODBYE, DAISY! SO LONG, COMIC BOOKS! I'LL MISS YOU, HAMMOCK!
FINAL CHECK! SEATBELTS FASTENED?
HELMETS SECURE? ... GOOD! REMEMBER ... I'LL BRING YOU BACK IN 48 HOURS' TIME!
TIME THAT WILL BECOME MONEY!
MISSION IS GO IN 3 ... 2 ... 1 ... ZERO!
BZZZ

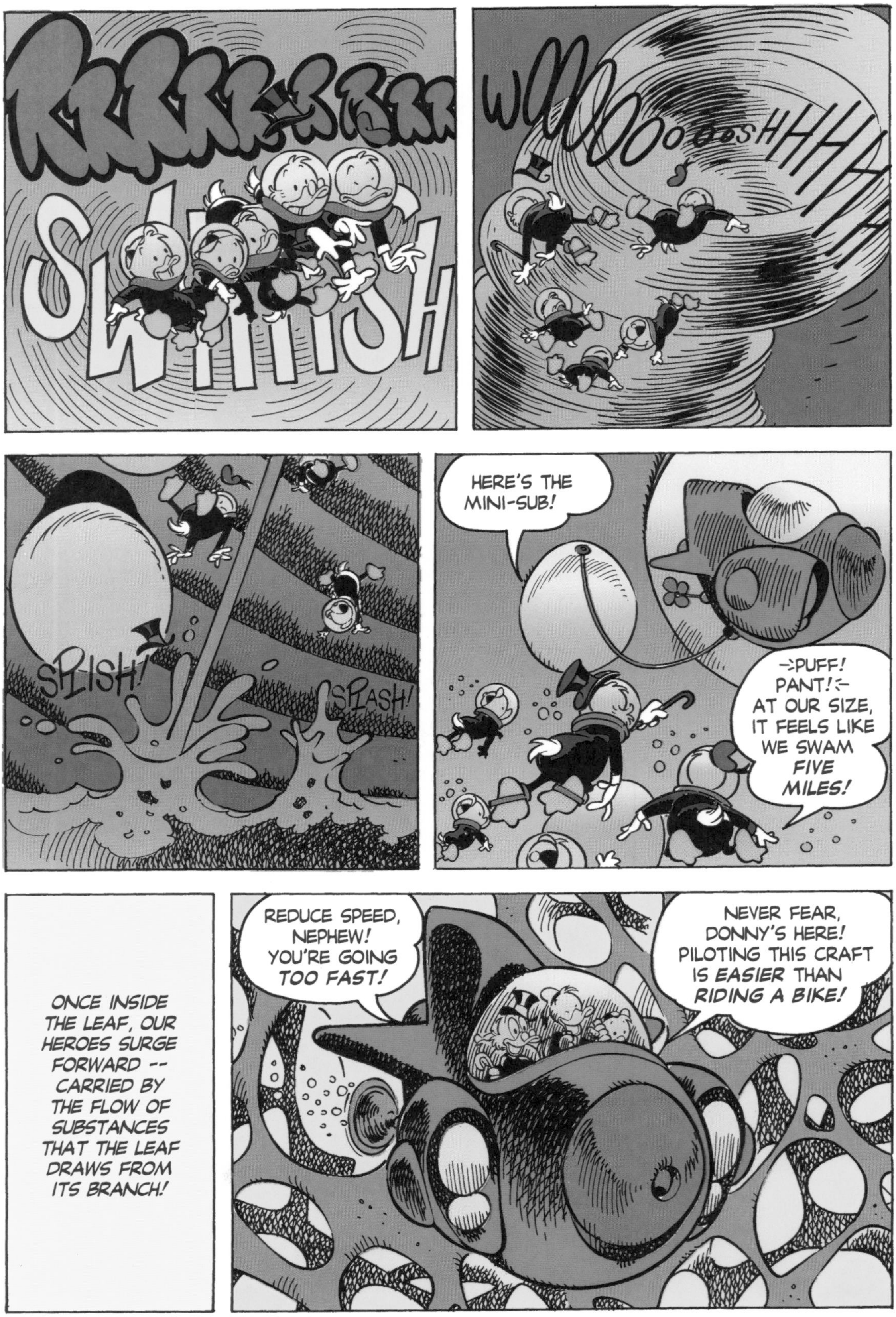
SPLISH!
SPLASH!
HERE'S THE MINI-SUB!
–PUFF! PANT!– AT OUR SIZE, IT FEELS LIKE WE SWAM FIVE MILES!
ONCE INSIDE THE LEAF, OUR HEROES SURGE FORWARD -- CARRIED BY THE FLOW OF SUBSTANCES THAT THE LEAF DRAWS FROM ITS BRANCH!
REDUCE SPEED, NEPHEW! YOU'RE GOING TOO FAST!
NEVER FEAR, DONNY'S HERE! PILOTING THIS CRAFT IS EASIER THAN RIDING A BIKE!

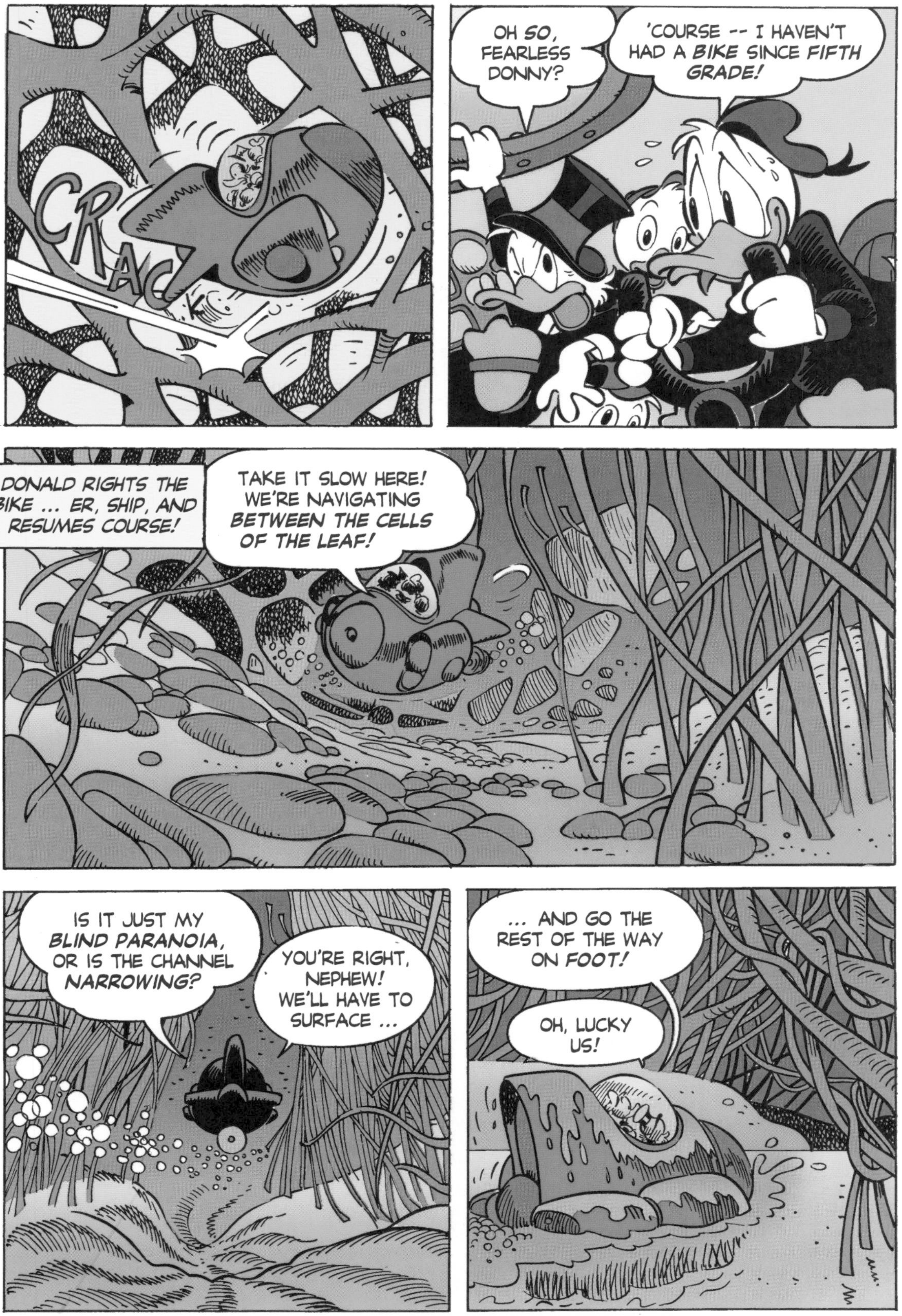
CRACK
OH SO, FEARLESS DONNY?
'COURSE -- I HAVEN'T HAD A BIKE SINCE FIFTH GRADE!
DONALD RIGHTS THE BIKE ... ER, SHIP, AND RESUMES COURSE!
TAKE IT SLOW HERE! WE'RE NAVIGATING BETWEEN THE CELLS OF THE LEAF!
IS IT JUST MY BLIND PARANOIA, OR IS THE CHANNEL NARROWING?
YOU'RE RIGHT, NEPHEW! WE'LL HAVE TO SURFACE ...
... AND GO THE REST OF THE WAY ON FOOT!
OH, LUCKY US!

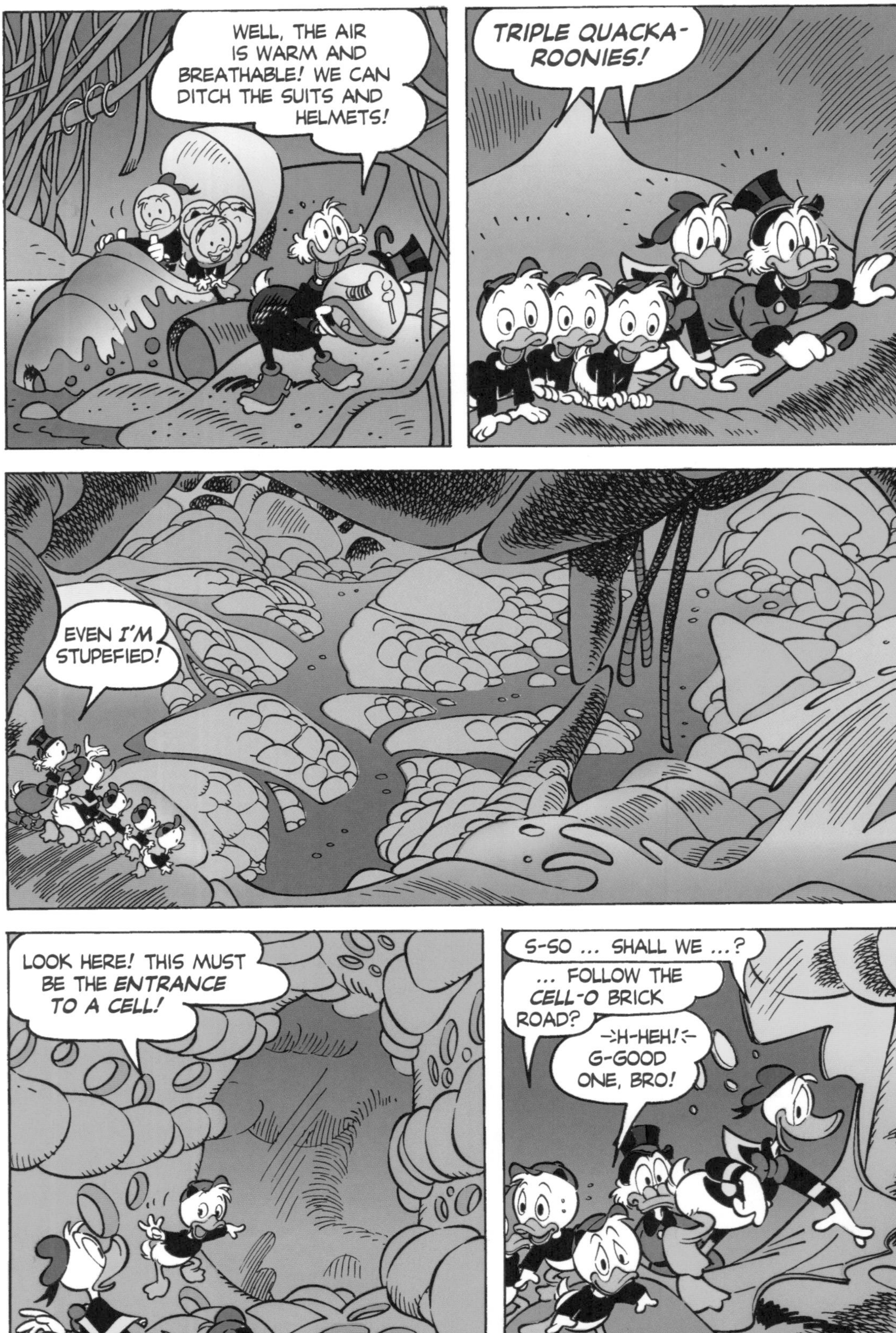
WELL, THE AIR IS WARM AND BREATHABLE! WE CAN DITCH THE SUITS AND HELMETS!
TRIPLE QUACKA-ROONIES!
EVEN I'M STUPEFIED!
LOOK HERE! THIS MUST BE THE ENTRANCE TO A CELL!
S-SO ... SHALL WE ...?
... FOLLOW THE CELL-O BRICK ROAD?
H-HEH! G-GOOD ONE, BRO!

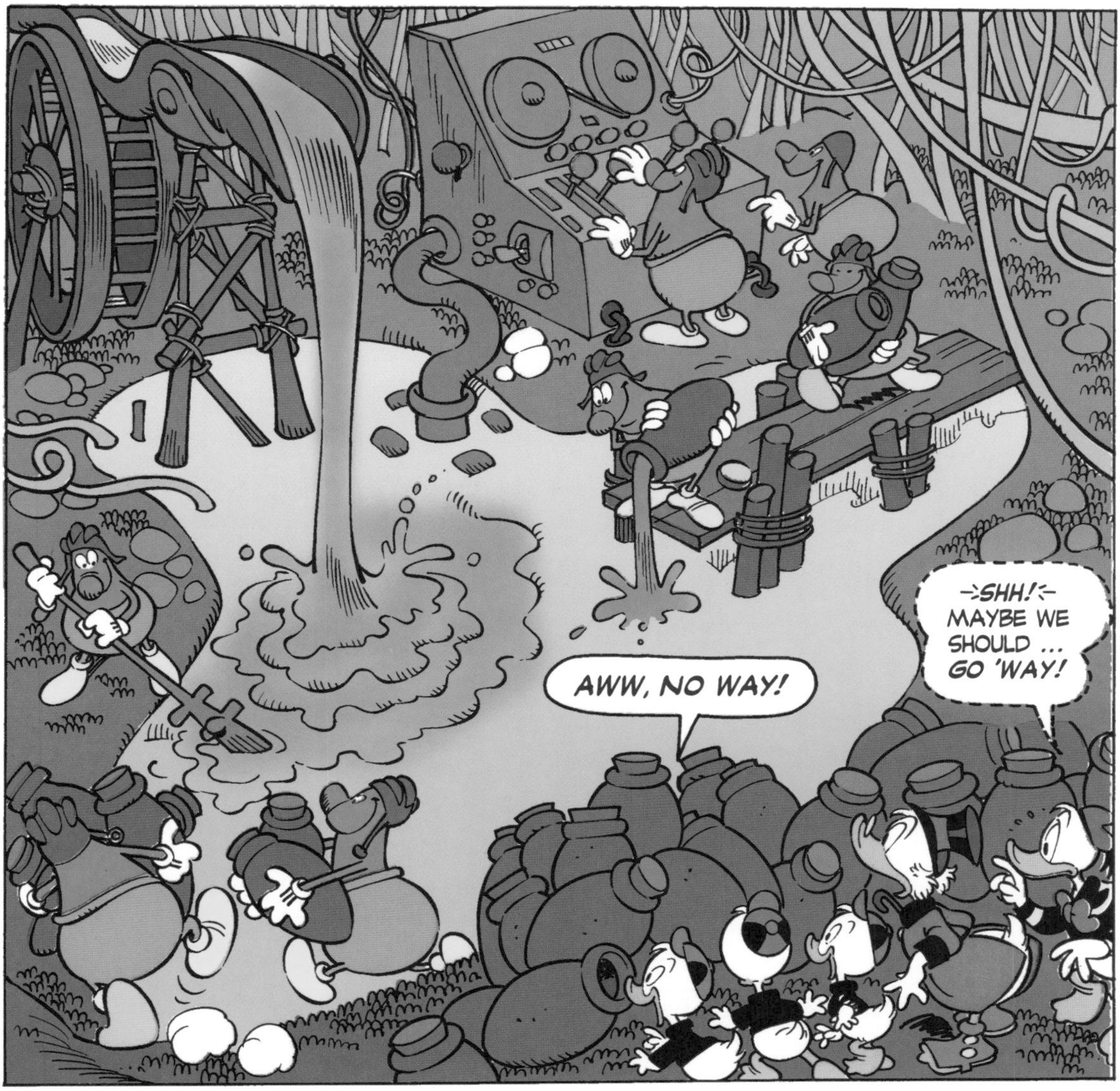
AWW, NO WAY!
-SHH!- MAYBE WE SHOULD ... GO 'WAY!

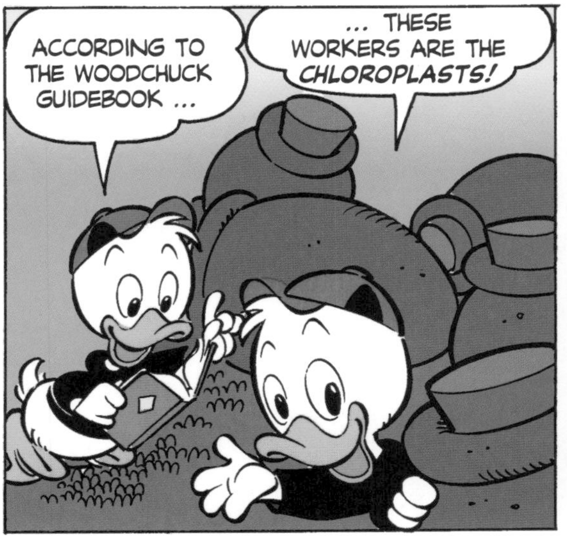
ACCORDING TO THE WOODCHUCK GUIDEBOOK ...
... THESE WORKERS ARE THE CHLOROPLASTS!

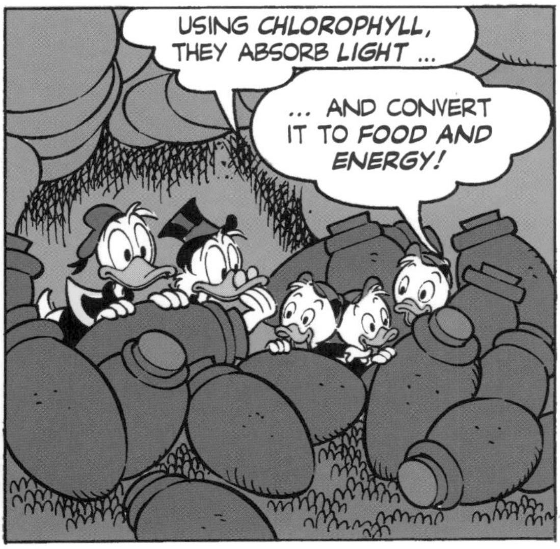
USING CHLOROPHYLL, THEY ABSORB LIGHT ...
... AND CONVERT IT TO FOOD AND ENERGY!

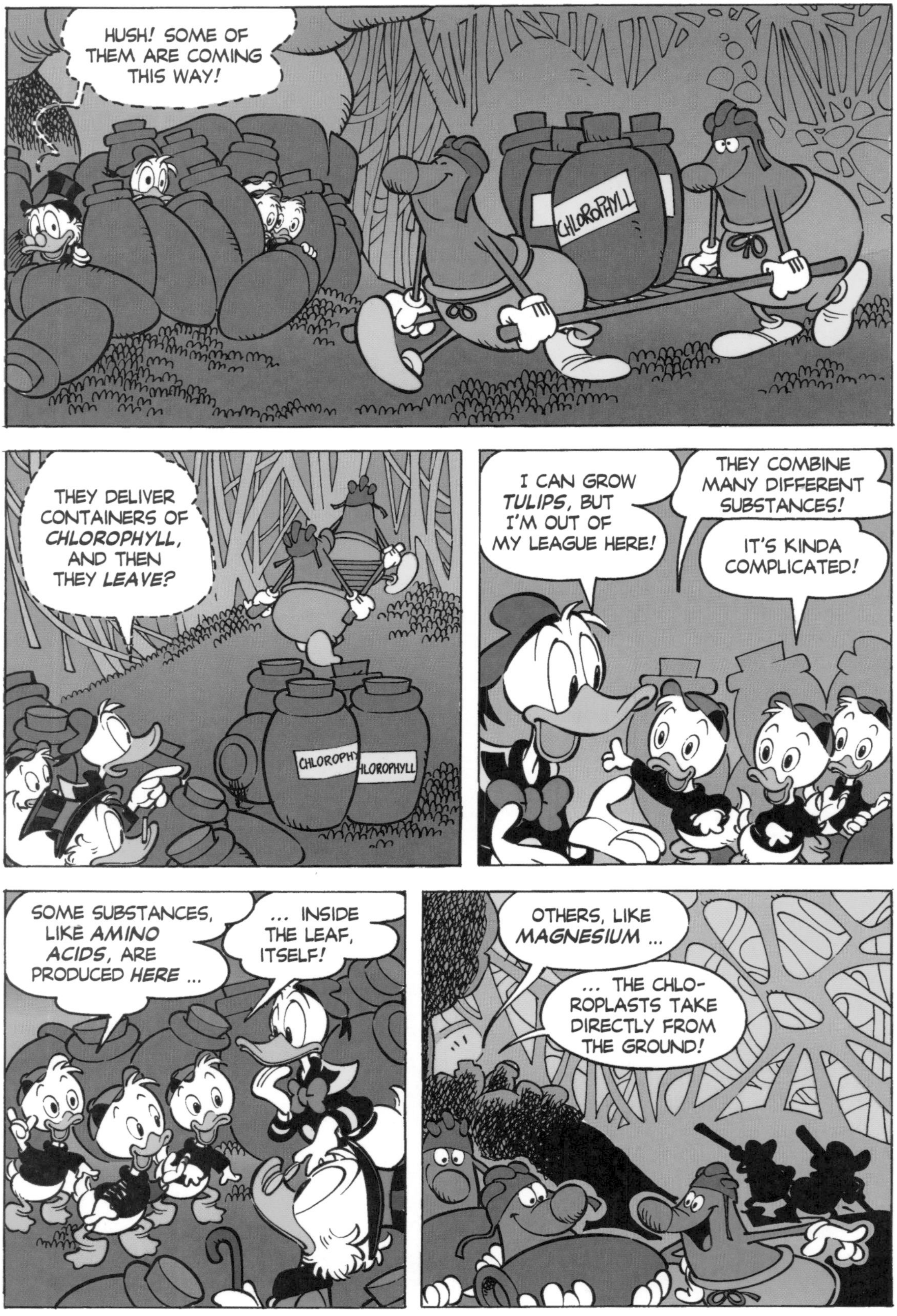
HUSH! SOME OF THEM ARE COMING THIS WAY!
CHLOROPHYLL
THEY DELIVER CONTAINERS OF CHLOROPHYLL, AND THEN THEY LEAVE?
CHLOROPHY
HLOROPHYLL
I CAN GROW TULIPS, BUT I'M OUT OF MY LEAGUE HERE!
THEY COMBINE MANY DIFFERENT SUBSTANCES!
IT'S KINDA COMPLICATED!
SOME SUBSTANCES, LIKE AMINO ACIDS, ARE PRODUCED HERE ...
... INSIDE THE LEAF, ITSELF!
OTHERS, LIKE MAGNESIUM ...
... THE CHLO-ROPLASTS TAKE DIRECTLY FROM THE GROUND!

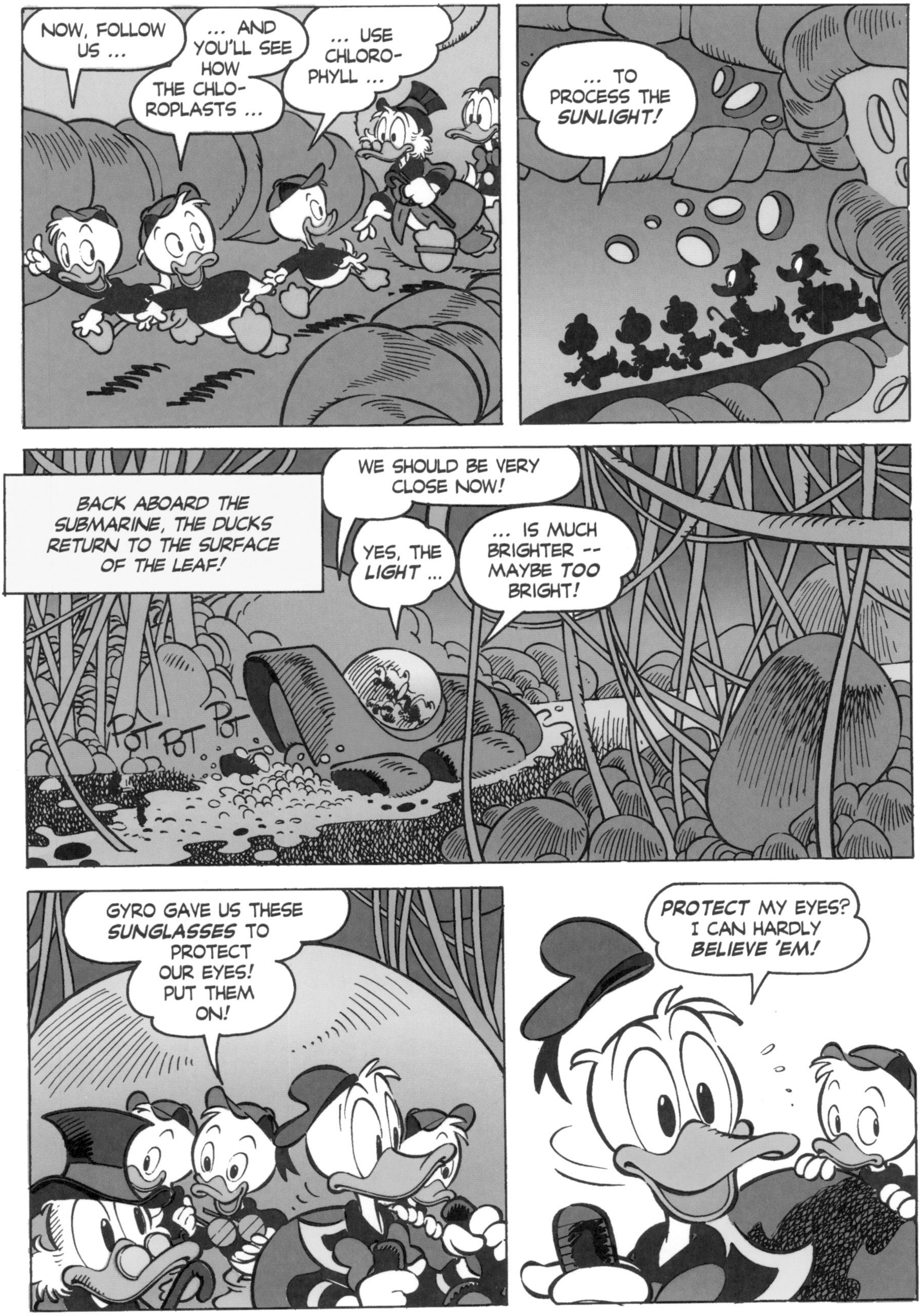
NOW, FOLLOW US ...
... AND YOU'LL SEE HOW THE CHLOROPLASTS ...
... USE CHLOROPHYLL ...
... TO PROCESS THE SUNLIGHT!
BACK ABOARD THE SUBMARINE, THE DUCKS RETURN TO THE SURFACE OF THE LEAF!
WE SHOULD BE VERY CLOSE NOW!
YES, THE LIGHT ...
... IS MUCH BRIGHTER -- MAYBE TOO BRIGHT!
POT POT POT
GYRO GAVE US THESE SUNGLASSES TO PROTECT OUR EYES! PUT THEM ON!
PROTECT MY EYES? I CAN HARDLY BELIEVE 'EM!

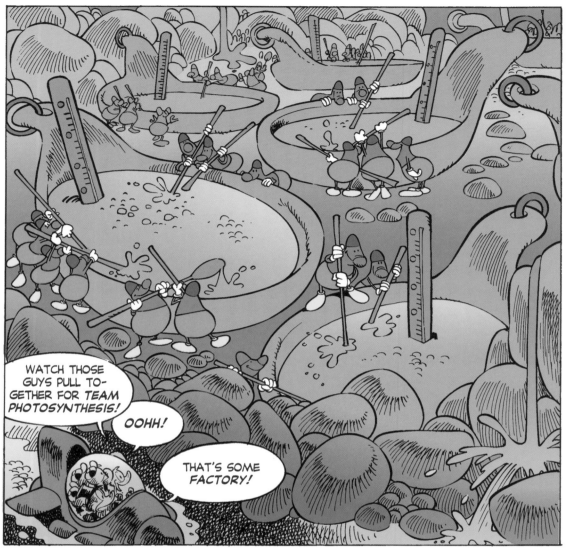

WATCH THOSE GUYS PULL TO-GETHER FOR *TEAM PHOTOSYNTHESIS!*

*OOHH!*

THAT'S SOME FACTORY!

THE CHLOROPLASTS USE A *LEAF'S SURFACE ...*

... LIKE A *LENS* TO CONCENTRATE THE SUN'S RAYS!

THE CHLOROPHYLL *ABSORBS* THOSE RAYS FOR PHOTO-SYNTHESIS!

AND THOSE *THERMOM-ETERS?*

BOT BOT BOT

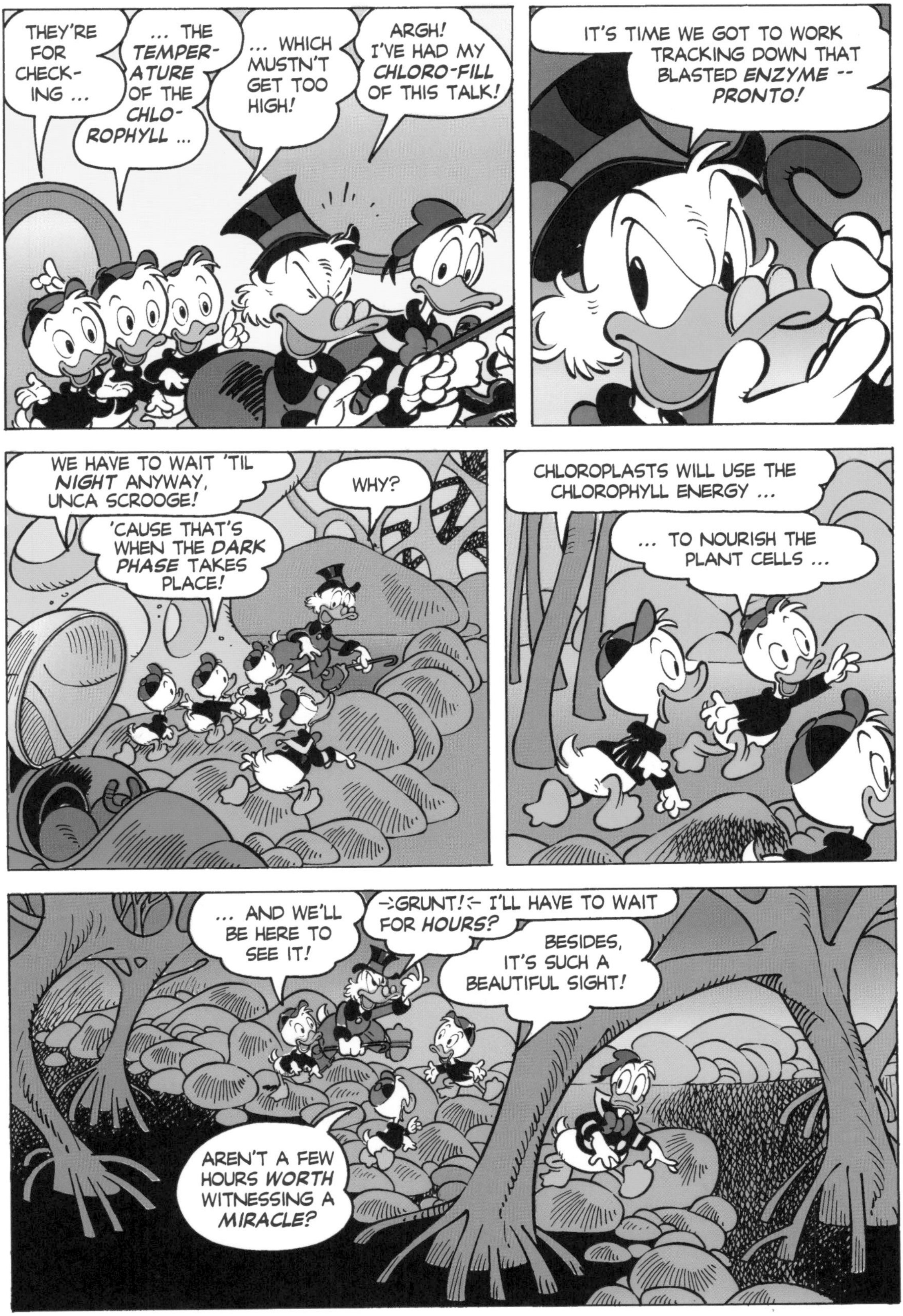
THEY'RE FOR CHECKING ...
... THE TEMPERATURE OF THE CHLOROPHYLL ...
... WHICH MUSTN'T GET TOO HIGH!
ARGH! I'VE HAD MY CHLORO-FILL OF THIS TALK!
IT'S TIME WE GOT TO WORK TRACKING DOWN THAT BLASTED ENZYME -- PRONTO!
WE HAVE TO WAIT 'TIL NIGHT ANYWAY, UNCA SCROOGE!
WHY?
'CAUSE THAT'S WHEN THE DARK PHASE TAKES PLACE!
CHLOROPLASTS WILL USE THE CHLOROPHYLL ENERGY ...
... TO NOURISH THE PLANT CELLS ...
... AND WE'LL BE HERE TO SEE IT!
-GRUNT!- I'LL HAVE TO WAIT FOR HOURS?
BESIDES, IT'S SUCH A BEAUTIFUL SIGHT!
AREN'T A FEW HOURS WORTH WITNESSING A MIRACLE?

FIE ON THAT ROMANTIC RUBBISH! I'M ONLY INTERESTED IN FINDING THAT *ENZYME!*

UM -- WHAT *IS* AN ENZYME? JUST ASKIN'!

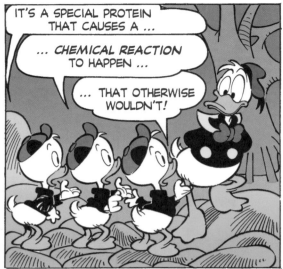

IT'S A SPECIAL PROTEIN THAT CAUSES A ...

... *CHEMICAL REACTION* TO HAPPEN ...

... THAT OTHERWISE WOULDN'T!

YOU KNOW, LIKE A CHEF ...

... *MIXES* DIFFERENT INGREDIENTS TO MAKE A MEAL!

SO WE COULD BE KNEE-DEEP IN *SPA-GHETTI AND MEATBALLS?* YUM!

CURB YOUR APPETITE, YOU GARRULOUS GOURMET! IT'S BACK TO THE SUB!

SINCE WE'RE GON-NA BE UP SO LATE, WE SHOULD *NAP* ...

... AND *WAKE* FOR THE DARK PHASE!

*NAP?* I'M IN!

⇒*SNORT!*⇐ OK! BUT WE'LL TAKE TURNS ON *GUARD DUTY!* I CAN'T AFFORD TO TAKE CHANCES!

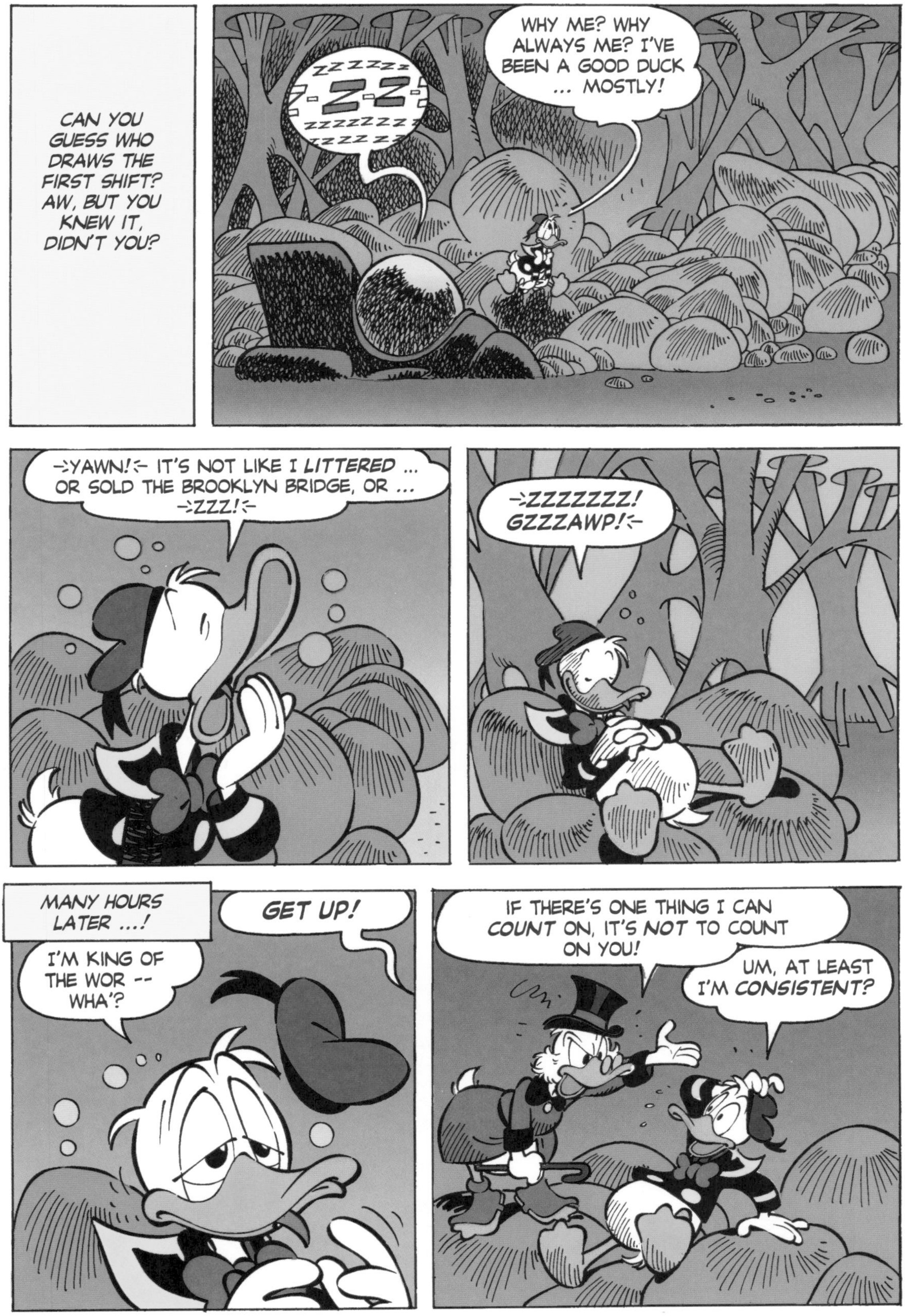
CAN YOU GUESS WHO DRAWS THE FIRST SHIFT? AW, BUT YOU KNEW IT, DIDN'T YOU?
ZZZZZZ -Z-Z- ZZZZZZZ ZZZZZ
WHY ME? WHY ALWAYS ME? I'VE BEEN A GOOD DUCK ... MOSTLY!
-YAWN!- IT'S NOT LIKE I LITTERED ... OR SOLD THE BROOKLYN BRIDGE, OR ... -ZZZ!-
-ZZZZZZZ! GZZZAWP!-
MANY HOURS LATER ...!
GET UP!
I'M KING OF THE WOR -- WHA'?
IF THERE'S ONE THING I CAN COUNT ON, IT'S NOT TO COUNT ON YOU!
UM, AT LEAST I'M CONSISTENT?

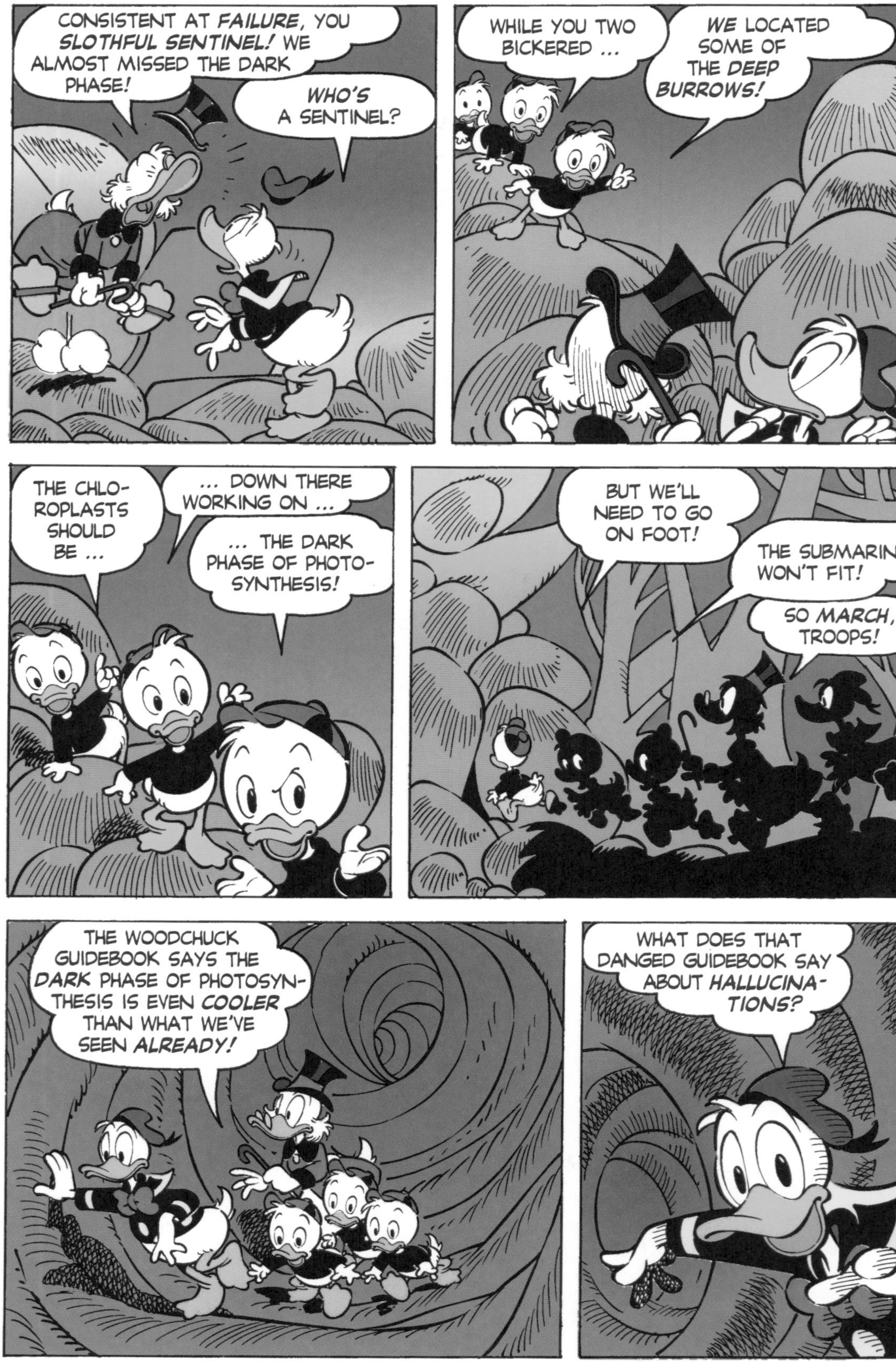

CONSISTENT AT FAILURE, YOU SLOTHFUL SENTINEL! WE ALMOST MISSED THE DARK PHASE!
WHO'S A SENTINEL?
WHILE YOU TWO BICKERED ...
WE LOCATED SOME OF THE DEEP BURROWS!
THE CHLO-ROPLASTS SHOULD BE ...
... DOWN THERE WORKING ON ...
... THE DARK PHASE OF PHOTO-SYNTHESIS!
BUT WE'LL NEED TO GO ON FOOT!
THE SUBMARINE WON'T FIT!
SO MARCH, TROOPS!
THE WOODCHUCK GUIDEBOOK SAYS THE DARK PHASE OF PHOTOSYN-THESIS IS EVEN COOLER THAN WHAT WE'VE SEEN ALREADY!
WHAT DOES THAT DANGED GUIDEBOOK SAY ABOUT HALLUCINA-TIONS?

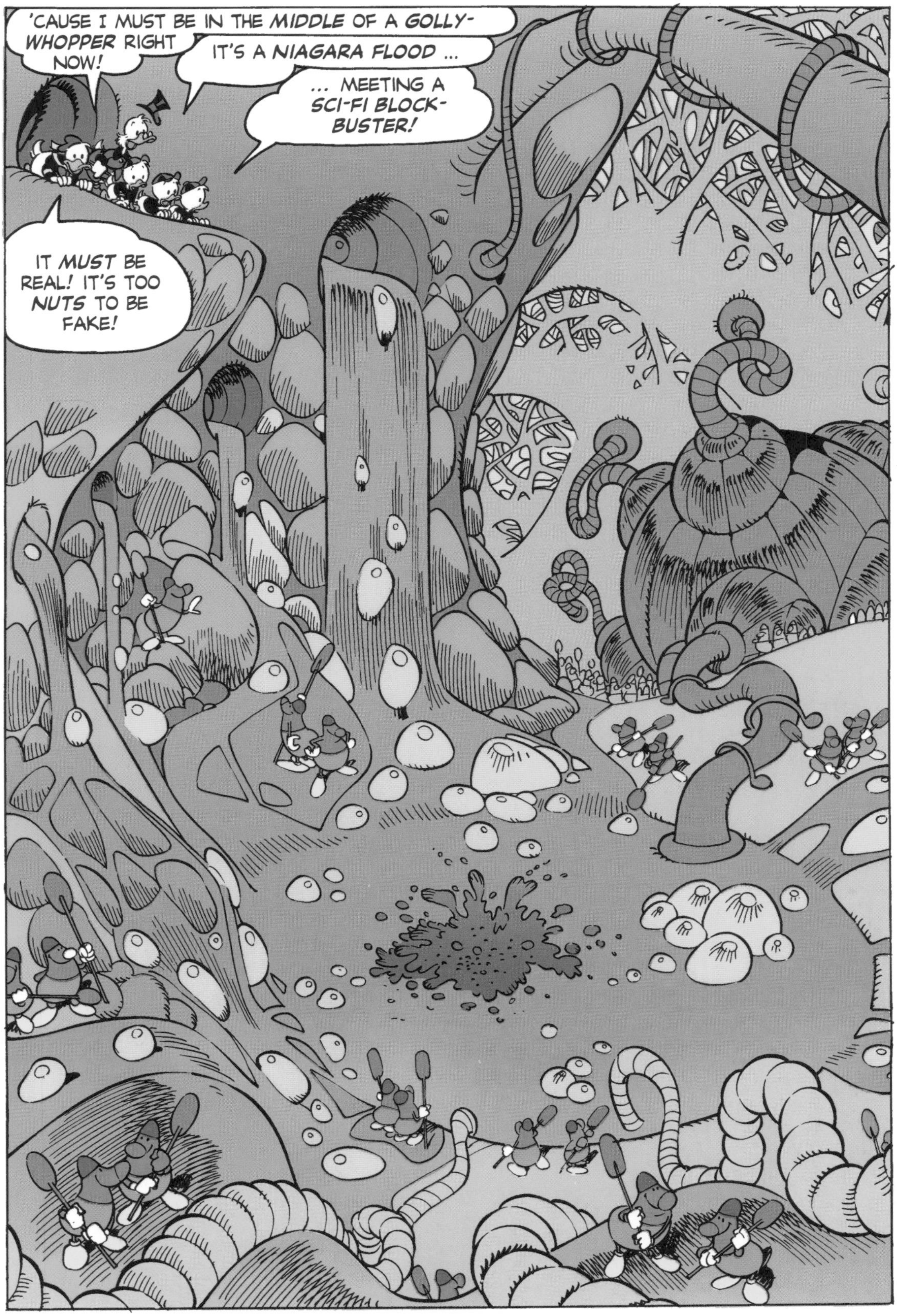
'CAUSE I MUST BE IN THE *MIDDLE* OF A *GOLLY-WHOPPER* RIGHT NOW!
IT'S A *NIAGARA FLOOD* ...
... MEETING A *SCI-FI BLOCK-BUSTER!*
IT *MUST* BE REAL! IT'S TOO *NUTS* TO BE FAKE!

THE CHLOROPHYLL IS COLLECTED IN THAT HUGE POND ...

... AND THEN PASSED THROUGH A SERIES OF COMPONENTS, LIKE IN AN *ASSEMBLY LINE!*

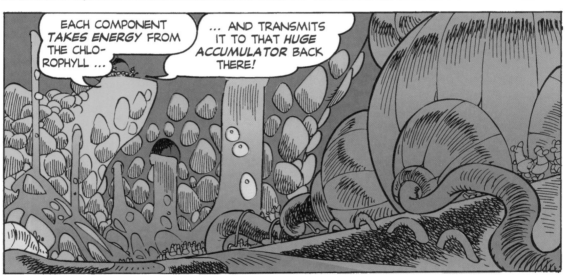

EACH COMPONENT *TAKES ENERGY* FROM THE CHLO-ROPHYLL ...

... AND TRANSMITS IT TO THAT *HUGE ACCUMULATOR* BACK THERE!

I KNOW I'LL REGRET SAYING THIS, BUT WE SHOULD GET CLOSER!

YES, AND GLOM ONTO SOME OF THAT *VALUABLE MISSING ENZYME!* ‹DROOL!›

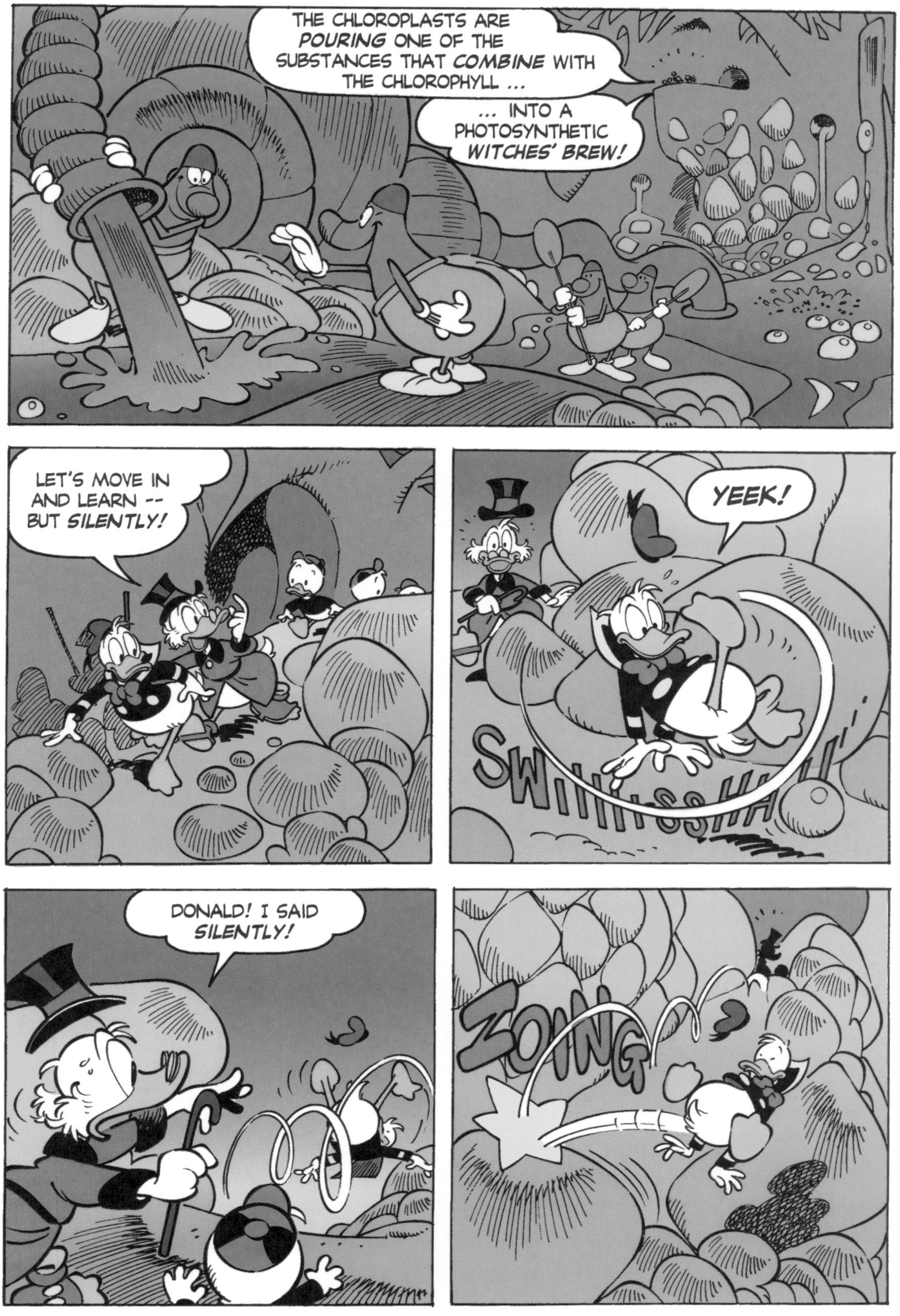
THE CHLOROPLASTS ARE POURING ONE OF THE SUBSTANCES THAT COMBINE WITH THE CHLOROPHYLL ...
... INTO A PHOTOSYNTHETIC WITCHES' BREW!
LET'S MOVE IN AND LEARN -- BUT SILENTLY!
YEEK!
SWIIIIISSHH
DONALD! I SAID SILENTLY!
ZOING

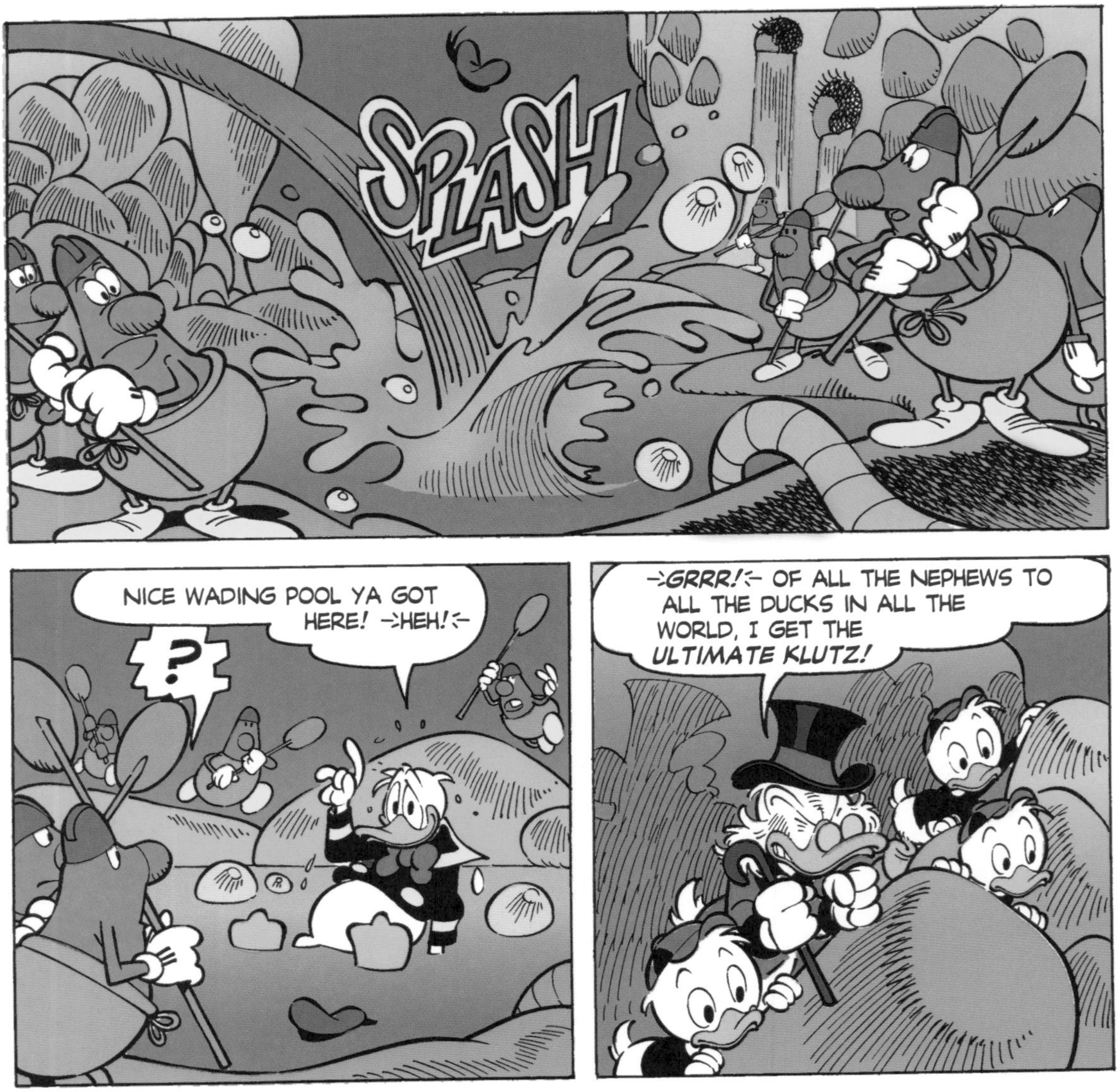
SPLASH
NICE WADING POOL YA GOT HERE! ⇾HEH!⇽
?
⇾GRRR!⇽ OF ALL THE NEPHEWS TO ALL THE DUCKS IN ALL THE WORLD, I GET THE ULTIMATE KLUTZ!

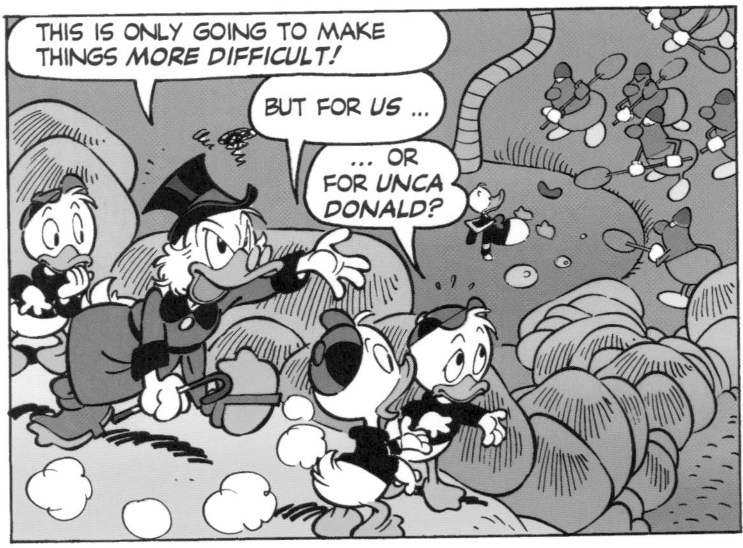
THIS IS ONLY GOING TO MAKE THINGS MORE DIFFICULT!
BUT FOR US ...
... OR FOR UNCA DONALD?

*POOR DONALD'S REALLY IN THE PRIMORDIAL SOUP THIS TIME! HE'D LIKE NOTHING MORE THAN TO **LEAF** FOR HOME! CAN HIS INTREPID NEPHEWS **STEM** THE TIDE OF MISFORTUNE? LET'S **ROOT** FOR THEM IN THE NEXT CHAPTER AND SEE ...*

# UNCLE $CROOGE IN PLANTASTIC VOYAGE

Walt Disney

CHAPTER 2

YIKES! AFTER BEING SHRUNKEN BY GYRO, SCROOGE, DONALD, AND THE BOYS HAVE ENTERED THE INTERNAL STRUCTURE OF A LEAF -- IN ORDER TO OBTAIN A CRITICAL ENZYME USED IN THE PROCESS OF PHOTOSYNTHESIS! DONALD, HOWEVER, SLIPS AND FINDS HIMSELF SURROUNDED BY CHLOROPLASTS! OH, DEAR ...

J-1456-B

WELL, *THIS* IS UNEXPECTED!

DID YOU *OVER-COOK* THE FOR-MULA AGAIN?

I FOLLOWED THE CHLOROPLASTIC COOKBOOK TO THE LETTER!

THEN READ IT AGAIN, MAN!

HAVE WE CAUGHT A *BACTERIAL SPY?*

OR MAYBE SOME *UNKNOWN SPECIES!*

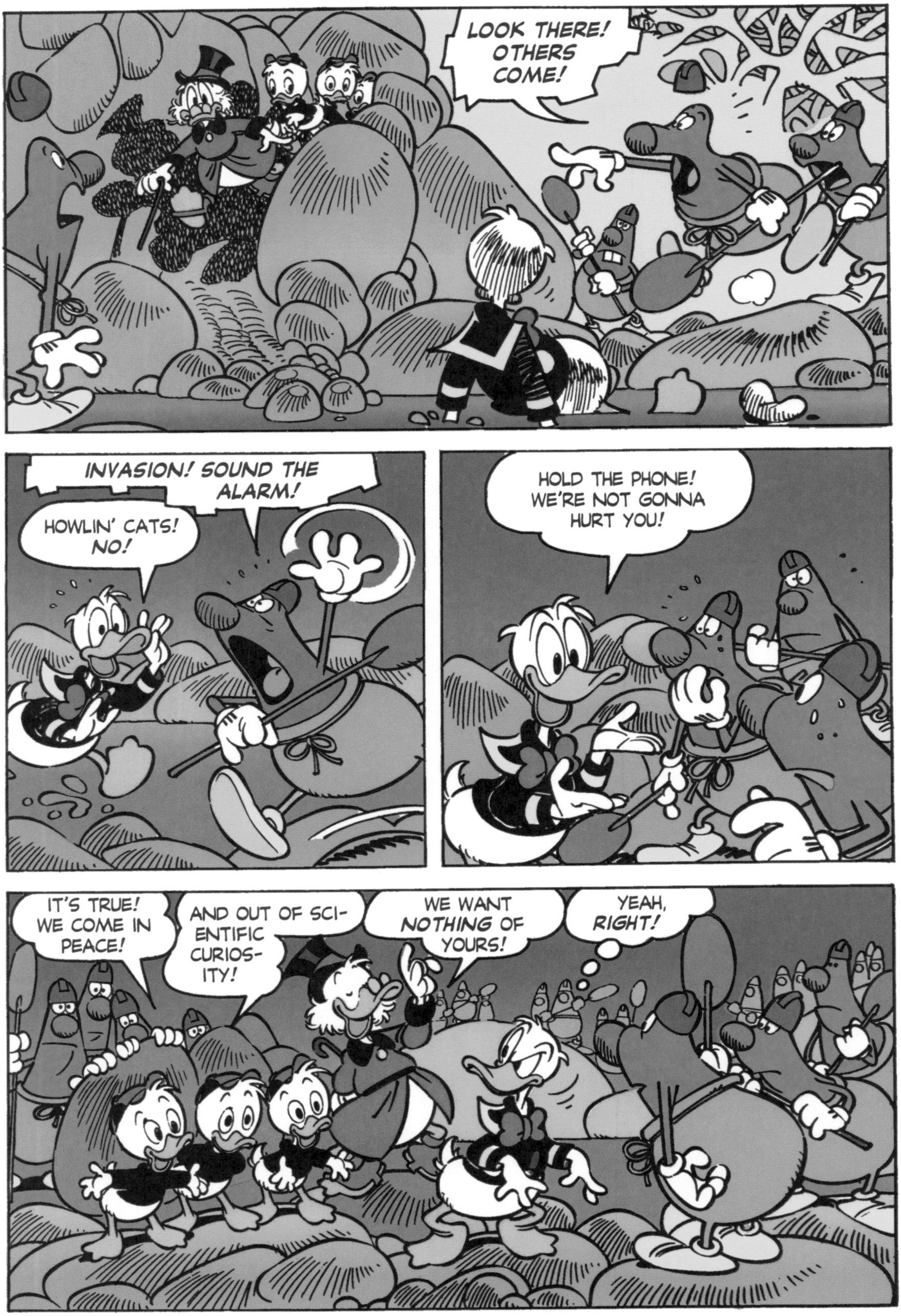
LOOK THERE! OTHERS COME!
INVASION! SOUND THE ALARM!
HOWLIN' CATS! NO!
HOLD THE PHONE! WE'RE NOT GONNA HURT YOU!
IT'S TRUE! WE COME IN PEACE!
AND OUT OF SCI-ENTIFIC CURIOS-ITY!
WE WANT NOTHING OF YOURS!
YEAH, RIGHT!

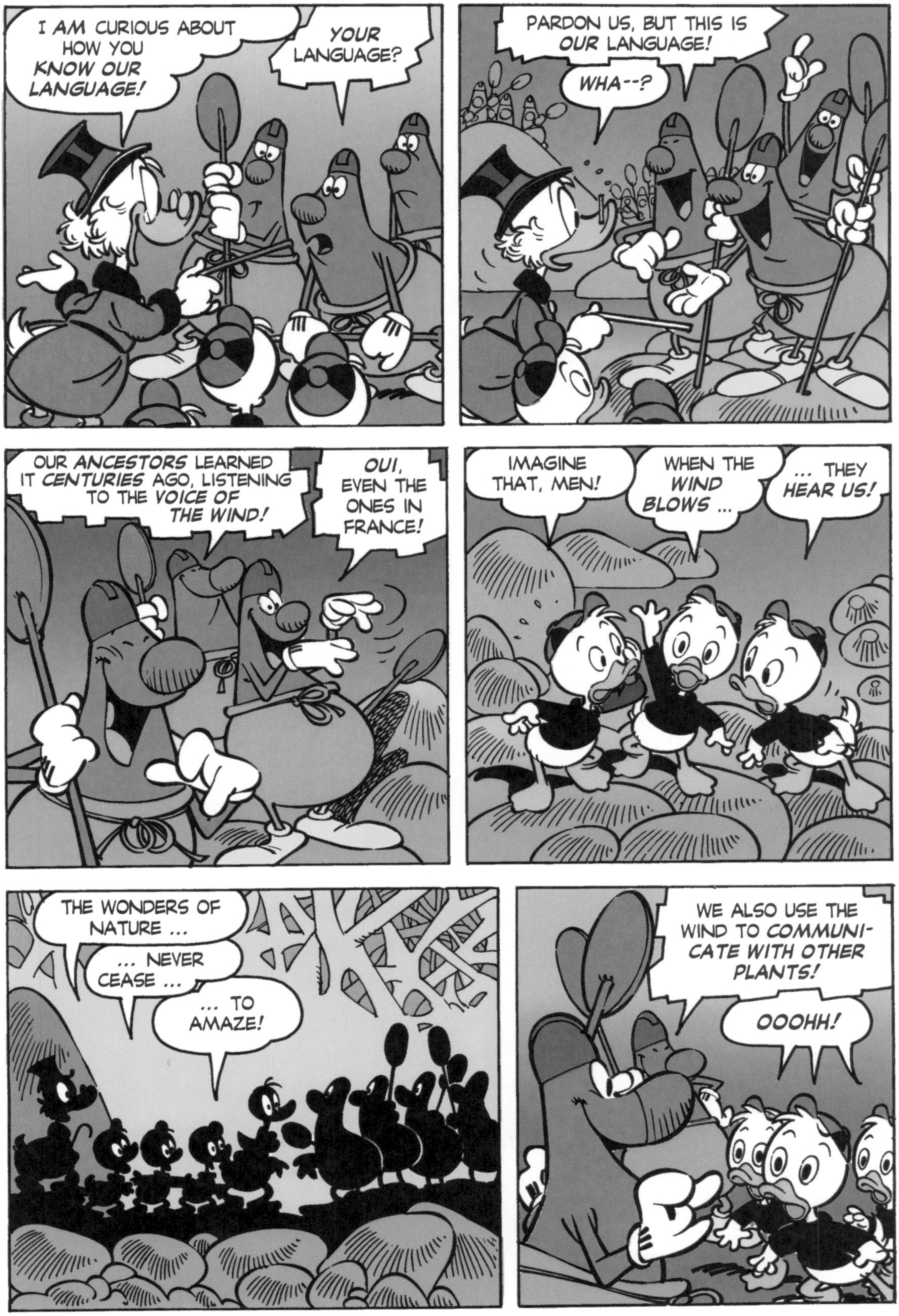
I AM CURIOUS ABOUT HOW YOU KNOW OUR LANGUAGE!
YOUR LANGUAGE?
PARDON US, BUT THIS IS OUR LANGUAGE!
WHA--?
OUR ANCESTORS LEARNED IT CENTURIES AGO, LISTENING TO THE VOICE OF THE WIND!
OUI, EVEN THE ONES IN FRANCE!
IMAGINE THAT, MEN!
WHEN THE WIND BLOWS ...
... THEY HEAR US!
THE WONDERS OF NATURE ...
... NEVER CEASE ...
... TO AMAZE!
WE ALSO USE THE WIND TO COMMUNICATE WITH OTHER PLANTS!
OOOHH!

WE **NEED** TO COMMUNICATE -- TO GUARD AGAINST *BACTERIA SPIES!*

?

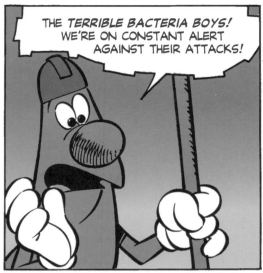

THE *TERRIBLE BACTERIA BOYS!* WE'RE ON CONSTANT ALERT AGAINST THEIR ATTACKS!

THEY GET MORE AND MORE *STUBBORN* ALL THE TIME ... BUT ENOUGH OF THAT! LET'S SHOW YOU SOMETHING *BEAUTIFUL!*

⇥*PSST!*⇤ AND WHAT COULD BE *MORE BEAUTIFUL* THAN THE SECRETS OF PHOTOSYNTHESIS, EH?

REIN IT IN, UNK!

CAREFUL, NOW! THESE STEPS CAN BE *SLIPPERY!*

DON'T TELL ME! TELL MY *PAINFUL FLASHBACKS!*

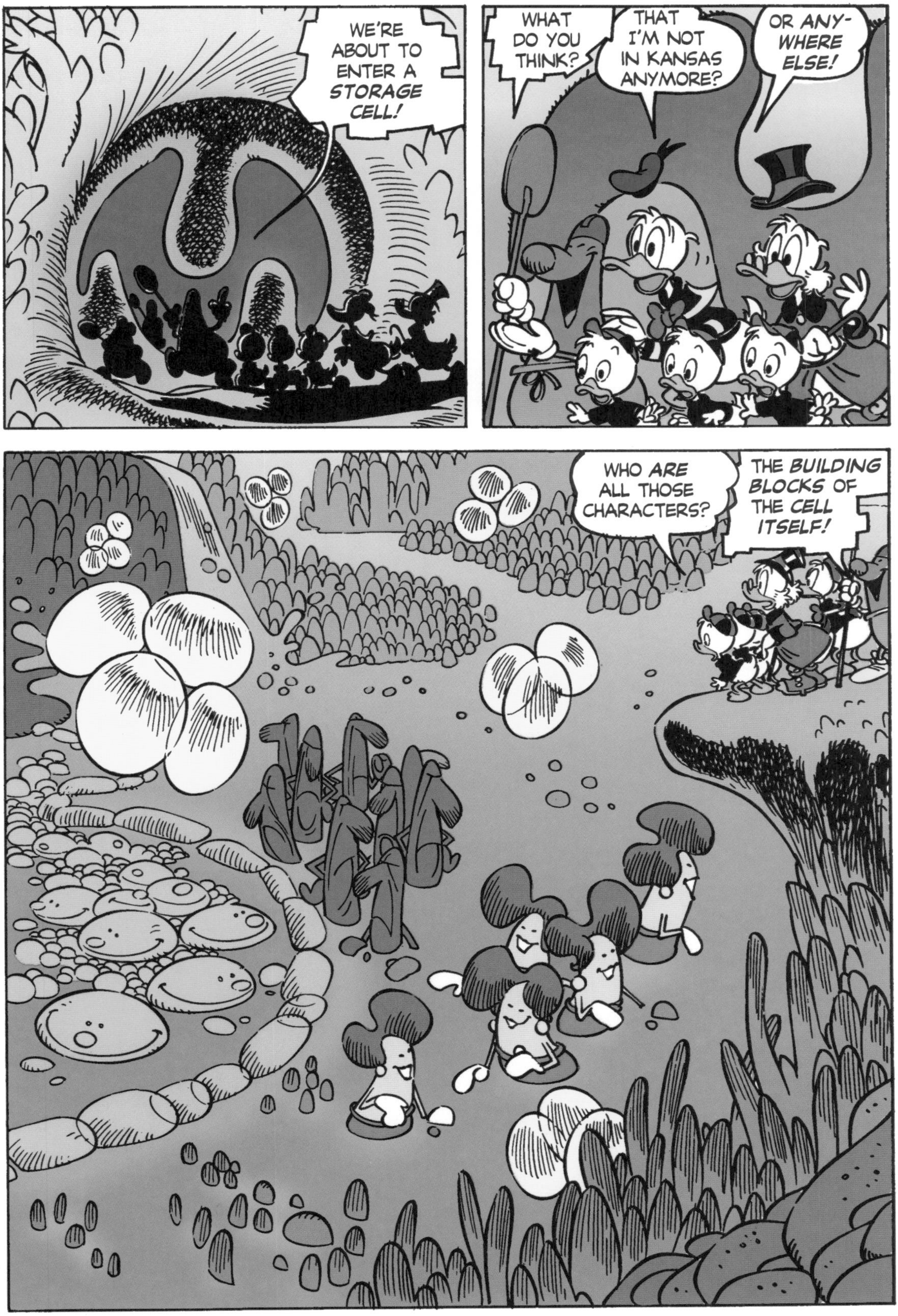
WE'RE ABOUT TO ENTER A STORAGE CELL!
WHAT DO YOU THINK?
THAT I'M NOT IN KANSAS ANYMORE?
OR ANY-WHERE ELSE!
WHO ARE ALL THOSE CHARACTERS?
THE BUILDING BLOCKS OF THE CELL ITSELF!

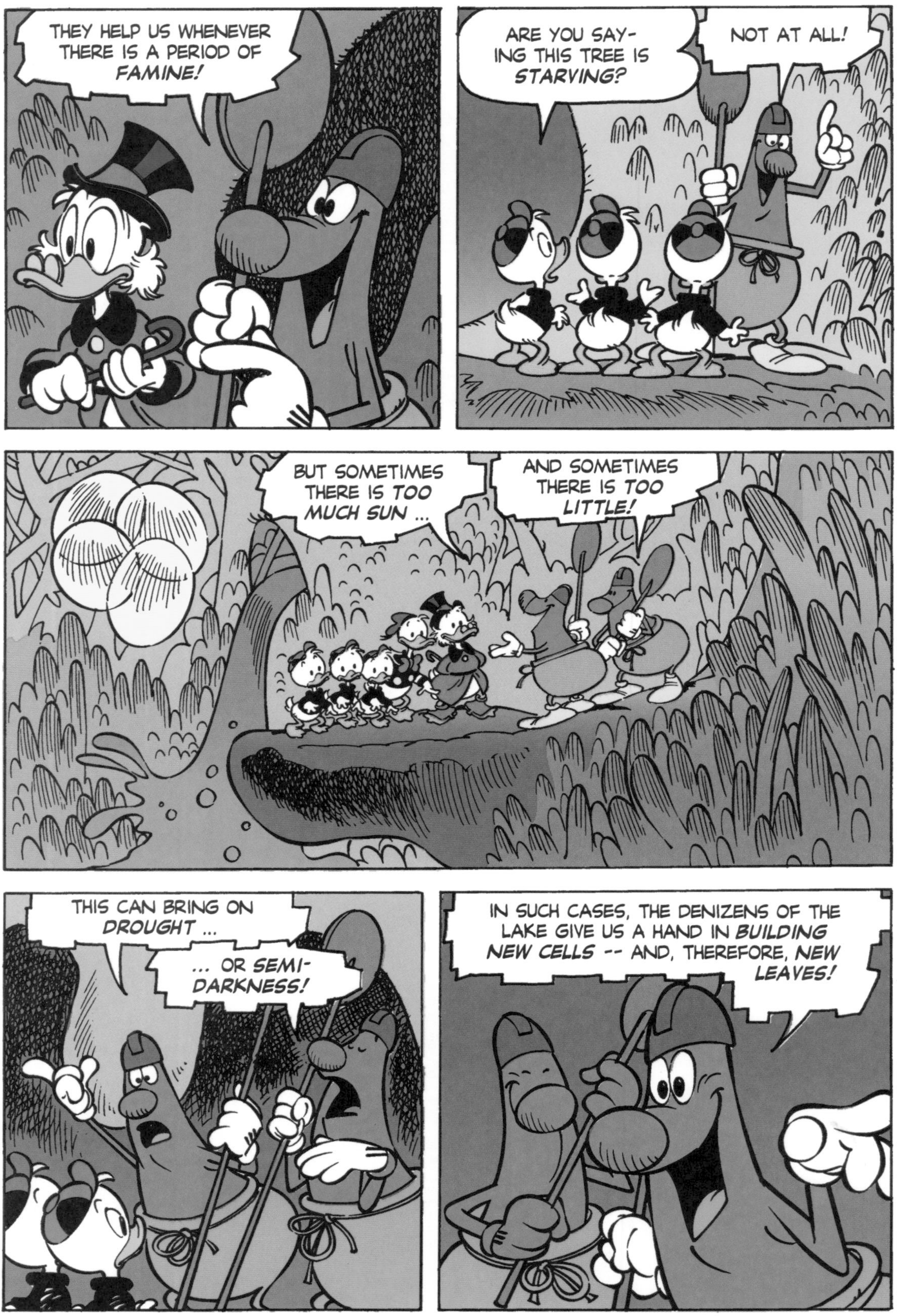
THEY HELP US WHENEVER THERE IS A PERIOD OF FAMINE!
ARE YOU SAYING THIS TREE IS STARVING?
NOT AT ALL!
BUT SOMETIMES THERE IS TOO MUCH SUN ...
AND SOMETIMES THERE IS TOO LITTLE!
THIS CAN BRING ON DROUGHT ...
... OR SEMI-DARKNESS!
IN SUCH CASES, THE DENIZENS OF THE LAKE GIVE US A HAND IN BUILDING NEW CELLS -- AND, THEREFORE, NEW LEAVES!

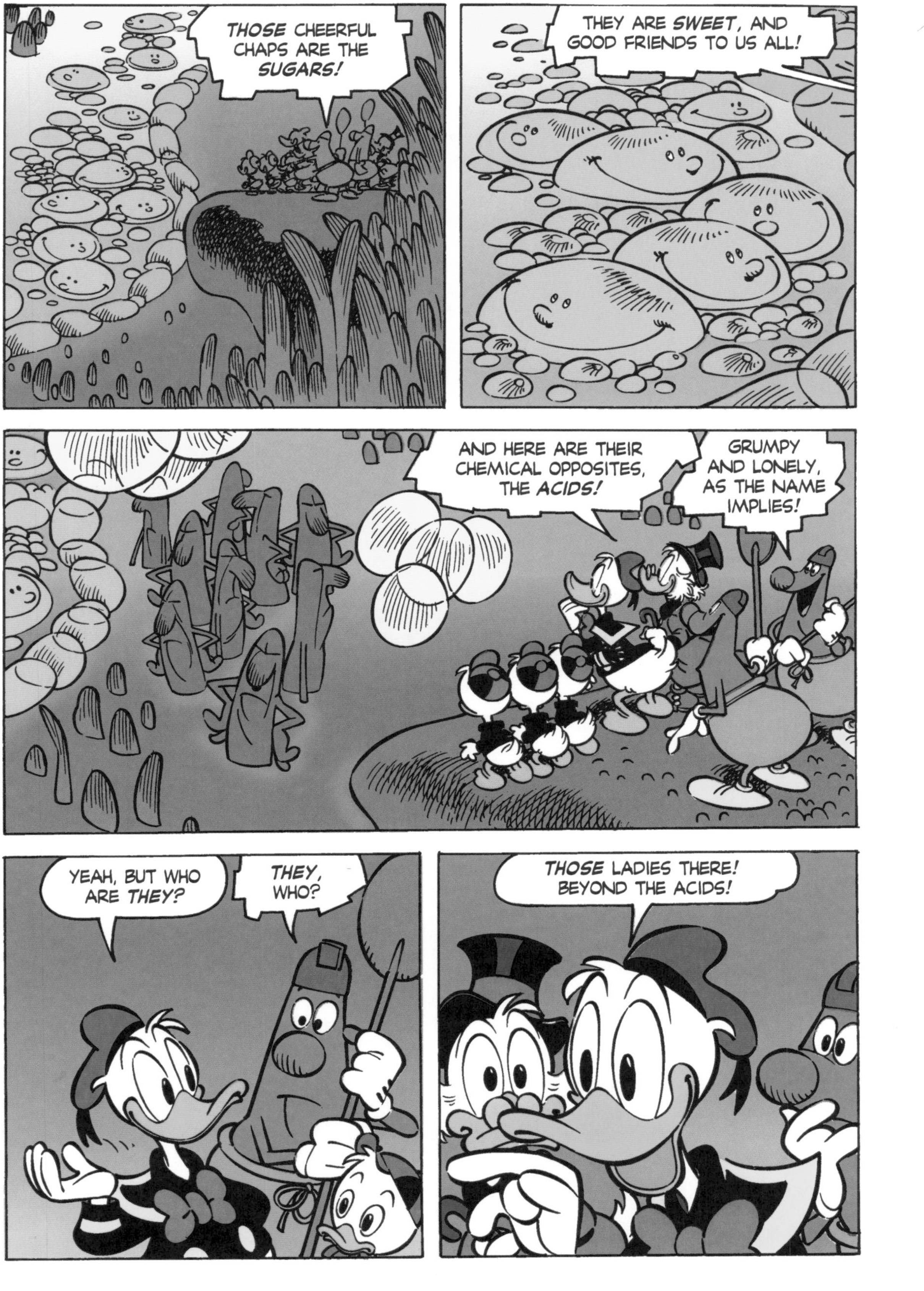
THOSE CHEERFUL CHAPS ARE THE SUGARS!
THEY ARE SWEET, AND GOOD FRIENDS TO US ALL!
AND HERE ARE THEIR CHEMICAL OPPOSITES, THE ACIDS!
GRUMPY AND LONELY, AS THE NAME IMPLIES!
YEAH, BUT WHO ARE THEY?
THEY, WHO?
THOSE LADIES THERE! BEYOND THE ACIDS!

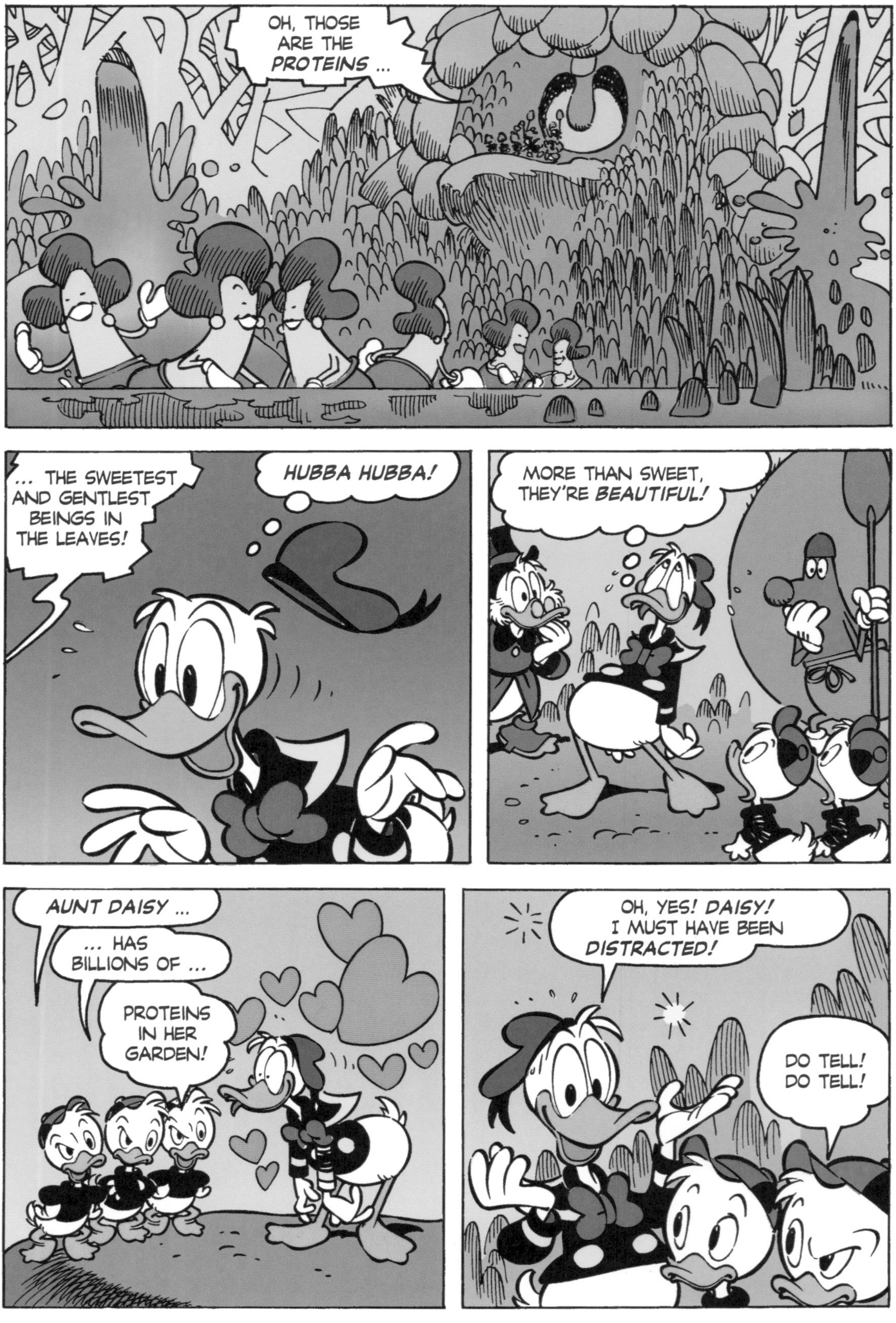
OH, THOSE ARE THE PROTEINS ...
... THE SWEETEST AND GENTLEST BEINGS IN THE LEAVES!
HUBBA HUBBA!
MORE THAN SWEET, THEY'RE BEAUTIFUL!
AUNT DAISY ...
... HAS BILLIONS OF ...
PROTEINS IN HER GARDEN!
OH, YES! DAISY! I MUST HAVE BEEN DISTRACTED!
DO TELL! DO TELL!

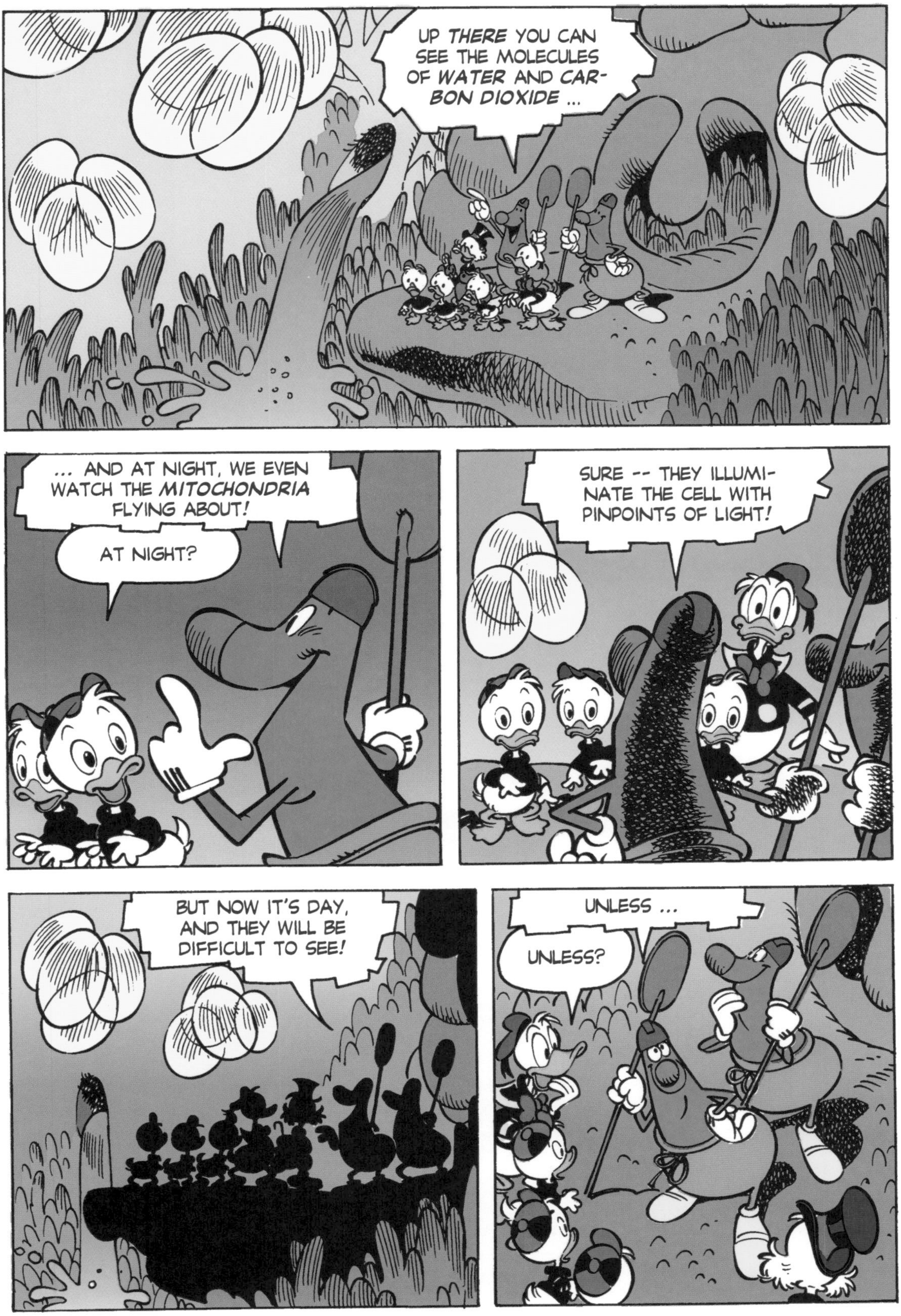
UP *THERE* YOU CAN SEE THE MOLECULES OF *WATER* AND *CAR-BON DIOXIDE* ...
... AND AT NIGHT, WE EVEN WATCH THE *MITOCHONDRIA* FLYING ABOUT!
AT NIGHT?
SURE -- THEY ILLUMI-NATE THE CELL WITH PINPOINTS OF LIGHT!
BUT NOW IT'S DAY, AND THEY WILL BE DIFFICULT TO SEE!
UNLESS ...
UNLESS?

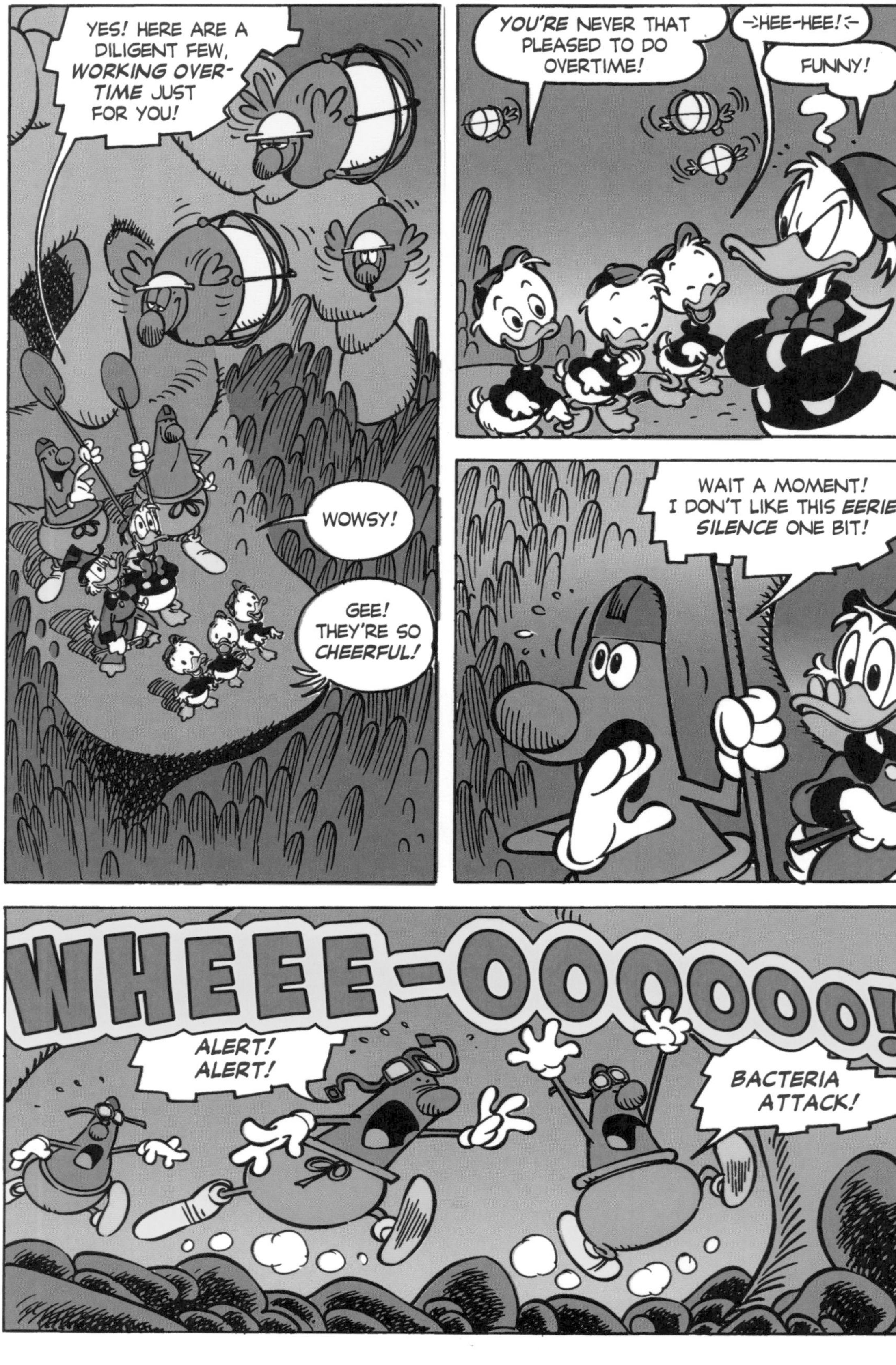
YES! HERE ARE A DILIGENT FEW, WORKING OVER-TIME JUST FOR YOU!
WOWSY!
GEE! THEY'RE SO CHEERFUL!
YOU'RE NEVER THAT PLEASED TO DO OVERTIME!
HEE-HEE!
FUNNY!
?
WAIT A MOMENT! I DON'T LIKE THIS EERIE SILENCE ONE BIT!
WHEEE-OOOOOO!
ALERT! ALERT!
BACTERIA ATTACK!

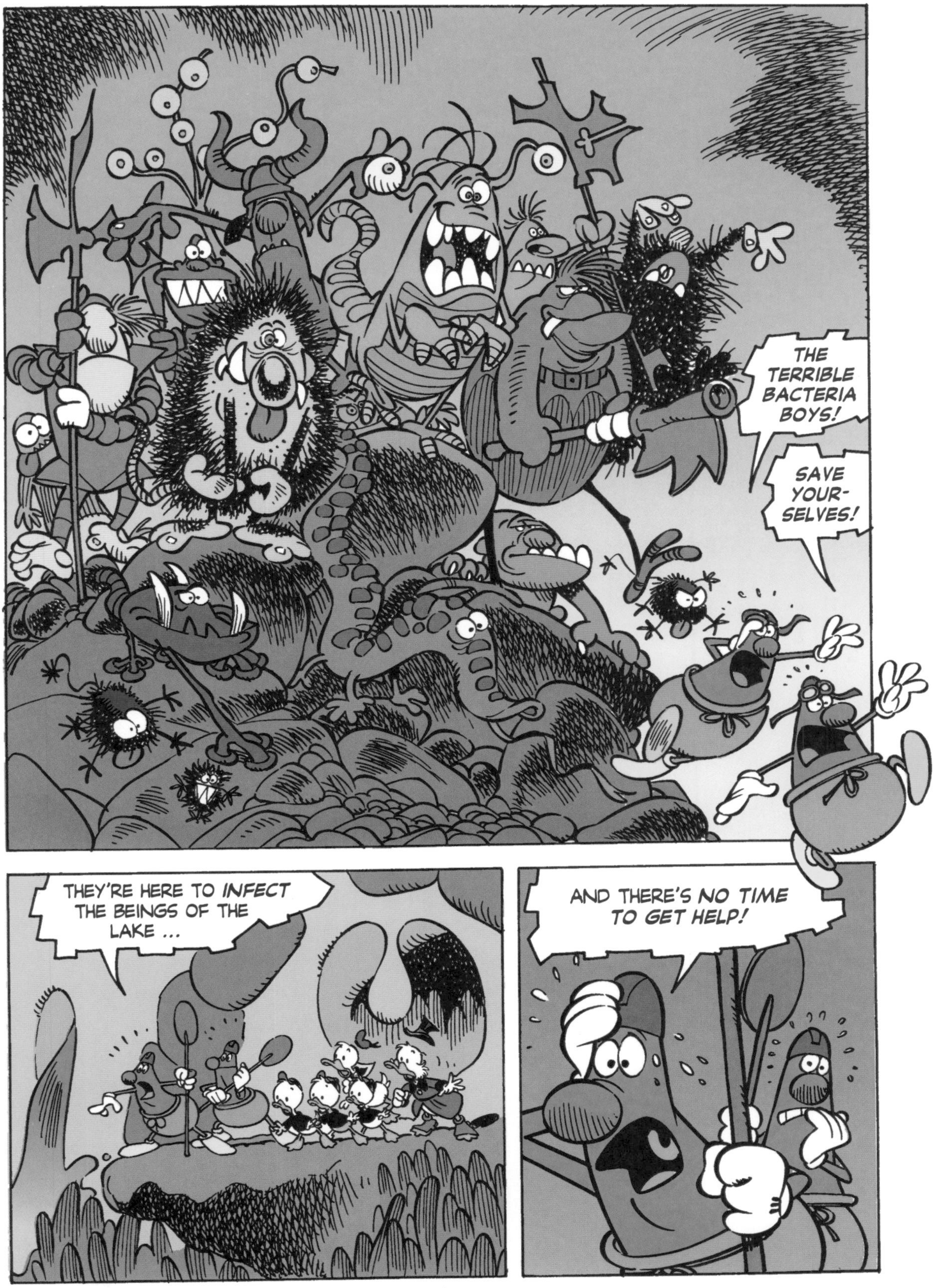
THE TERRIBLE BACTERIA BOYS!
SAVE YOUR-SELVES!
THEY'RE HERE TO INFECT THE BEINGS OF THE LAKE ...
AND THERE'S NO TIME TO GET HELP!

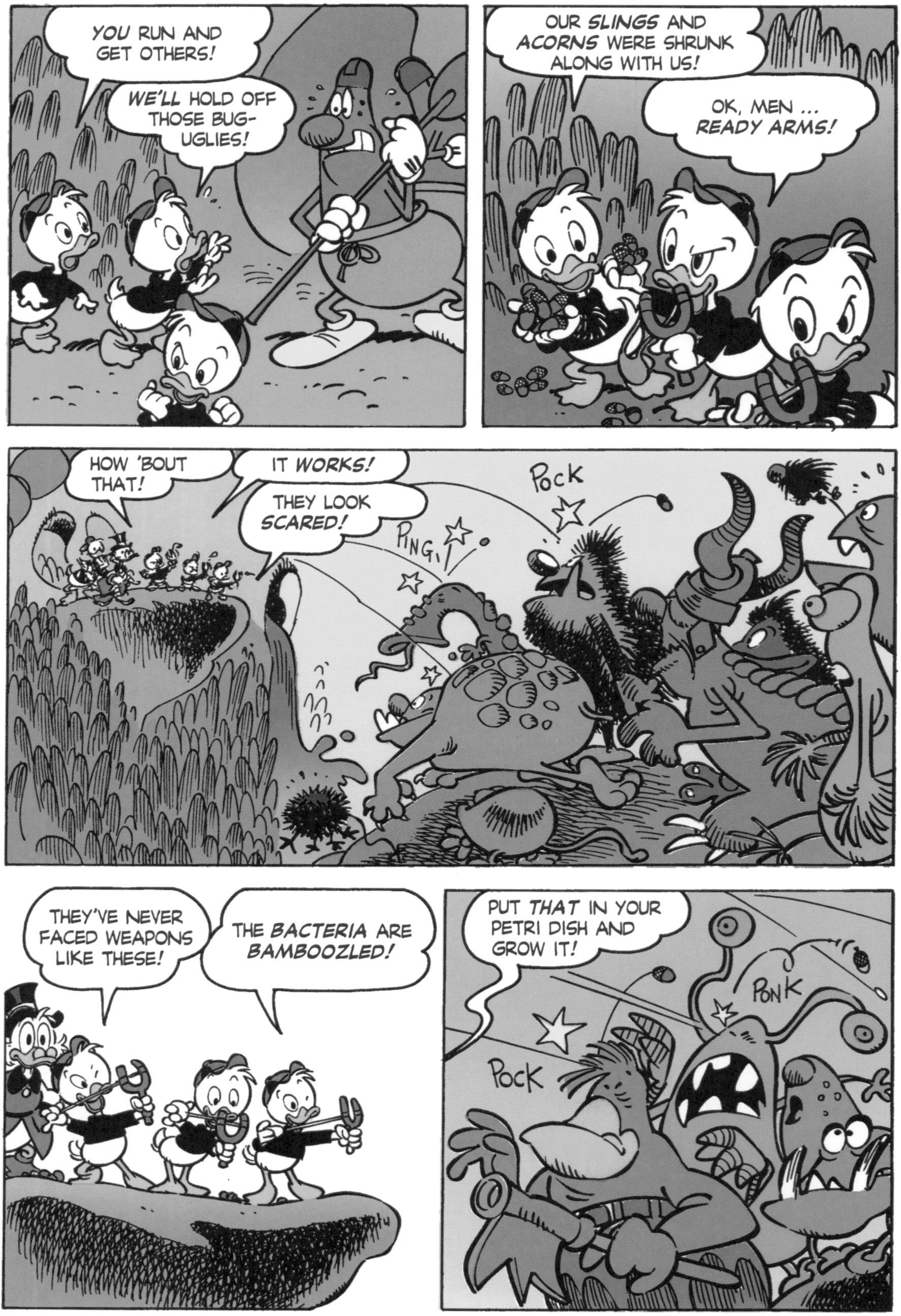
YOU RUN AND GET OTHERS!
WE'LL HOLD OFF THOSE BUG-UGLIES!
OUR SLINGS AND ACORNS WERE SHRUNK ALONG WITH US!
OK, MEN ... READY ARMS!
HOW 'BOUT THAT!
IT WORKS!
THEY LOOK SCARED!
POCK
PING!
THEY'VE NEVER FACED WEAPONS LIKE THESE!
THE BACTERIA ARE BAMBOOZLED!
PUT THAT IN YOUR PETRI DISH AND GROW IT!
PONK
POCK

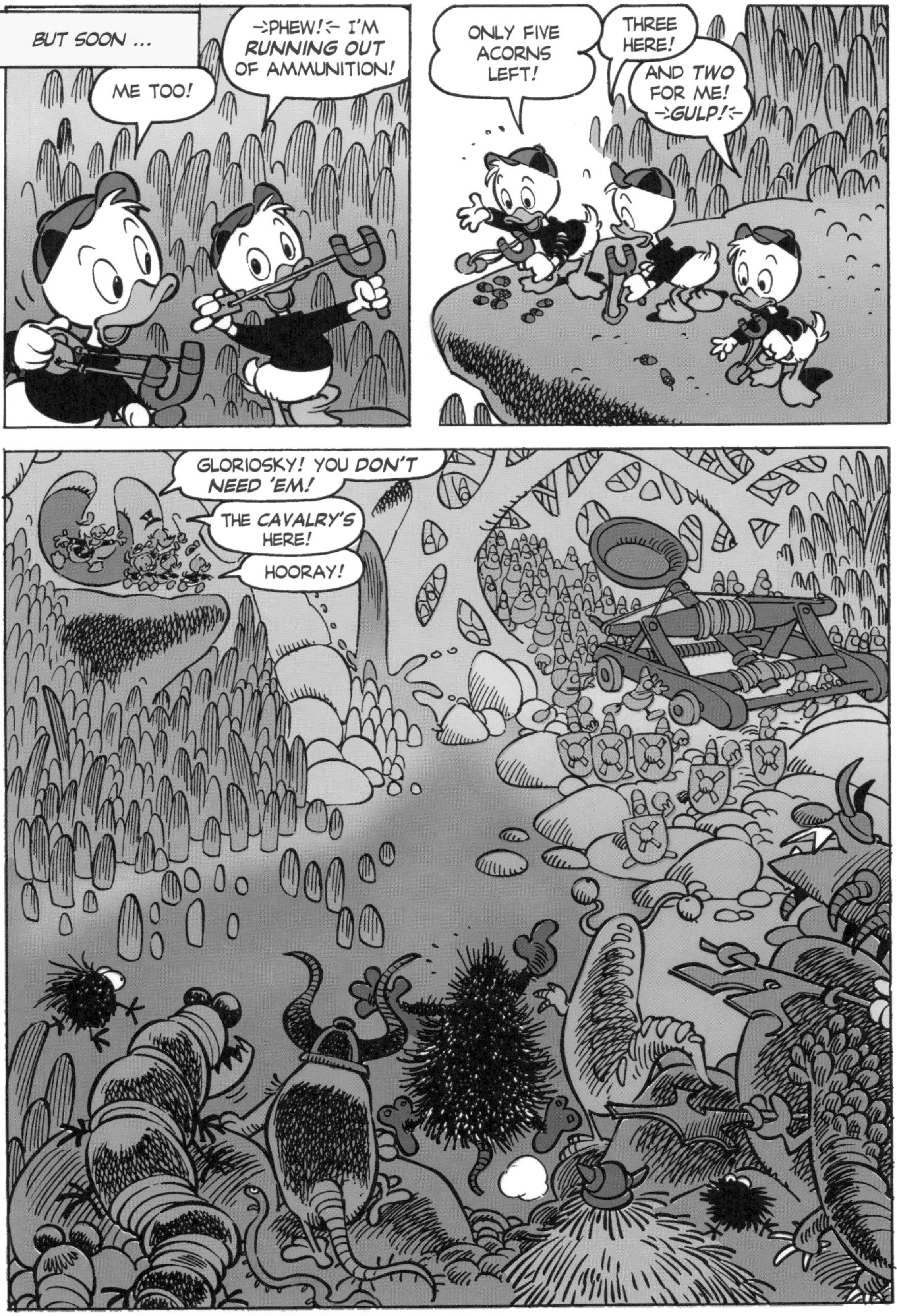

BUT SOON ...
–PHEW!– I'M RUNNING OUT OF AMMUNITION!
ME TOO!
ONLY FIVE ACORNS LEFT!
THREE HERE!
AND TWO FOR ME! –GULP!–
GLORIOSKY! YOU DON'T NEED 'EM!
THE CAVALRY'S HERE!
HOORAY!

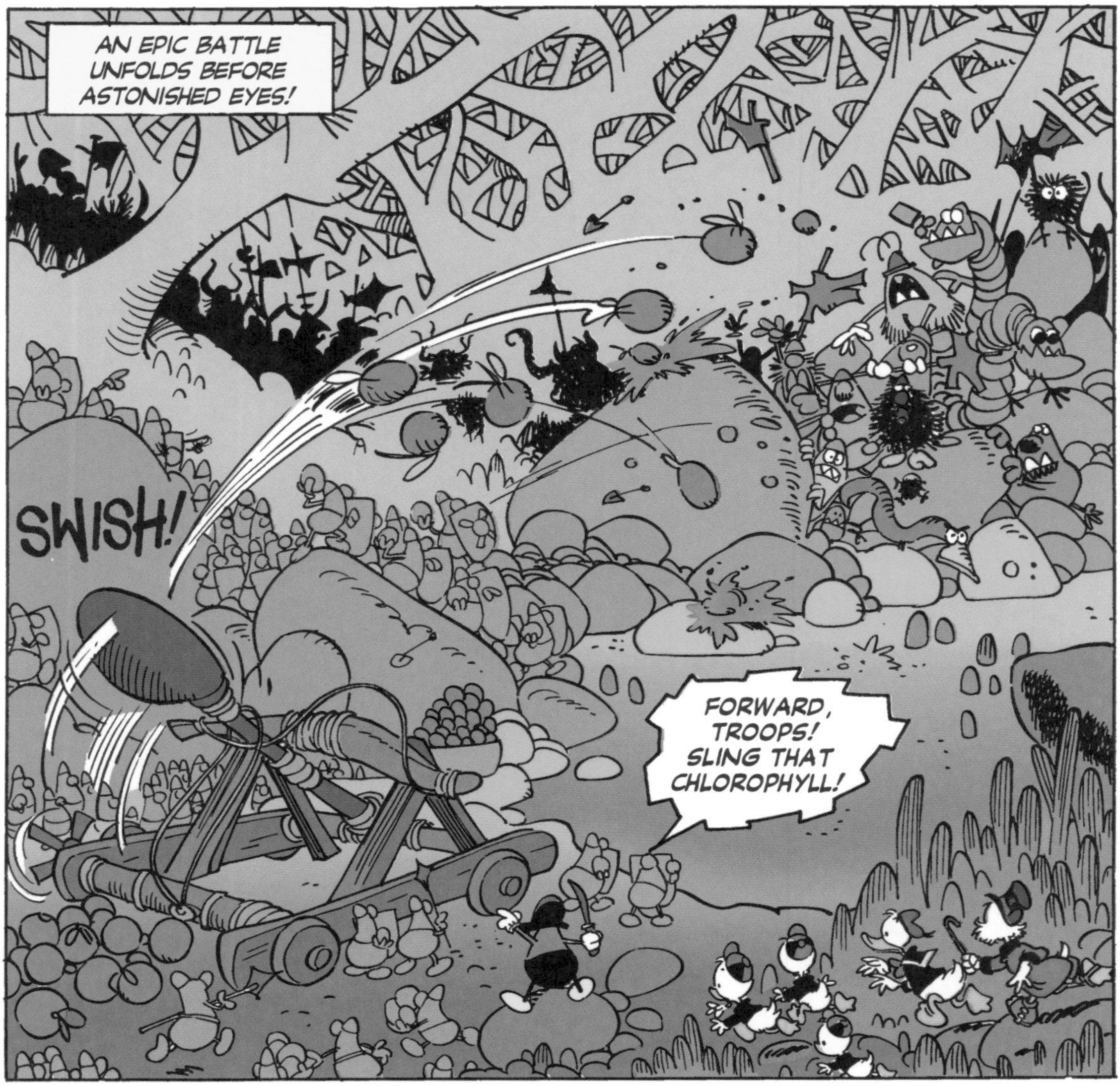
AN EPIC BATTLE UNFOLDS BEFORE ASTONISHED EYES!
SWISH!
FORWARD, TROOPS! SLING THAT CHLOROPHYLL!

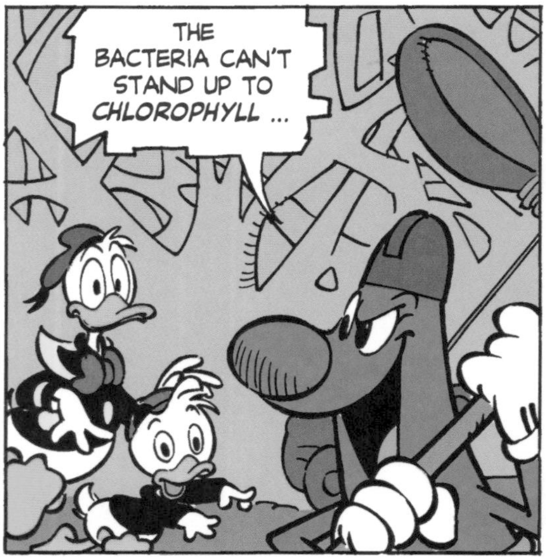
THE BACTERIA CAN'T STAND UP TO CHLOROPHYLL ...

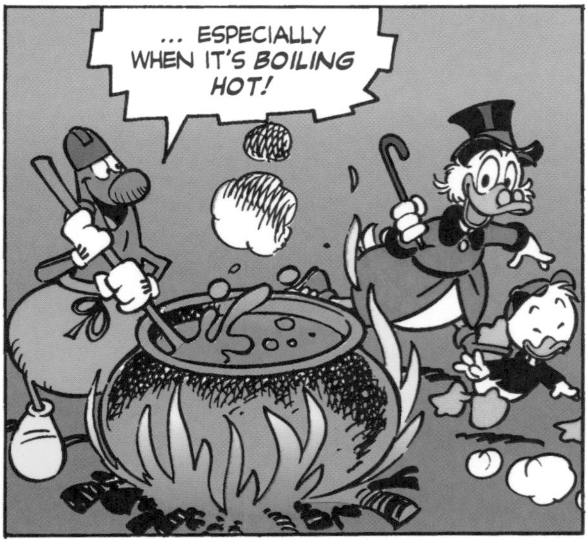
... ESPECIALLY WHEN IT'S BOILING HOT!

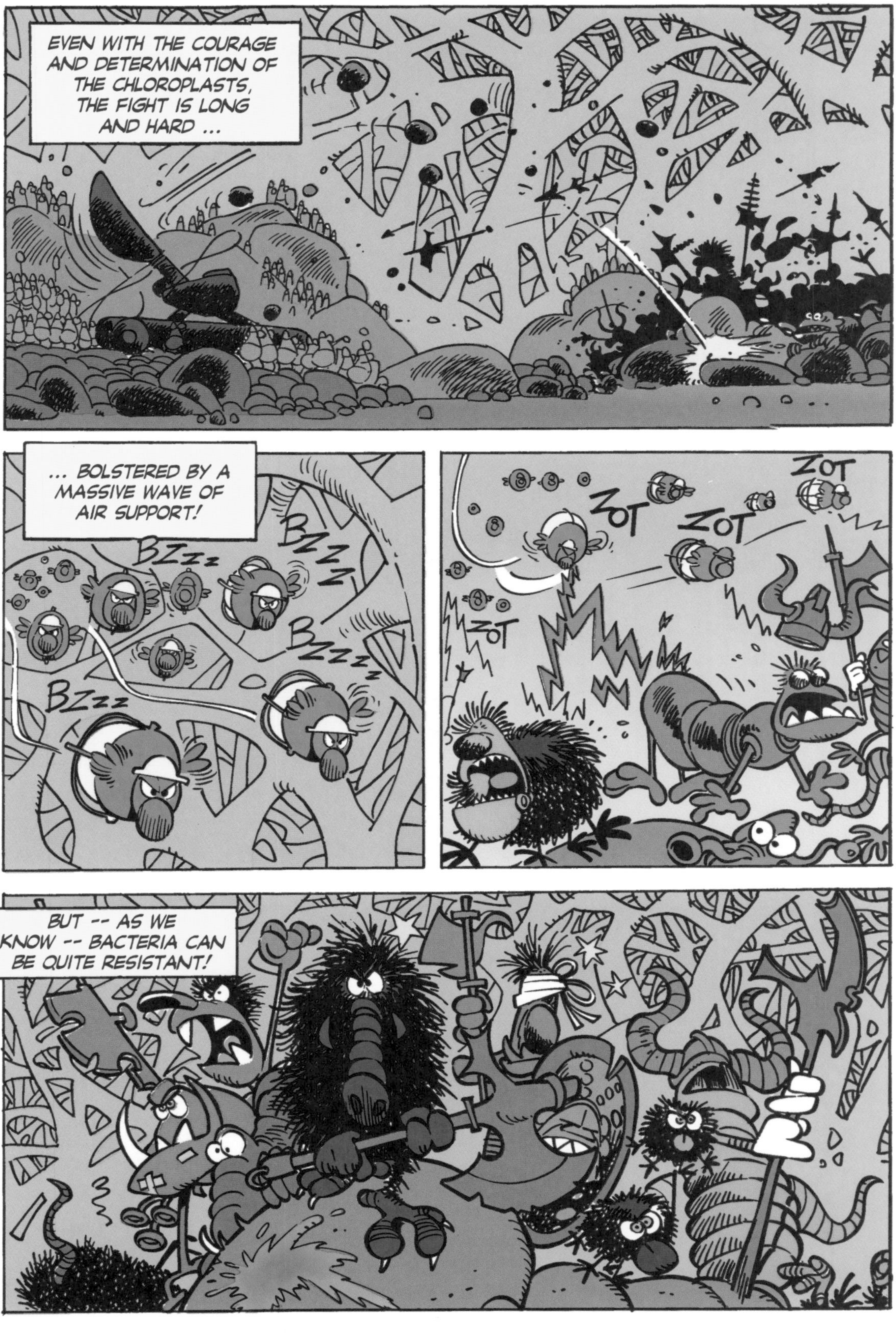
EVEN WITH THE COURAGE AND DETERMINATION OF THE CHLOROPLASTS, THE FIGHT IS LONG AND HARD ...
... BOLSTERED BY A MASSIVE WAVE OF AIR SUPPORT!
BZzzz
BZZZZ
BZzz
BZzzzz
ZOT
ZOT
ZOT
ZOT
BUT -- AS WE KNOW -- BACTERIA CAN BE QUITE RESISTANT!

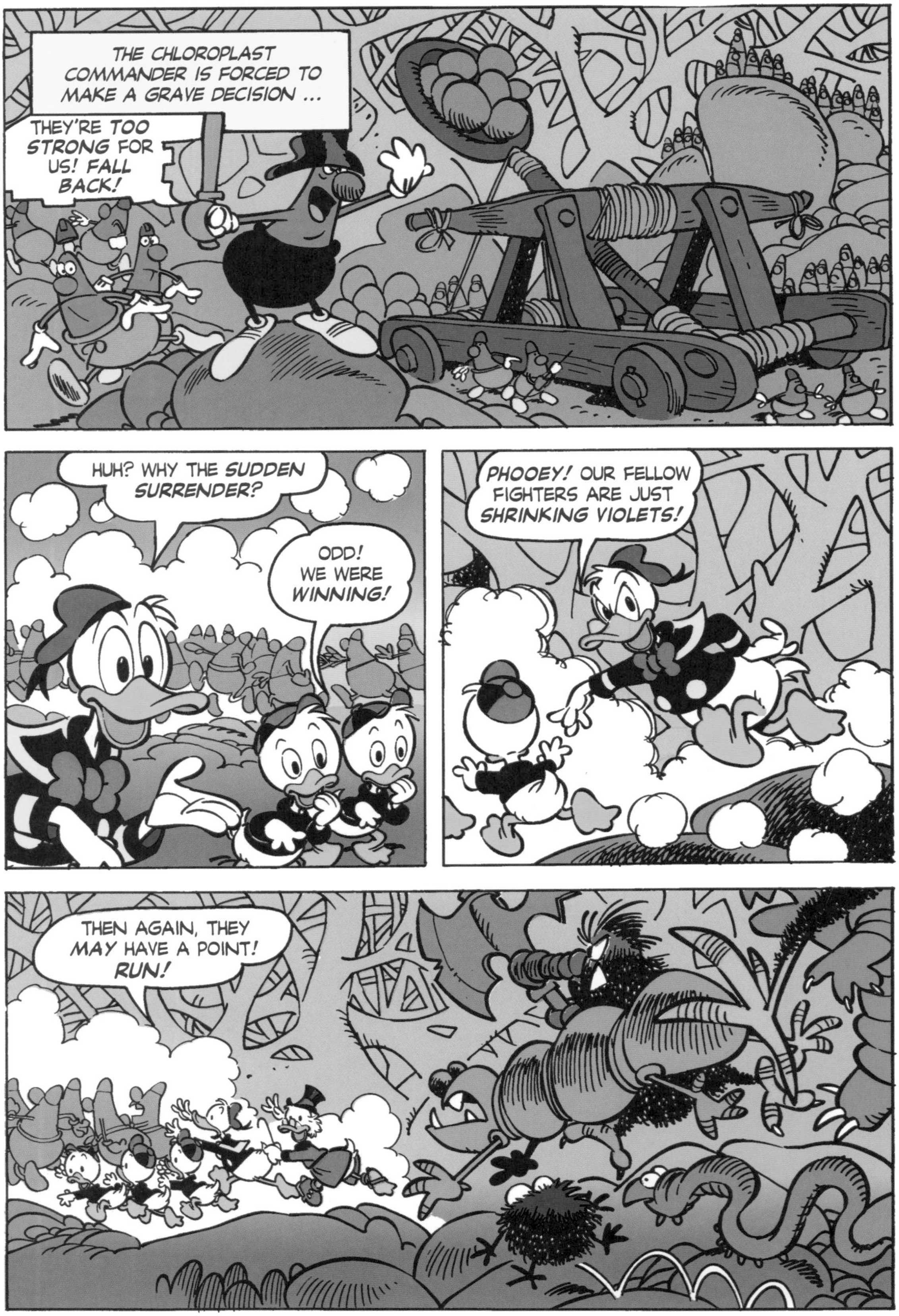
THE CHLOROPLAST COMMANDER IS FORCED TO MAKE A GRAVE DECISION ...
THEY'RE TOO STRONG FOR US! FALL BACK!
HUH? WHY THE SUDDEN SURRENDER?
ODD! WE WERE WINNING!
PHOOEY! OUR FELLOW FIGHTERS ARE JUST SHRINKING VIOLETS!
THEN AGAIN, THEY MAY HAVE A POINT! RUN!

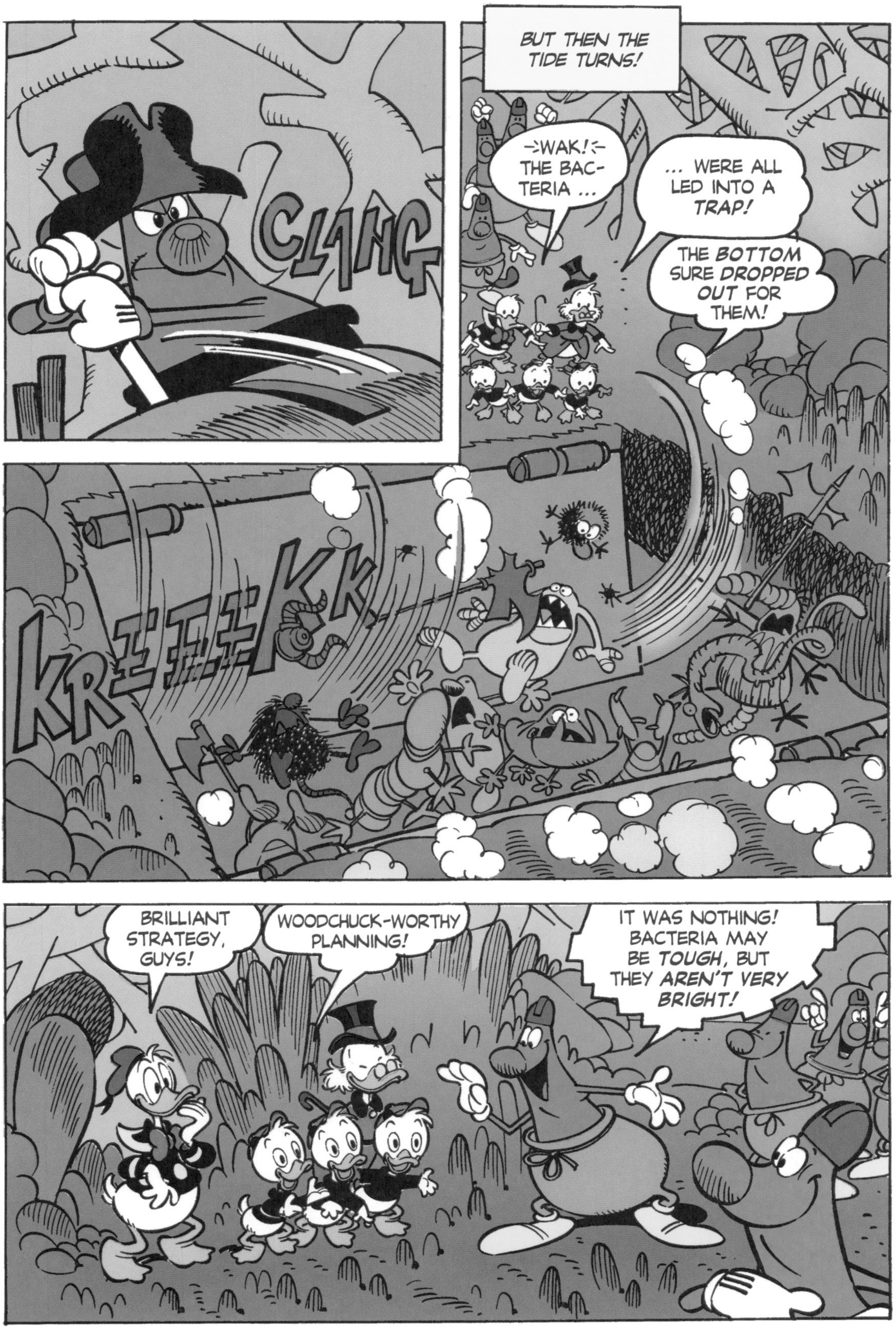
CLANG
BUT THEN THE TIDE TURNS!
WAK! THE BACTERIA ...
... WERE ALL LED INTO A TRAP!
THE BOTTOM SURE DROPPED OUT FOR THEM!
KREEEEKK
BRILLIANT STRATEGY, GUYS!
WOODCHUCK-WORTHY PLANNING!
IT WAS NOTHING! BACTERIA MAY BE TOUGH, BUT THEY AREN'T VERY BRIGHT!

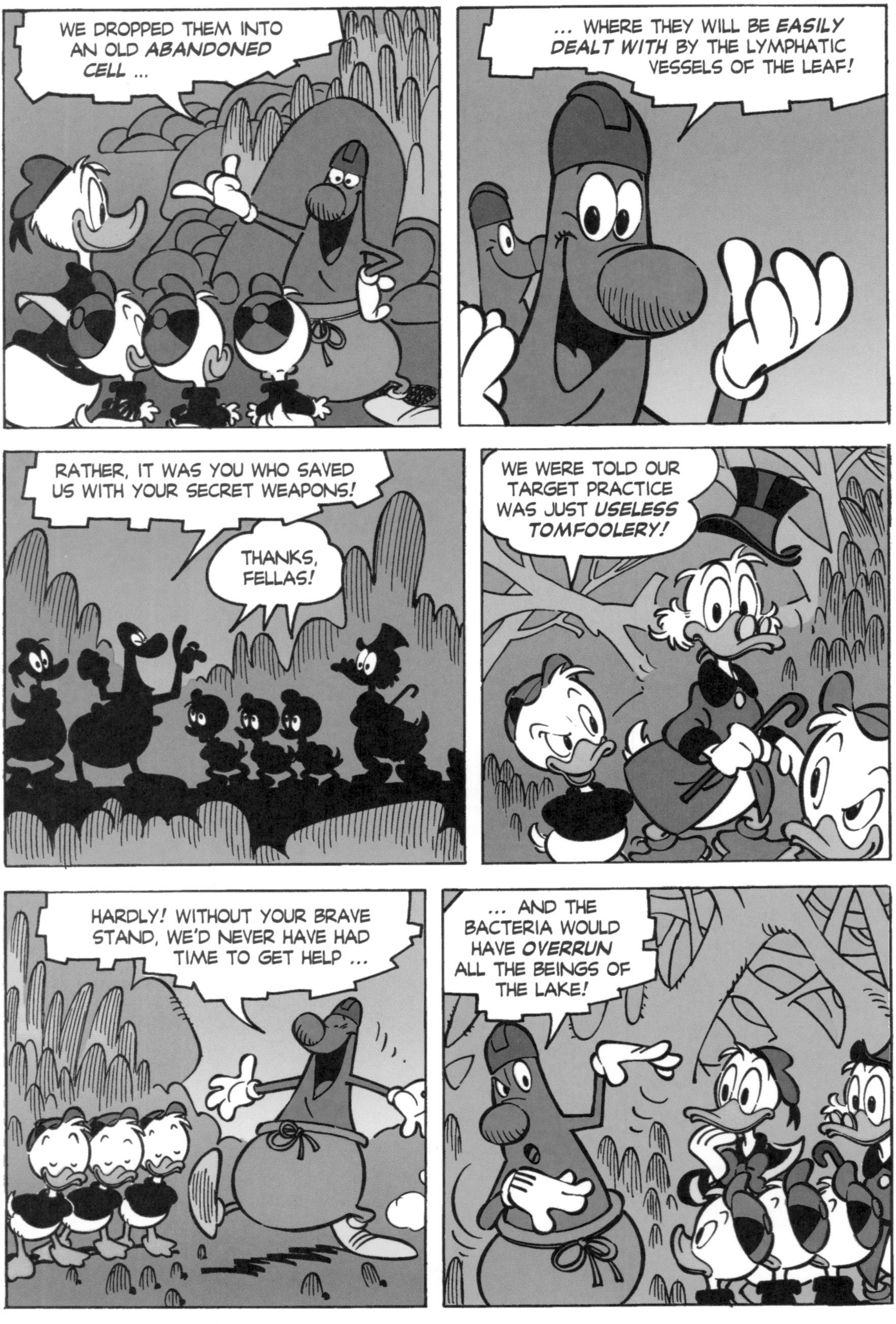
WE DROPPED THEM INTO AN OLD ABANDONED CELL ...
... WHERE THEY WILL BE EASILY DEALT WITH BY THE LYMPHATIC VESSELS OF THE LEAF!
RATHER, IT WAS YOU WHO SAVED US WITH YOUR SECRET WEAPONS!
THANKS, FELLAS!
WE WERE TOLD OUR TARGET PRACTICE WAS JUST USELESS TOMFOOLERY!
HARDLY! WITHOUT YOUR BRAVE STAND, WE'D NEVER HAVE HAD TIME TO GET HELP ...
... AND THE BACTERIA WOULD HAVE OVERRUN ALL THE BEINGS OF THE LAKE!

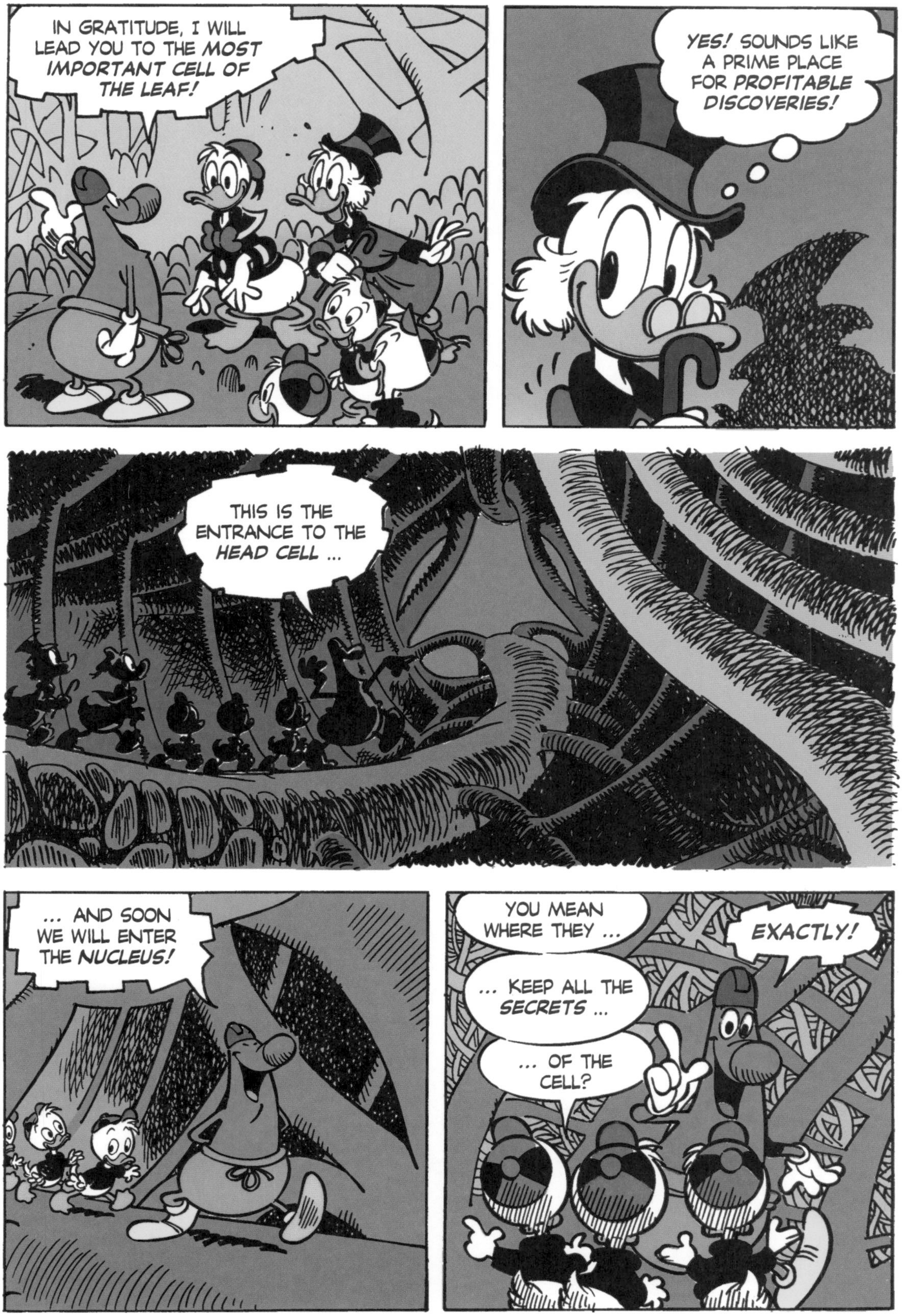
IN GRATITUDE, I WILL LEAD YOU TO THE *MOST IMPORTANT CELL OF THE LEAF!*
*YES!* SOUNDS LIKE A PRIME PLACE FOR *PROFITABLE DISCOVERIES!*
THIS IS THE ENTRANCE TO THE *HEAD CELL* ...
... AND SOON WE WILL ENTER THE *NUCLEUS!*
YOU MEAN WHERE THEY ...
... KEEP ALL THE *SECRETS* ...
... OF THE CELL?
*EXACTLY!*

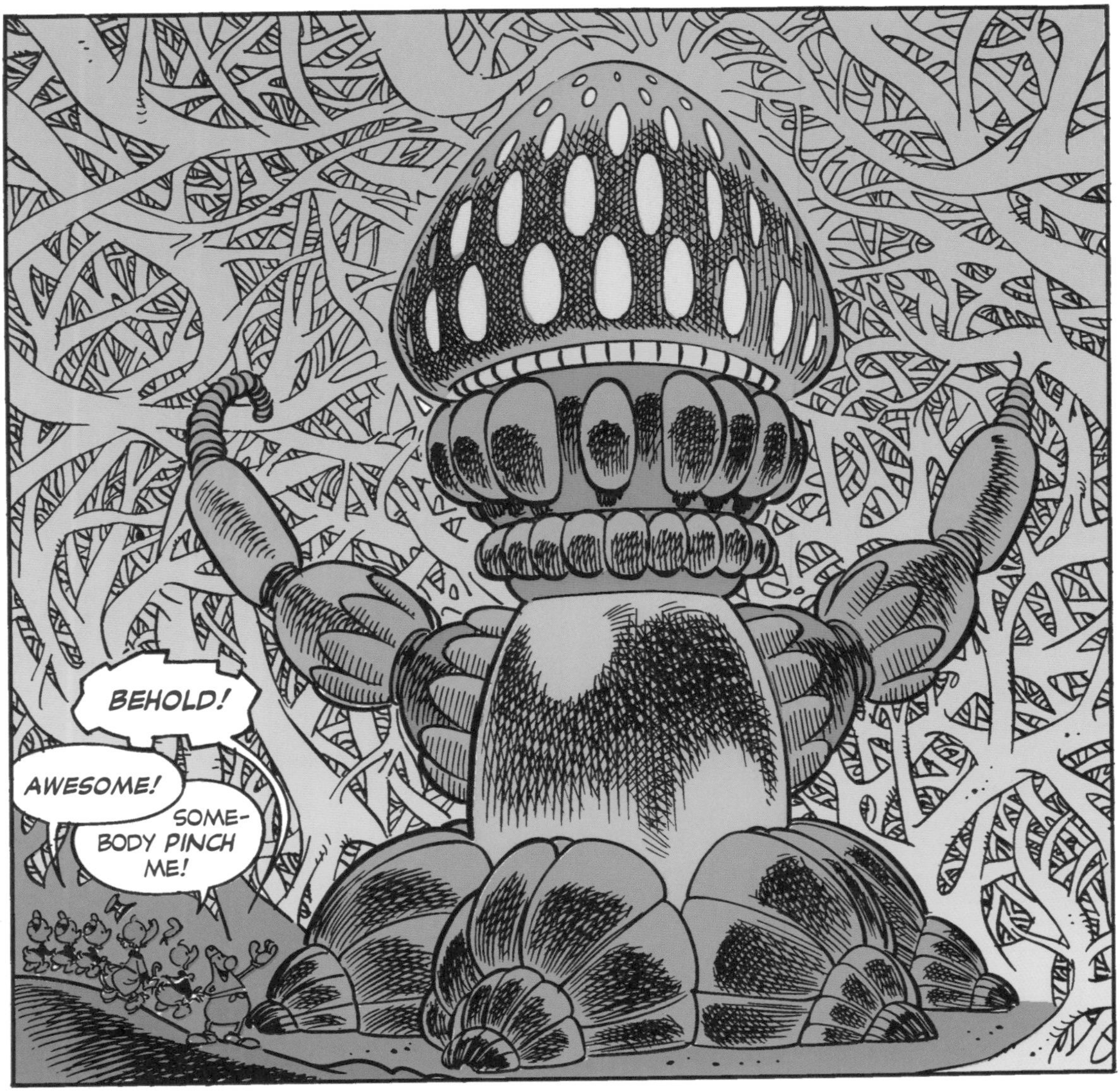
BEHOLD!
AWESOME!
SOME-BODY PINCH ME!

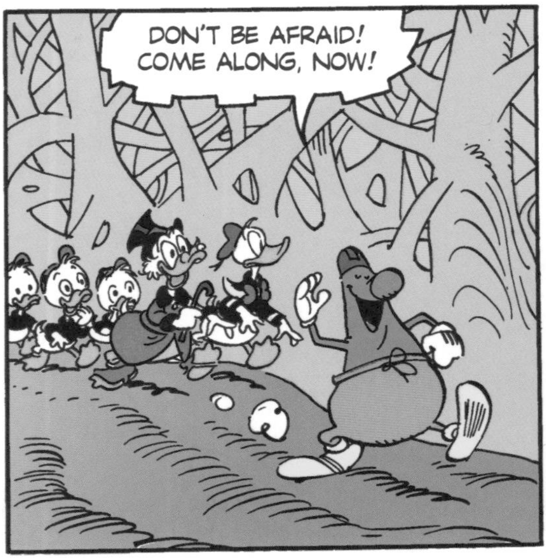
DON'T BE AFRAID! COME ALONG, NOW!

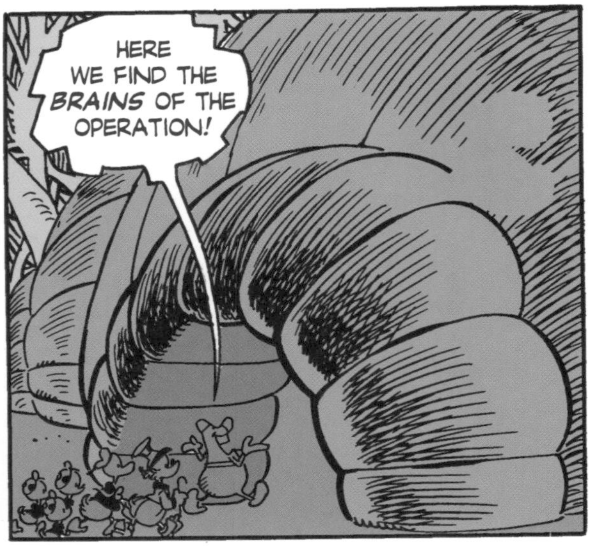
HERE WE FIND THE BRAINS OF THE OPERATION!

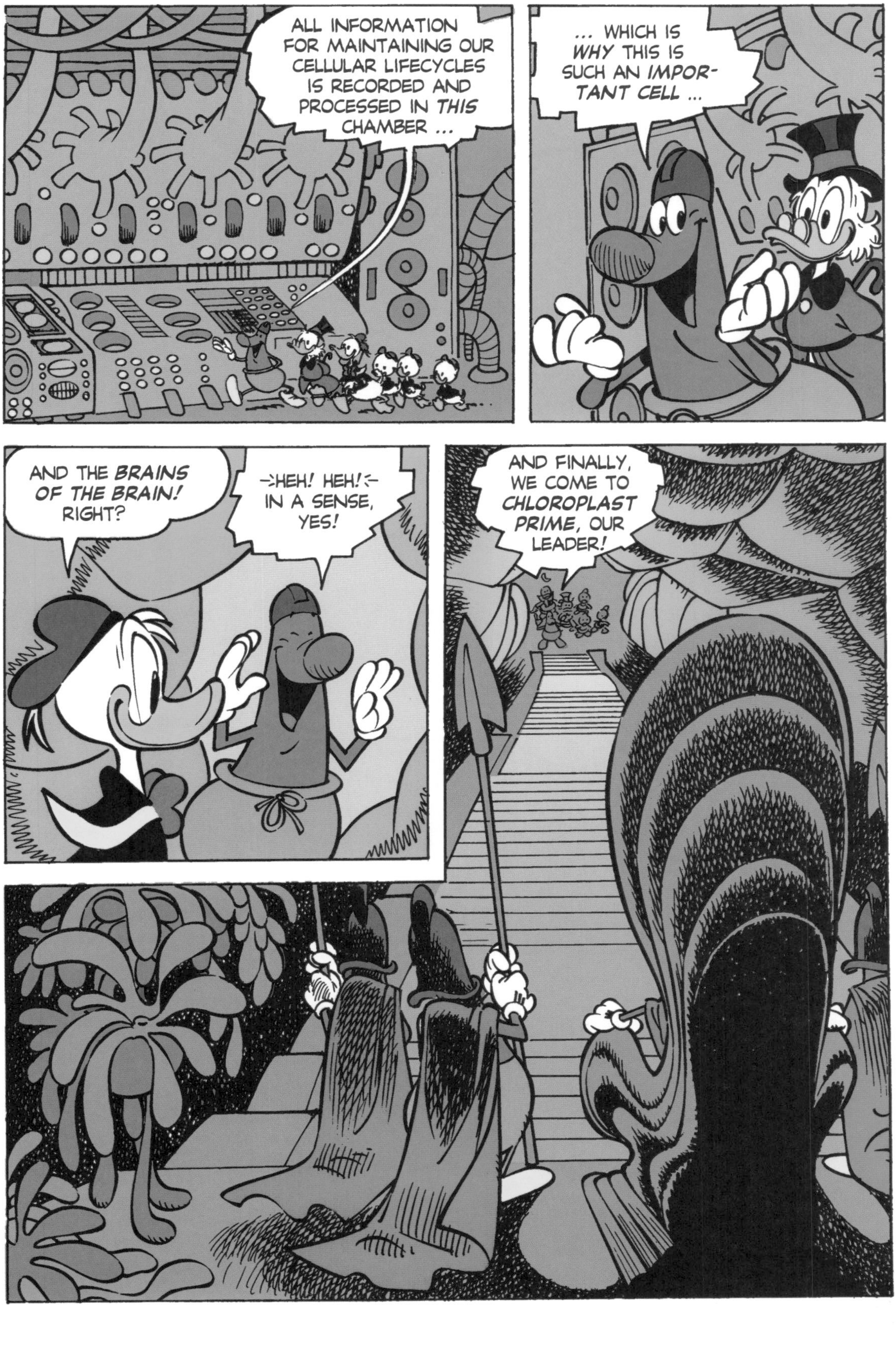
ALL INFORMATION FOR MAINTAINING OUR CELLULAR LIFECYCLES IS RECORDED AND PROCESSED IN THIS CHAMBER ...
... WHICH IS WHY THIS IS SUCH AN IMPORTANT CELL ...
AND THE BRAINS OF THE BRAIN! RIGHT?
-HEH! HEH!- IN A SENSE, YES!
AND FINALLY, WE COME TO CHLOROPLAST PRIME, OUR LEADER!

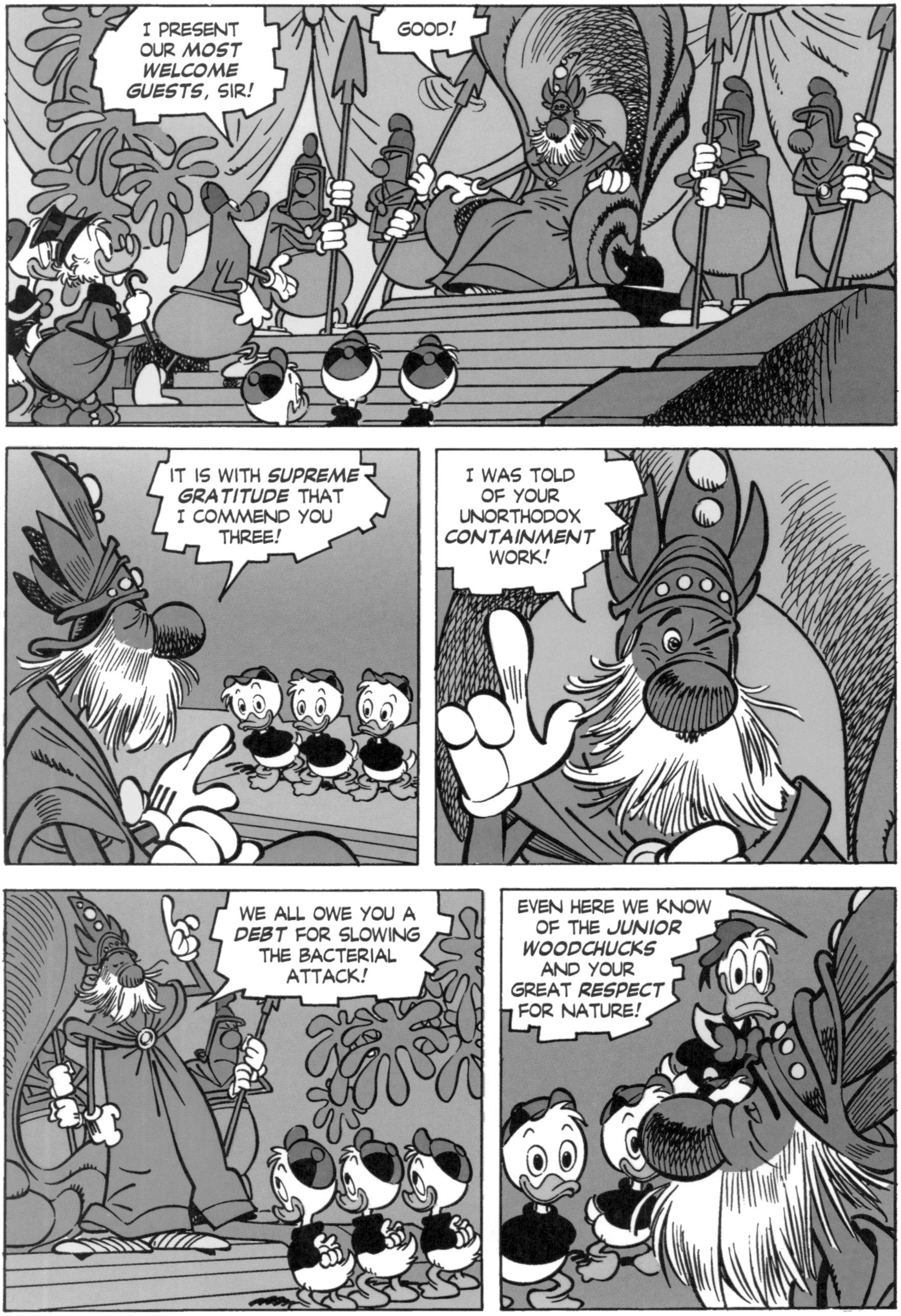
I PRESENT OUR MOST WELCOME GUESTS, SIR!
GOOD!
IT IS WITH SUPREME GRATITUDE THAT I COMMEND YOU THREE!
I WAS TOLD OF YOUR UNORTHODOX CONTAINMENT WORK!
WE ALL OWE YOU A DEBT FOR SLOWING THE BACTERIAL ATTACK!
EVEN HERE WE KNOW OF THE JUNIOR WOODCHUCKS AND YOUR GREAT RESPECT FOR NATURE!

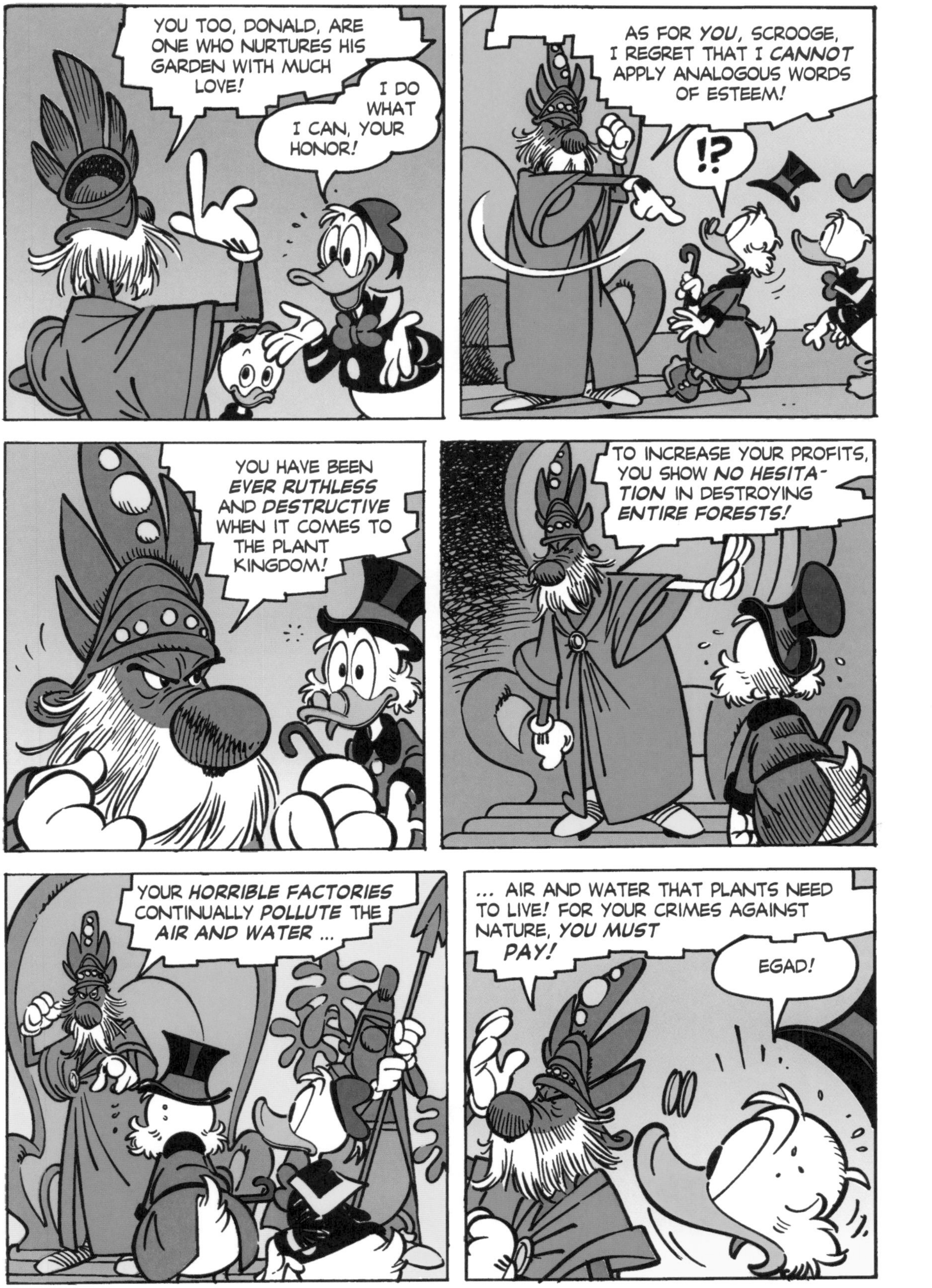
YOU TOO, DONALD, ARE ONE WHO NURTURES HIS GARDEN WITH MUCH LOVE!
I DO WHAT I CAN, YOUR HONOR!
AS FOR YOU, SCROOGE, I REGRET THAT I CANNOT APPLY ANALOGOUS WORDS OF ESTEEM!
!?
YOU HAVE BEEN EVER RUTHLESS AND DESTRUCTIVE WHEN IT COMES TO THE PLANT KINGDOM!
TO INCREASE YOUR PROFITS, YOU SHOW NO HESITATION IN DESTROYING ENTIRE FORESTS!
YOUR HORRIBLE FACTORIES CONTINUALLY POLLUTE THE AIR AND WATER ...
... AIR AND WATER THAT PLANTS NEED TO LIVE! FOR YOUR CRIMES AGAINST NATURE, YOU MUST PAY!
EGAD!

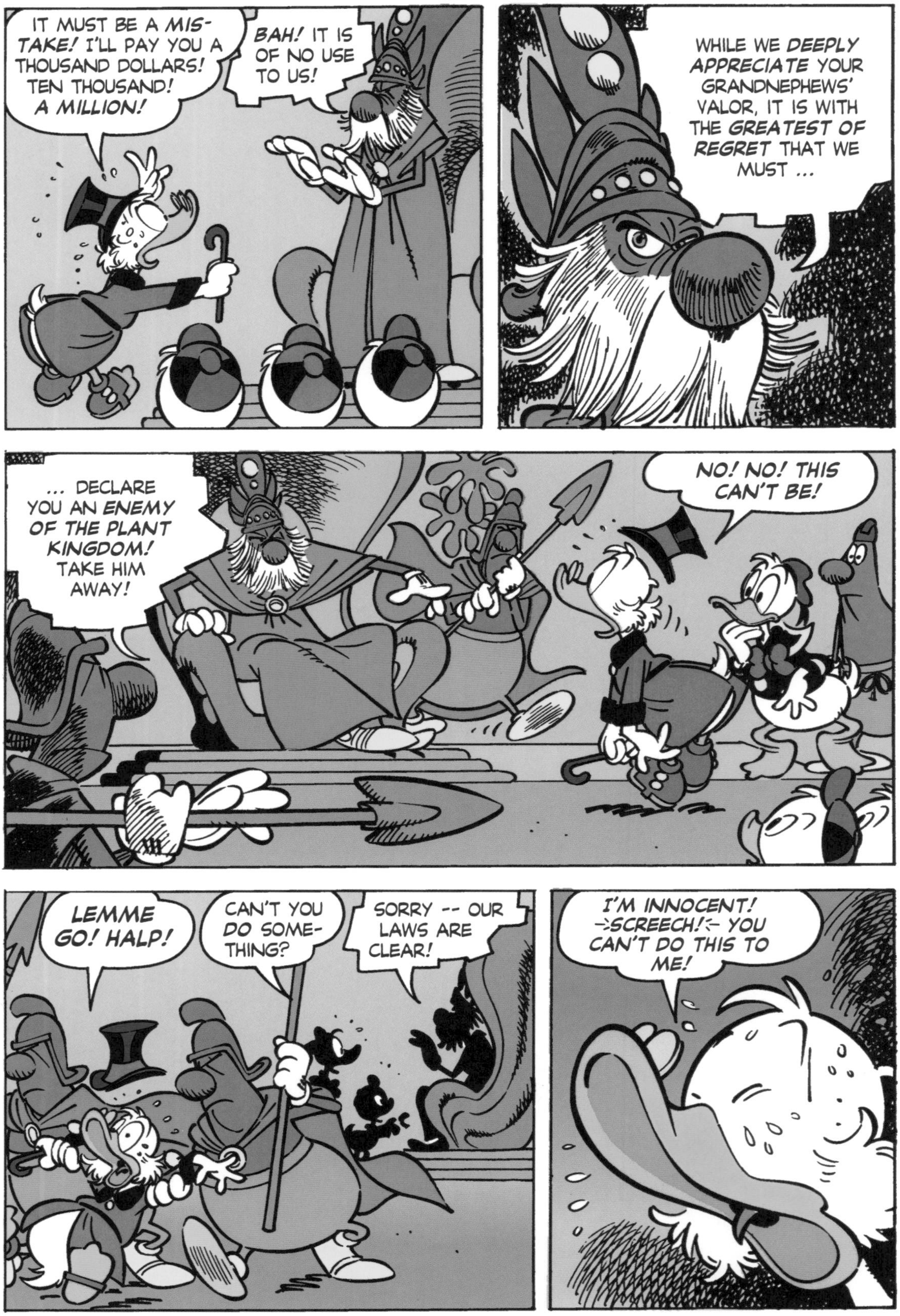
IT MUST BE A MIS-TAKE! I'LL PAY YOU A THOUSAND DOLLARS! TEN THOUSAND! A MILLION!
BAH! IT IS OF NO USE TO US!
WHILE WE DEEPLY APPRECIATE YOUR GRANDNEPHEWS' VALOR, IT IS WITH THE GREATEST OF REGRET THAT WE MUST ...
... DECLARE YOU AN ENEMY OF THE PLANT KINGDOM! TAKE HIM AWAY!
NO! NO! THIS CAN'T BE!
LEMME GO! HALP!
CAN'T YOU DO SOME-THING?
SORRY -- OUR LAWS ARE CLEAR!
I'M INNOCENT! -SCREECH!- YOU CAN'T DO THIS TO ME!

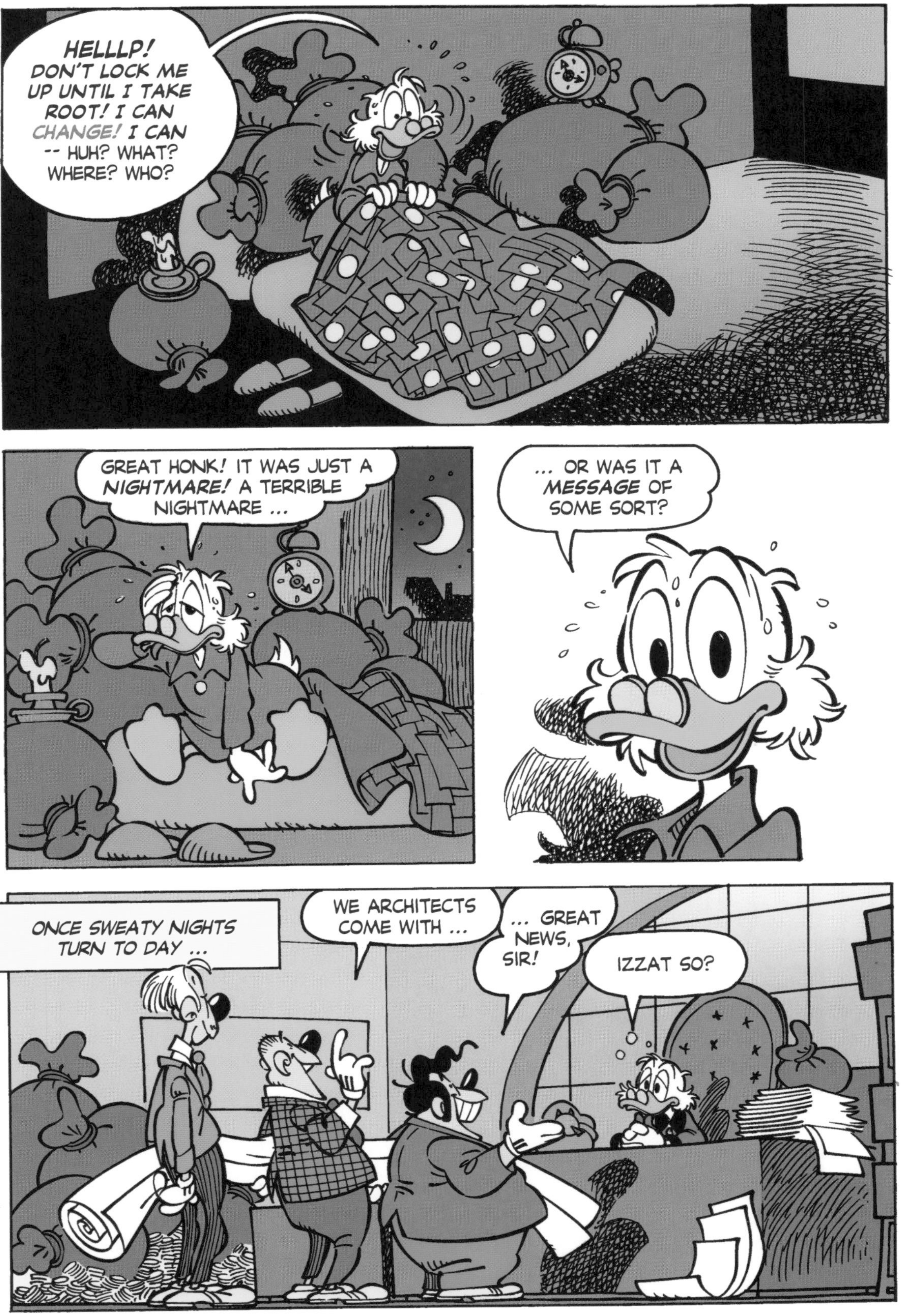
HELLLP! DON'T LOCK ME UP UNTIL I TAKE ROOT! I CAN CHANGE! I CAN -- HUH? WHAT? WHERE? WHO?
GREAT HONK! IT WAS JUST A NIGHTMARE! A TERRIBLE NIGHTMARE ...
... OR WAS IT A MESSAGE OF SOME SORT?
ONCE SWEATY NIGHTS TURN TO DAY ...
WE ARCHITECTS COME WITH ...
... GREAT NEWS, SIR!
IZZAT SO?

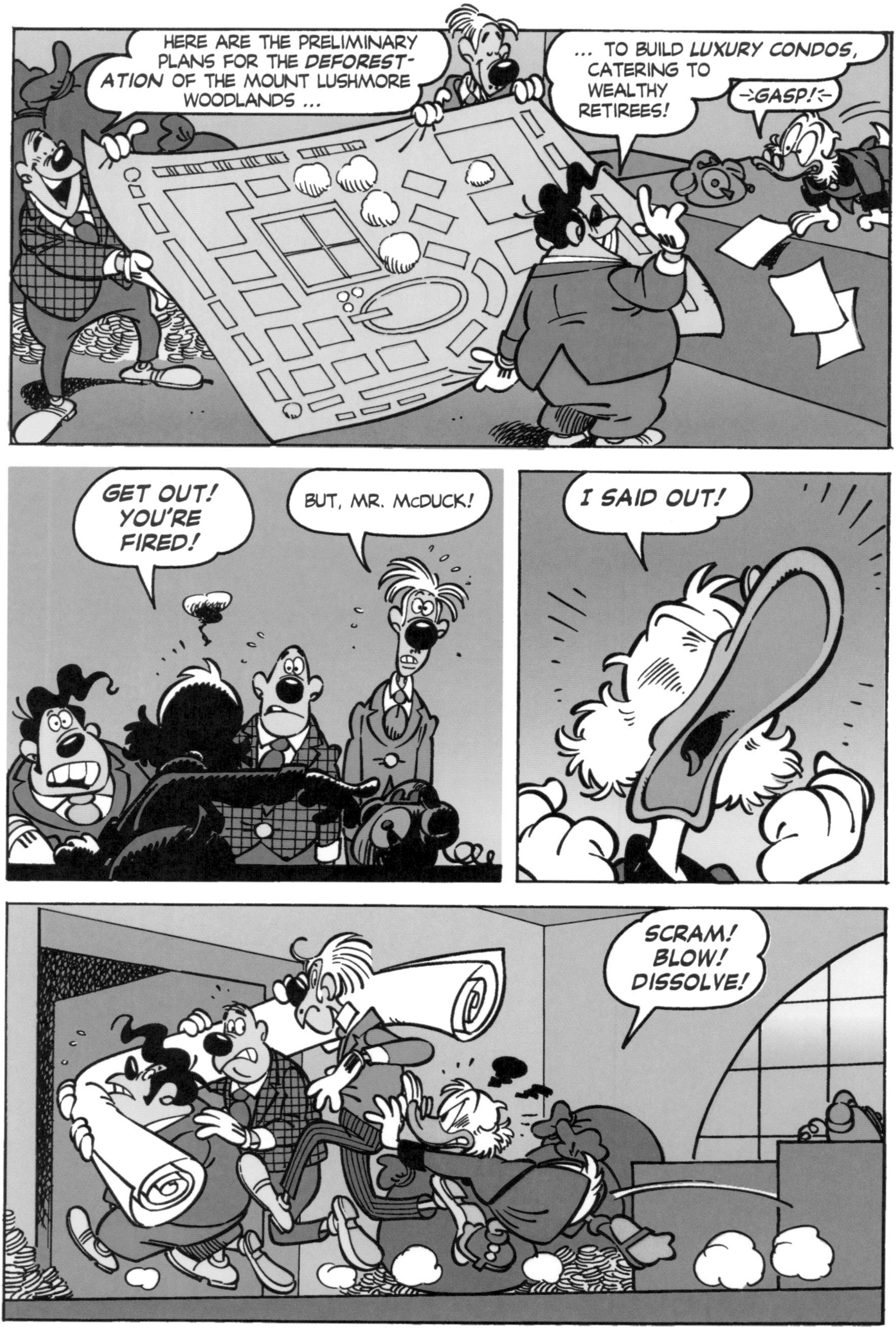
HERE ARE THE PRELIMINARY PLANS FOR THE *DEFORESTATION* OF THE MOUNT LUSHMORE WOODLANDS ...
... TO BUILD *LUXURY CONDOS*, CATERING TO WEALTHY RETIREES!
GASP!
GET OUT! YOU'RE FIRED!
BUT, MR. McDUCK!
I SAID OUT!
SCRAM! BLOW! DISSOLVE!

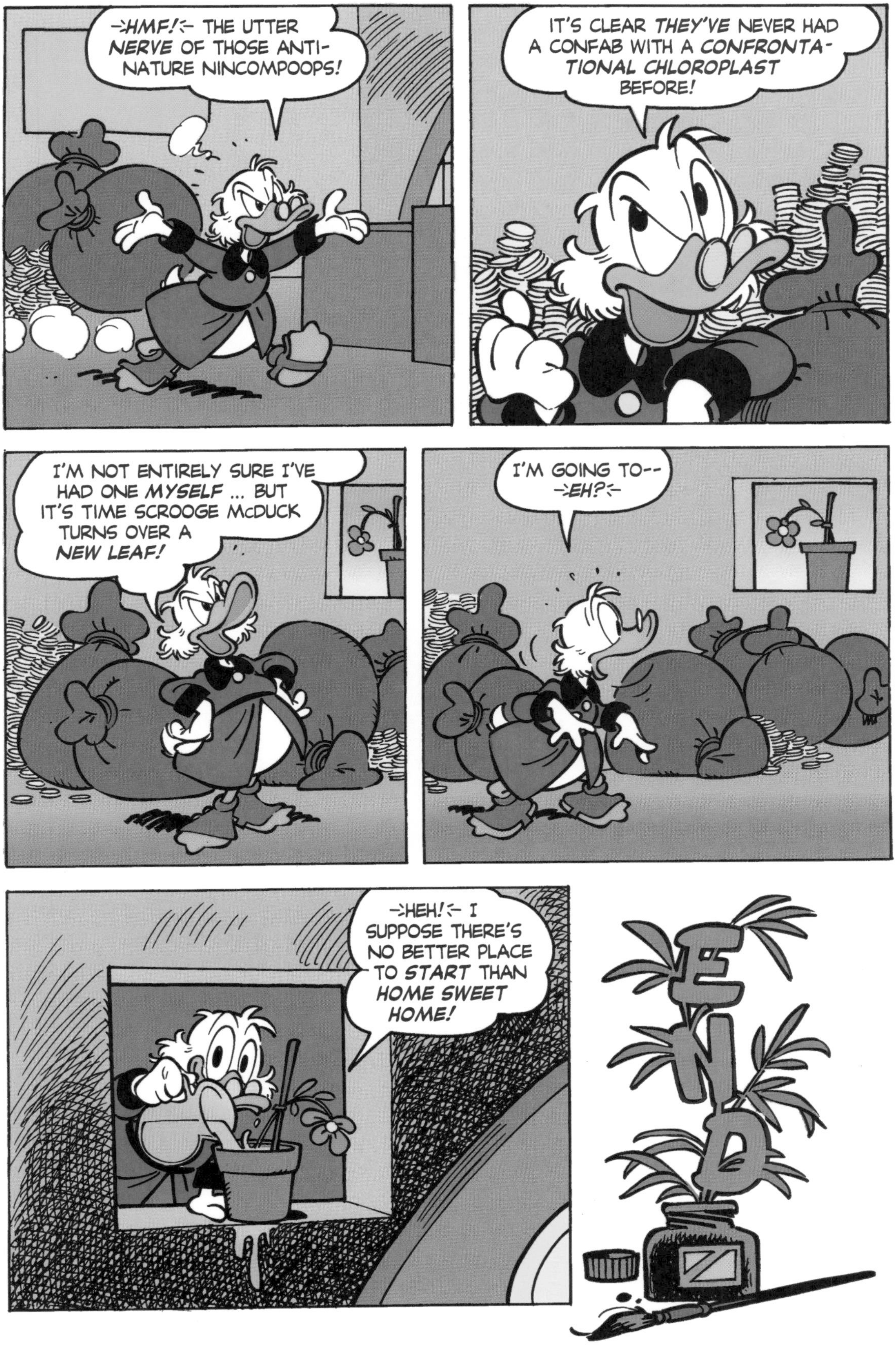

-HMF!- THE UTTER NERVE OF THOSE ANTI-NATURE NINCOMPOOPS!
IT'S CLEAR THEY'VE NEVER HAD A CONFAB WITH A CONFRONTATIONAL CHLOROPLAST BEFORE!
I'M NOT ENTIRELY SURE I'VE HAD ONE MYSELF ... BUT IT'S TIME SCROOGE McDUCK TURNS OVER A NEW LEAF!
I'M GOING TO-- -EH?-
-HEH!- I SUPPOSE THERE'S NO BETTER PLACE TO START THAN HOME SWEET HOME!
END

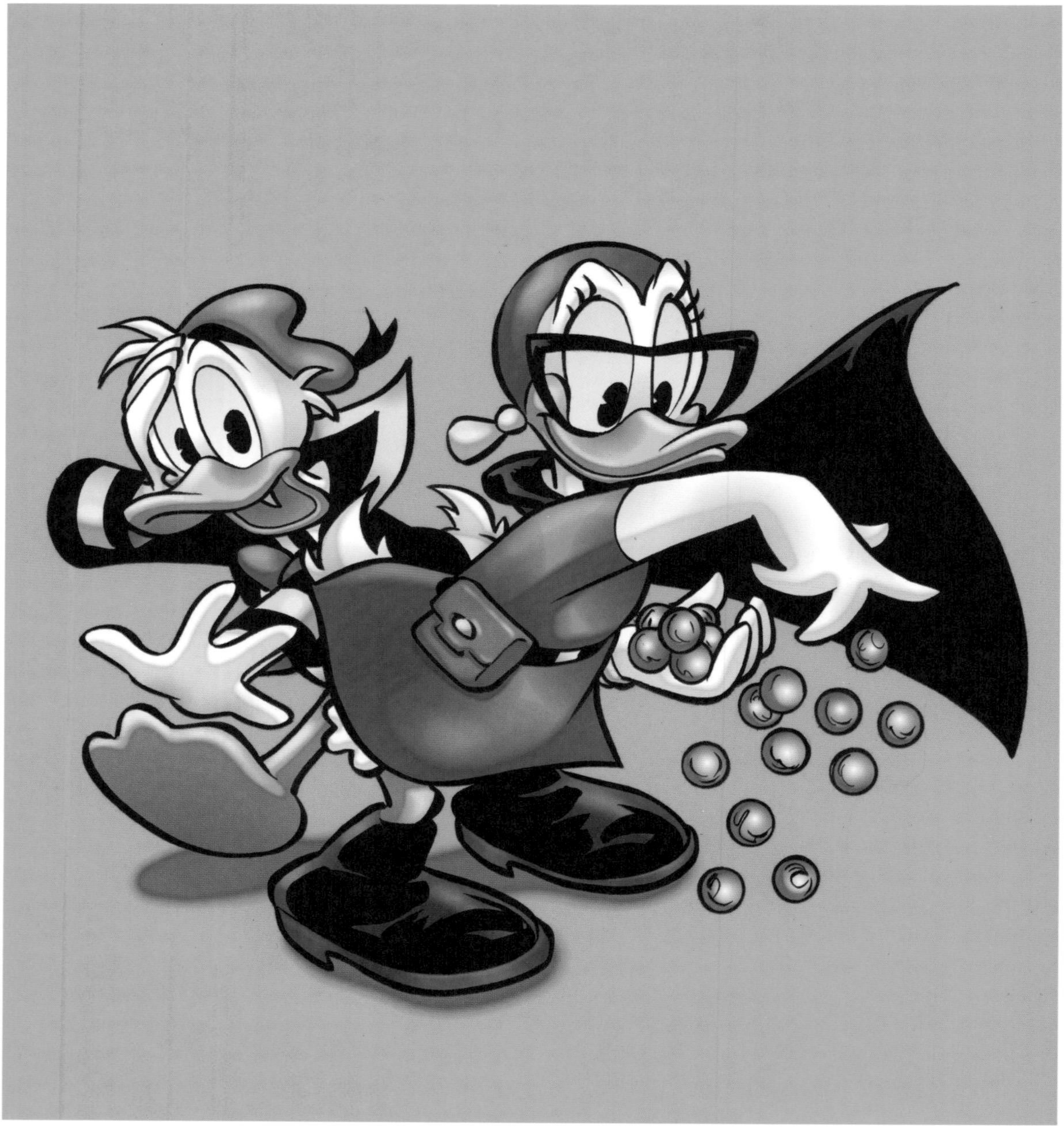

Donald had spent four years as the "super-anti-hero" Duck Avenger when — in 1973 — the *Topolino* staff struck a blow for women's equality. "The Dazzling Duck She-Venger" (opposite), written by Guido Martina and drawn by Cavazzano, starts out like many a 1950s Duck story, with Donald viewing Daisy as little more than a pest. But then the story takes what at the time was a historic turnabout, making Daisy the reader identification character and sending her on her own avenging adventure. Above: Cavazzano's 2017 cover for a recent Italian reprint of the story.

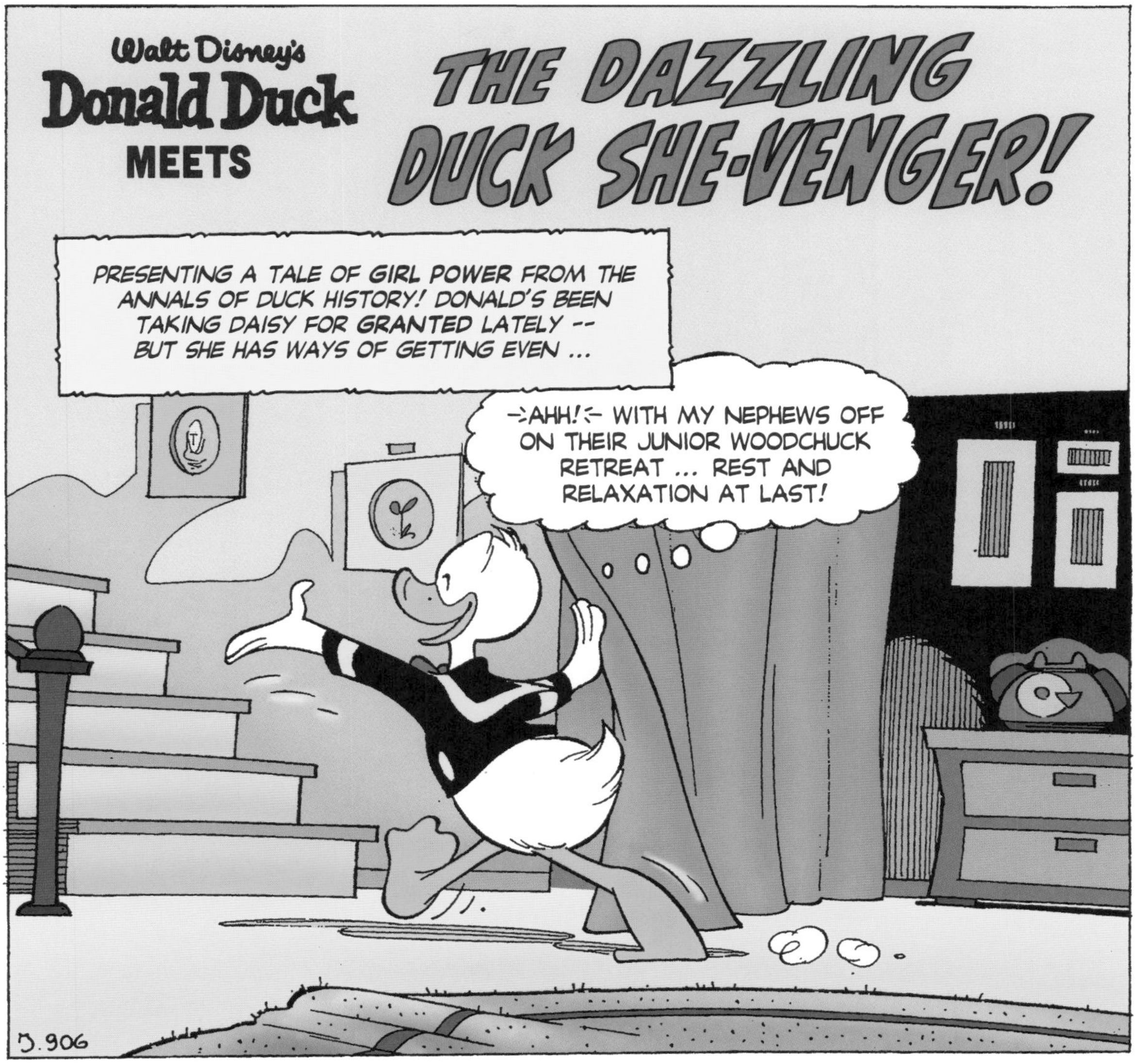
Walt Disney's
Donald Duck
MEETS
THE DAZZLING DUCK SHE-VENGER!
PRESENTING A TALE OF GIRL POWER FROM THE ANNALS OF DUCK HISTORY! DONALD'S BEEN TAKING DAISY FOR GRANTED LATELY -- BUT SHE HAS WAYS OF GETTING EVEN ...
AHH! WITH MY NEPHEWS OFF ON THEIR JUNIOR WOODCHUCK RETREAT ... REST AND RELAXATION AT LAST!
J. 906

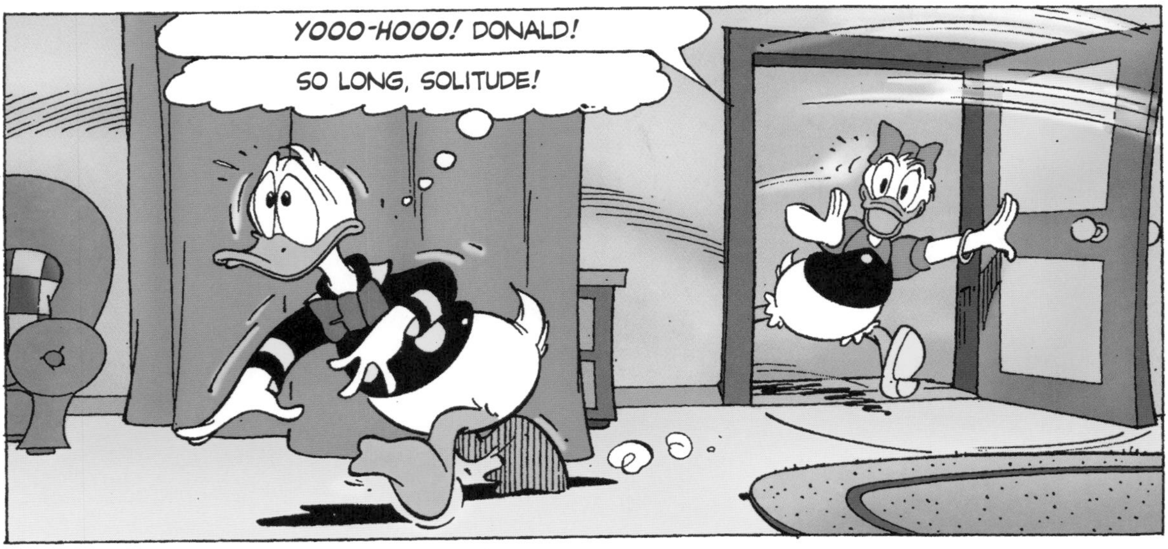
YOOO-HOOO! DONALD!
SO LONG, SOLITUDE!

STORY BY GUIDO MARTINA • ART BY GIORGIO CAVAZZANO • TRANSLATION AND DIALOGUE BY THAD KOMOROWSKI
EDITING BY J. MICHAEL CATRON AND DAVID GERSTEIN

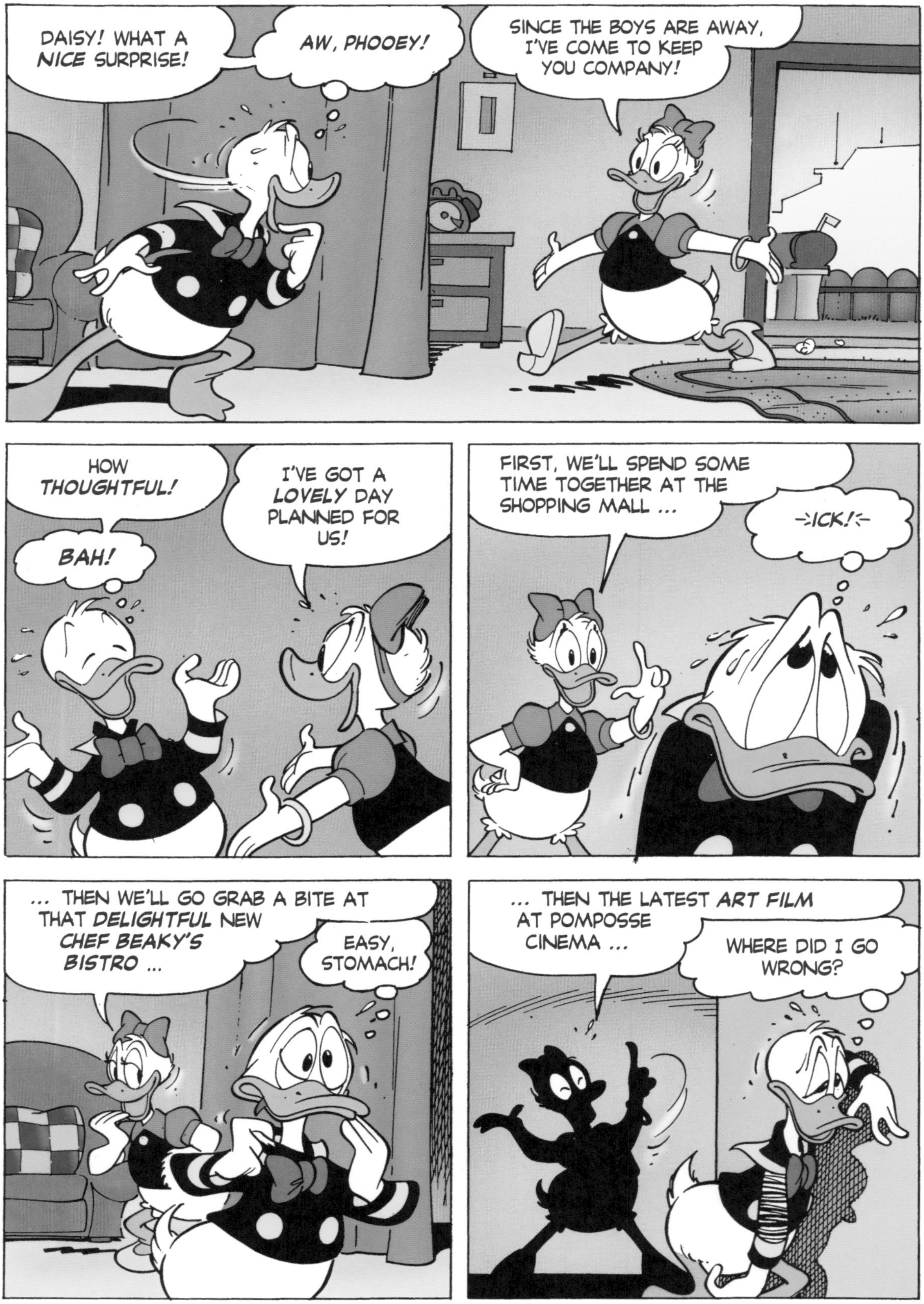
DAISY! WHAT A NICE SURPRISE!
AW, PHOOEY!
SINCE THE BOYS ARE AWAY, I'VE COME TO KEEP YOU COMPANY!
HOW THOUGHTFUL!
BAH!
I'VE GOT A LOVELY DAY PLANNED FOR US!
FIRST, WE'LL SPEND SOME TIME TOGETHER AT THE SHOPPING MALL ...
ICK!
... THEN WE'LL GO GRAB A BITE AT THAT DELIGHTFUL NEW CHEF BEAKY'S BISTRO ...
EASY, STOMACH!
... THEN THE LATEST ART FILM AT POMPOSSE CINEMA ...
WHERE DID I GO WRONG?

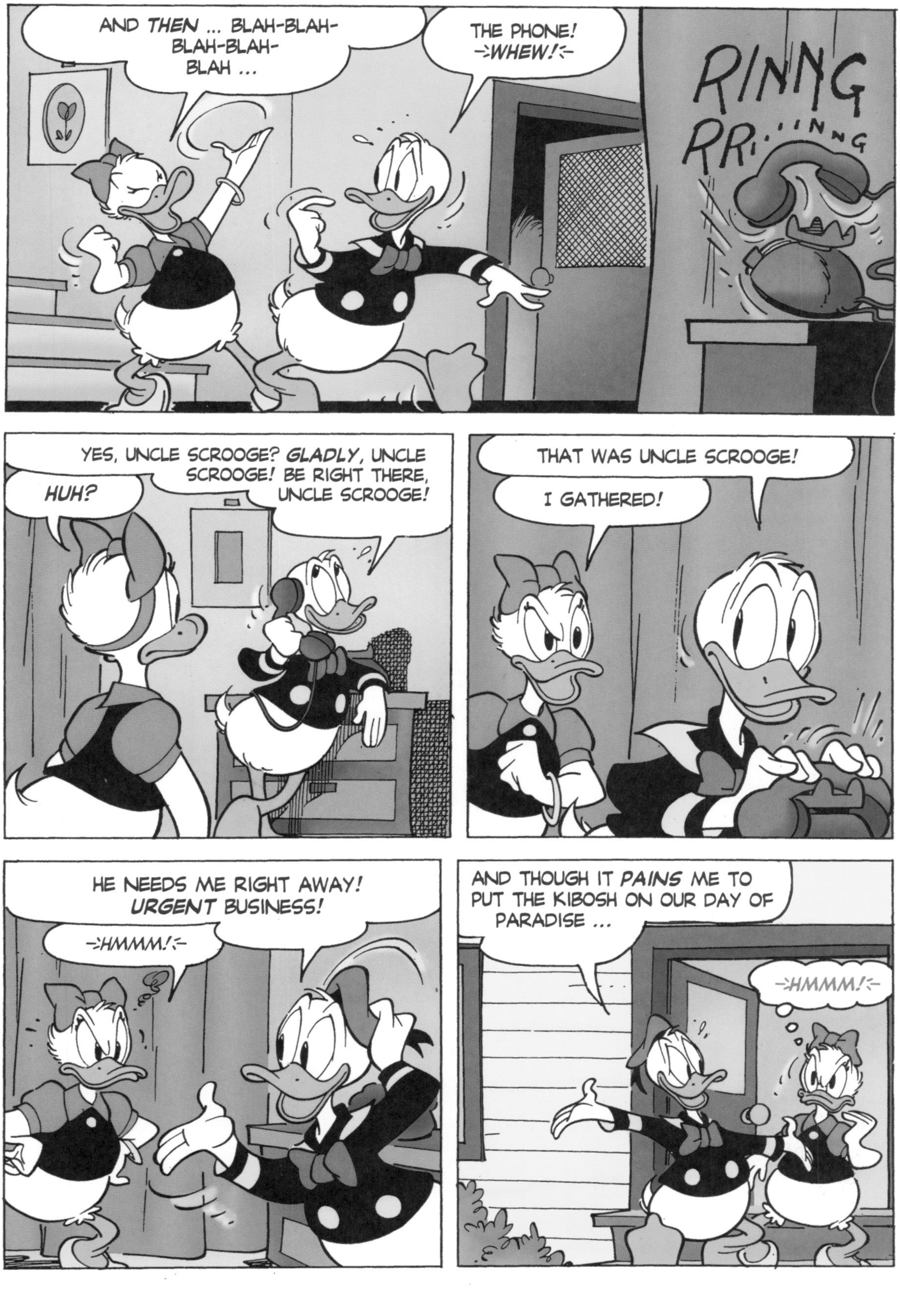
AND THEN ... BLAH-BLAH-BLAH-BLAH-BLAH ...
THE PHONE! WHEW!
RINNG
RRiiiNNG
YES, UNCLE SCROOGE? GLADLY, UNCLE SCROOGE! BE RIGHT THERE, UNCLE SCROOGE!
HUH?
THAT WAS UNCLE SCROOGE!
I GATHERED!
HE NEEDS ME RIGHT AWAY! URGENT BUSINESS!
HMMM!
AND THOUGH IT PAINS ME TO PUT THE KIBOSH ON OUR DAY OF PARADISE ...
HMMM!

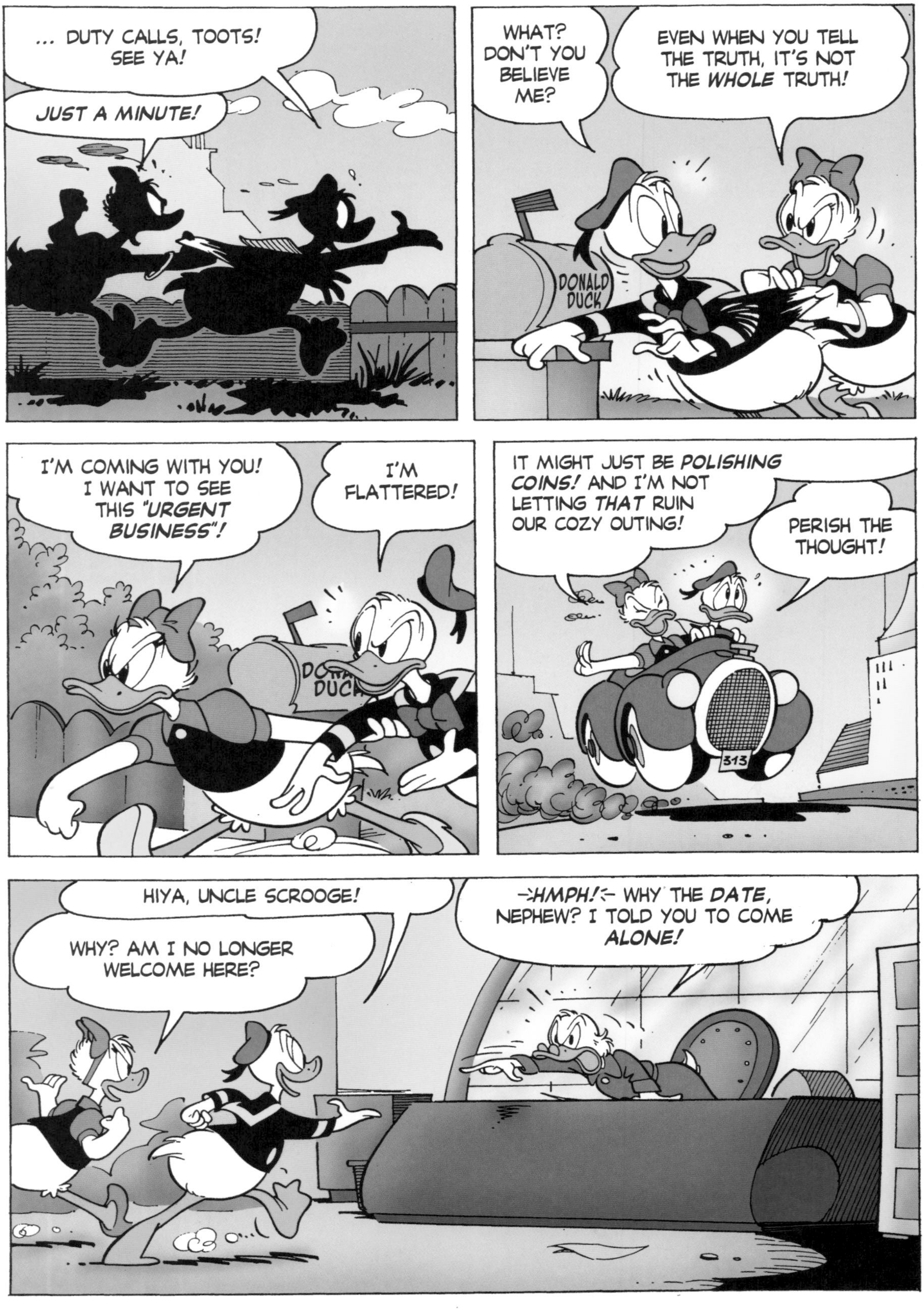
... DUTY CALLS, TOOTS! SEE YA!
JUST A MINUTE!
WHAT? DON'T YOU BELIEVE ME?
EVEN WHEN YOU TELL THE TRUTH, IT'S NOT THE WHOLE TRUTH!
DONALD DUCK
I'M COMING WITH YOU! I WANT TO SEE THIS "URGENT BUSINESS"!
I'M FLATTERED!
IT MIGHT JUST BE POLISHING COINS! AND I'M NOT LETTING THAT RUIN OUR COZY OUTING!
PERISH THE THOUGHT!
313
HIYA, UNCLE SCROOGE!
WHY? AM I NO LONGER WELCOME HERE?
-HMPH!- WHY THE DATE, NEPHEW? I TOLD YOU TO COME ALONE!

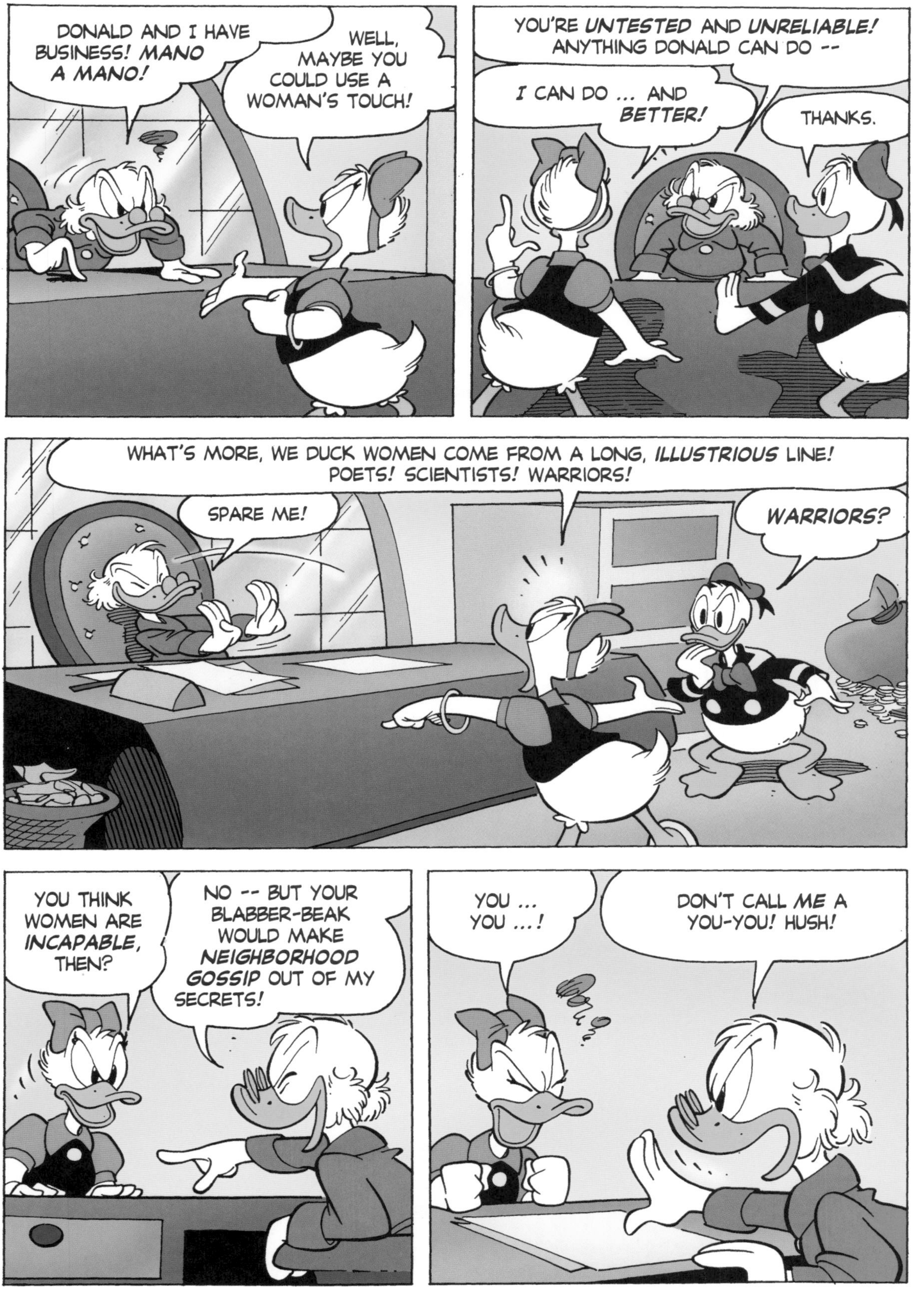
DONALD AND I HAVE BUSINESS! MANO A MANO!
WELL, MAYBE YOU COULD USE A WOMAN'S TOUCH!
YOU'RE UNTESTED AND UNRELIABLE! ANYTHING DONALD CAN DO --
I CAN DO ... AND BETTER!
THANKS.
WHAT'S MORE, WE DUCK WOMEN COME FROM A LONG, ILLUSTRIOUS LINE! POETS! SCIENTISTS! WARRIORS!
SPARE ME!
WARRIORS?
YOU THINK WOMEN ARE INCAPABLE, THEN?
NO -- BUT YOUR BLABBER-BEAK WOULD MAKE NEIGHBORHOOD GOSSIP OUT OF MY SECRETS!
YOU ... YOU ...!
DON'T CALL ME A YOU-YOU! HUSH!

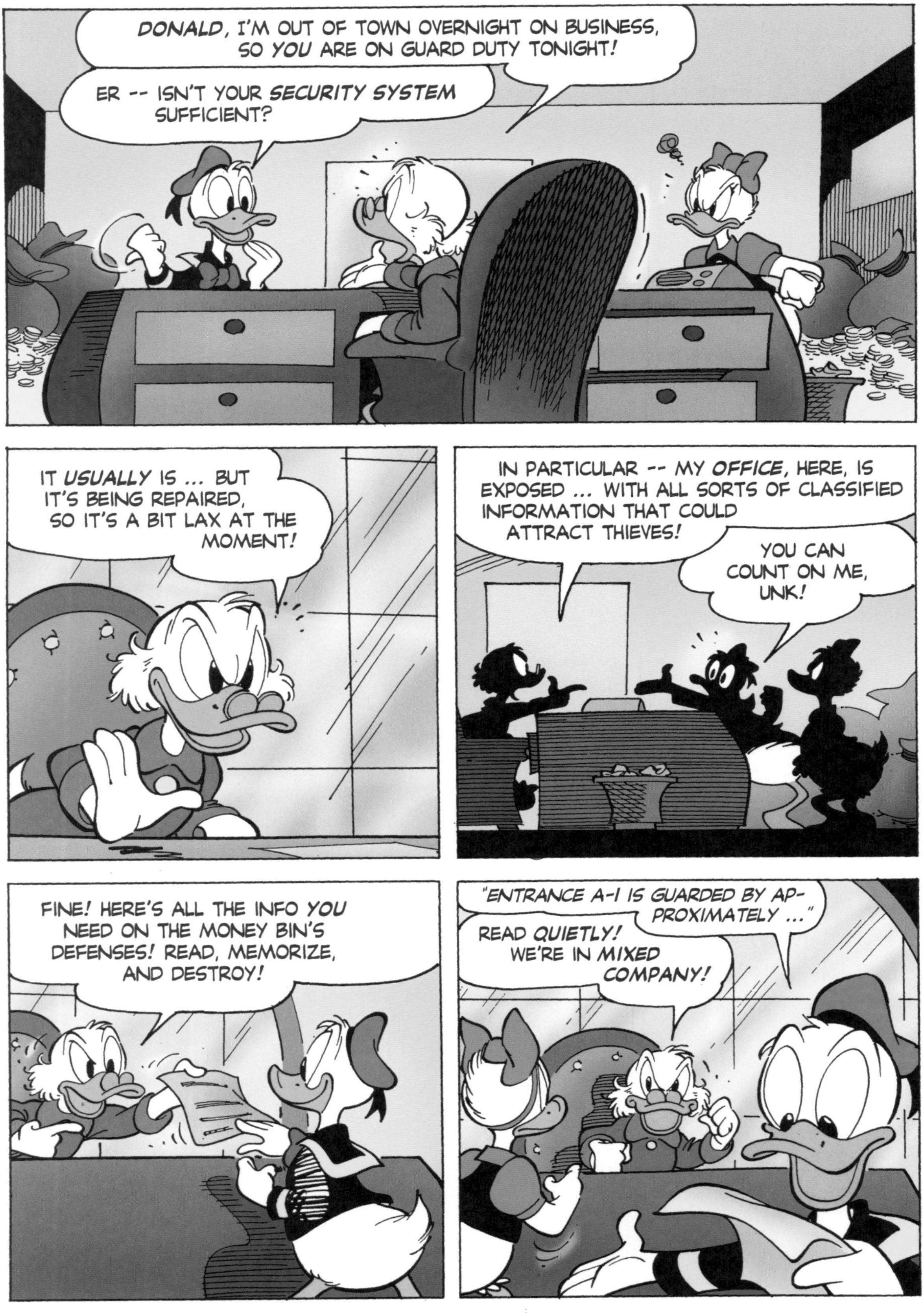
DONALD, I'M OUT OF TOWN OVERNIGHT ON BUSINESS, SO YOU ARE ON GUARD DUTY TONIGHT!
ER -- ISN'T YOUR SECURITY SYSTEM SUFFICIENT?
IT USUALLY IS ... BUT IT'S BEING REPAIRED, SO IT'S A BIT LAX AT THE MOMENT!
IN PARTICULAR -- MY OFFICE, HERE, IS EXPOSED ... WITH ALL SORTS OF CLASSIFIED INFORMATION THAT COULD ATTRACT THIEVES!
YOU CAN COUNT ON ME, UNK!
FINE! HERE'S ALL THE INFO YOU NEED ON THE MONEY BIN'S DEFENSES! READ, MEMORIZE, AND DESTROY!
"ENTRANCE A-1 IS GUARDED BY APPROXIMATELY ..."
READ QUIETLY! WE'RE IN MIXED COMPANY!

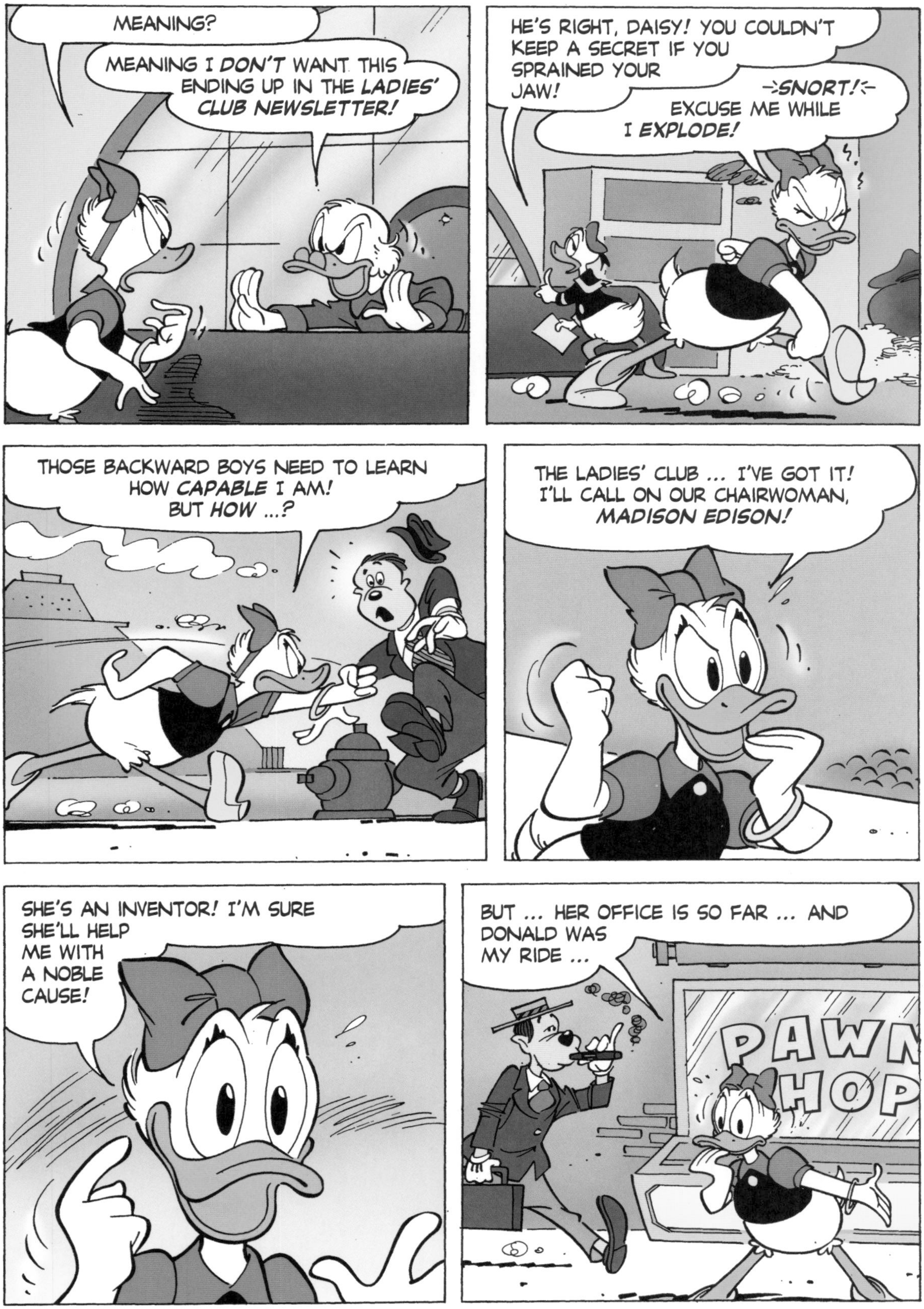
MEANING?
MEANING I DON'T WANT THIS ENDING UP IN THE LADIES' CLUB NEWSLETTER!
HE'S RIGHT, DAISY! YOU COULDN'T KEEP A SECRET IF YOU SPRAINED YOUR JAW!
SNORT! EXCUSE ME WHILE I EXPLODE!
THOSE BACKWARD BOYS NEED TO LEARN HOW CAPABLE I AM! BUT HOW ...?
THE LADIES' CLUB ... I'VE GOT IT! I'LL CALL ON OUR CHAIRWOMAN, MADISON EDISON!
SHE'S AN INVENTOR! I'M SURE SHE'LL HELP ME WITH A NOBLE CAUSE!
BUT ... HER OFFICE IS SO FAR ... AND DONALD WAS MY RIDE ...
PAWN SHOP

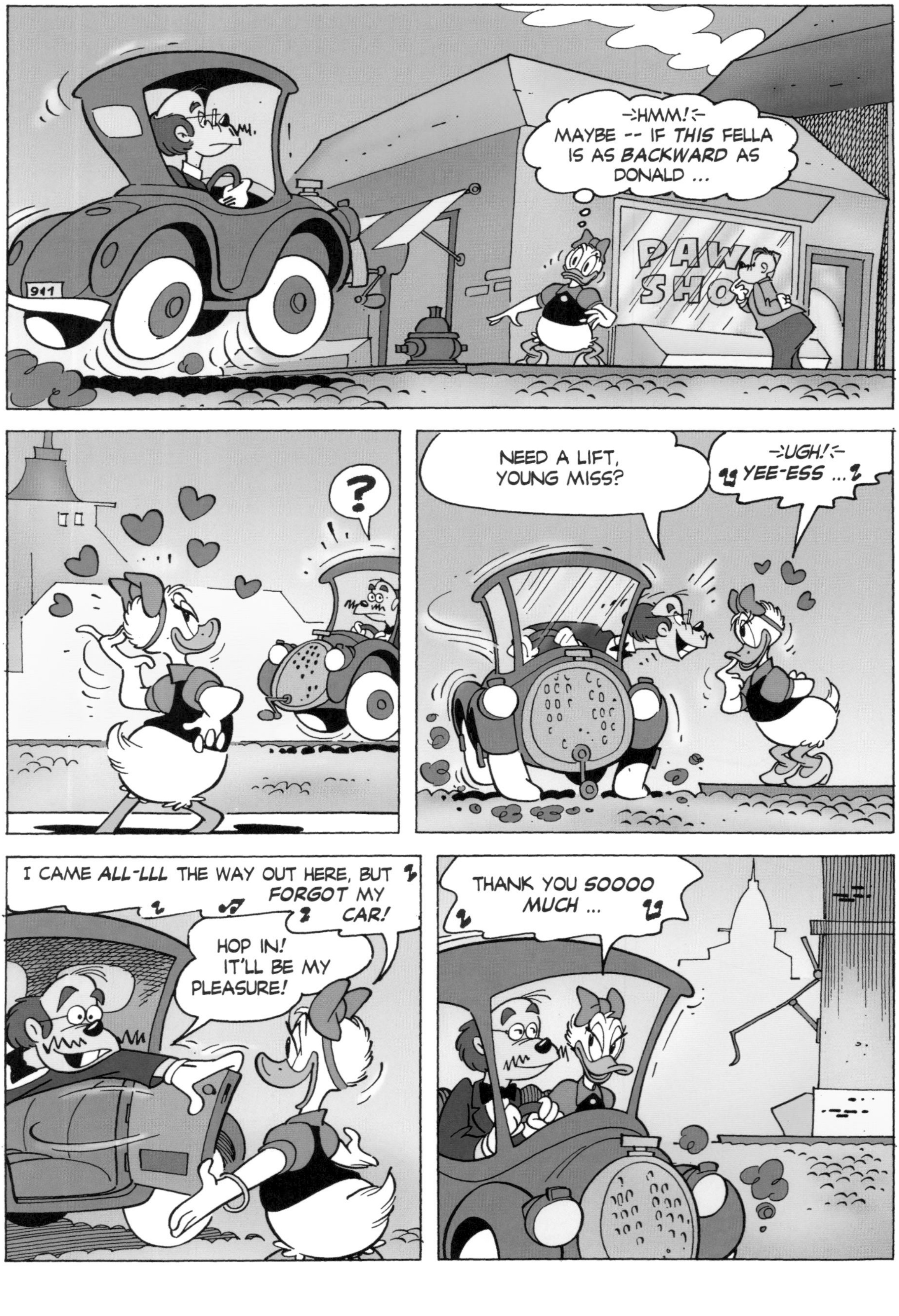
HMM!
MAYBE -- IF THIS FELLA IS AS BACKWARD AS DONALD ...
911
PAWN SHOP
?
NEED A LIFT, YOUNG MISS?
UGH!
YEE-ESS ...
I CAME ALL-LLL THE WAY OUT HERE, BUT FORGOT MY CAR!
HOP IN! IT'LL BE MY PLEASURE!
THANK YOU SOOOO MUCH ...

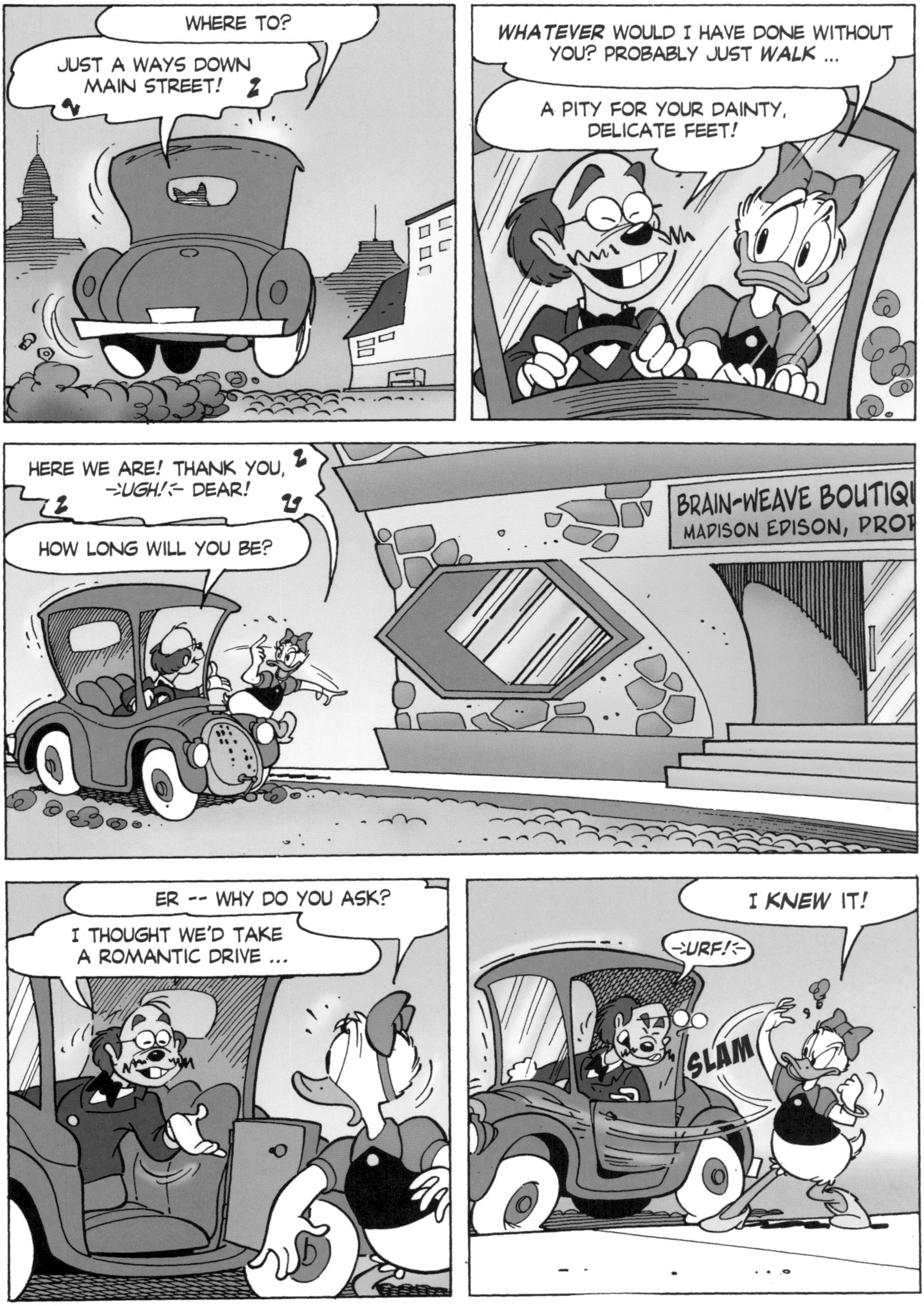
WHERE TO?
JUST A WAYS DOWN MAIN STREET!
WHATEVER WOULD I HAVE DONE WITHOUT YOU? PROBABLY JUST WALK ...
A PITY FOR YOUR DAINTY, DELICATE FEET!
HERE WE ARE! THANK YOU, -UGH!- DEAR!
HOW LONG WILL YOU BE?
BRAIN-WEAVE BOUTIQ
MADISON EDISON, PRO
ER -- WHY DO YOU ASK?
I THOUGHT WE'D TAKE A ROMANTIC DRIVE ...
I KNEW IT!
-URF!-
SLAM

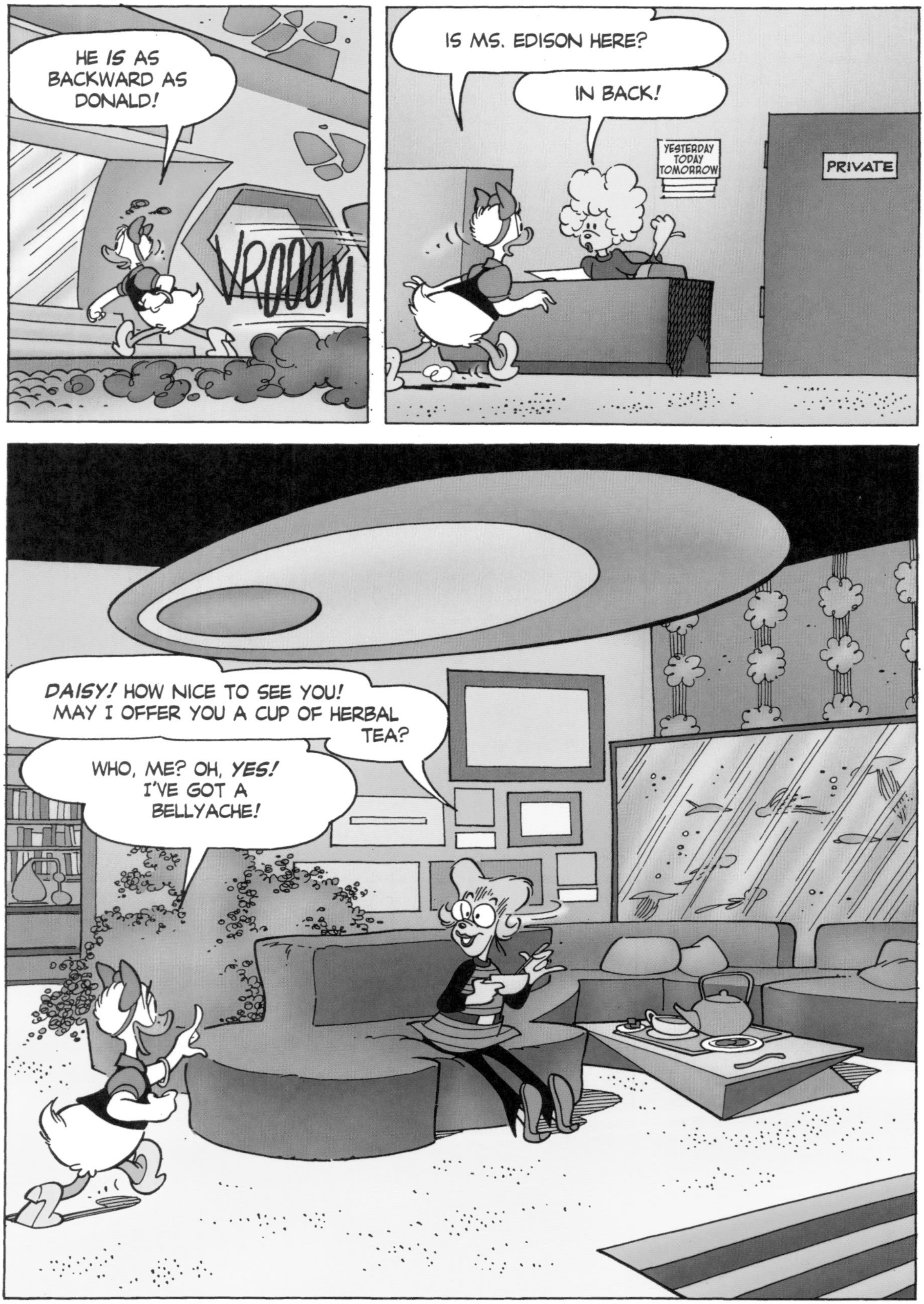
HE IS AS BACKWARD AS DONALD!
VROOOM
IS MS. EDISON HERE?
IN BACK!
YESTERDAY TODAY TOMORROW
PRIVATE
DAISY! HOW NICE TO SEE YOU! MAY I OFFER YOU A CUP OF HERBAL TEA?
WHO, ME? OH, YES! I'VE GOT A BELLYACHE!

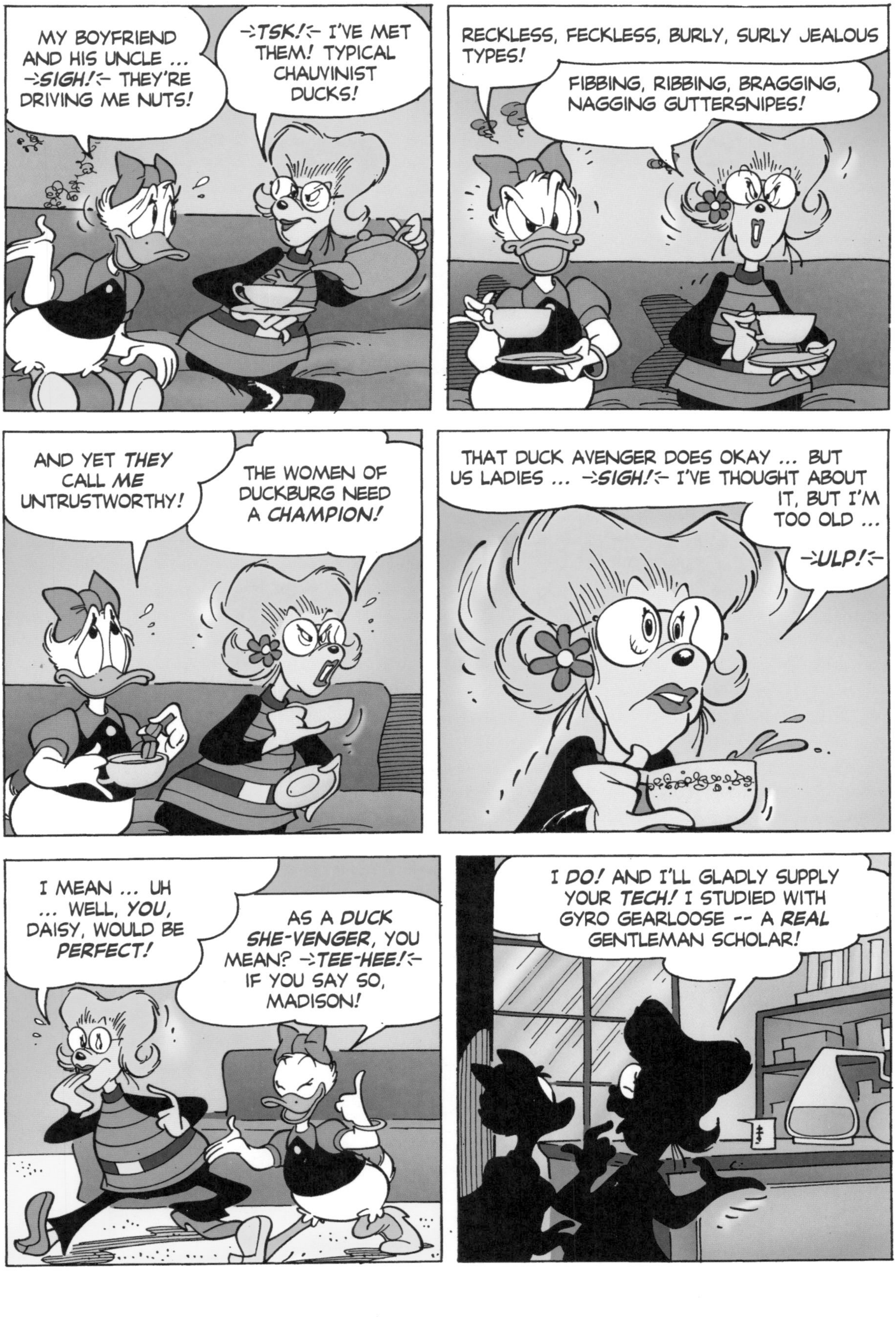
MY BOYFRIEND AND HIS UNCLE ... –>SIGH!<– THEY'RE DRIVING ME NUTS!
–>TSK!<– I'VE MET THEM! TYPICAL CHAUVINIST DUCKS!
RECKLESS, FECKLESS, BURLY, SURLY JEALOUS TYPES!
FIBBING, RIBBING, BRAGGING, NAGGING GUTTERSNIPES!
AND YET THEY CALL ME UNTRUSTWORTHY!
THE WOMEN OF DUCKBURG NEED A CHAMPION!
THAT DUCK AVENGER DOES OKAY ... BUT US LADIES ... –>SIGH!<– I'VE THOUGHT ABOUT IT, BUT I'M TOO OLD ...
–>ULP!<–
I MEAN ... UH ... WELL, YOU, DAISY, WOULD BE PERFECT!
AS A DUCK SHE-VENGER, YOU MEAN? –>TEE-HEE!<– IF YOU SAY SO, MADISON!
I DO! AND I'LL GLADLY SUPPLY YOUR TECH! I STUDIED WITH GYRO GEARLOOSE -- A REAL GENTLEMAN SCHOLAR!

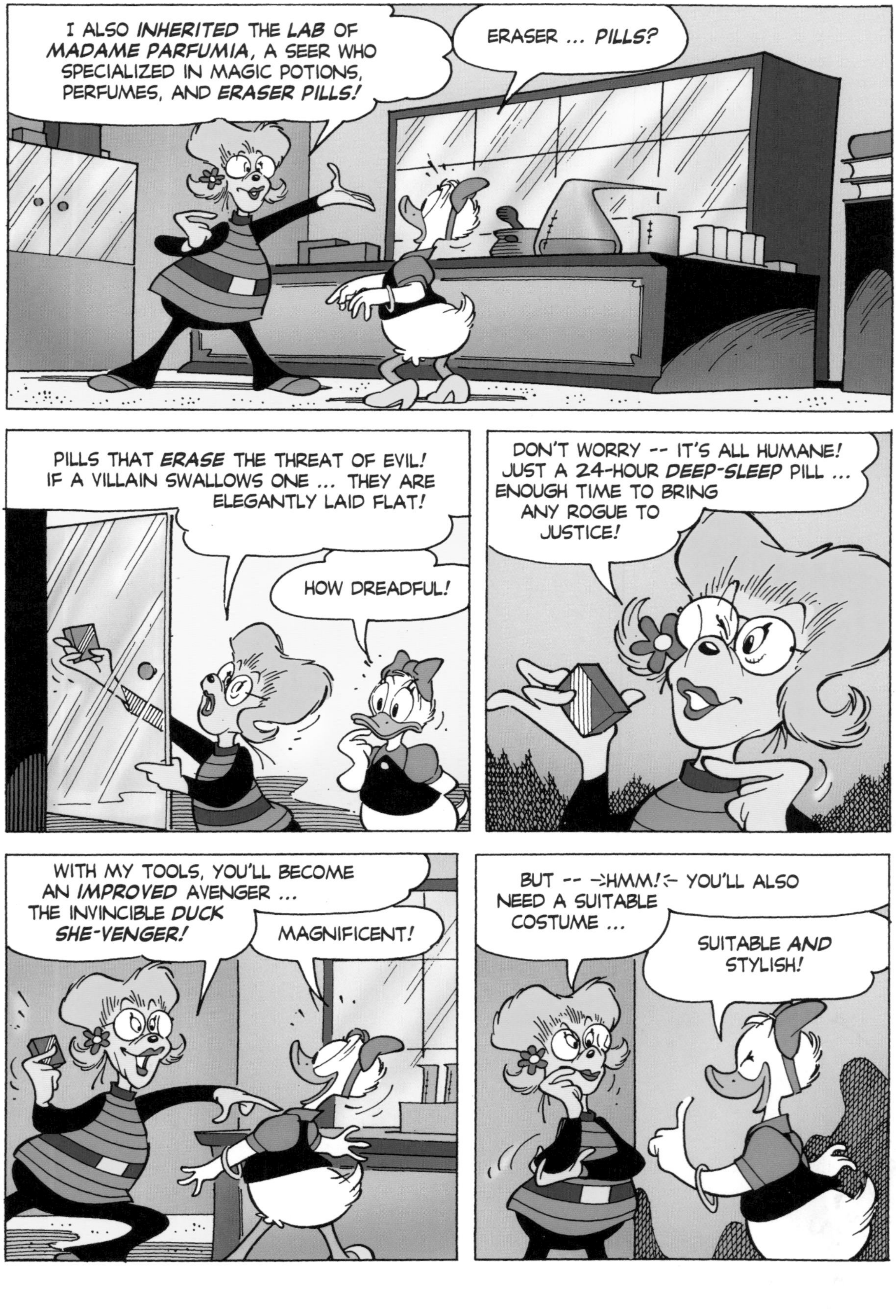
I ALSO *INHERITED* THE *LAB* OF *MADAME PARFUMIA*, A SEER WHO SPECIALIZED IN MAGIC POTIONS, PERFUMES, AND *ERASER PILLS!*
ERASER ... *PILLS?*
PILLS THAT *ERASE* THE THREAT OF EVIL! IF A VILLAIN SWALLOWS ONE ... THEY ARE ELEGANTLY LAID FLAT!
HOW DREADFUL!
DON'T WORRY -- IT'S ALL HUMANE! JUST A 24-HOUR *DEEP-SLEEP* PILL ... ENOUGH TIME TO BRING ANY ROGUE TO JUSTICE!
WITH MY TOOLS, YOU'LL BECOME AN *IMPROVED* AVENGER ... THE INVINCIBLE *DUCK SHE-VENGER!*
MAGNIFICENT!
BUT -- HMM! -- YOU'LL ALSO NEED A SUITABLE COSTUME ...
SUITABLE *AND* STYLISH!

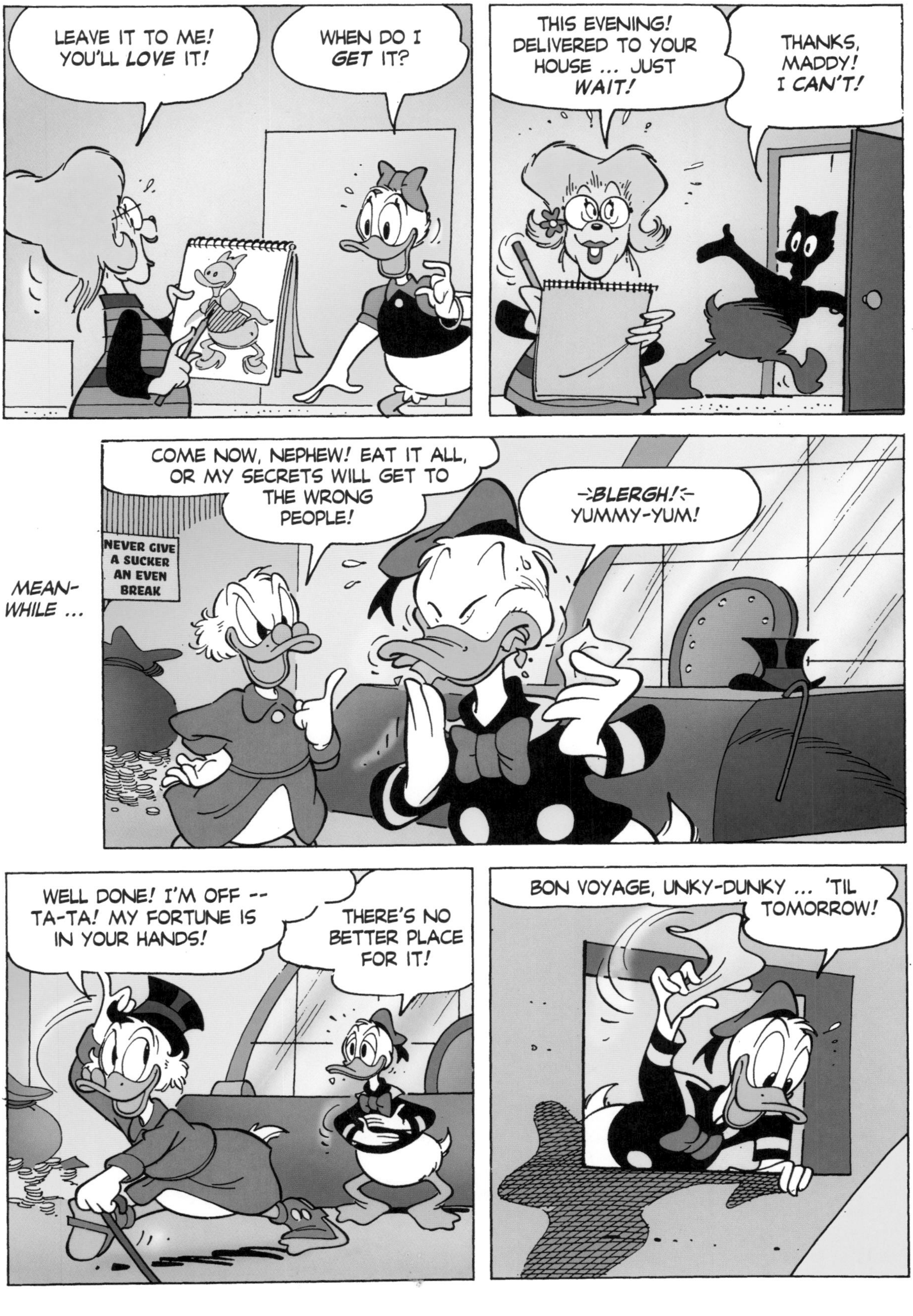
LEAVE IT TO ME! YOU'LL LOVE IT!
WHEN DO I GET IT?
THIS EVENING! DELIVERED TO YOUR HOUSE ... JUST WAIT!
THANKS, MADDY! I CAN'T!
MEAN-WHILE ...
COME NOW, NEPHEW! EAT IT ALL, OR MY SECRETS WILL GET TO THE WRONG PEOPLE!
NEVER GIVE A SUCKER AN EVEN BREAK
BLERGH! YUMMY-YUM!
WELL DONE! I'M OFF -- TA-TA! MY FORTUNE IS IN YOUR HANDS!
THERE'S NO BETTER PLACE FOR IT!
BON VOYAGE, UNKY-DUNKY ... 'TIL TOMORROW!

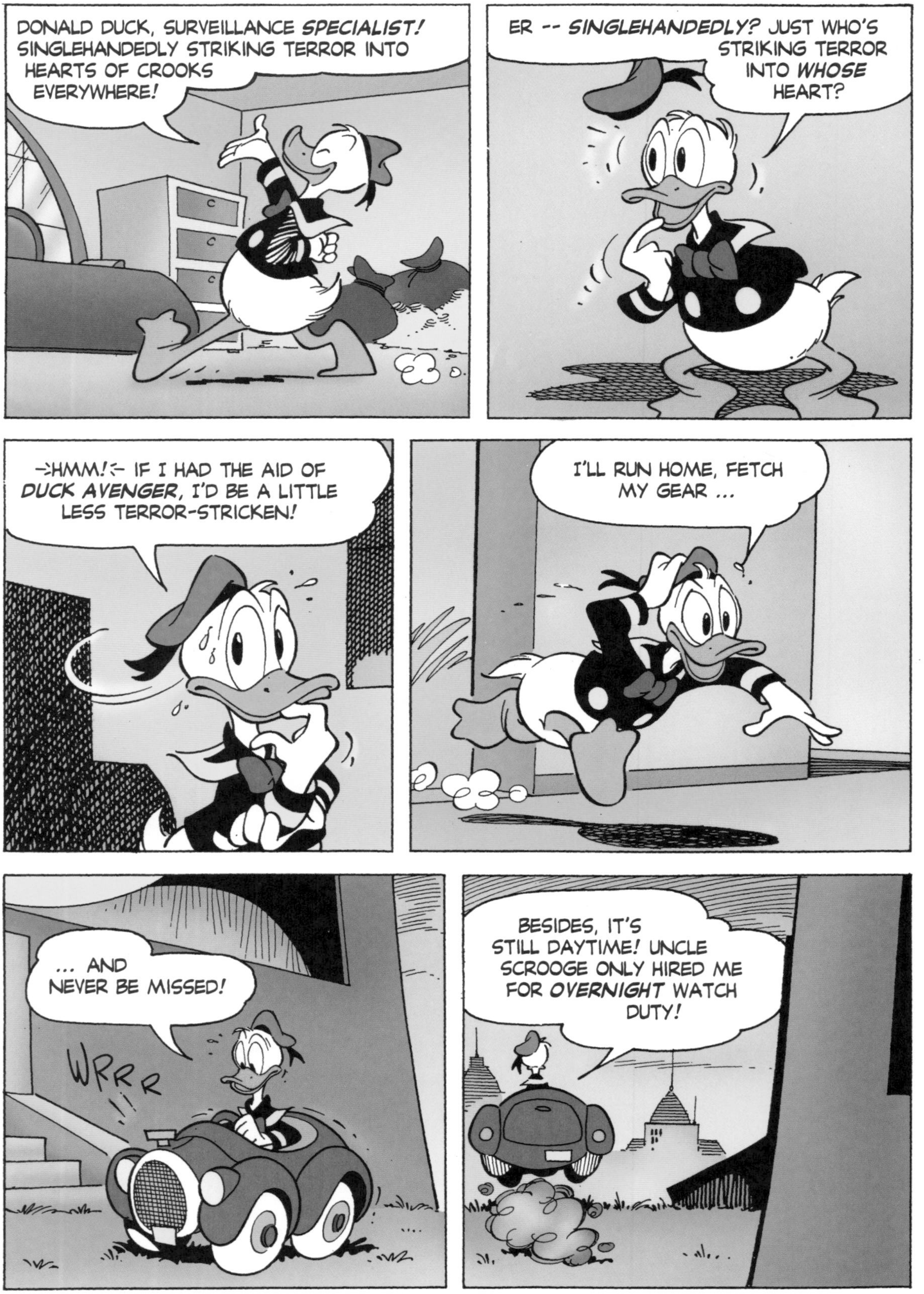
DONALD DUCK, SURVEILLANCE *SPECIALIST!* SINGLEHANDEDLY STRIKING TERROR INTO HEARTS OF CROOKS EVERYWHERE!
ER -- *SINGLEHANDEDLY?* JUST WHO'S STRIKING TERROR INTO *WHOSE* HEART?
HMM! IF I HAD THE AID OF *DUCK AVENGER*, I'D BE A LITTLE LESS TERROR-STRICKEN!
I'LL RUN HOME, FETCH MY GEAR ...
... AND NEVER BE MISSED!
WRRR
BESIDES, IT'S STILL DAYTIME! UNCLE SCROOGE ONLY HIRED ME FOR *OVERNIGHT* WATCH DUTY!

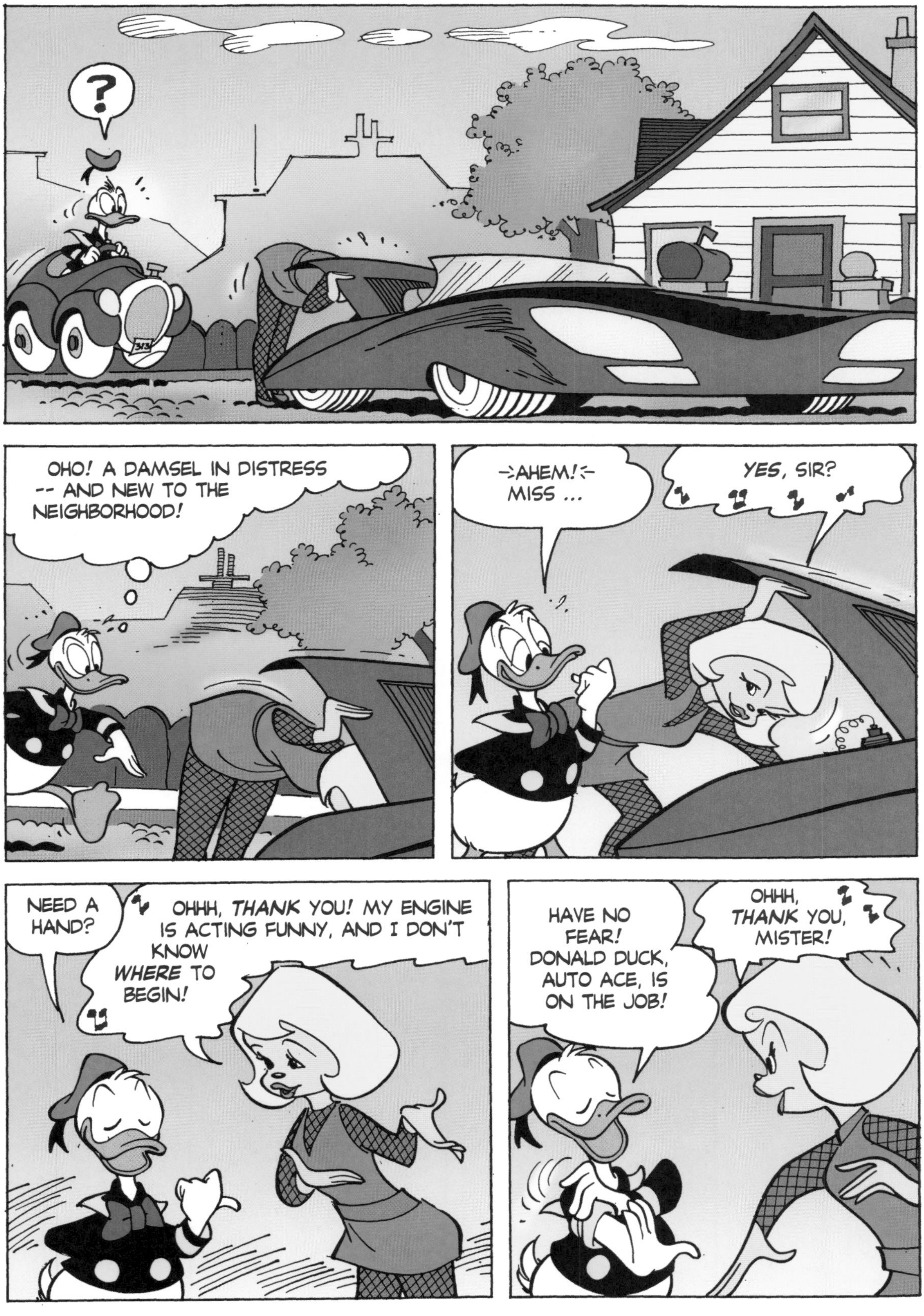
?
OHO! A DAMSEL IN DISTRESS -- AND NEW TO THE NEIGHBORHOOD!
AHEM! MISS ...
YES, SIR?
NEED A HAND?
OHHH, THANK YOU! MY ENGINE IS ACTING FUNNY, AND I DON'T KNOW WHERE TO BEGIN!
HAVE NO FEAR! DONALD DUCK, AUTO ACE, IS ON THE JOB!
OHHH, THANK YOU, MISTER!

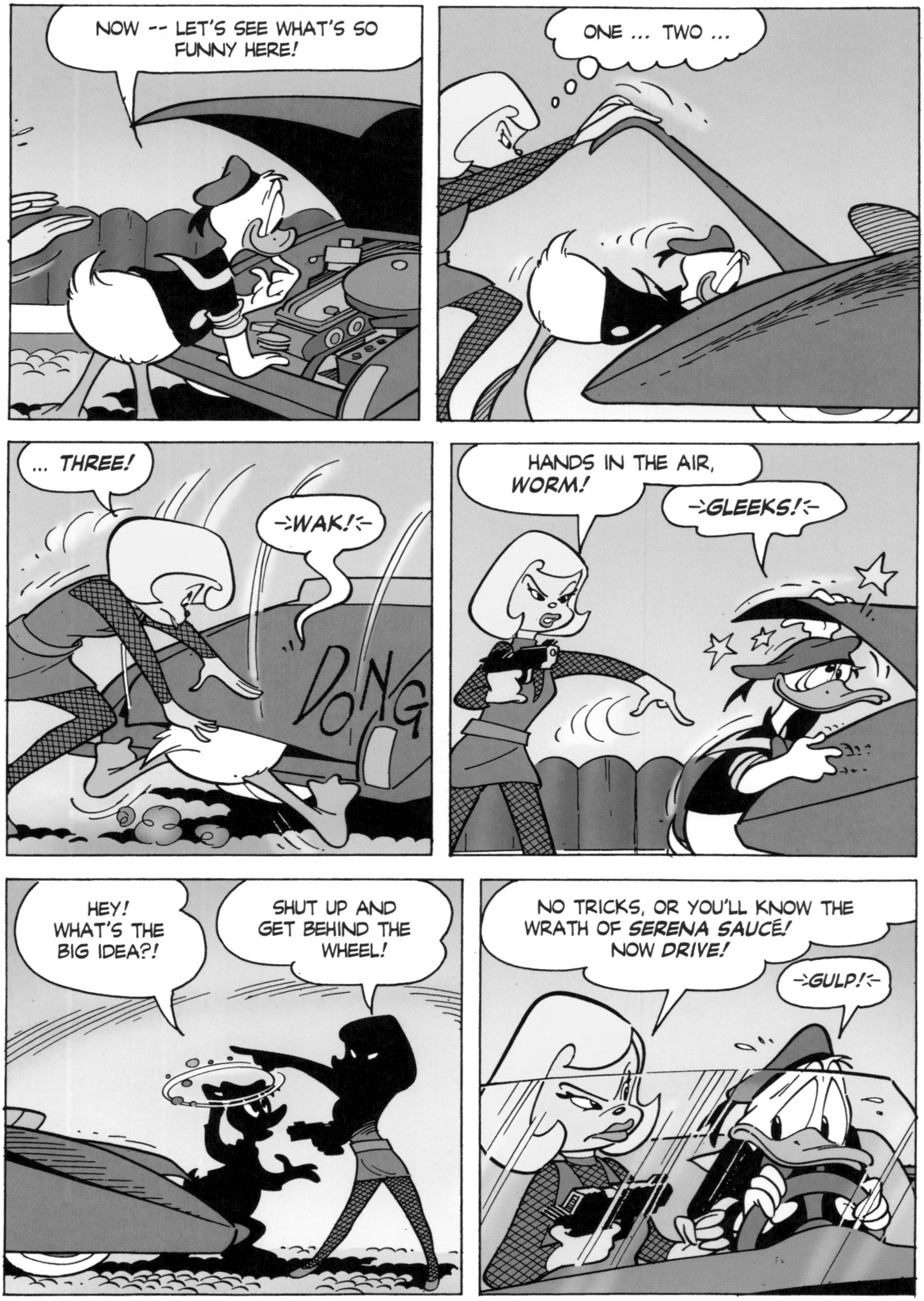
NOW -- LET'S SEE WHAT'S SO FUNNY HERE!
ONE ... TWO ...
... THREE!
-WAK!-
DONG
HANDS IN THE AIR, WORM!
-GLEEKS!-
HEY! WHAT'S THE BIG IDEA?!
SHUT UP AND GET BEHIND THE WHEEL!
NO TRICKS, OR YOU'LL KNOW THE WRATH OF SERENA SAUCÉ! NOW DRIVE!
-GULP!-

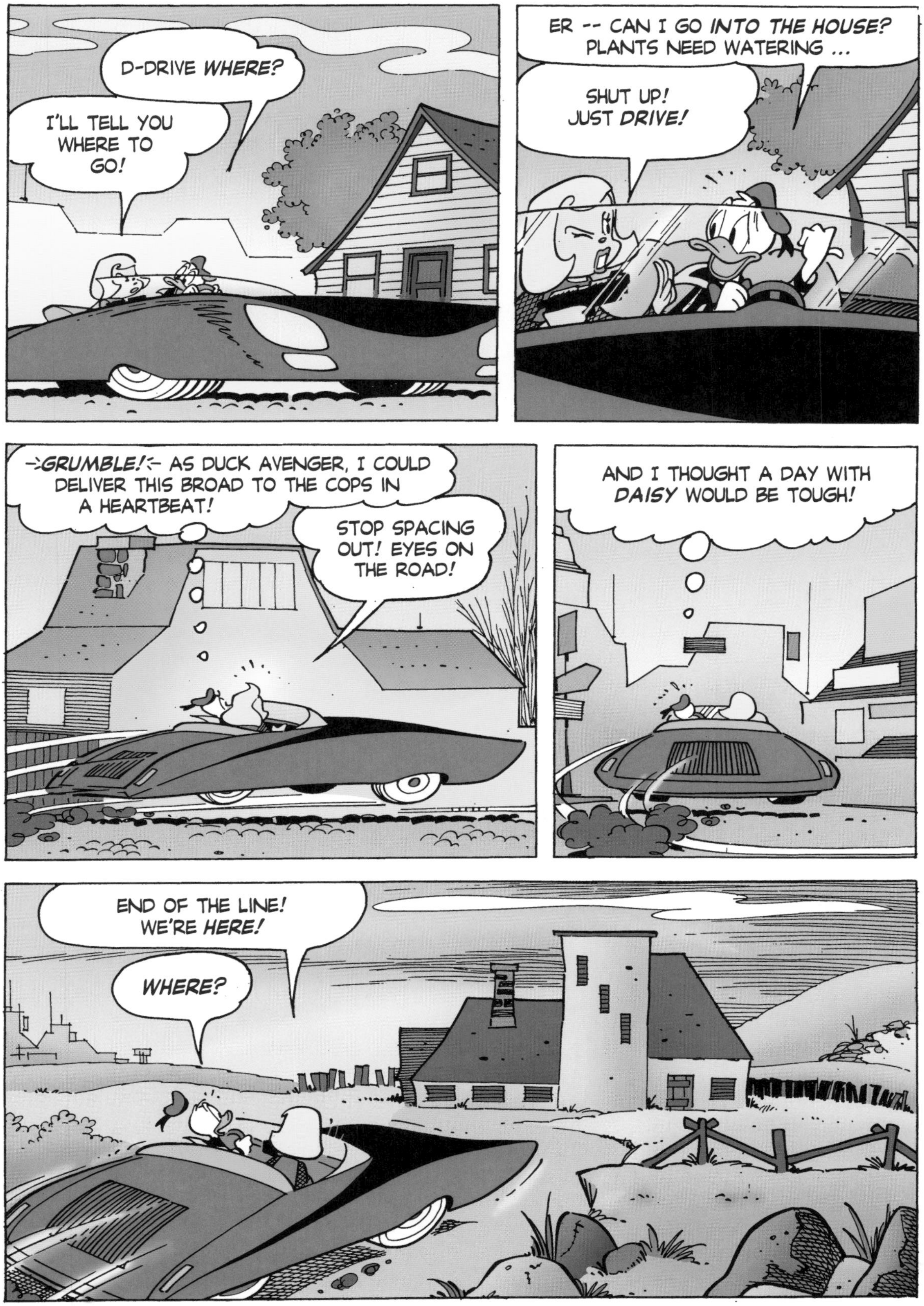
D-DRIVE WHERE?
I'LL TELL YOU WHERE TO GO!
ER -- CAN I GO INTO THE HOUSE? PLANTS NEED WATERING ...
SHUT UP! JUST DRIVE!
-GRUMBLE!- AS DUCK AVENGER, I COULD DELIVER THIS BROAD TO THE COPS IN A HEARTBEAT!
STOP SPACING OUT! EYES ON THE ROAD!
AND I THOUGHT A DAY WITH DAISY WOULD BE TOUGH!
END OF THE LINE! WE'RE HERE!
WHERE?

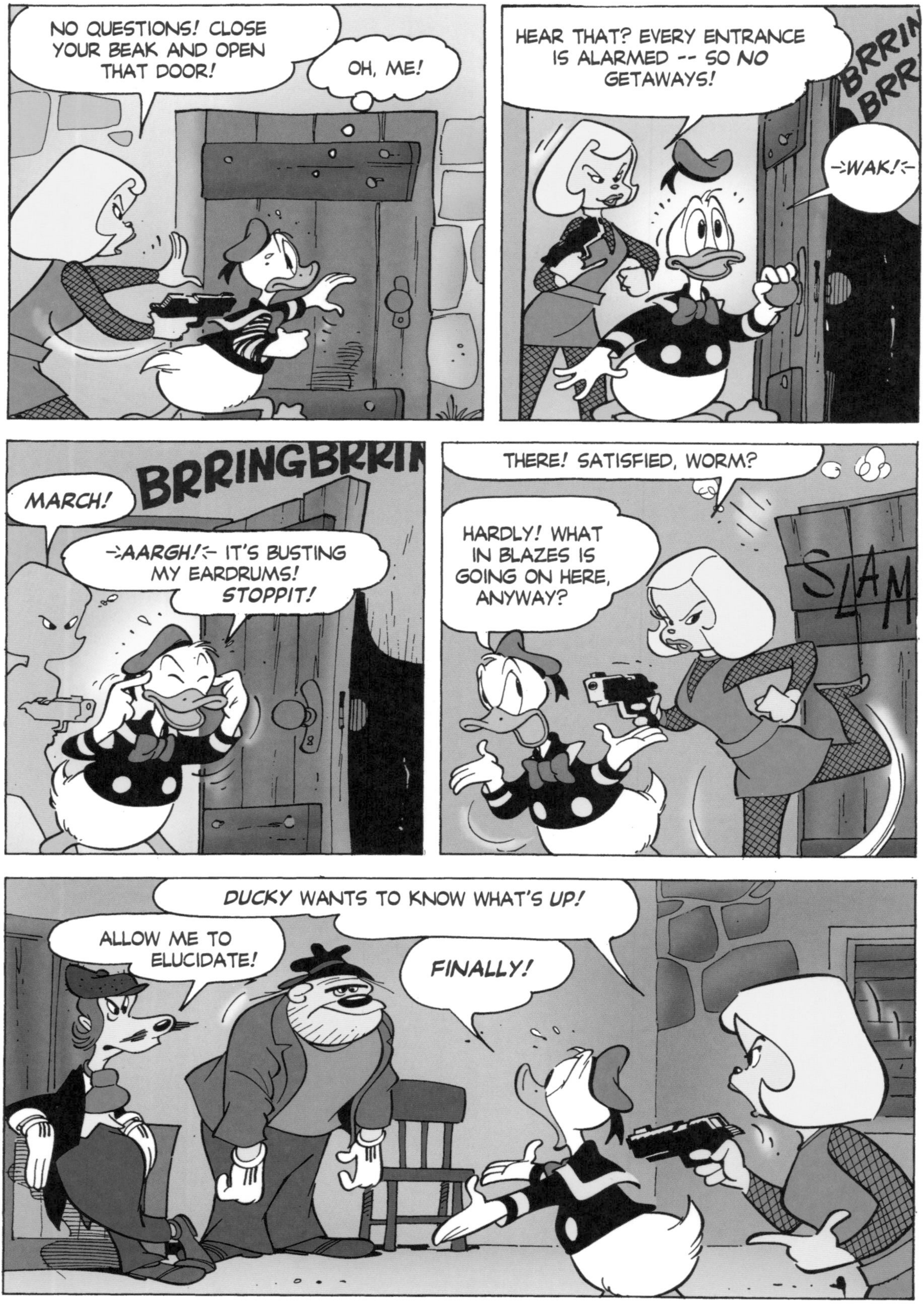
NO QUESTIONS! CLOSE YOUR BEAK AND OPEN THAT DOOR!
OH, ME!
HEAR THAT? EVERY ENTRANCE IS ALARMED -- SO NO GETAWAYS!
BRRIN BRR
-WAK!-
MARCH!
BRRINGBRRIN
-AARGH!- IT'S BUSTING MY EARDRUMS! STOPPIT!
THERE! SATISFIED, WORM?
HARDLY! WHAT IN BLAZES IS GOING ON HERE, ANYWAY?
SLAM
DUCKY WANTS TO KNOW WHAT'S UP!
ALLOW ME TO ELUCIDATE!
FINALLY!

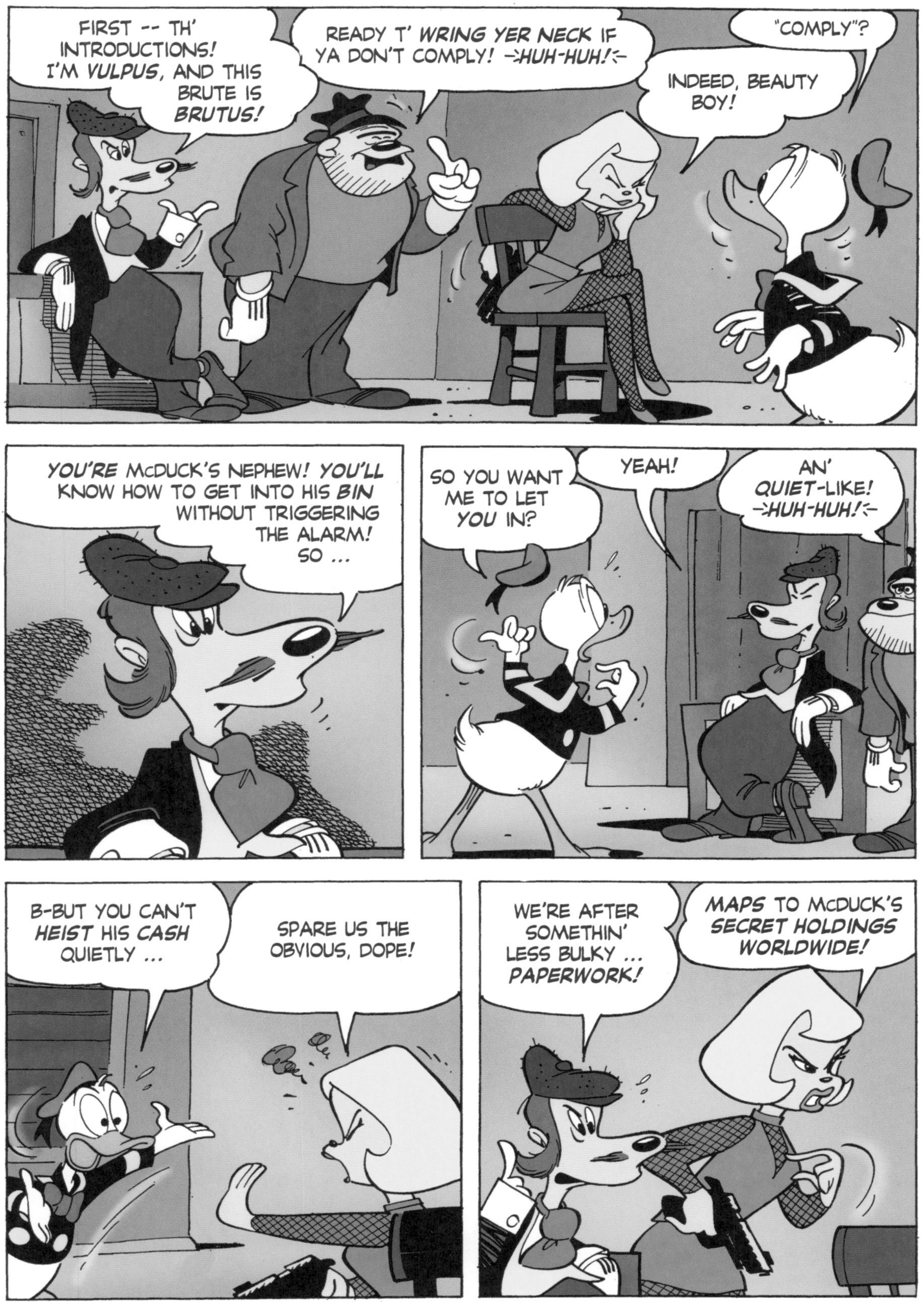
FIRST -- TH' INTRODUCTIONS! I'M VULPUS, AND THIS BRUTE IS BRUTUS!
READY T' WRING YER NECK IF YA DON'T COMPLY! ~HUH-HUH!~
"COMPLY"?
INDEED, BEAUTY BOY!
YOU'RE McDUCK'S NEPHEW! YOU'LL KNOW HOW TO GET INTO HIS BIN WITHOUT TRIGGERING THE ALARM! SO ...
SO YOU WANT ME TO LET YOU IN?
YEAH!
AN' QUIET-LIKE! ~HUH-HUH!~
B-BUT YOU CAN'T HEIST HIS CASH QUIETLY ...
SPARE US THE OBVIOUS, DOPE!
WE'RE AFTER SOMETHIN' LESS BULKY ... PAPERWORK!
MAPS TO McDUCK'S SECRET HOLDINGS WORLDWIDE!

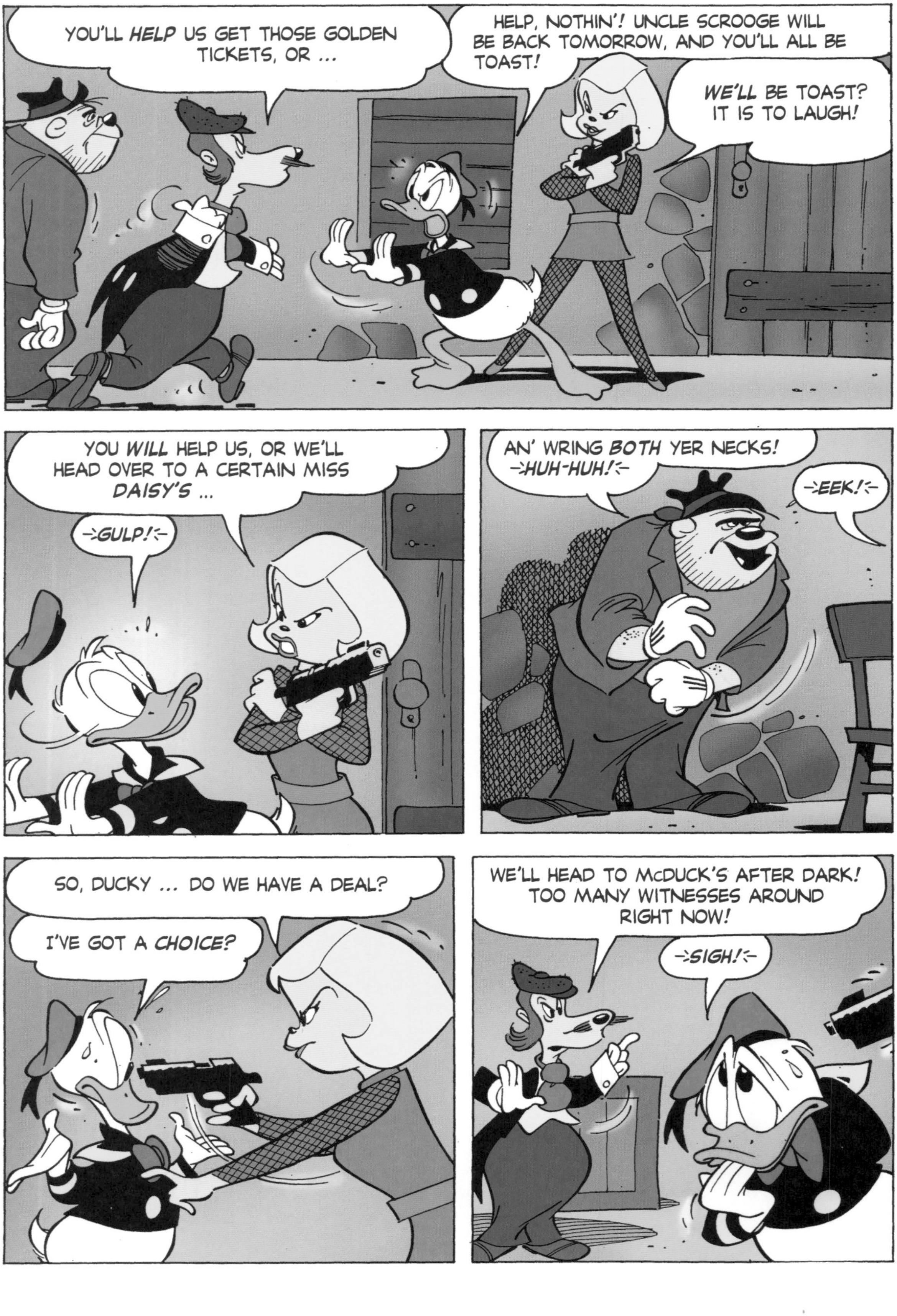
YOU'LL HELP US GET THOSE GOLDEN TICKETS, OR ...
HELP, NOTHIN'! UNCLE SCROOGE WILL BE BACK TOMORROW, AND YOU'LL ALL BE TOAST!
WE'LL BE TOAST? IT IS TO LAUGH!
YOU WILL HELP US, OR WE'LL HEAD OVER TO A CERTAIN MISS DAISY'S ...
GULP!
AN' WRING BOTH YER NECKS! HUH-HUH!
EEK!
SO, DUCKY ... DO WE HAVE A DEAL?
I'VE GOT A CHOICE?
WE'LL HEAD TO McDUCK'S AFTER DARK! TOO MANY WITNESSES AROUND RIGHT NOW!
SIGH!

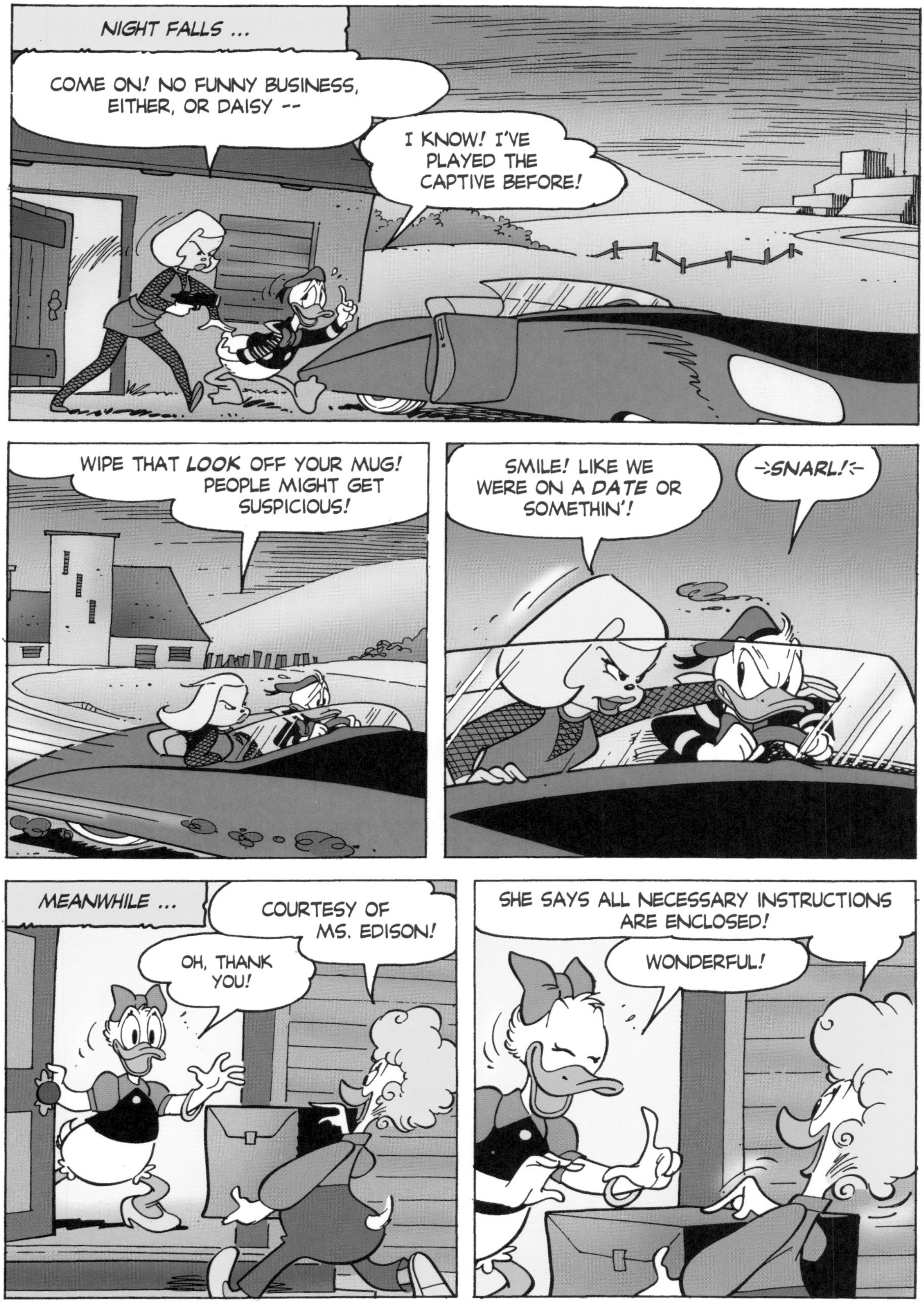
NIGHT FALLS ...
COME ON! NO FUNNY BUSINESS, EITHER, OR DAISY --
I KNOW! I'VE PLAYED THE CAPTIVE BEFORE!
WIPE THAT LOOK OFF YOUR MUG! PEOPLE MIGHT GET SUSPICIOUS!
SMILE! LIKE WE WERE ON A DATE OR SOMETHIN'!
SNARL!
MEANWHILE ...
COURTESY OF MS. EDISON!
OH, THANK YOU!
SHE SAYS ALL NECESSARY INSTRUCTIONS ARE ENCLOSED!
WONDERFUL!

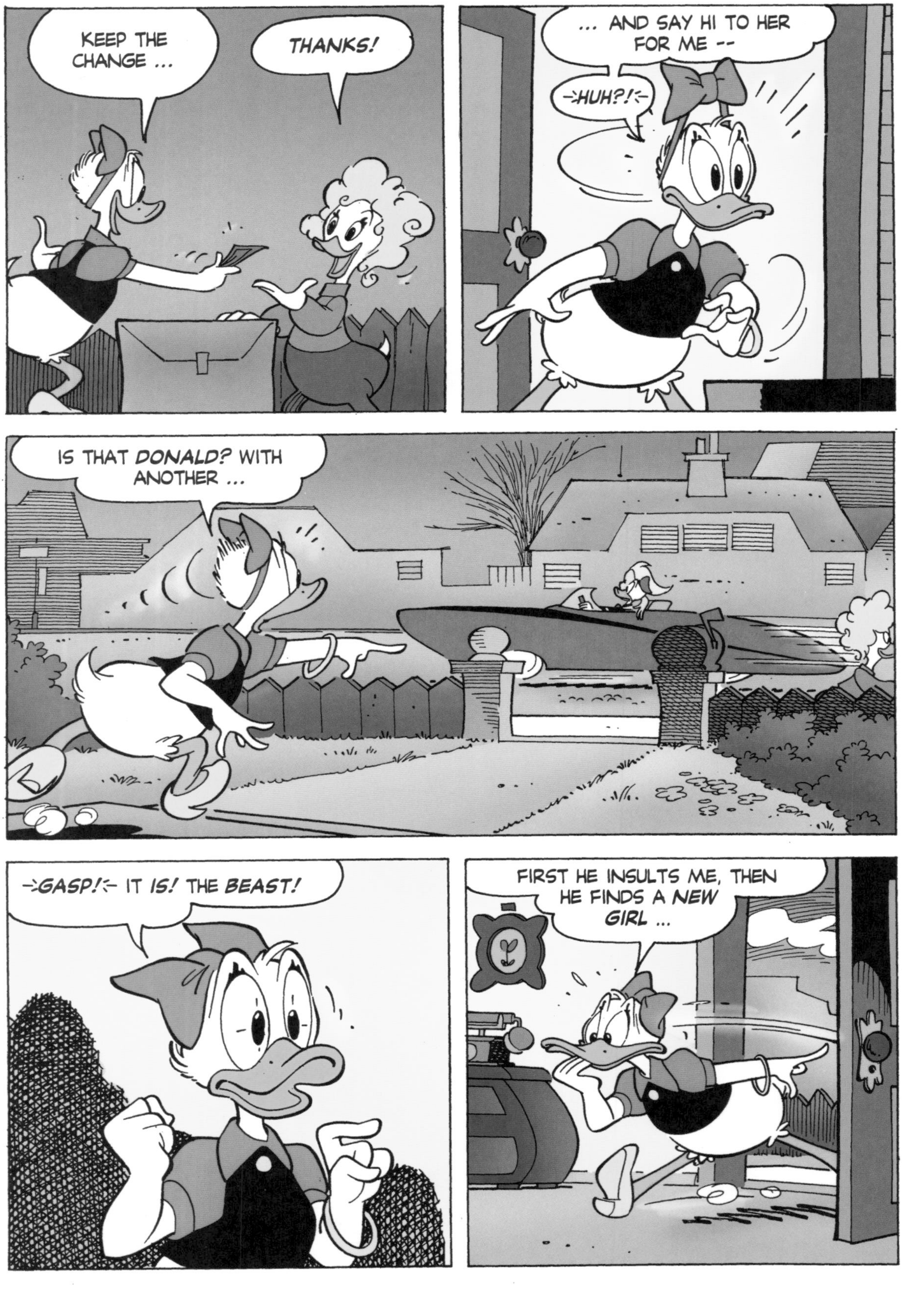
KEEP THE CHANGE ...
THANKS!
... AND SAY HI TO HER FOR ME --
-HUH?!-
IS THAT DONALD? WITH ANOTHER ...
-GASP!- IT IS! THE BEAST!
FIRST HE INSULTS ME, THEN HE FINDS A NEW GIRL ...

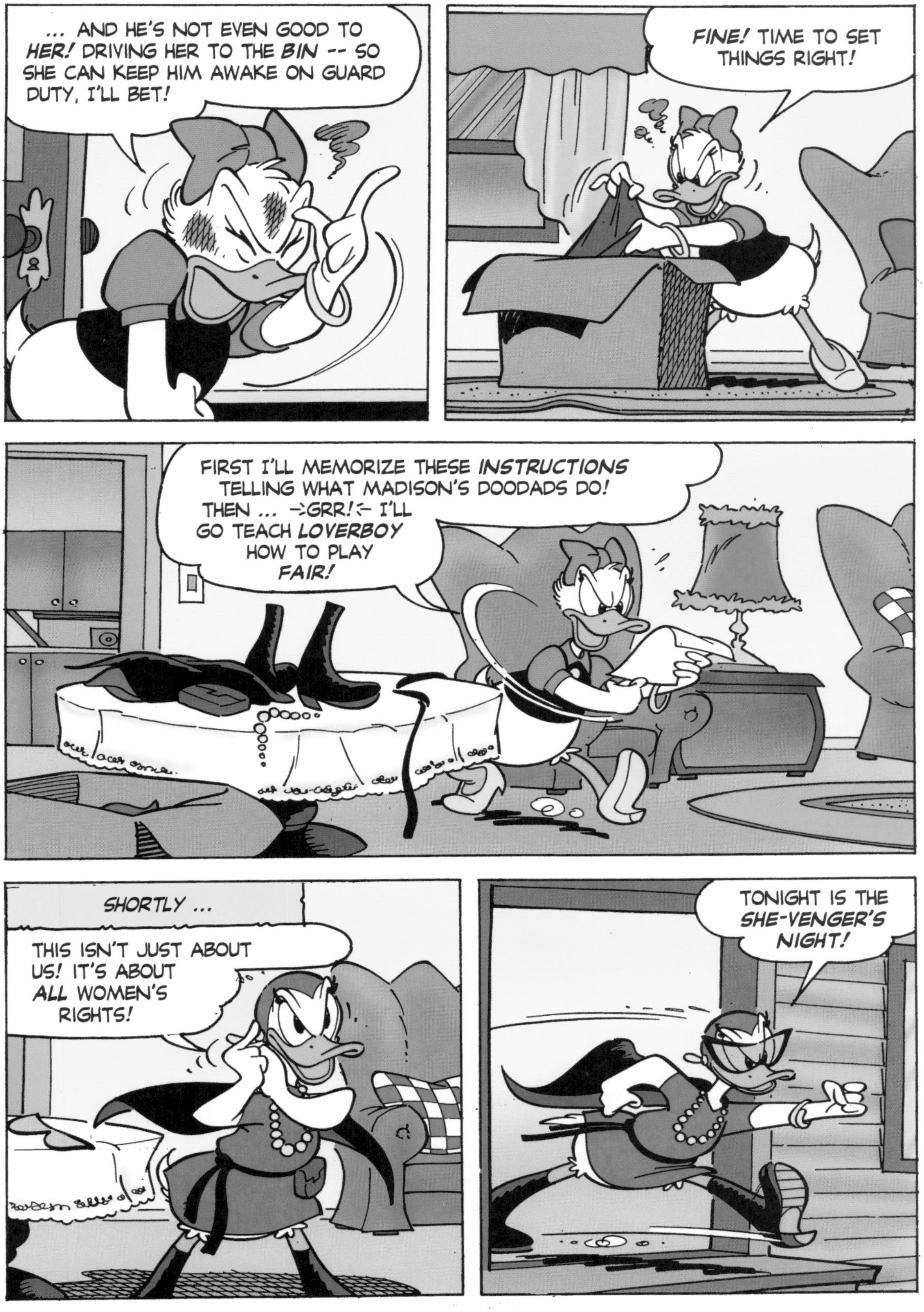
... AND HE'S NOT EVEN GOOD TO HER! DRIVING HER TO THE BIN -- SO SHE CAN KEEP HIM AWAKE ON GUARD DUTY, I'LL BET!
FINE! TIME TO SET THINGS RIGHT!
FIRST I'LL MEMORIZE THESE INSTRUCTIONS TELLING WHAT MADISON'S DOODADS DO! THEN ... ->GRR!<- I'LL GO TEACH LOVERBOY HOW TO PLAY FAIR!
SHORTLY ...
THIS ISN'T JUST ABOUT US! IT'S ABOUT ALL WOMEN'S RIGHTS!
TONIGHT IS THE SHE-VENGER'S NIGHT!

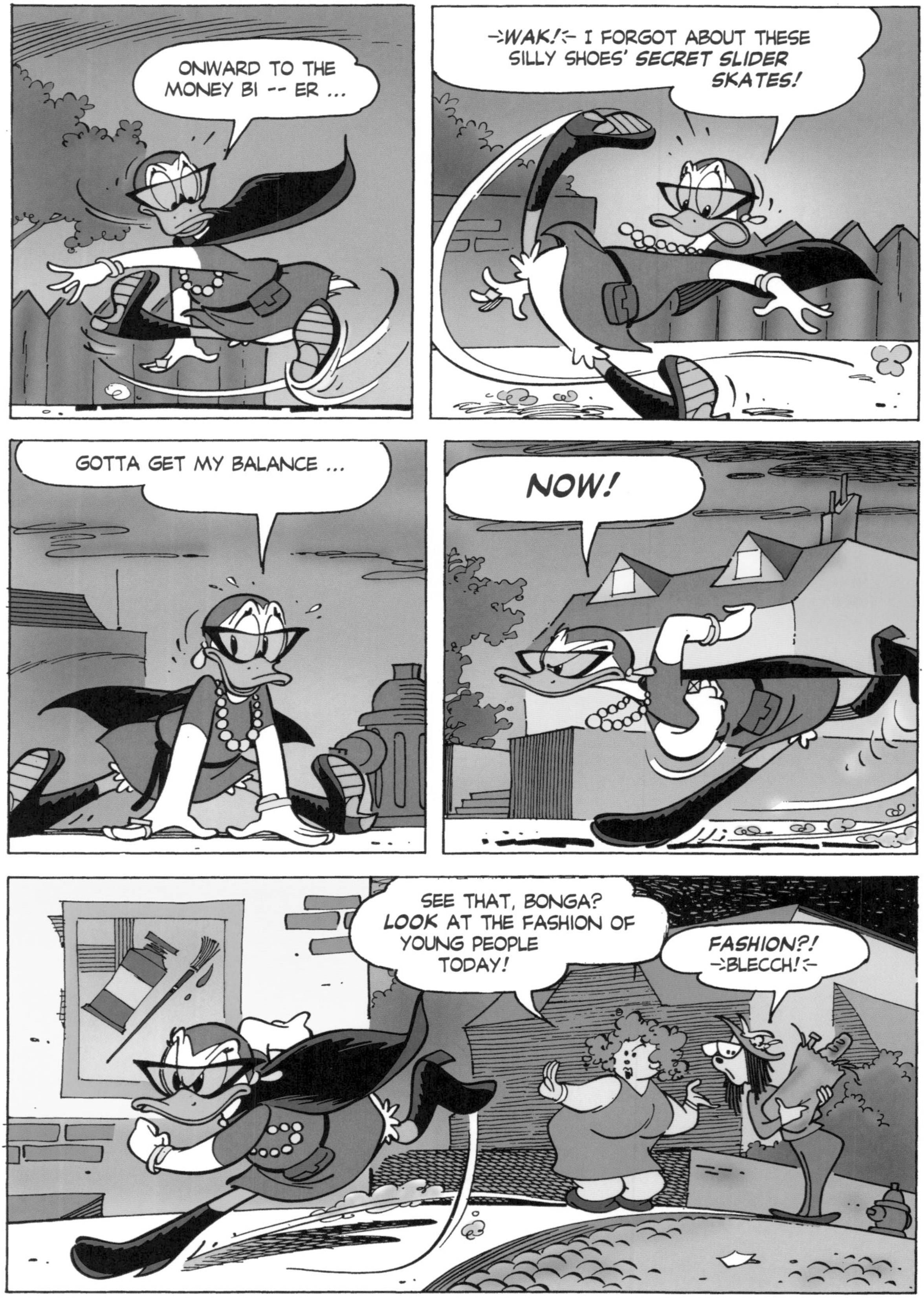
ONWARD TO THE MONEY BI -- ER ...
WAK! I FORGOT ABOUT THESE SILLY SHOES' SECRET SLIDER SKATES!
GOTTA GET MY BALANCE ...
NOW!
SEE THAT, BONGA? LOOK AT THE FASHION OF YOUNG PEOPLE TODAY!
FASHION?! BLECCH!

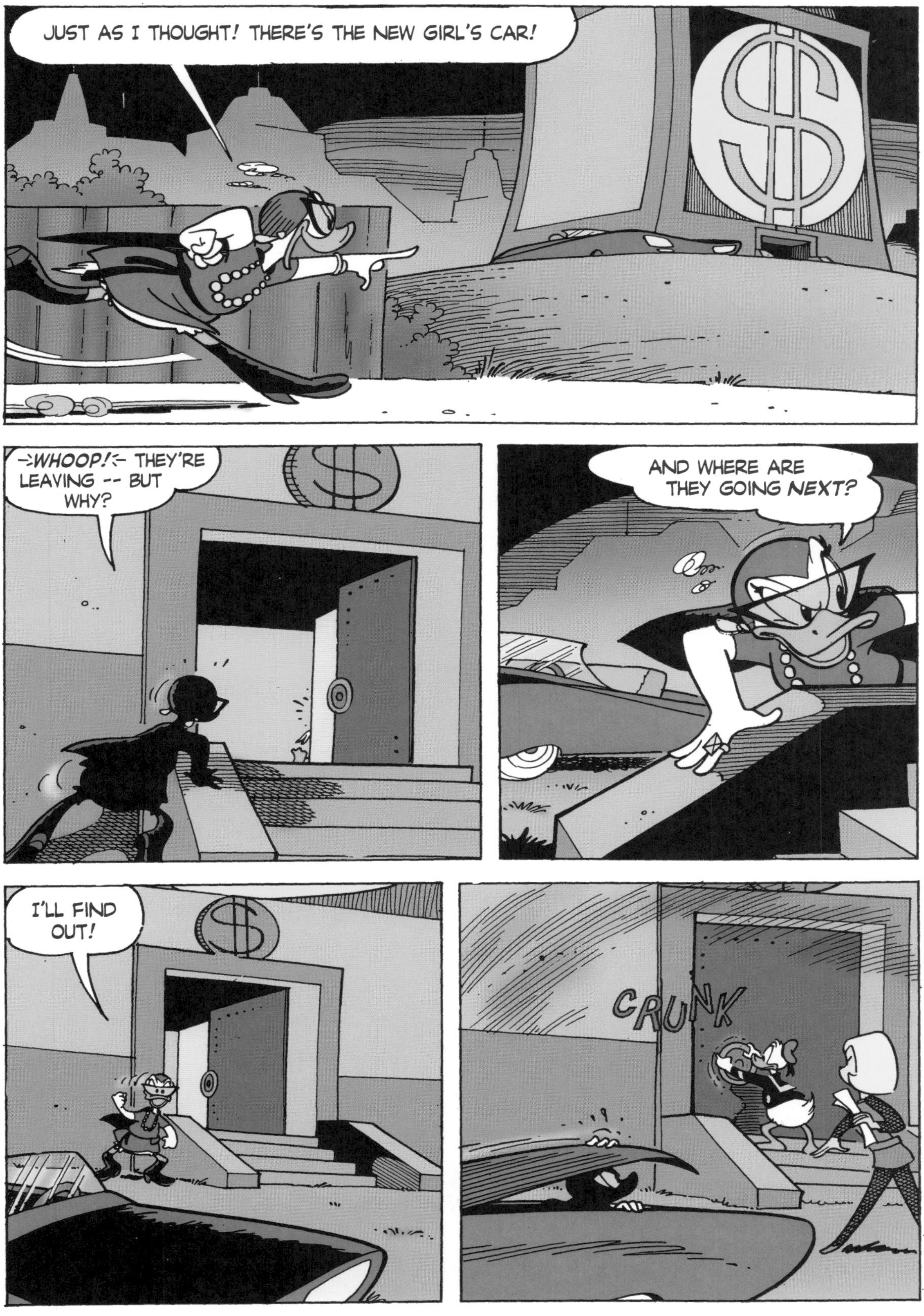
JUST AS I THOUGHT! THERE'S THE NEW GIRL'S CAR!
-WHOOP!- THEY'RE LEAVING -- BUT WHY?
AND WHERE ARE THEY GOING NEXT?
I'LL FIND OUT!
CRUNK

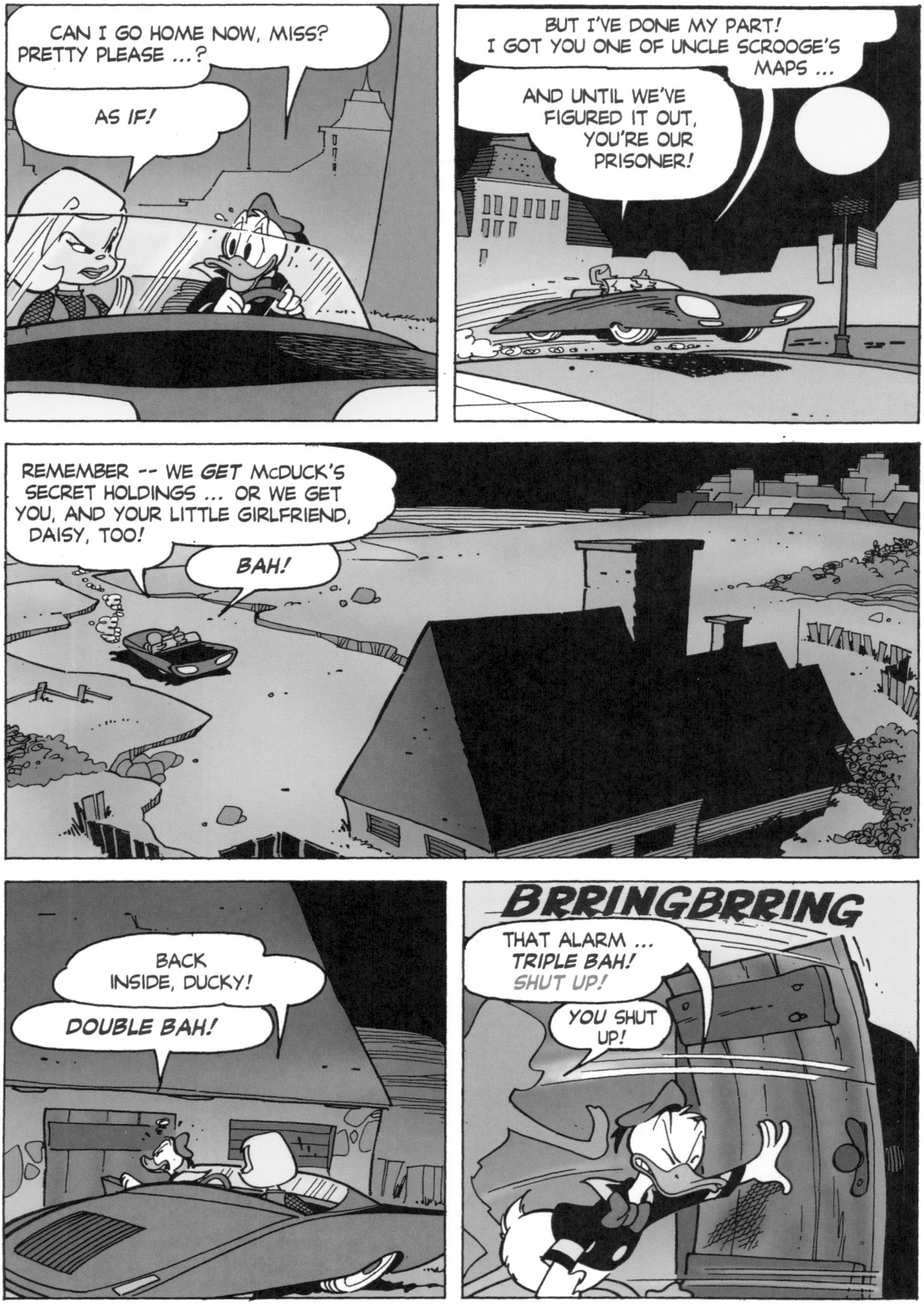
CAN I GO HOME NOW, MISS? PRETTY PLEASE ...?
AS IF!
BUT I'VE DONE MY PART! I GOT YOU ONE OF UNCLE SCROOGE'S MAPS ...
AND UNTIL WE'VE FIGURED IT OUT, YOU'RE OUR PRISONER!
REMEMBER -- WE GET McDUCK'S SECRET HOLDINGS ... OR WE GET YOU, AND YOUR LITTLE GIRLFRIEND, DAISY, TOO!
BAH!
BACK INSIDE, DUCKY!
DOUBLE BAH!
BRRINGBRRING
THAT ALARM ... TRIPLE BAH! SHUT UP!
YOU SHUT UP!

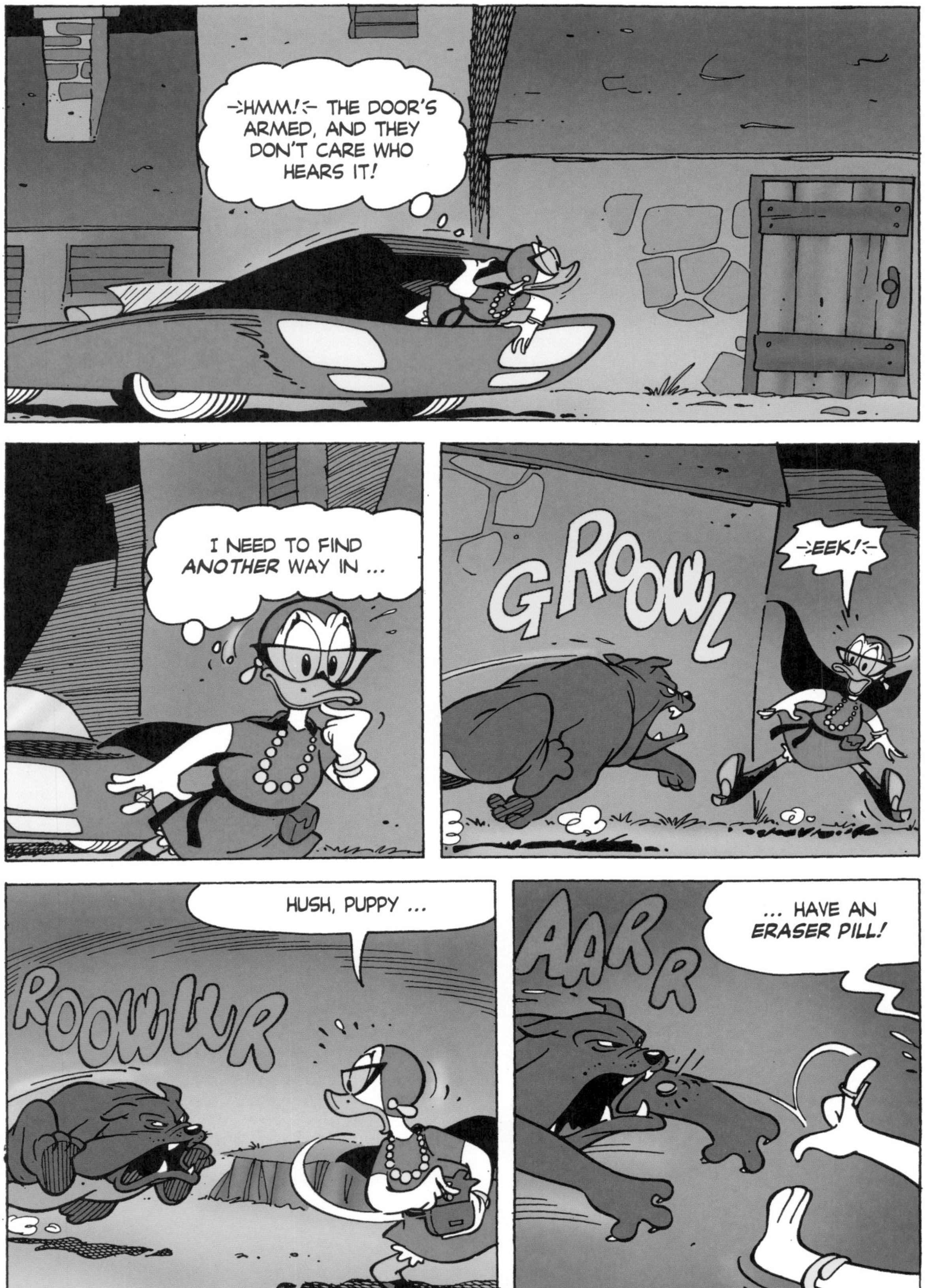
-HMM!- THE DOOR'S ARMED, AND THEY DON'T CARE WHO HEARS IT!
I NEED TO FIND ANOTHER WAY IN ...
GROOWL
-EEK!-
HUSH, PUPPY ...
ROOWLUR
AARR
... HAVE AN ERASER PILL!

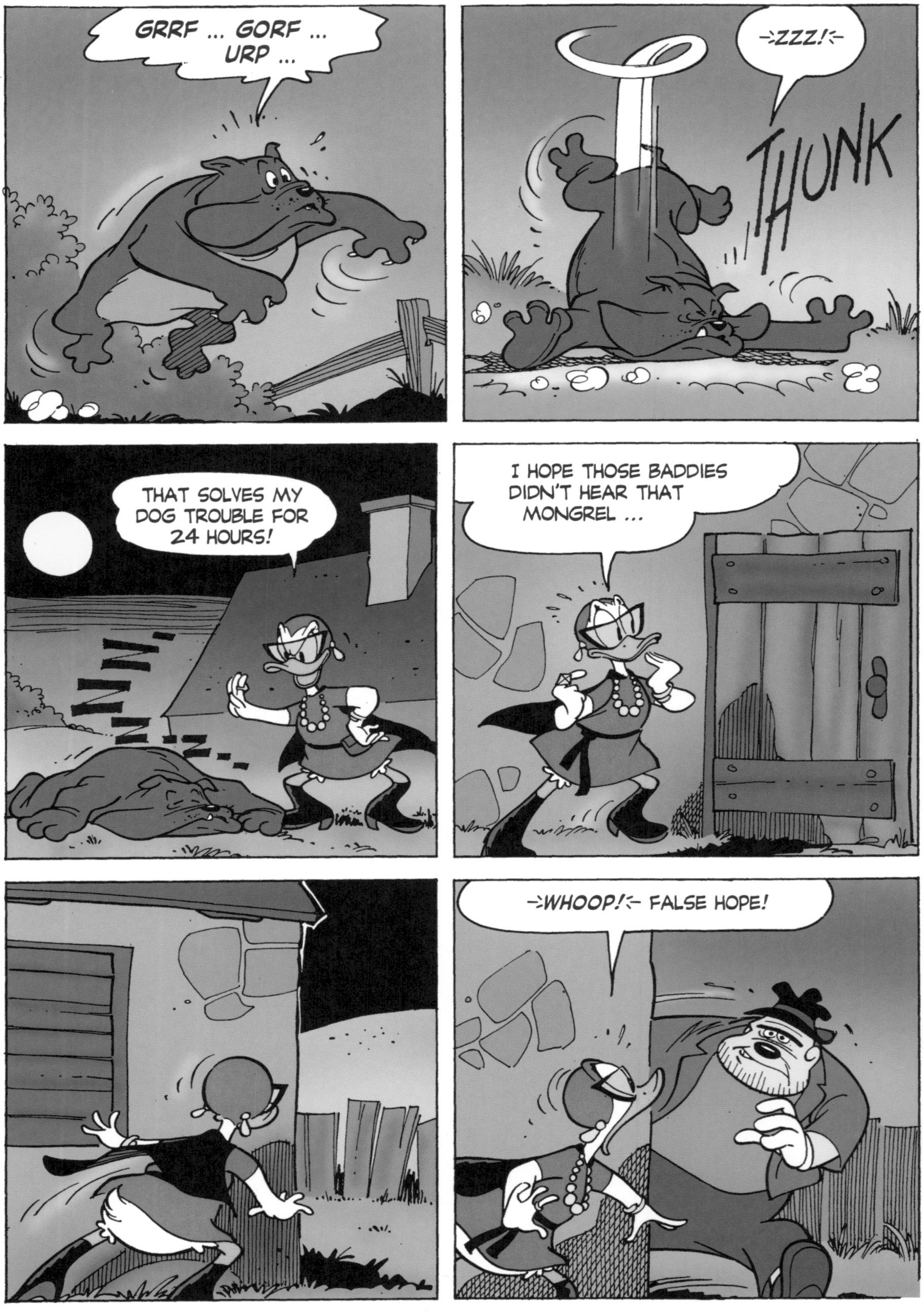
GRRF ... GORF ... URP ...
-ZZZ!-
THUNK
THAT SOLVES MY DOG TROUBLE FOR 24 HOURS!
I HOPE THOSE BADDIES DIDN'T HEAR THAT MONGREL ...
-WHOOP!- FALSE HOPE!

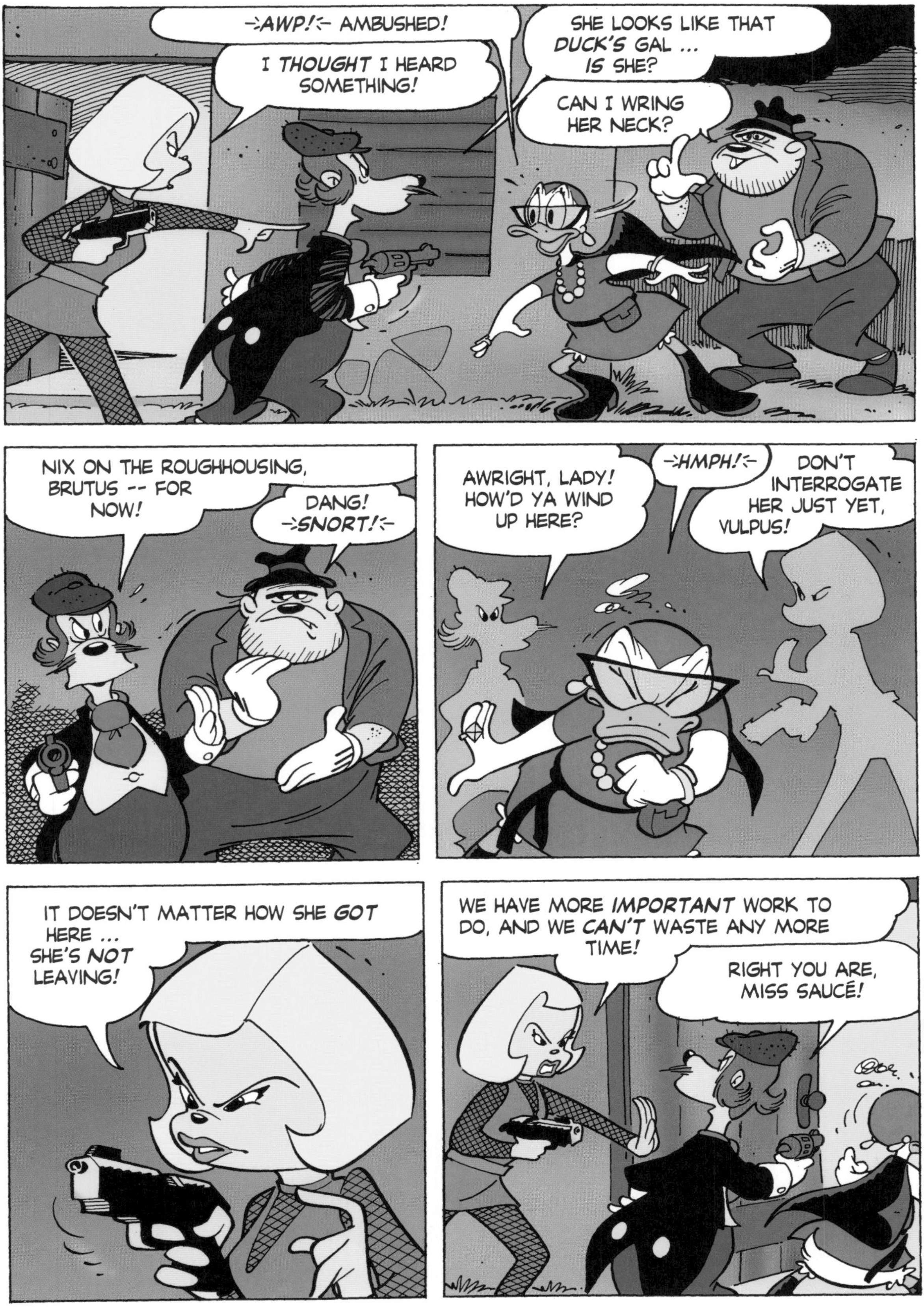
-AWP!- AMBUSHED!
I THOUGHT I HEARD SOMETHING!
SHE LOOKS LIKE THAT DUCK'S GAL ... IS SHE?
CAN I WRING HER NECK?
NIX ON THE ROUGHHOUSING, BRUTUS -- FOR NOW!
DANG! -SNORT!-
AWRIGHT, LADY! HOW'D YA WIND UP HERE?
-HMPH!-
DON'T INTERROGATE HER JUST YET, VULPUS!
IT DOESN'T MATTER HOW SHE GOT HERE ... SHE'S NOT LEAVING!
WE HAVE MORE IMPORTANT WORK TO DO, AND WE CAN'T WASTE ANY MORE TIME!
RIGHT YOU ARE, MISS SAUCÉ!

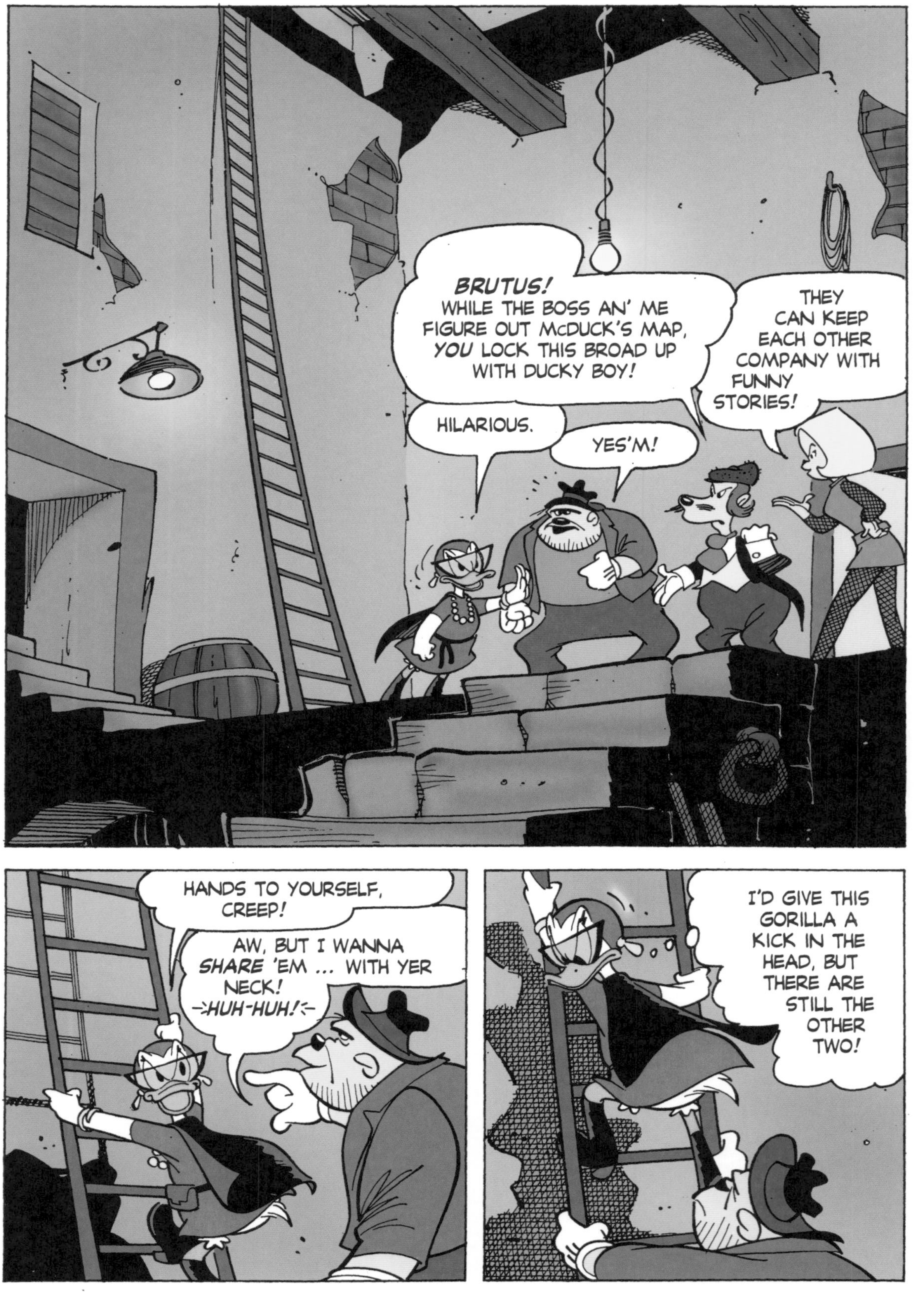
BRUTUS! WHILE THE BOSS AN' ME FIGURE OUT McDUCK'S MAP, YOU LOCK THIS BROAD UP WITH DUCKY BOY!
THEY CAN KEEP EACH OTHER COMPANY WITH FUNNY STORIES!
HILARIOUS.
YES'M!
HANDS TO YOURSELF, CREEP!
AW, BUT I WANNA SHARE 'EM ... WITH YER NECK! -HUH-HUH!-
I'D GIVE THIS GORILLA A KICK IN THE HEAD, BUT THERE ARE STILL THE OTHER TWO!

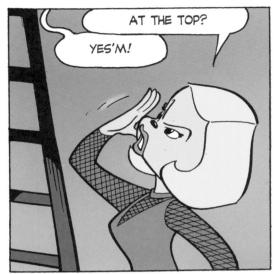

AT THE TOP?

YES'M!

SOMEHOW I DON'T TRUST HIS BRAIN-POWER! TAKE THE LADDER AS A PRECAUTION!

FORWARD MARCH!

NOW'S MY CHANCE!

HEY! NO FUNNY BUSINESS!

LOUT! CAN'T A LADY *POWDER HER NOSE* IN PEACE?

LEMME SEE DAT!

GLADLY!

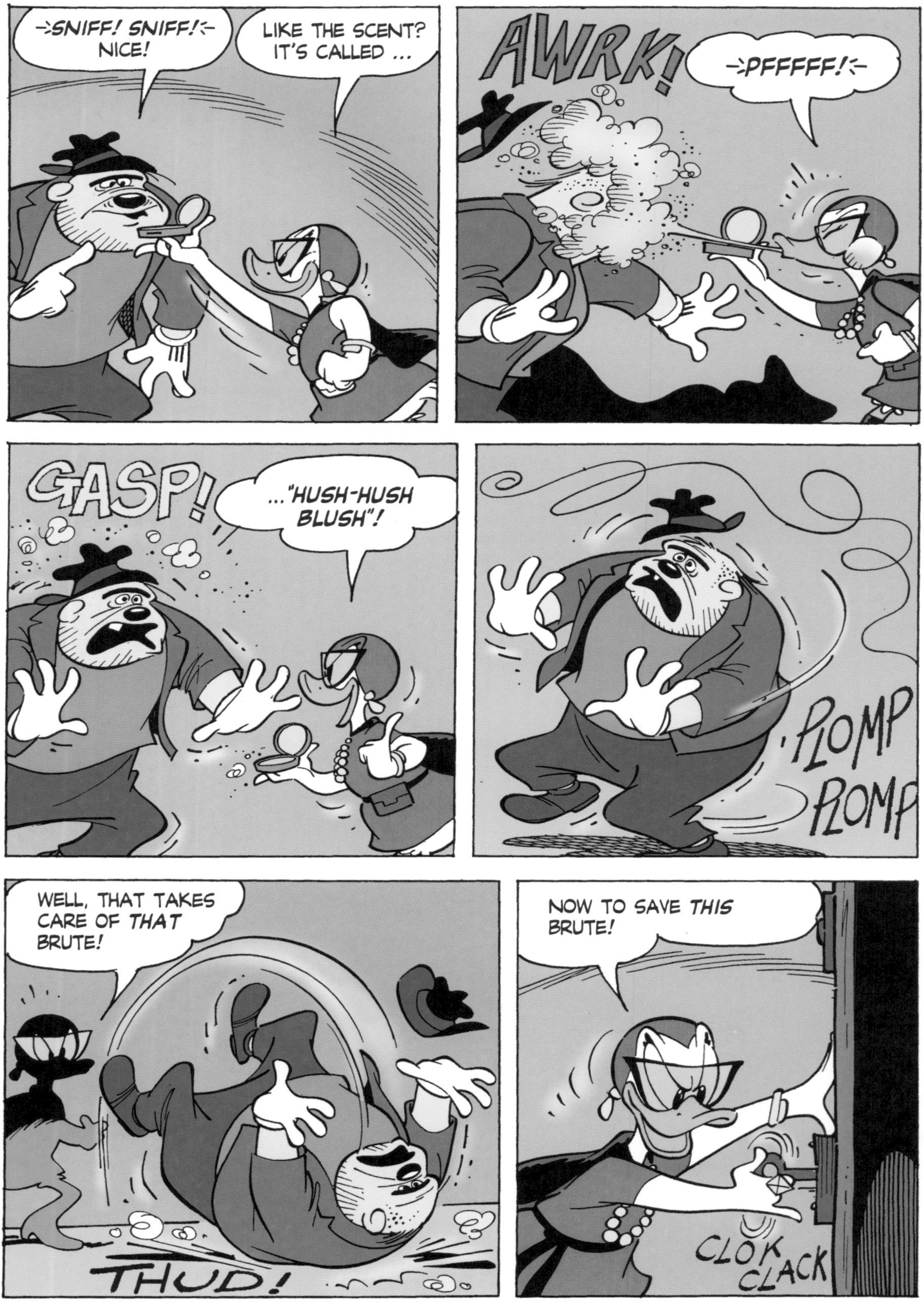

-SNIFF! SNIFF!- NICE!
LIKE THE SCENT? IT'S CALLED ...
AWRK!
-PFFFFF!-
GASP!
..."HUSH-HUSH BLUSH"!
PLOMP PLOMP
WELL, THAT TAKES CARE OF THAT BRUTE!
THUD!
NOW TO SAVE THIS BRUTE!
CLOK CLACK

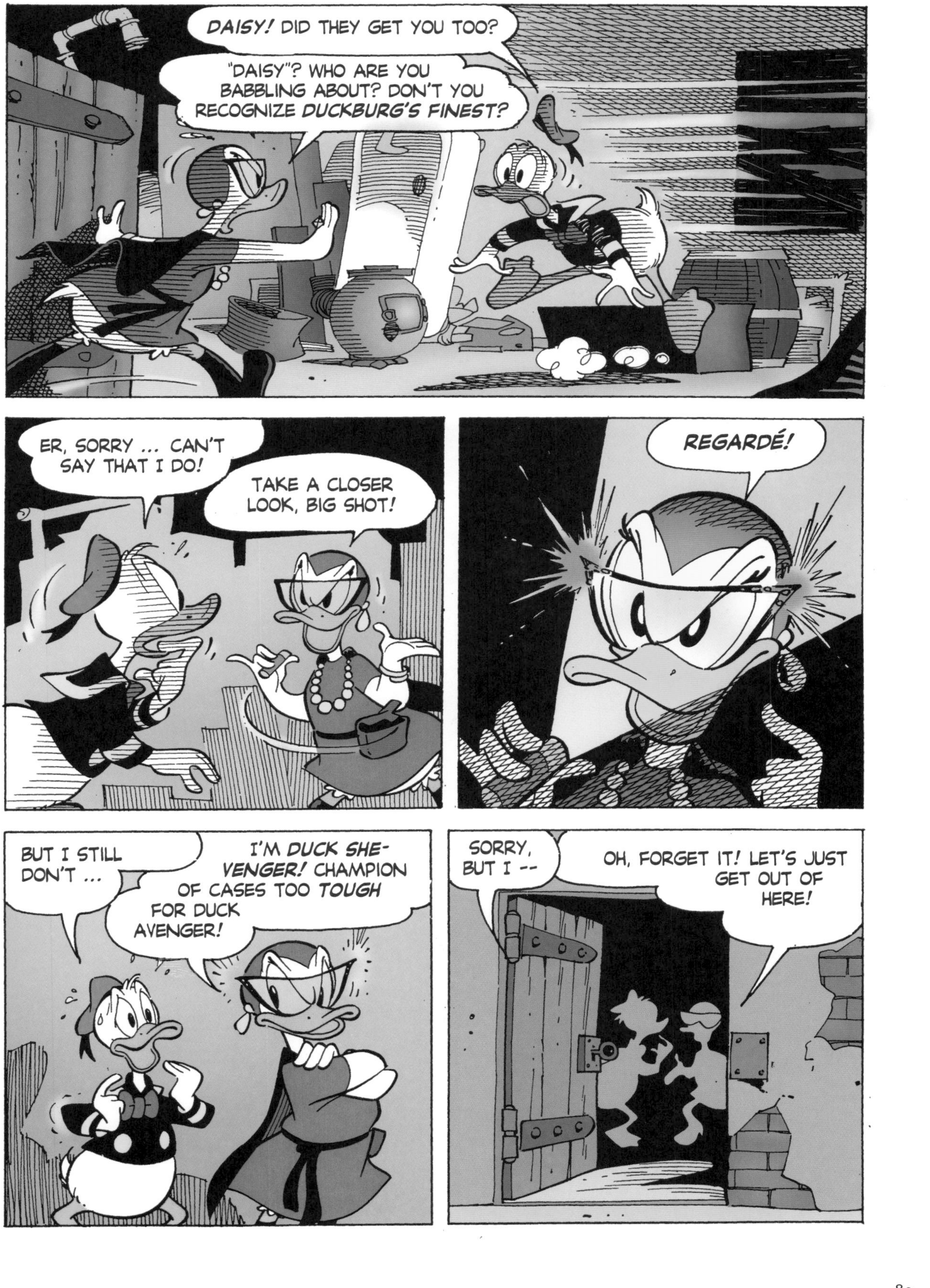
DAISY! DID THEY GET YOU TOO?
"DAISY"? WHO ARE YOU BABBLING ABOUT? DON'T YOU RECOGNIZE DUCKBURG'S FINEST?
ER, SORRY ... CAN'T SAY THAT I DO!
TAKE A CLOSER LOOK, BIG SHOT!
REGARDÉ!
BUT I STILL DON'T ...
I'M DUCK SHE-VENGER! CHAMPION OF CASES TOO TOUGH FOR DUCK AVENGER!
SORRY, BUT I --
OH, FORGET IT! LET'S JUST GET OUT OF HERE!

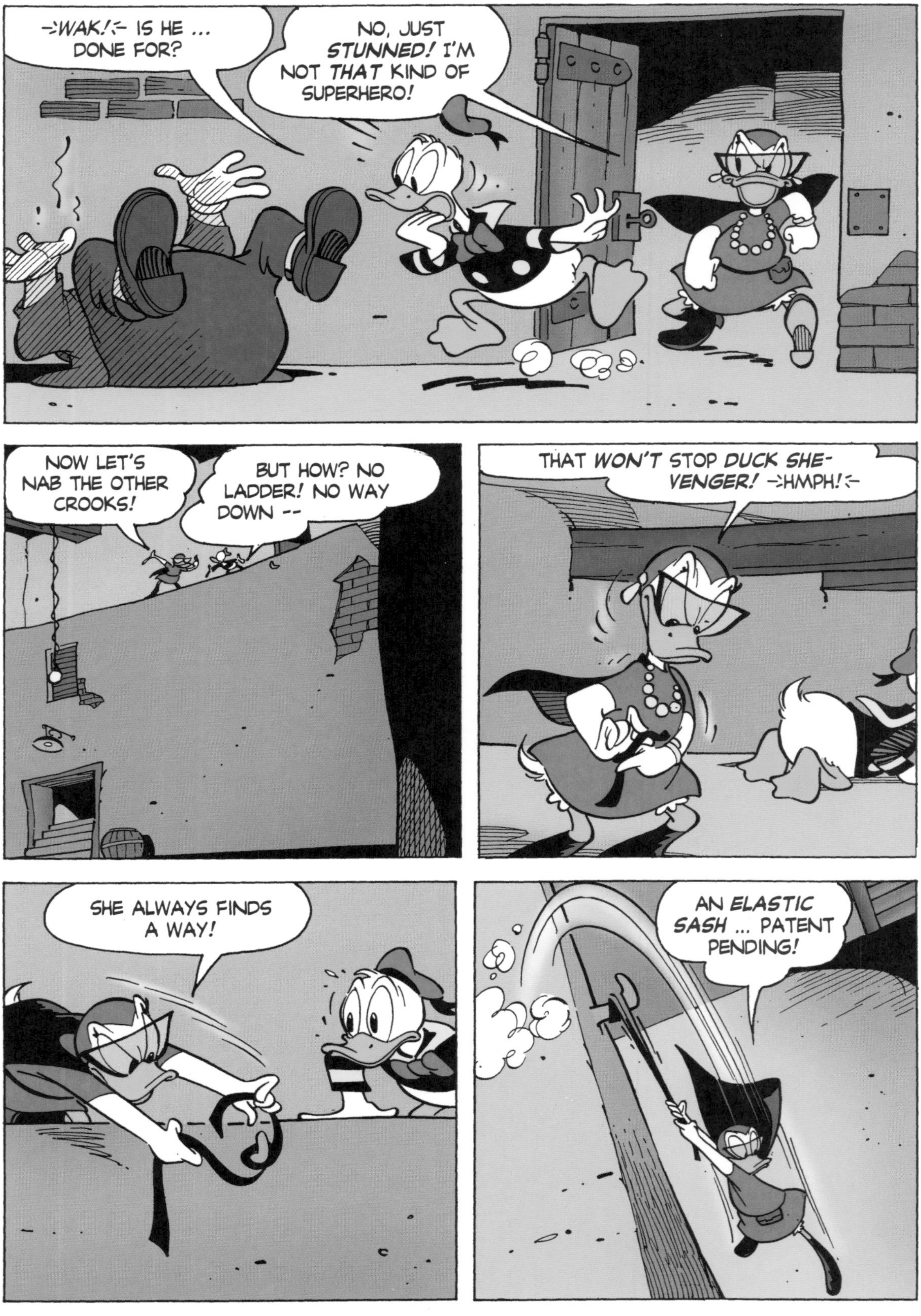
-WAK!- IS HE ... DONE FOR?
NO, JUST STUNNED! I'M NOT THAT KIND OF SUPERHERO!
NOW LET'S NAB THE OTHER CROOKS!
BUT HOW? NO LADDER! NO WAY DOWN --
THAT WON'T STOP DUCK SHE-VENGER! -HMPH!-
SHE ALWAYS FINDS A WAY!
AN ELASTIC SASH ... PATENT PENDING!

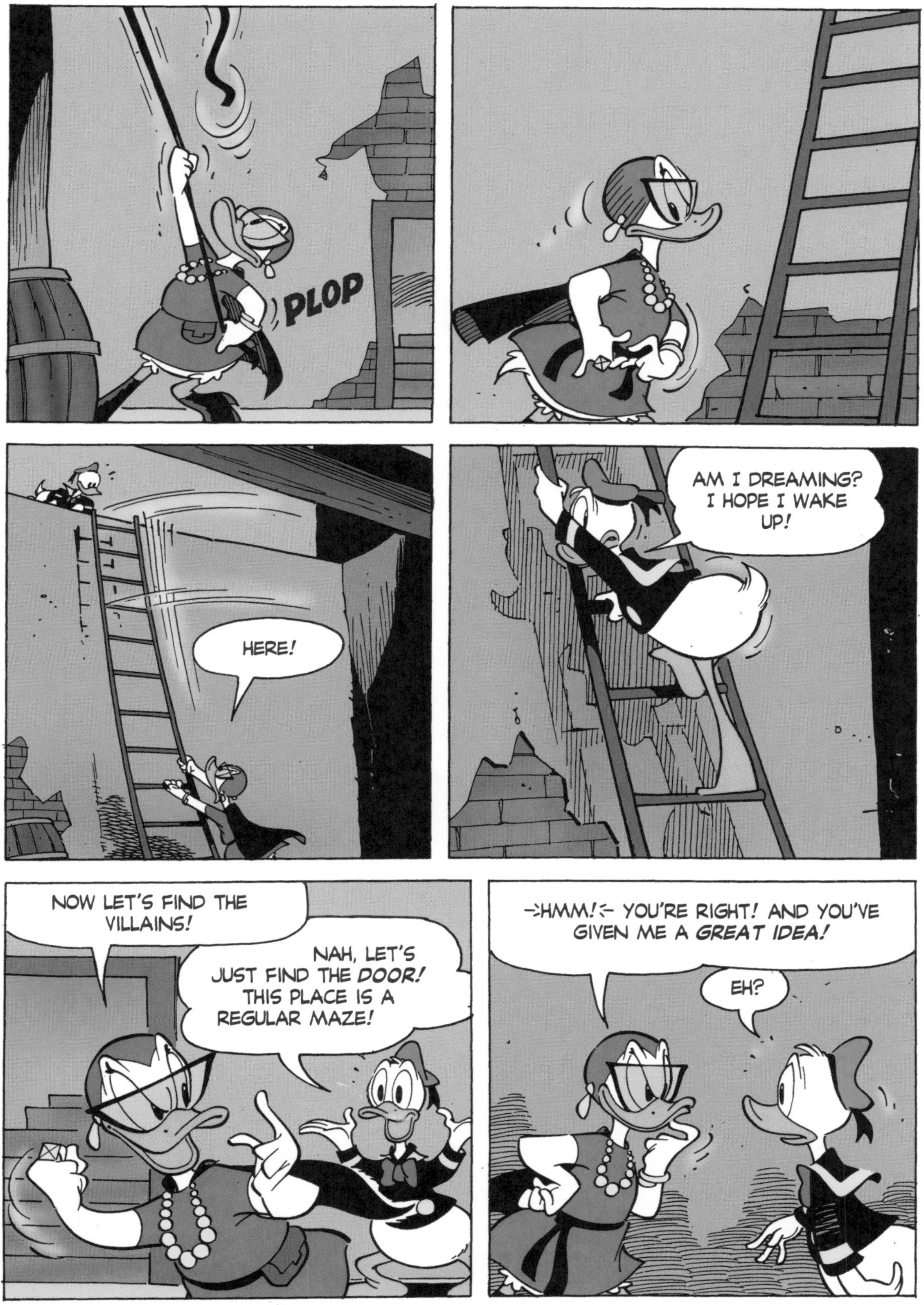
PLOP
HERE!
AM I DREAMING? I HOPE I WAKE UP!
NOW LET'S FIND THE VILLAINS!
NAH, LET'S JUST FIND THE *DOOR!* THIS PLACE IS A REGULAR MAZE!
HMM! YOU'RE RIGHT! AND YOU'VE GIVEN ME A *GREAT IDEA!*
EH?

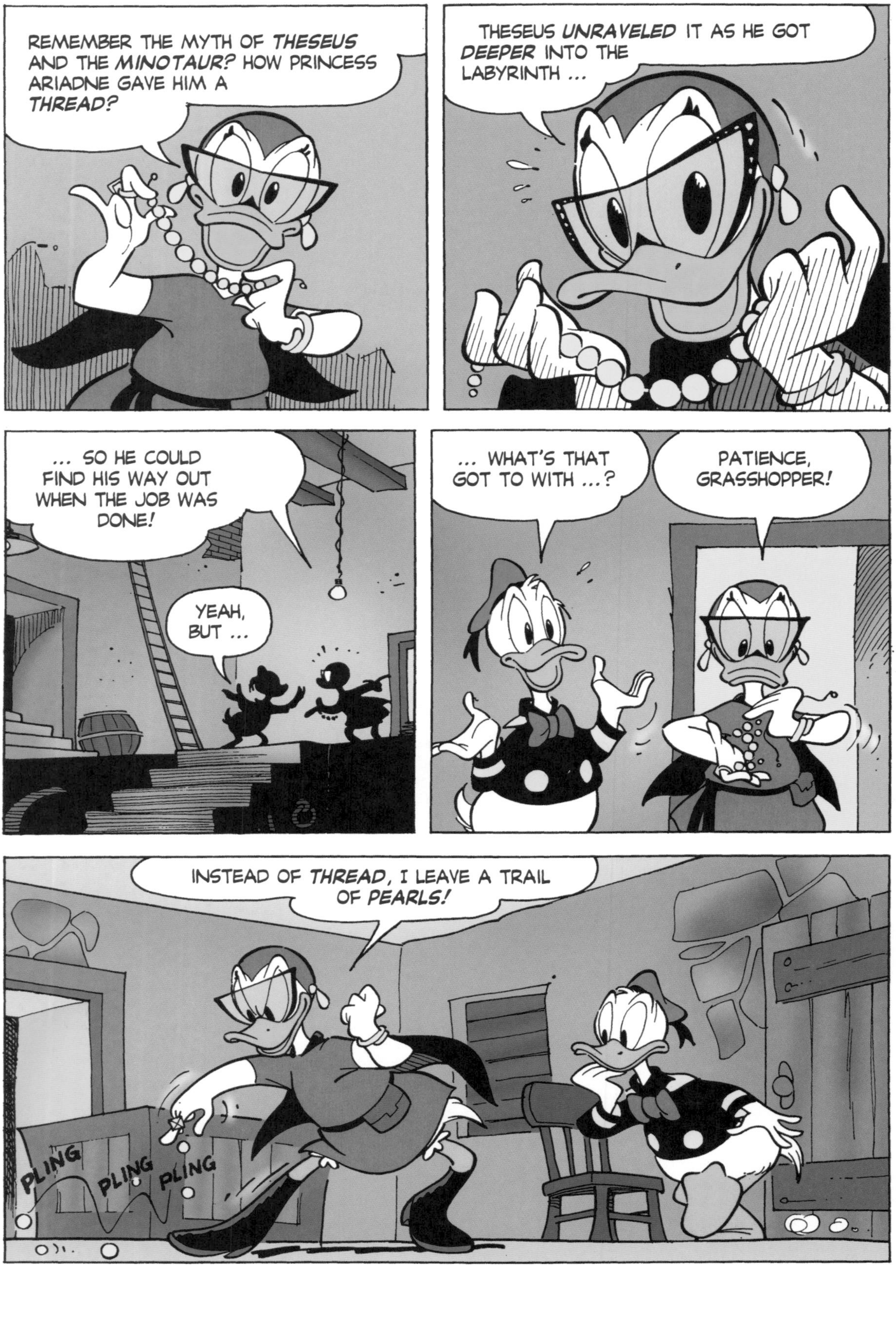
REMEMBER THE MYTH OF THESEUS AND THE MINOTAUR? HOW PRINCESS ARIADNE GAVE HIM A THREAD?
THESEUS UNRAVELED IT AS HE GOT DEEPER INTO THE LABYRINTH ...
... SO HE COULD FIND HIS WAY OUT WHEN THE JOB WAS DONE!
YEAH, BUT ...
... WHAT'S THAT GOT TO WITH ...?
PATIENCE, GRASSHOPPER!
INSTEAD OF THREAD, I LEAVE A TRAIL OF PEARLS!
PLING
PLING
PLING

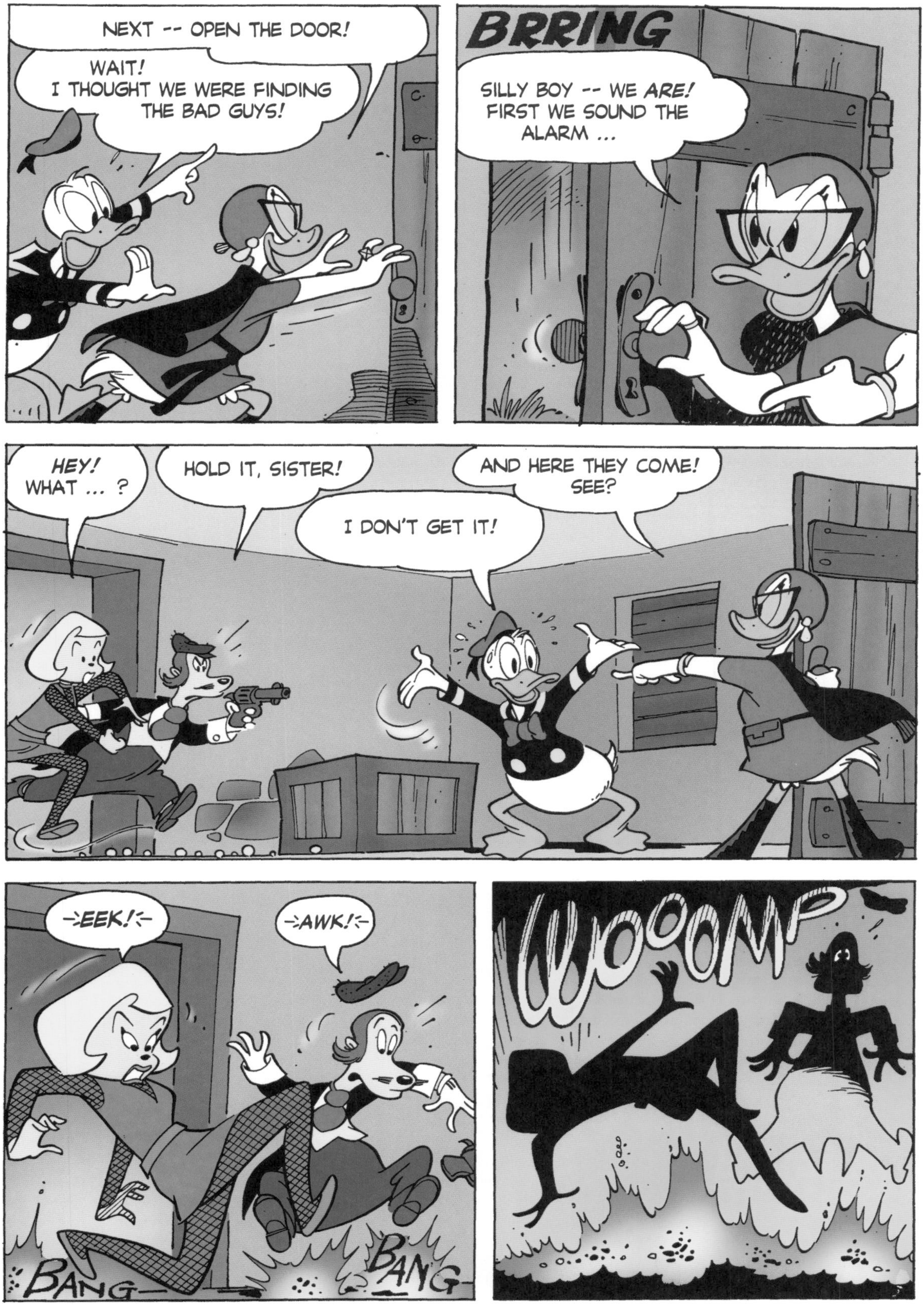
NEXT -- OPEN THE DOOR!
WAIT! I THOUGHT WE WERE FINDING THE BAD GUYS!
BRRING
SILLY BOY -- WE *ARE!* FIRST WE SOUND THE ALARM ...
*HEY!* WHAT ... ?
HOLD IT, SISTER!
AND HERE THEY COME! SEE?
I DON'T GET IT!
EEK!
AWK!
BANG
BANG
WOOOMP

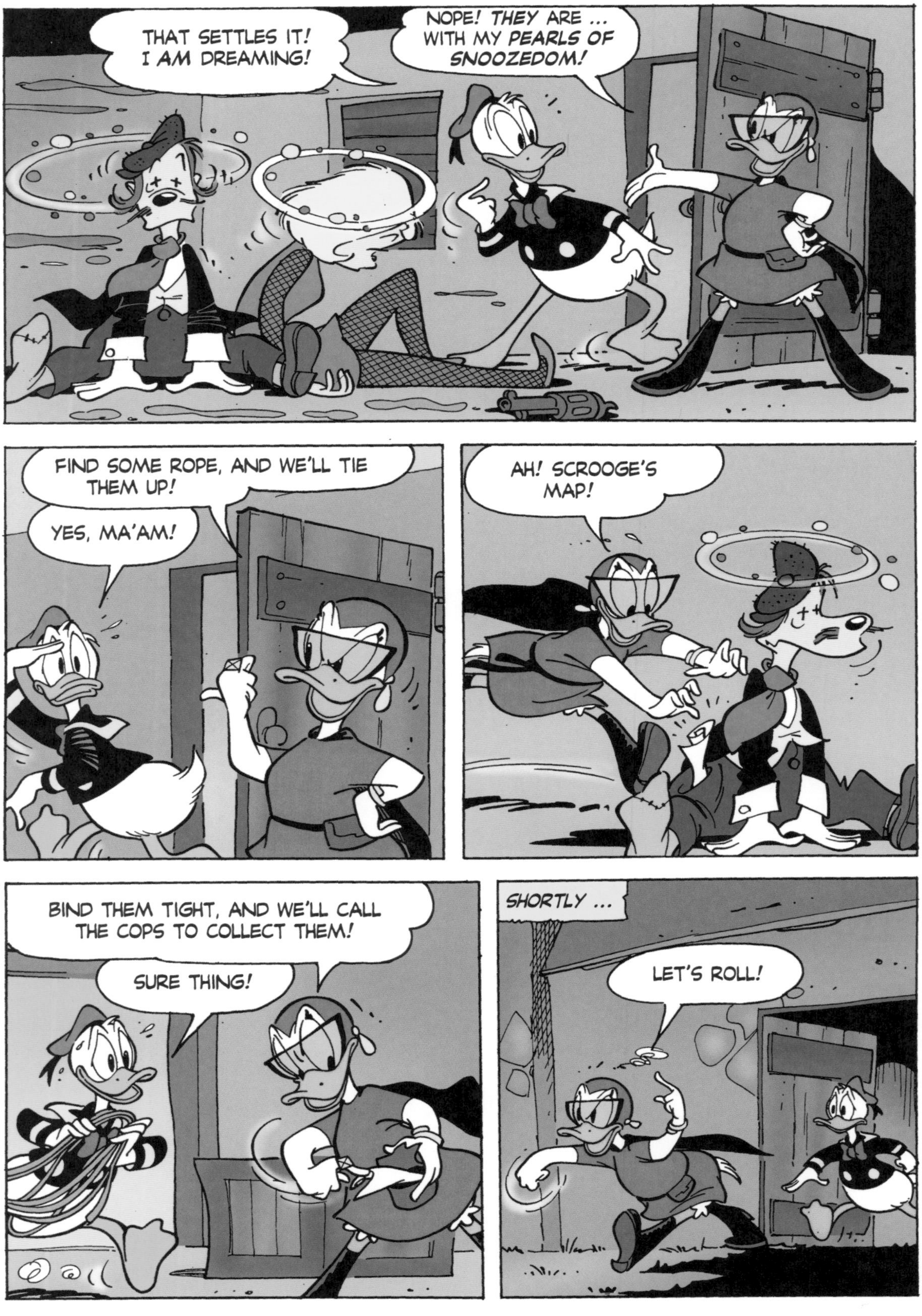
THAT SETTLES IT! I AM DREAMING!
NOPE! THEY ARE ... WITH MY PEARLS OF SNOOZEDOM!
FIND SOME ROPE, AND WE'LL TIE THEM UP!
YES, MA'AM!
AH! SCROOGE'S MAP!
BIND THEM TIGHT, AND WE'LL CALL THE COPS TO COLLECT THEM!
SURE THING!
SHORTLY ...
LET'S ROLL!

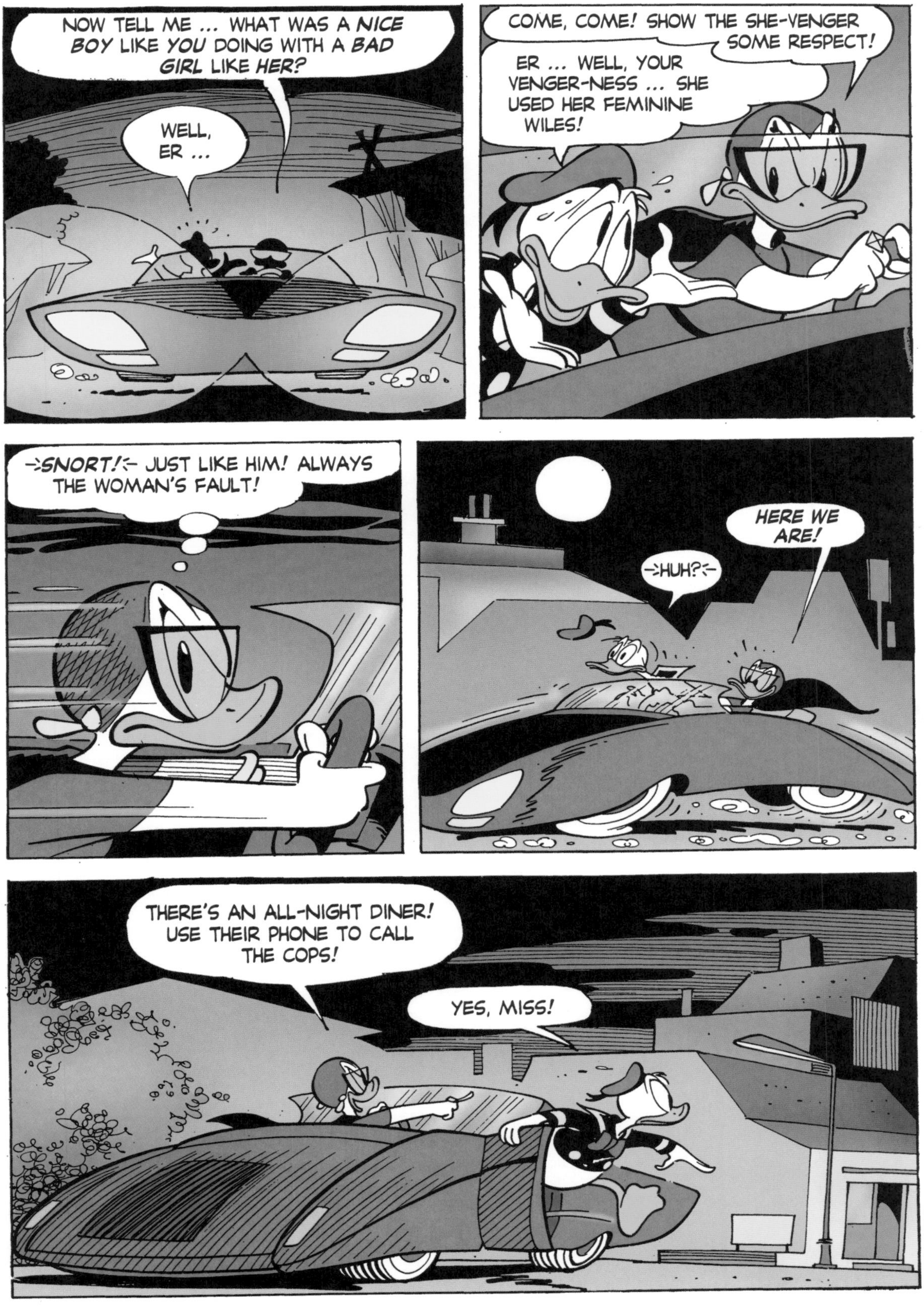
NOW TELL ME ... WHAT WAS A NICE BOY LIKE YOU DOING WITH A BAD GIRL LIKE HER?
WELL, ER ...
COME, COME! SHOW THE SHE-VENGER SOME RESPECT!
ER ... WELL, YOUR VENGER-NESS ... SHE USED HER FEMININE WILES!
-SNORT!- JUST LIKE HIM! ALWAYS THE WOMAN'S FAULT!
HERE WE ARE!
-HUH?-
THERE'S AN ALL-NIGHT DINER! USE THEIR PHONE TO CALL THE COPS!
YES, MISS!

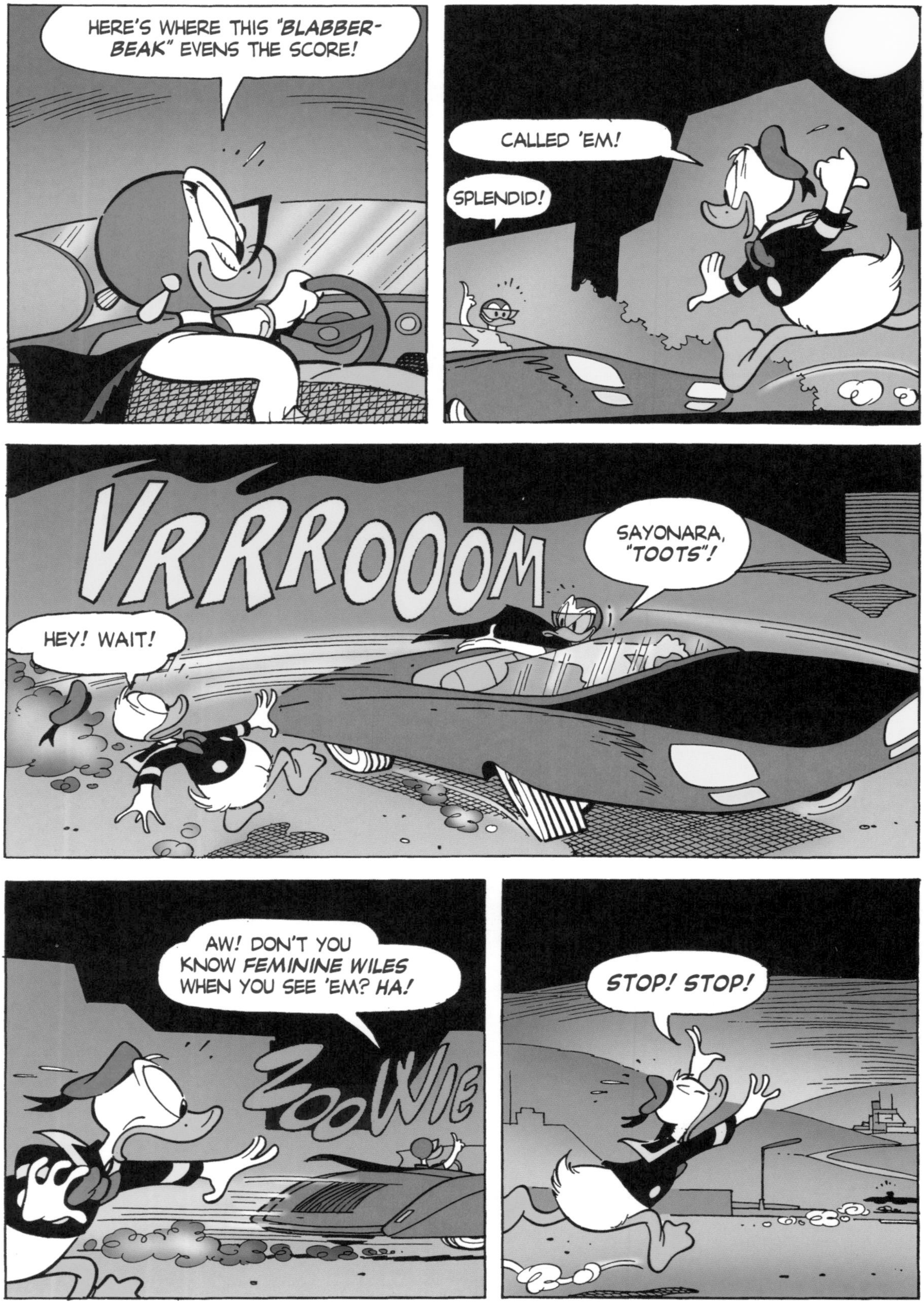
HERE'S WHERE THIS "BLABBER-BEAK" EVENS THE SCORE!
CALLED 'EM!
SPLENDID!
VRRROOOM
SAYONARA, "TOOTS"!
HEY! WAIT!
AW! DON'T YOU KNOW FEMININE WILES WHEN YOU SEE 'EM? HA!
ZOOWIE
STOP! STOP!

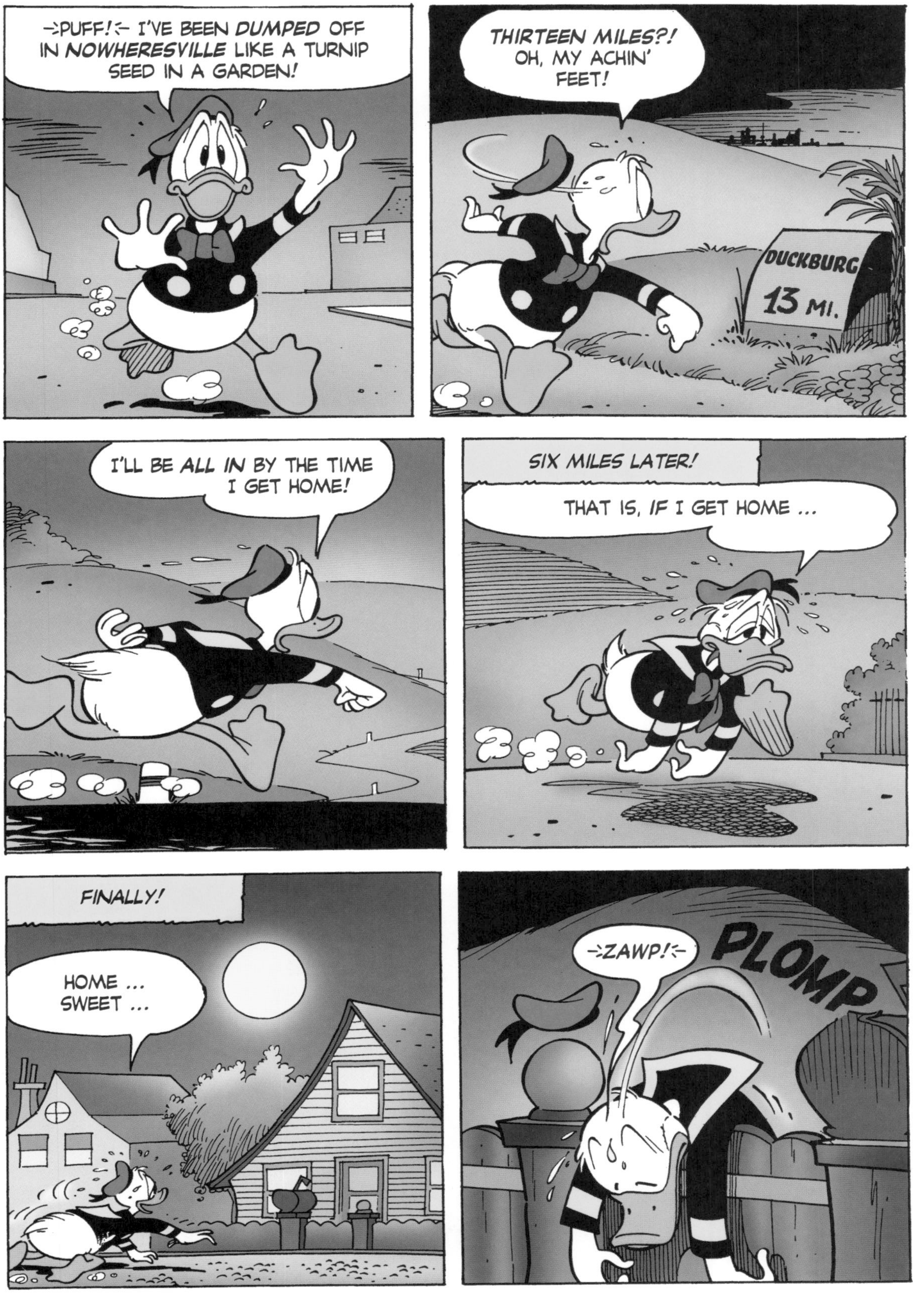
—PUFF!— I'VE BEEN DUMPED OFF IN NOWHERESVILLE LIKE A TURNIP SEED IN A GARDEN!
THIRTEEN MILES?! OH, MY ACHIN' FEET!
DUCKBURG 13 MI.
I'LL BE ALL IN BY THE TIME I GET HOME!
SIX MILES LATER!
THAT IS, IF I GET HOME ...
FINALLY!
HOME ... SWEET ...
—ZAWP!—
PLOMP

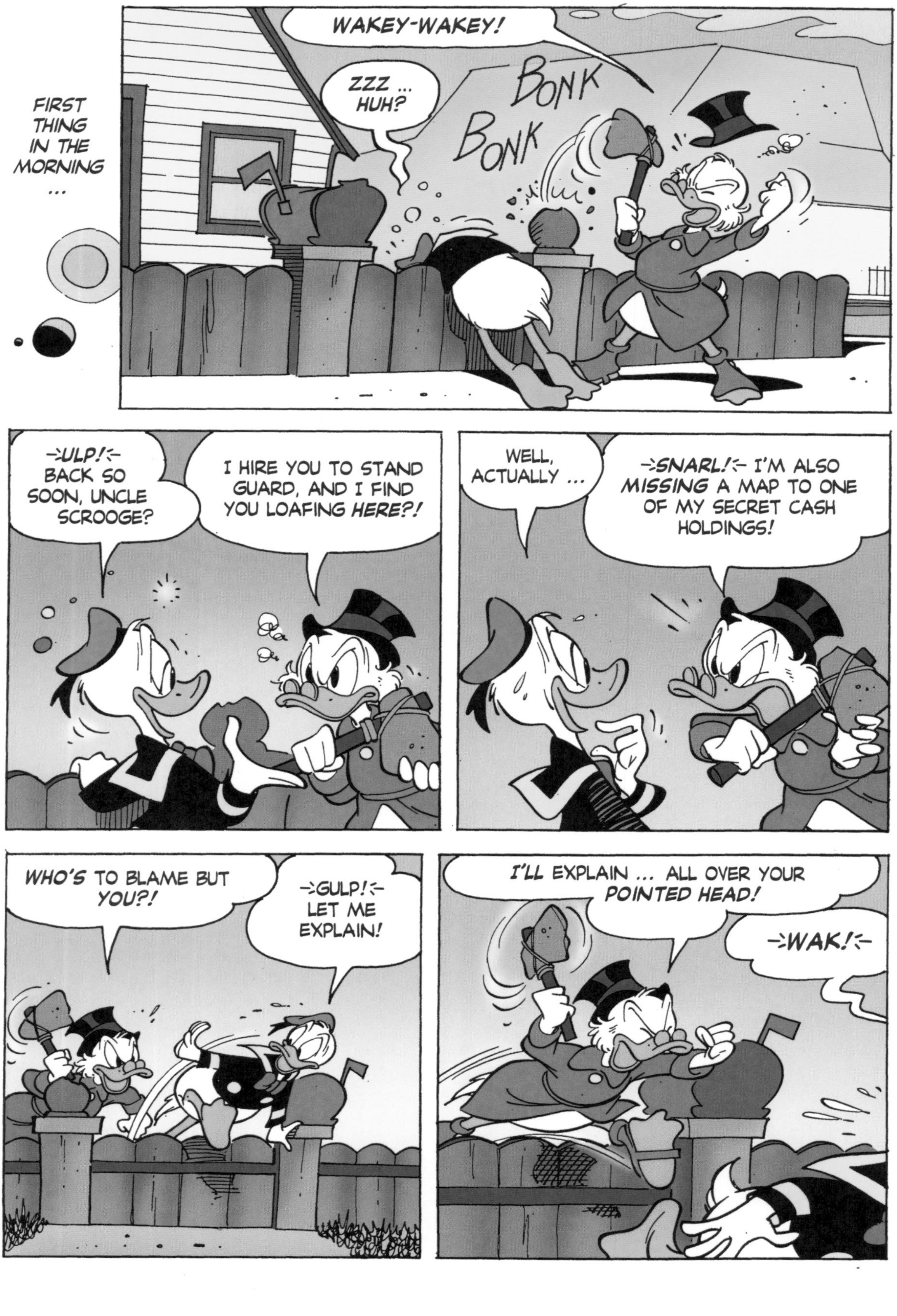
FIRST THING IN THE MORNING ...
WAKEY-WAKEY!
ZZZ ... HUH?
BONK
BONK
-ULP!- BACK SO SOON, UNCLE SCROOGE?
I HIRE YOU TO STAND GUARD, AND I FIND YOU LOAFING HERE?!
WELL, ACTUALLY ...
-SNARL!- I'M ALSO MISSING A MAP TO ONE OF MY SECRET CASH HOLDINGS!
WHO'S TO BLAME BUT YOU?!
-GULP!- LET ME EXPLAIN!
I'LL EXPLAIN ... ALL OVER YOUR POINTED HEAD!
-WAK!-

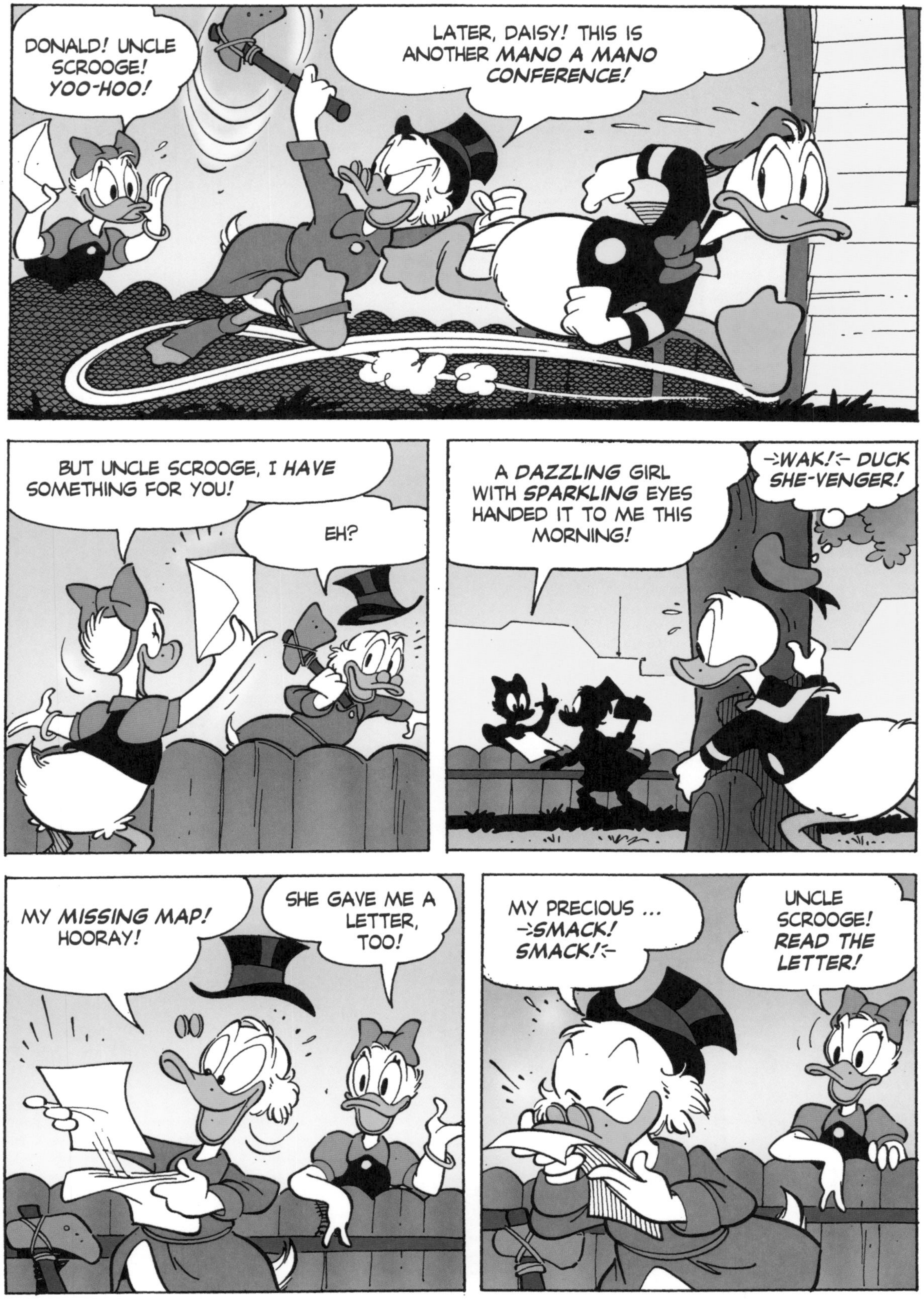

DONALD! UNCLE SCROOGE! YOO-HOO!
LATER, DAISY! THIS IS ANOTHER MANO A MANO CONFERENCE!
BUT UNCLE SCROOGE, I HAVE SOMETHING FOR YOU!
EH?
A DAZZLING GIRL WITH SPARKLING EYES HANDED IT TO ME THIS MORNING!
-WAK!- DUCK SHE-VENGER!
MY MISSING MAP! HOORAY!
SHE GAVE ME A LETTER, TOO!
MY PRECIOUS ... -SMACK! SMACK!-
UNCLE SCROOGE! READ THE LETTER!

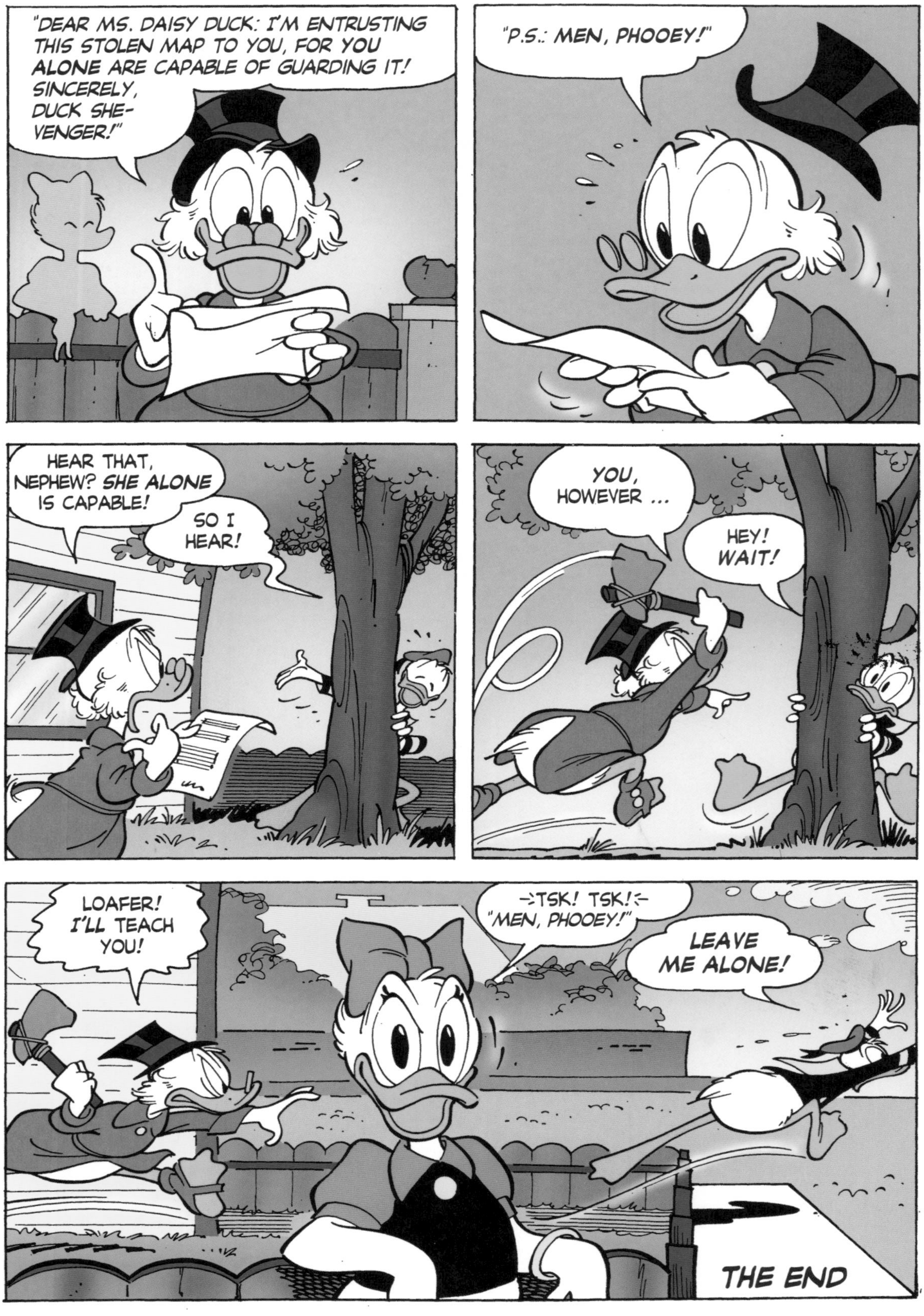
"DEAR MS. DAISY DUCK: I'M ENTRUSTING THIS STOLEN MAP TO YOU, FOR YOU ALONE ARE CAPABLE OF GUARDING IT! SINCERELY, DUCK SHE-VENGER!"
"P.S.: MEN, PHOOEY!"
HEAR THAT, NEPHEW? SHE ALONE IS CAPABLE!
SO I HEAR!
YOU, HOWEVER ...
HEY! WAIT!
LOAFER! I'LL TEACH YOU!
TSK! TSK! "MEN, PHOOEY!"
LEAVE ME ALONE!
THE END

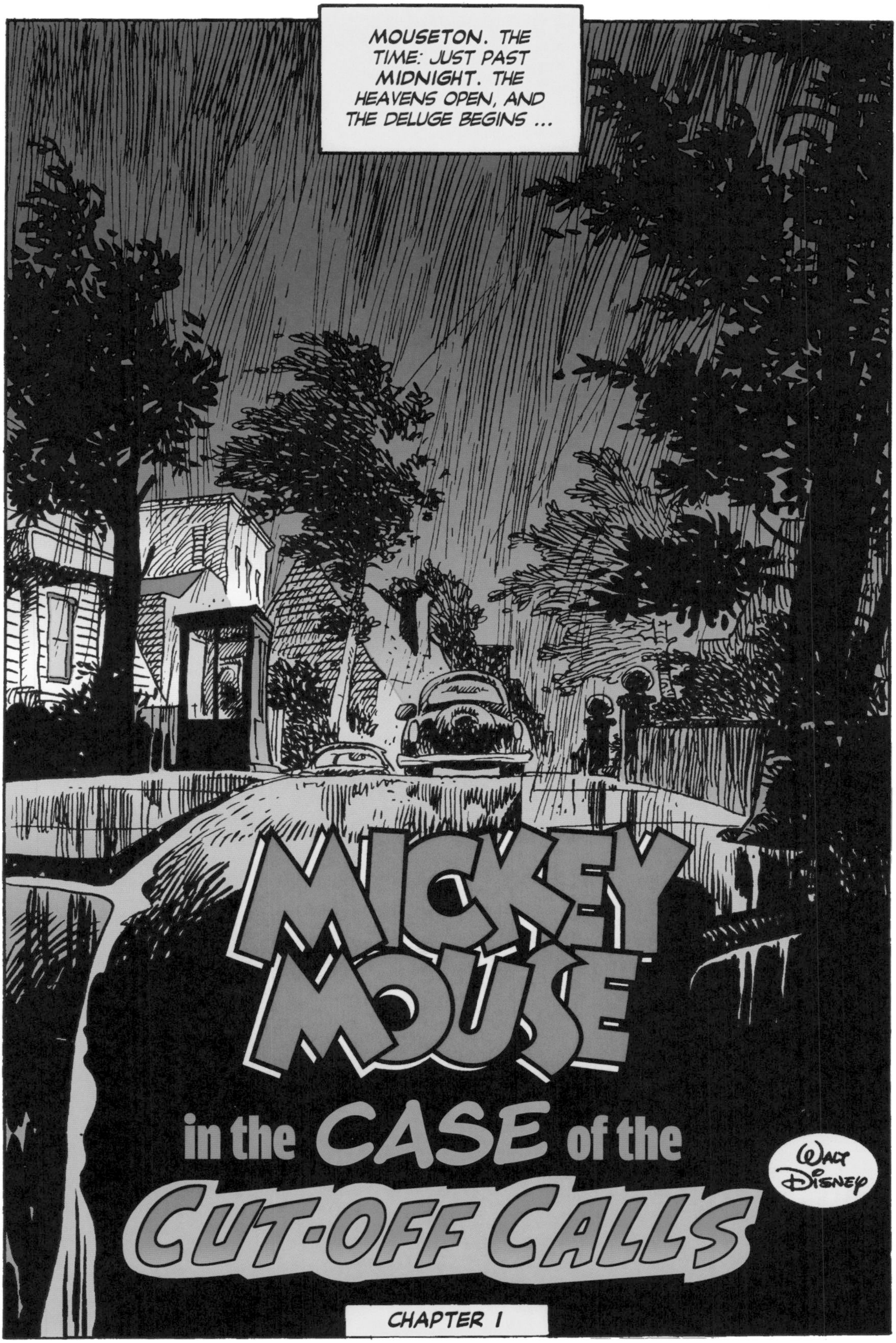
MOUSETON. THE TIME: JUST PAST MIDNIGHT. THE HEAVENS OPEN, AND THE DELUGE BEGINS ...
MICKEY MOUSE
in the CASE of the
CUT-OFF CALLS
WALT DISNEY
CHAPTER 1

STORY BY SILVANO MEZZAVILLA • ART BY GIORGIO CAVAZZANO • TRANSLATION AND DIALOGUE BY JONATHAN GRAY
EDITING BY J. MICHAEL CATRON AND DAVID GERSTEIN

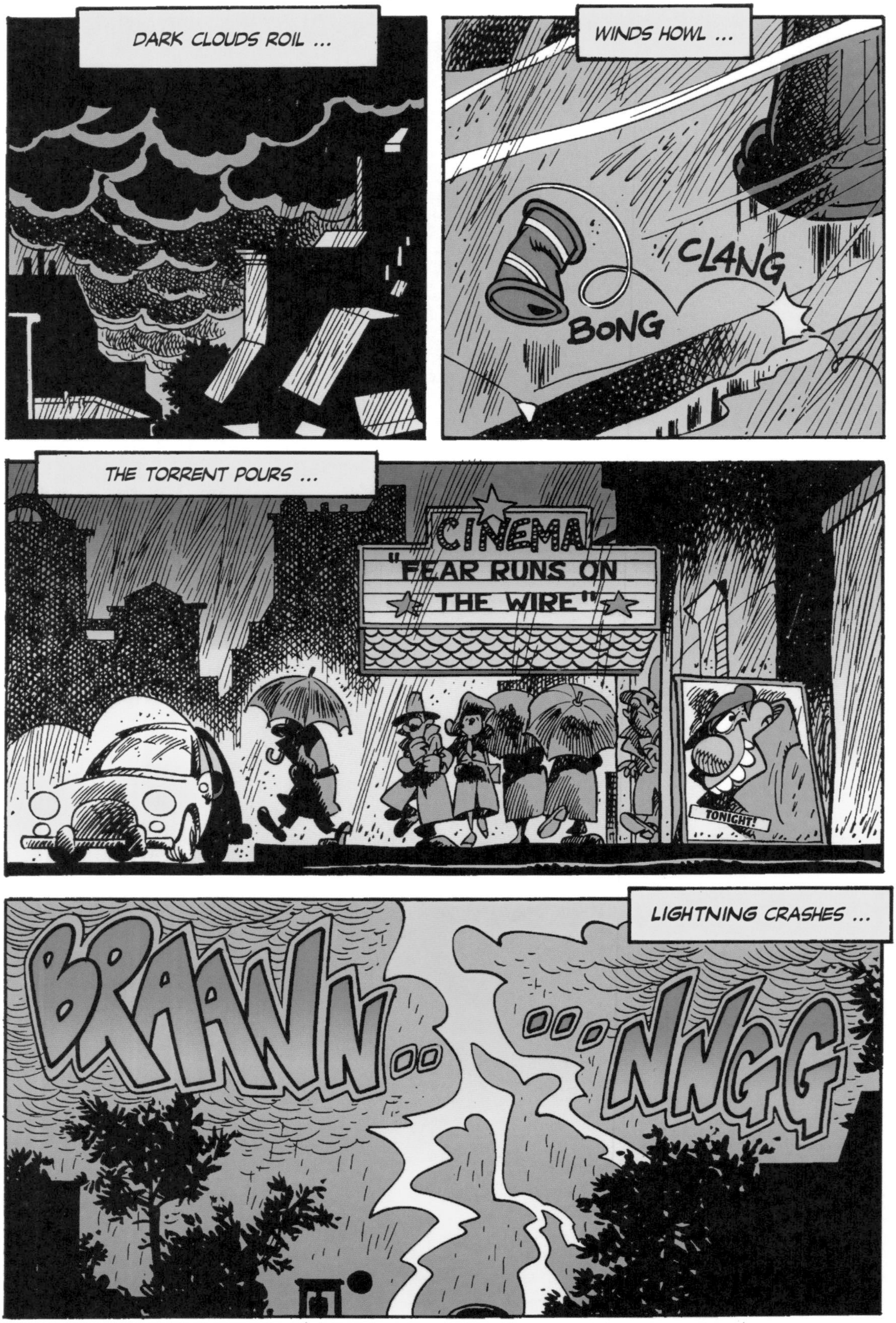

DARK CLOUDS ROIL ...
WINDS HOWL ...
CL4NG
BONG
THE TORRENT POURS ...
CINEMA
"FEAR RUNS ON THE WIRE"
TONIGHT!
LIGHTNING CRASHES ...
BRAAWN..
...NNGG

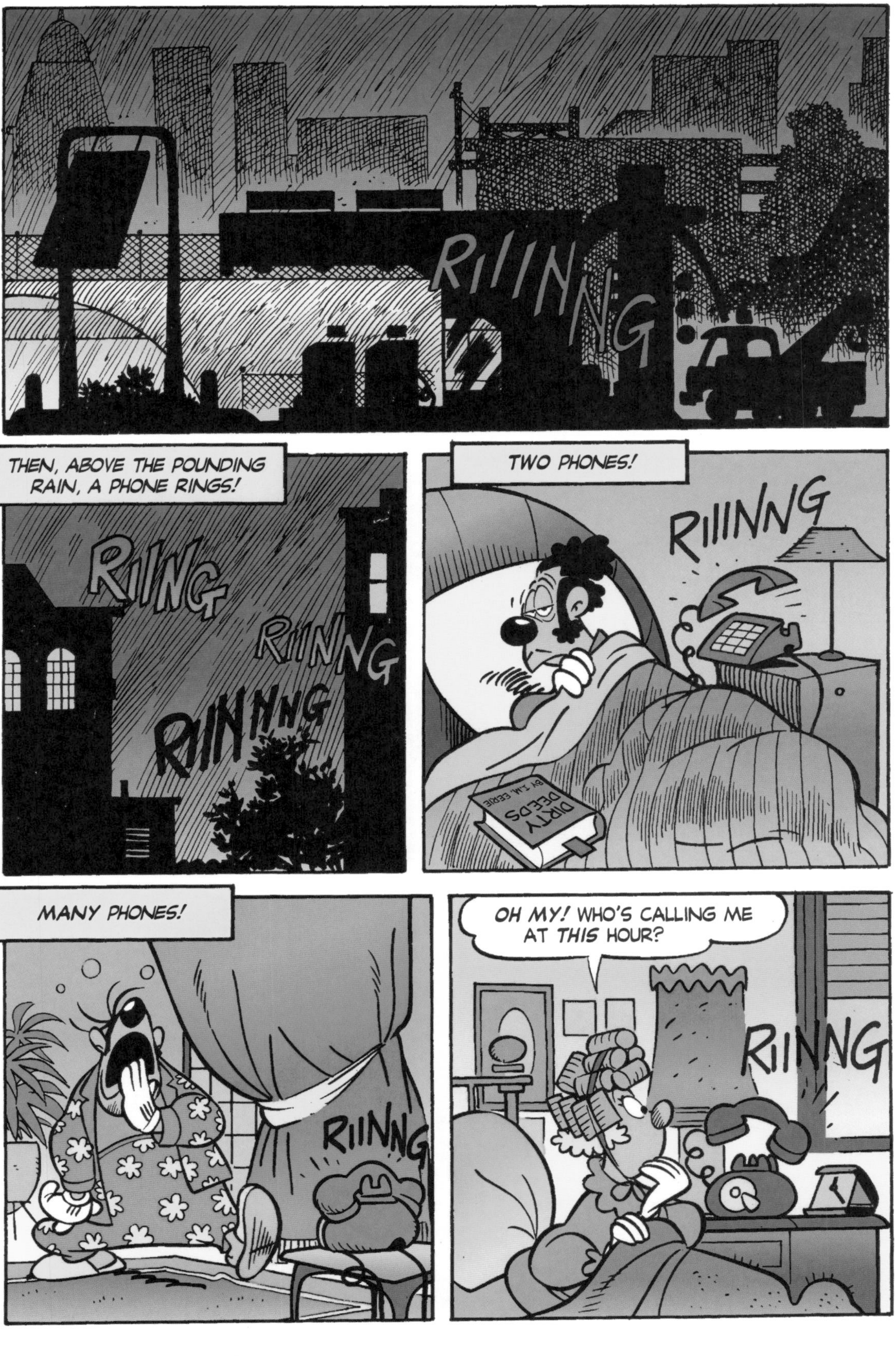
RIIINNG
THEN, ABOVE THE POUNDING RAIN, A PHONE RINGS!
RIING
RIINNG
RIINNNG
TWO PHONES!
RIIINNG
DIRTY DEEDS BY I.M. EERIE
MANY PHONES!
RIINNG
OH MY! WHO'S CALLING ME AT THIS HOUR?
RIINNG

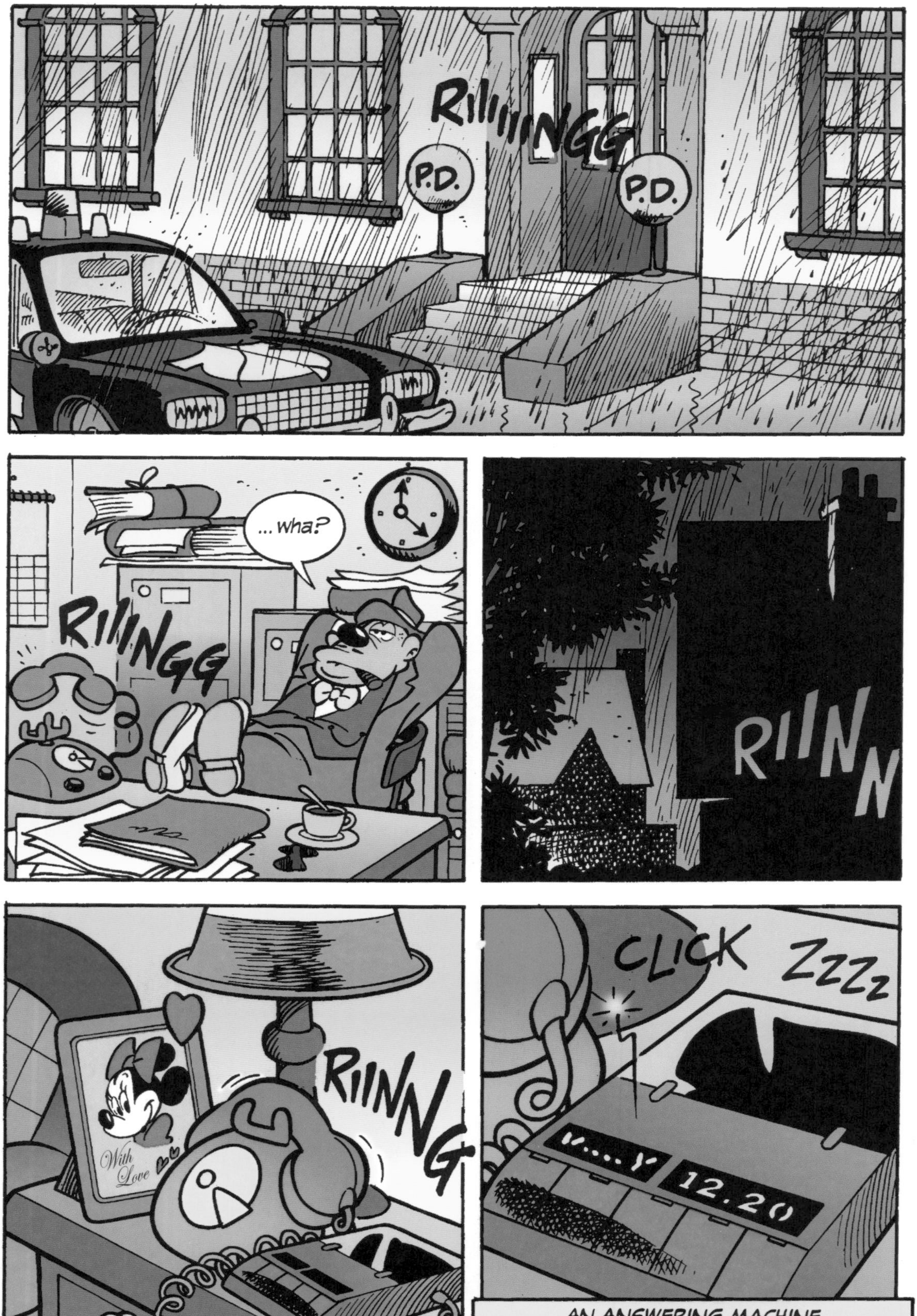
RIIIIINGG
P.D.
P.D.
RIIINGG
...wha?
RIINN
With Love
RIINNG
CLICK
ZZZz
12.20
AN ANSWERING MACHINE AUTOMATICALLY DOES ITS WORK ...

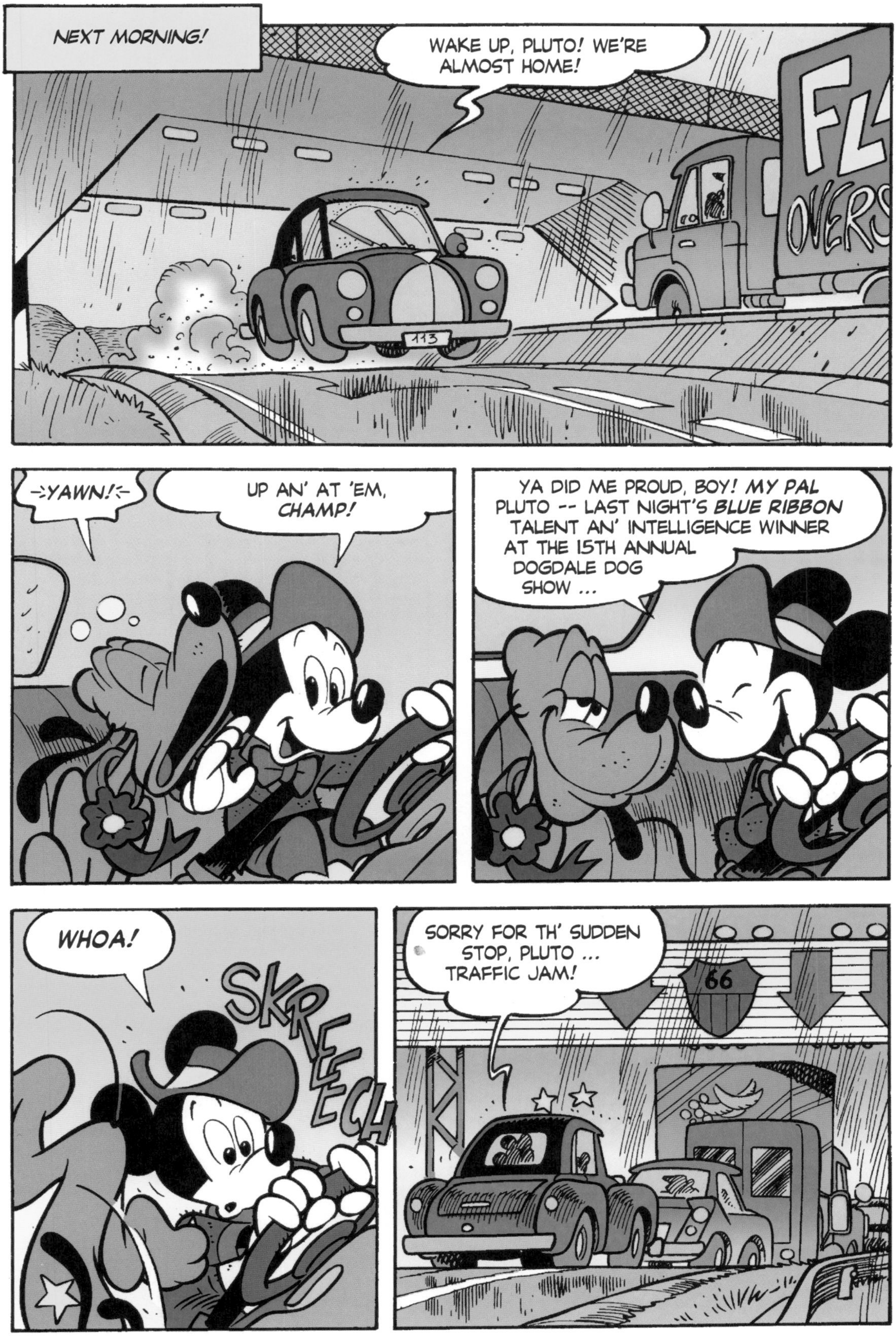
NEXT MORNING!
WAKE UP, PLUTO! WE'RE ALMOST HOME!
113
-YAWN!-
UP AN' AT 'EM, CHAMP!
YA DID ME PROUD, BOY! MY PAL PLUTO -- LAST NIGHT'S BLUE RIBBON TALENT AN' INTELLIGENCE WINNER AT THE 15TH ANNUAL DOGDALE DOG SHOW ...
WHOA!
SKREECH
SORRY FOR TH' SUDDEN STOP, PLUTO ... TRAFFIC JAM!
66

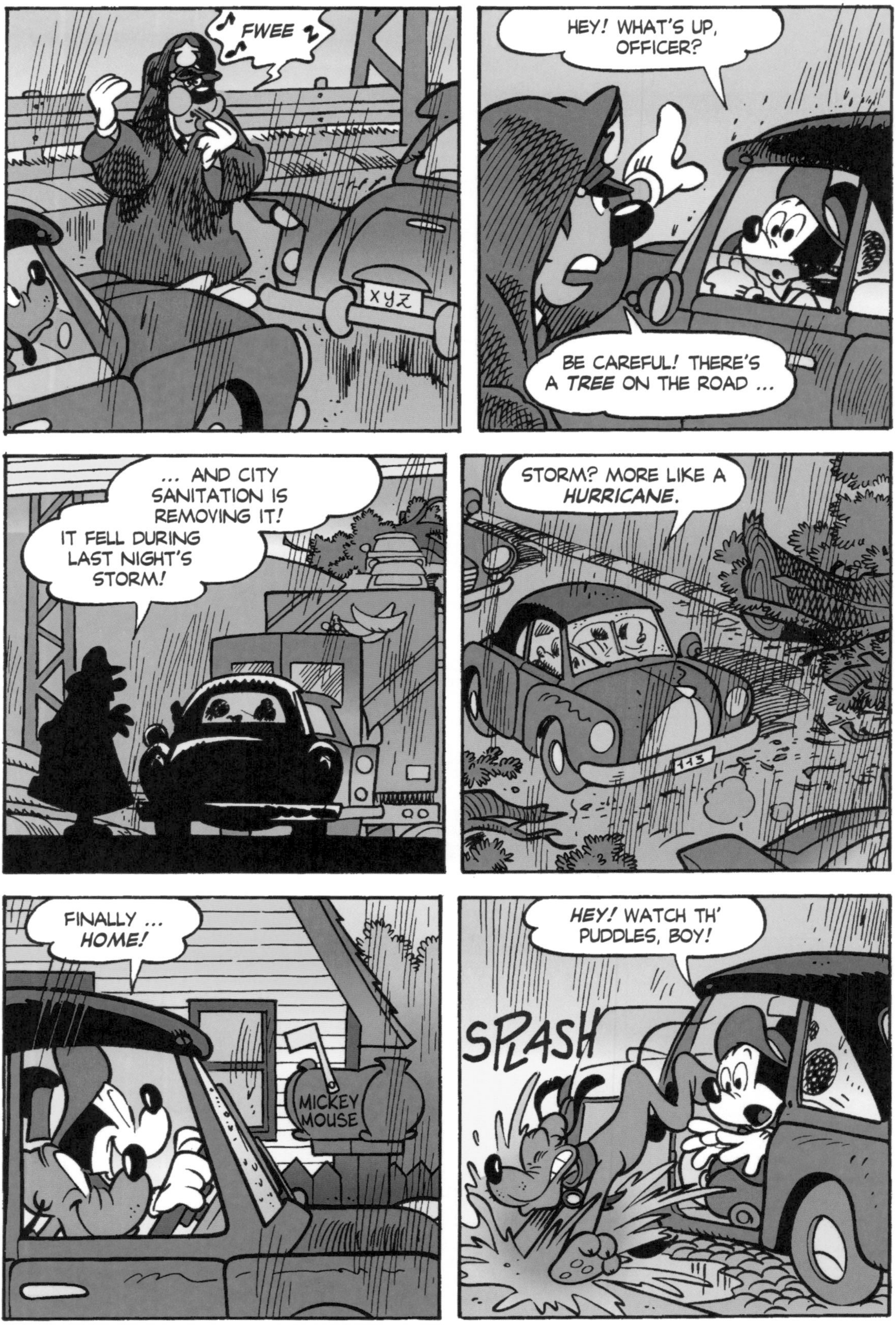
FWEE
HEY! WHAT'S UP, OFFICER?
BE CAREFUL! THERE'S A TREE ON THE ROAD ...
XYZ
... AND CITY SANITATION IS REMOVING IT!
IT FELL DURING LAST NIGHT'S STORM!
STORM? MORE LIKE A HURRICANE.
113
FINALLY ... HOME!
MICKEY MOUSE
HEY! WATCH TH' PUDDLES, BOY!
SPLASH

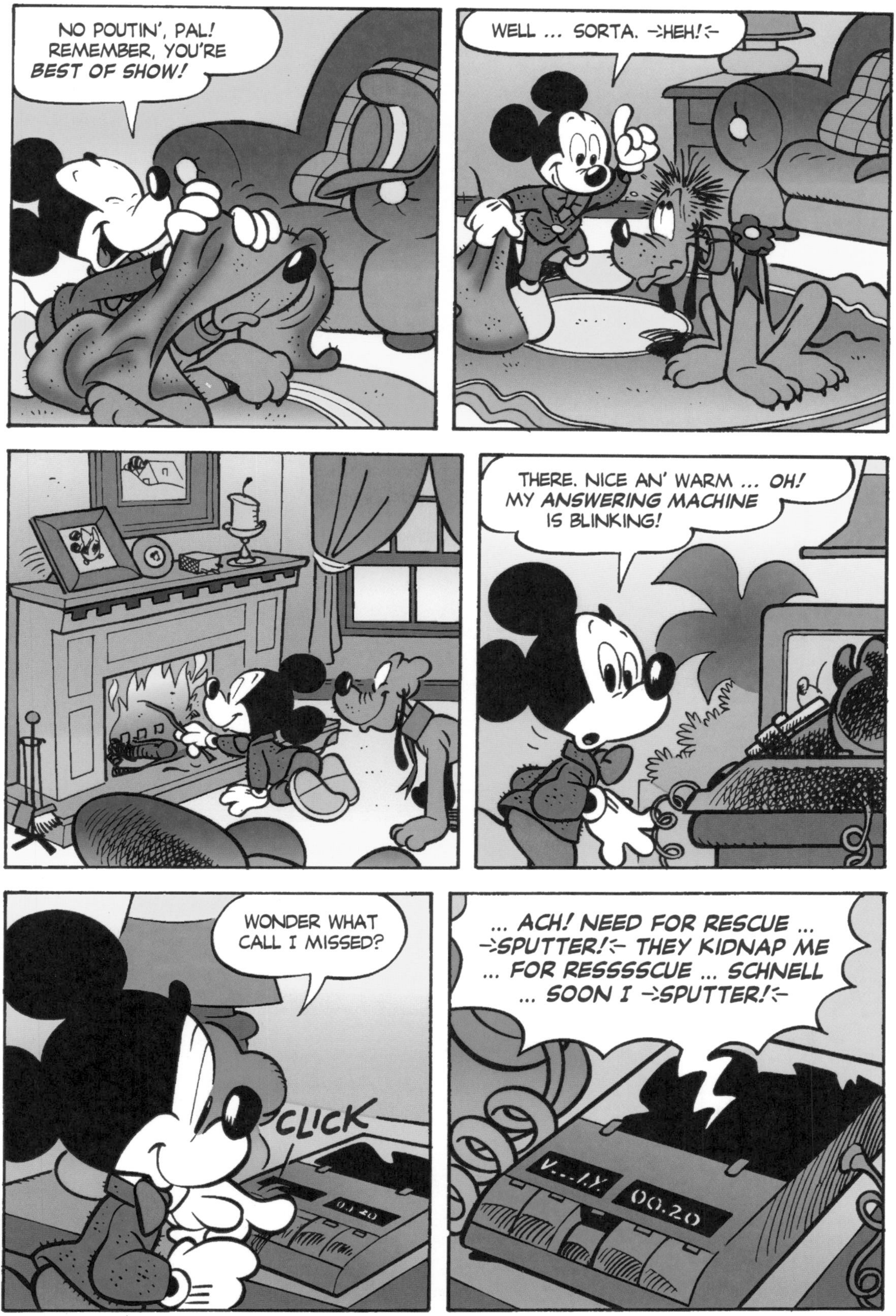
NO POUTIN', PAL! REMEMBER, YOU'RE BEST OF SHOW!
WELL ... SORTA. HEH!
THERE. NICE AN' WARM ... OH! MY ANSWERING MACHINE IS BLINKING!
WONDER WHAT CALL I MISSED?
CLICK
... ACH! NEED FOR RESCUE ... SPUTTER! THEY KIDNAP ME ... FOR RESSSSCUE ... SCHNELL ... SOON I SPUTTER!

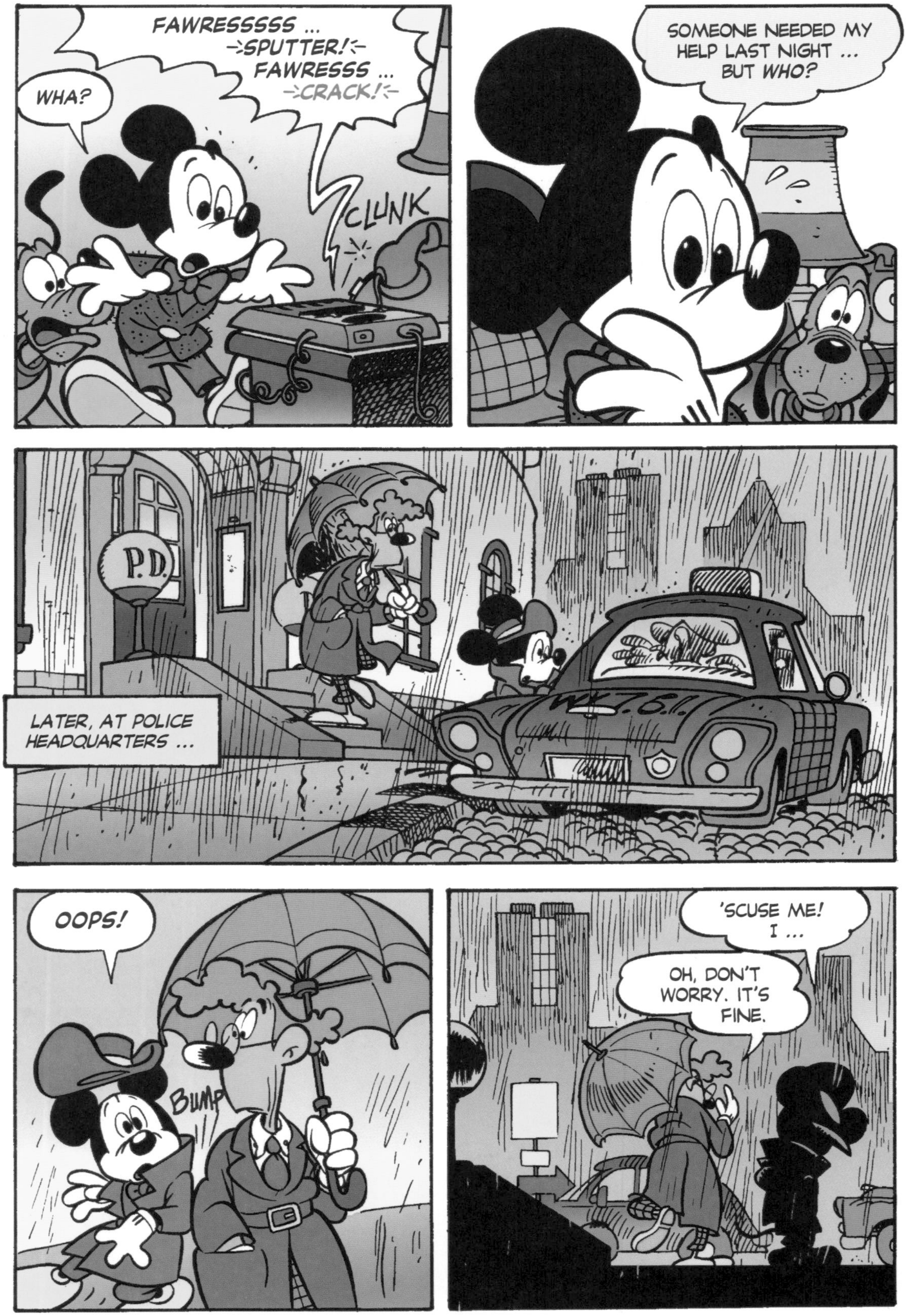
FAWRESSSSS ...
SPUTTER!
FAWRESSS ...
CRACK!
WHA?
CLUNK
SOMEONE NEEDED MY HELP LAST NIGHT ... BUT WHO?
P.D.
LATER, AT POLICE HEADQUARTERS ...
OOPS!
BUMP
'SCUSE ME! I ...
OH, DON'T WORRY. IT'S FINE.

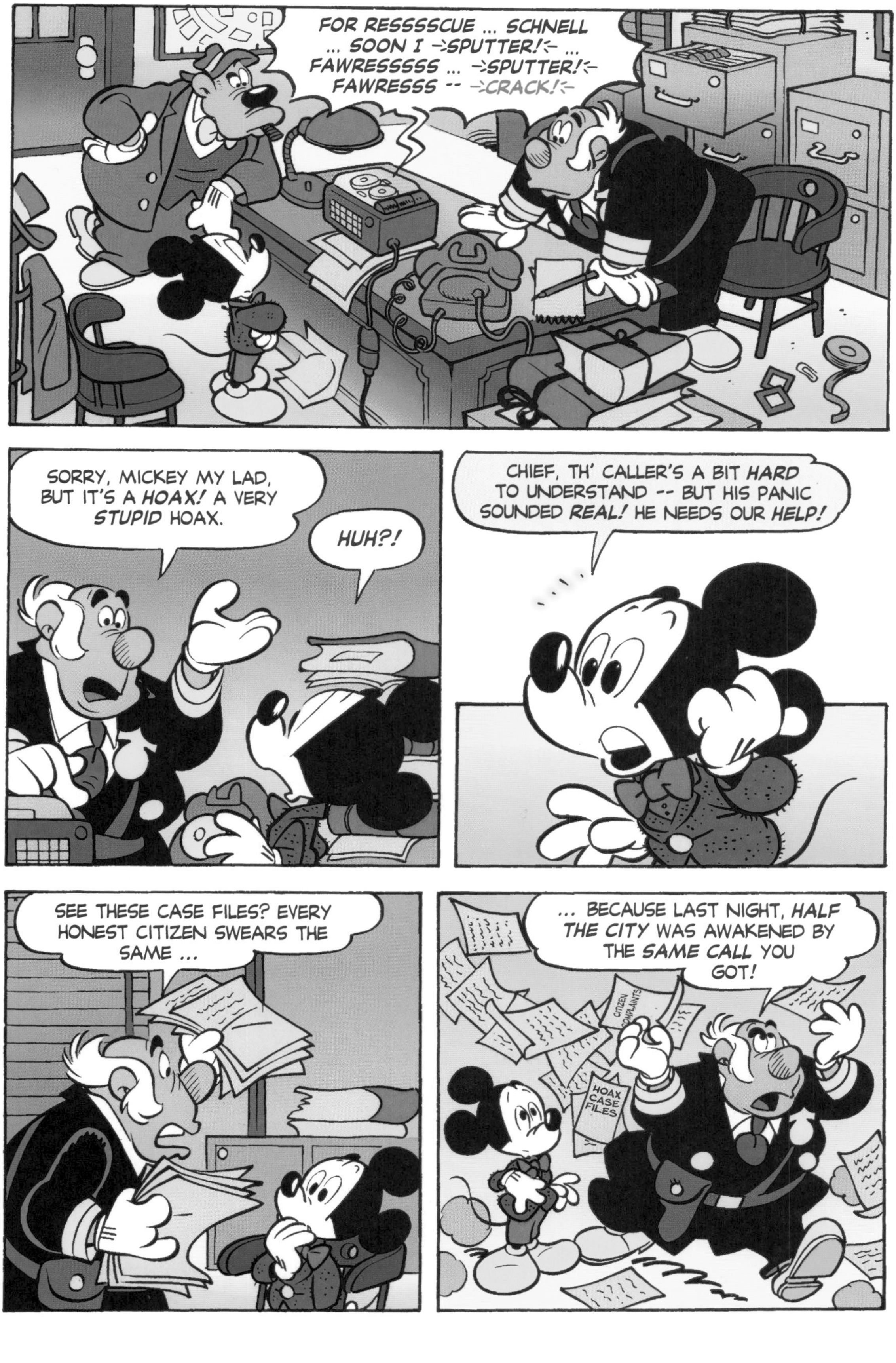
FOR RESSSSCUE ... SCHNELL ... SOON I ->SPUTTER!<- ... FAWRESSSSS ... ->SPUTTER!<- FAWRESSS -- ->CRACK!<-
SORRY, MICKEY MY LAD, BUT IT'S A HOAX! A VERY STUPID HOAX.
HUH?!
CHIEF, TH' CALLER'S A BIT HARD TO UNDERSTAND -- BUT HIS PANIC SOUNDED REAL! HE NEEDS OUR HELP!
SEE THESE CASE FILES? EVERY HONEST CITIZEN SWEARS THE SAME ...
... BECAUSE LAST NIGHT, HALF THE CITY WAS AWAKENED BY THE SAME CALL YOU GOT!
CITIZEN COMPLAINTS
HOAX CASE FILES

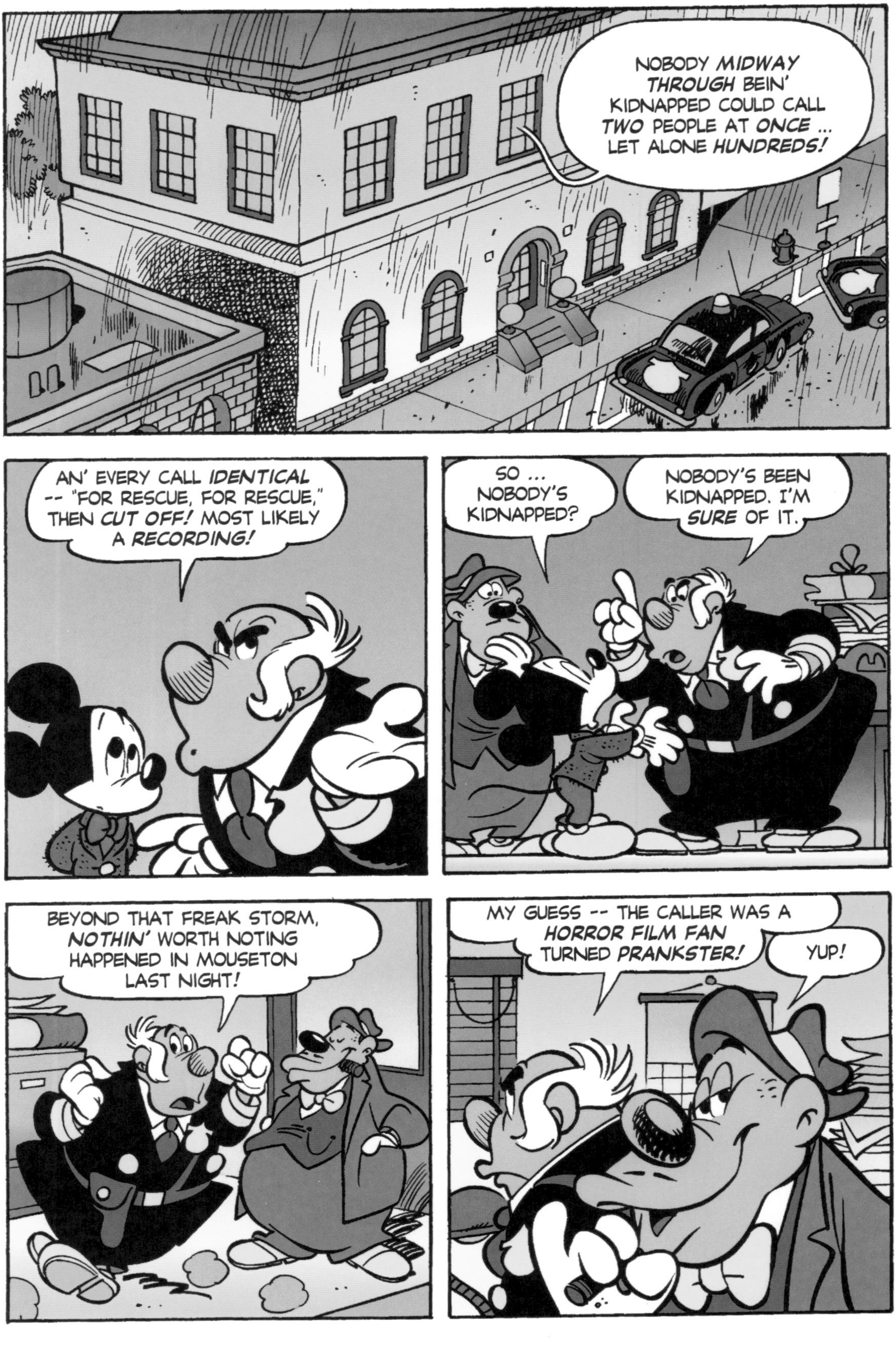
NOBODY MIDWAY THROUGH BEIN' KIDNAPPED COULD CALL TWO PEOPLE AT ONCE ... LET ALONE HUNDREDS!
AN' EVERY CALL IDENTICAL -- "FOR RESCUE, FOR RESCUE," THEN CUT OFF! MOST LIKELY A RECORDING!
SO ... NOBODY'S KIDNAPPED?
NOBODY'S BEEN KIDNAPPED. I'M SURE OF IT.
BEYOND THAT FREAK STORM, NOTHIN' WORTH NOTING HAPPENED IN MOUSETON LAST NIGHT!
MY GUESS -- THE CALLER WAS A HORROR FILM FAN TURNED PRANKSTER!
YUP!

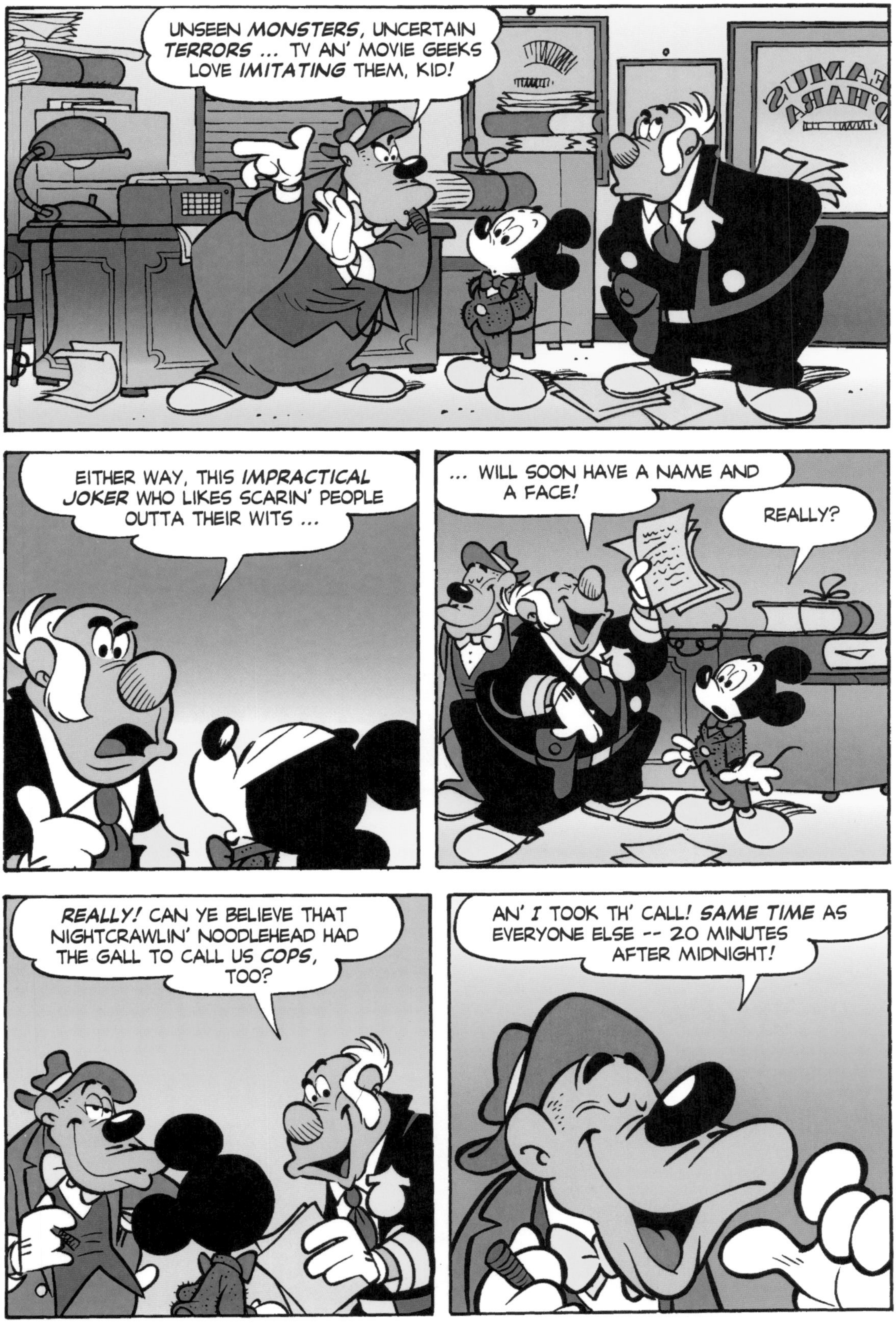
UNSEEN MONSTERS, UNCERTAIN TERRORS ... TV AN' MOVIE GEEKS LOVE IMITATING THEM, KID!
EITHER WAY, THIS IMPRACTICAL JOKER WHO LIKES SCARIN' PEOPLE OUTTA THEIR WITS ...
... WILL SOON HAVE A NAME AND A FACE!
REALLY?
REALLY! CAN YE BELIEVE THAT NIGHTCRAWLIN' NOODLEHEAD HAD THE GALL TO CALL US COPS, TOO?
AN' I TOOK TH' CALL! SAME TIME AS EVERYONE ELSE -- 20 MINUTES AFTER MIDNIGHT!

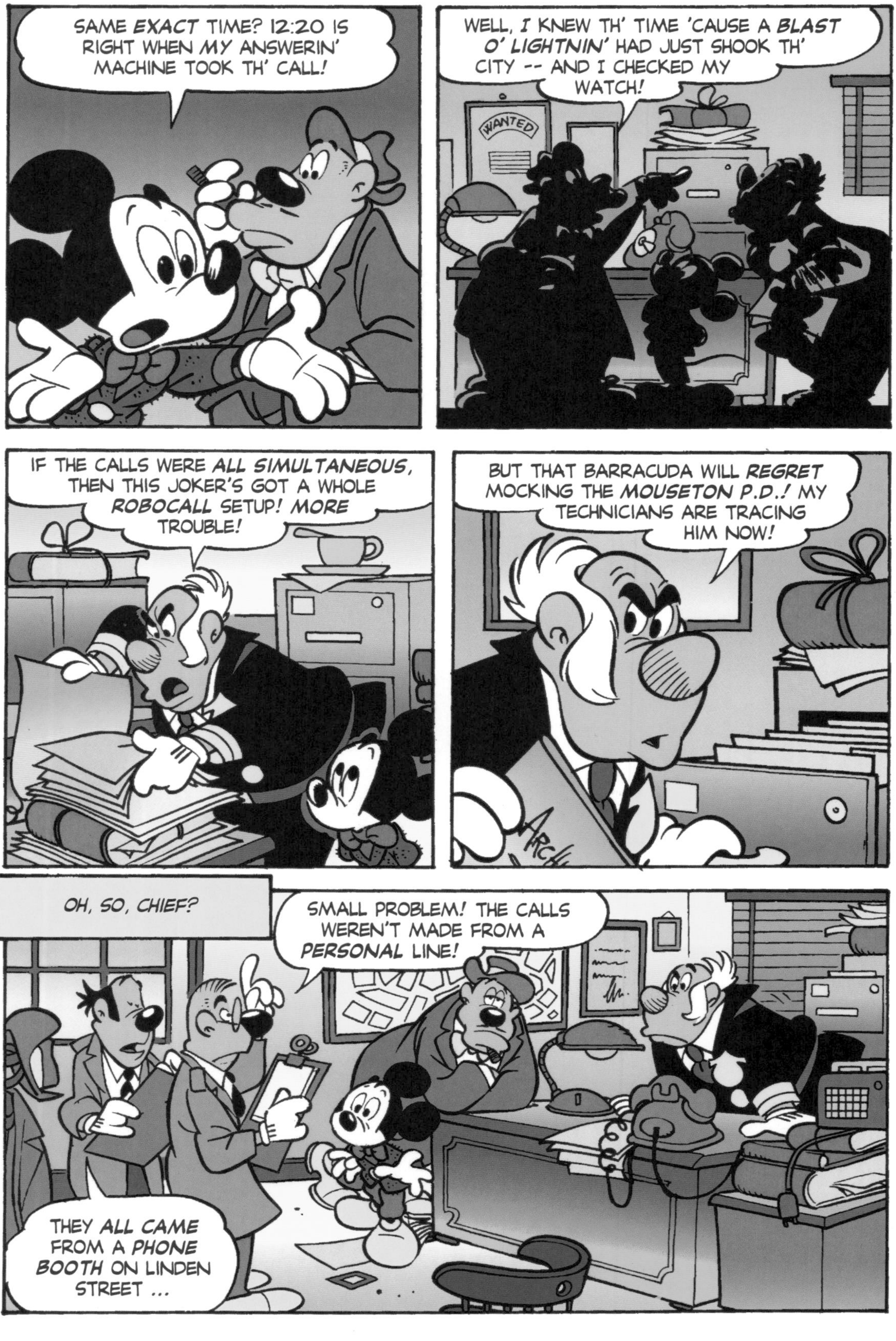
SAME EXACT TIME? 12:20 IS RIGHT WHEN MY ANSWERIN' MACHINE TOOK TH' CALL!
WELL, I KNEW TH' TIME 'CAUSE A BLAST O' LIGHTNIN' HAD JUST SHOOK TH' CITY -- AND I CHECKED MY WATCH!
WANTED
IF THE CALLS WERE ALL SIMULTANEOUS, THEN THIS JOKER'S GOT A WHOLE ROBOCALL SETUP! MORE TROUBLE!
BUT THAT BARRACUDA WILL REGRET MOCKING THE MOUSETON P.D.! MY TECHNICIANS ARE TRACING HIM NOW!
OH, SO, CHIEF?
SMALL PROBLEM! THE CALLS WEREN'T MADE FROM A PERSONAL LINE!
THEY ALL CAME FROM A PHONE BOOTH ON LINDEN STREET ...

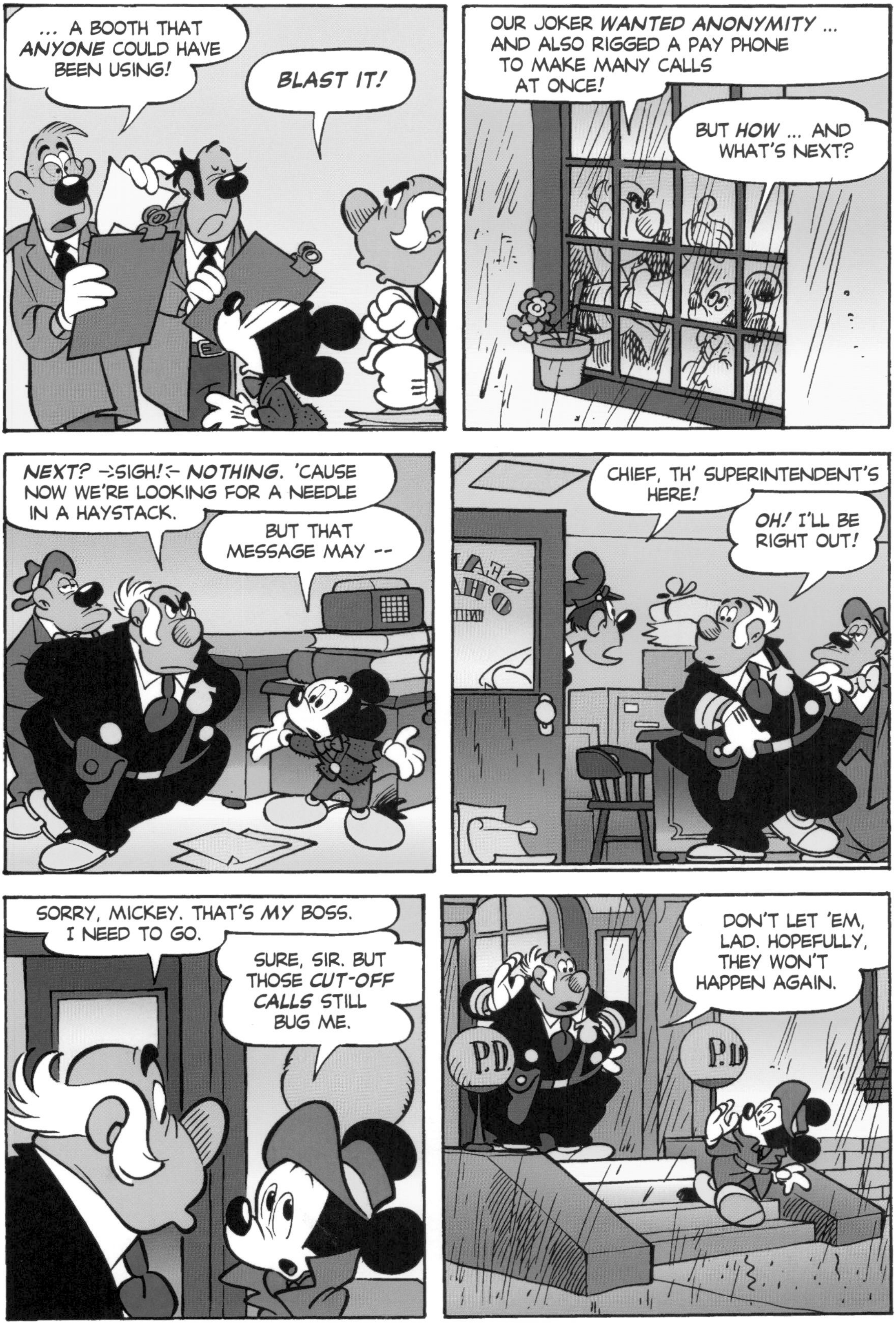
... A BOOTH THAT ANYONE COULD HAVE BEEN USING!
BLAST IT!
OUR JOKER WANTED ANONYMITY ... AND ALSO RIGGED A PAY PHONE TO MAKE MANY CALLS AT ONCE!
BUT HOW ... AND WHAT'S NEXT?
NEXT? -SIGH!- NOTHING. 'CAUSE NOW WE'RE LOOKING FOR A NEEDLE IN A HAYSTACK.
BUT THAT MESSAGE MAY --
CHIEF, TH' SUPERINTENDENT'S HERE!
OH! I'LL BE RIGHT OUT!
SORRY, MICKEY. THAT'S MY BOSS. I NEED TO GO.
SURE, SIR. BUT THOSE CUT-OFF CALLS STILL BUG ME.
DON'T LET 'EM, LAD. HOPEFULLY, THEY WON'T HAPPEN AGAIN.
P.D.

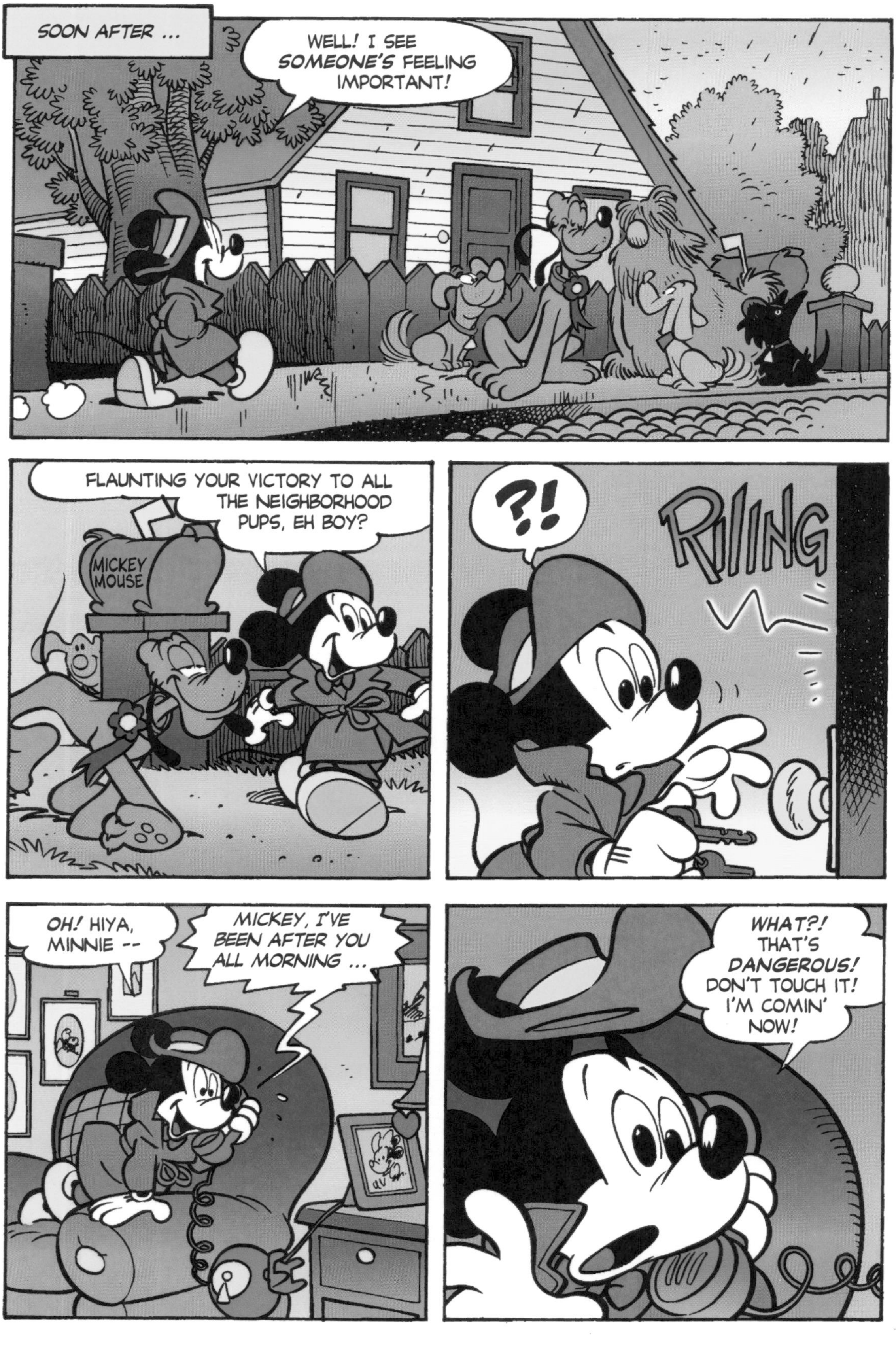
SOON AFTER ...
WELL! I SEE SOMEONE'S FEELING IMPORTANT!
FLAUNTING YOUR VICTORY TO ALL THE NEIGHBORHOOD PUPS, EH BOY?
MICKEY MOUSE
?!
RIIING
OH! HIYA, MINNIE --
MICKEY, I'VE BEEN AFTER YOU ALL MORNING ...
WHAT?! THAT'S DANGEROUS! DON'T TOUCH IT! I'M COMIN' NOW!

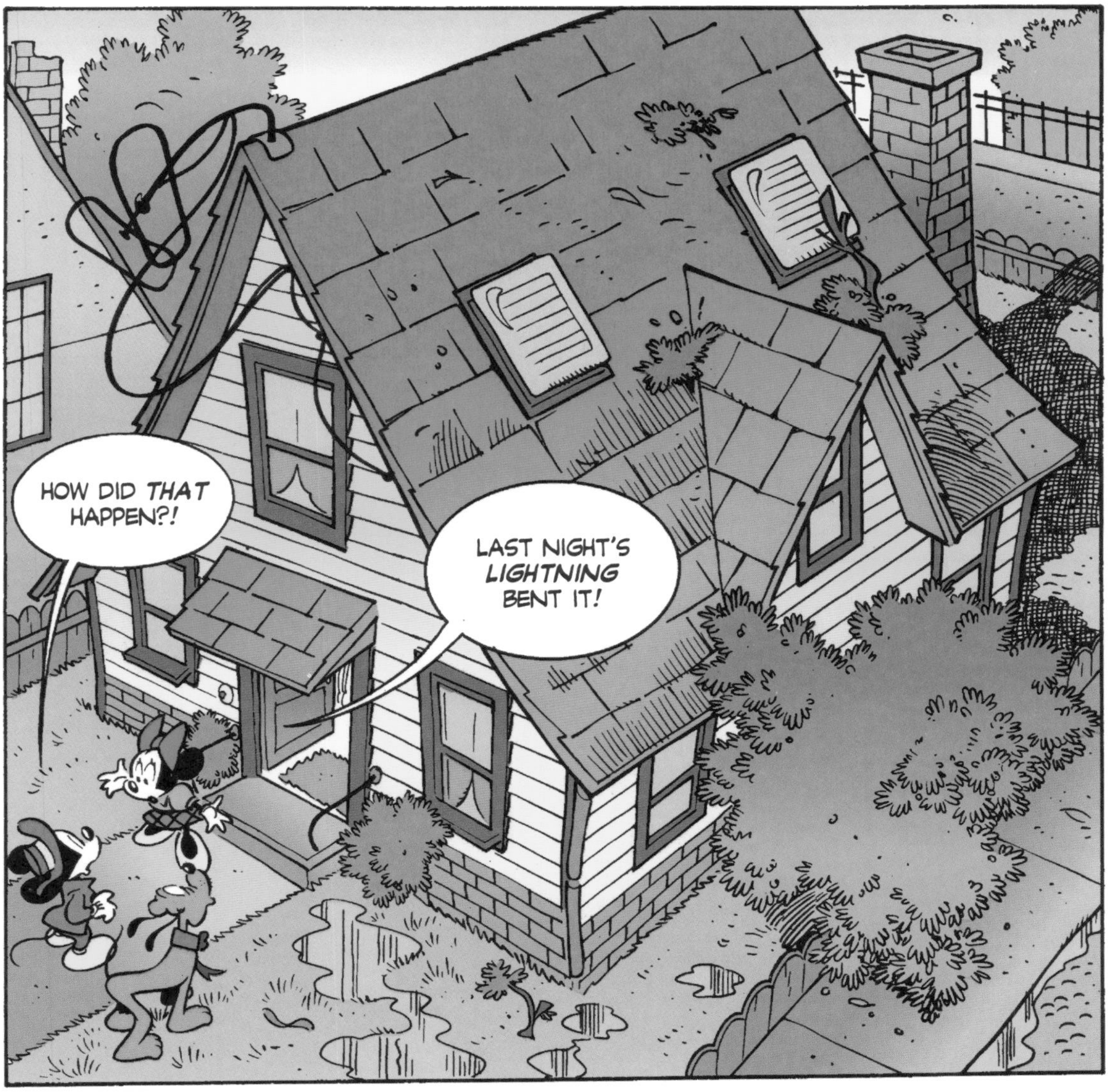
HOW DID *THAT* HAPPEN?!
LAST NIGHT'S ***LIGHTNING*** BENT IT!

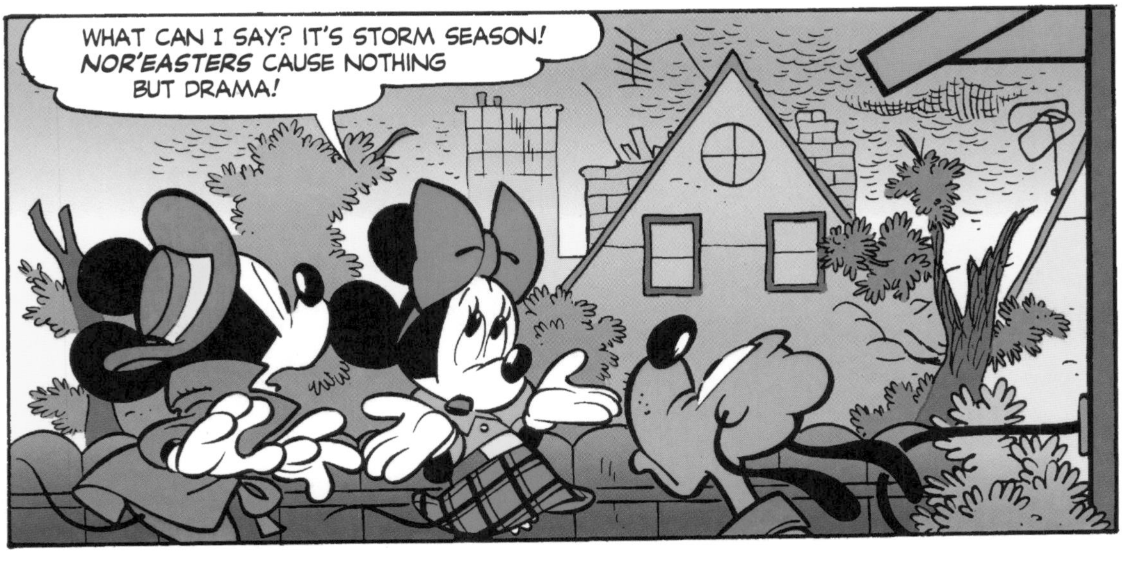
WHAT CAN I SAY? IT'S STORM SEASON! ***NOR'EASTERS*** CAUSE NOTHING BUT DRAMA!

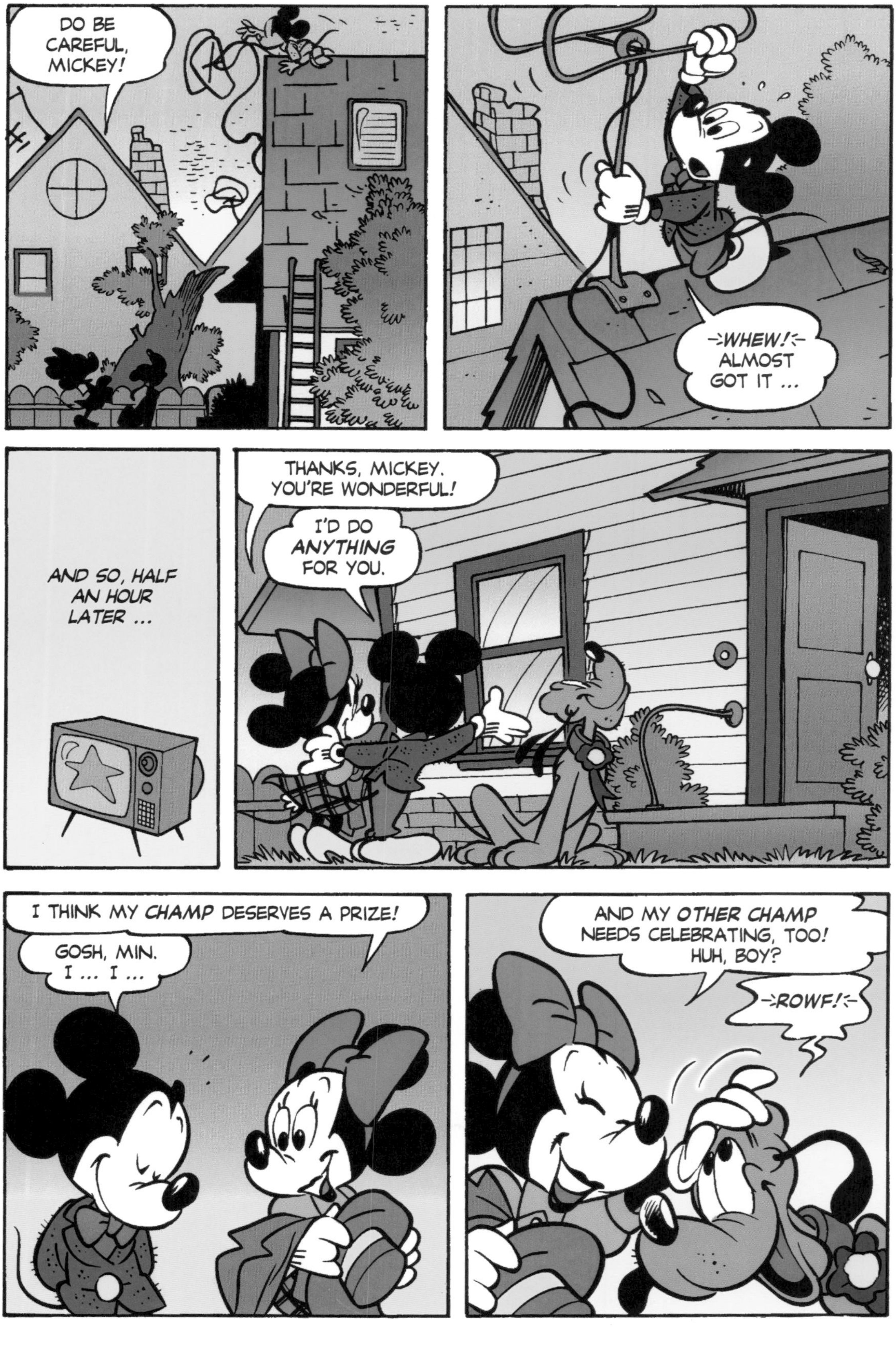
DO BE CAREFUL, MICKEY!
-WHEW!- ALMOST GOT IT ...
AND SO, HALF AN HOUR LATER ...
THANKS, MICKEY. YOU'RE WONDERFUL!
I'D DO ANYTHING FOR YOU.
I THINK MY CHAMP DESERVES A PRIZE!
GOSH, MIN. I ... I ...
AND MY OTHER CHAMP NEEDS CELEBRATING, TOO! HUH, BOY?
-ROWF!-

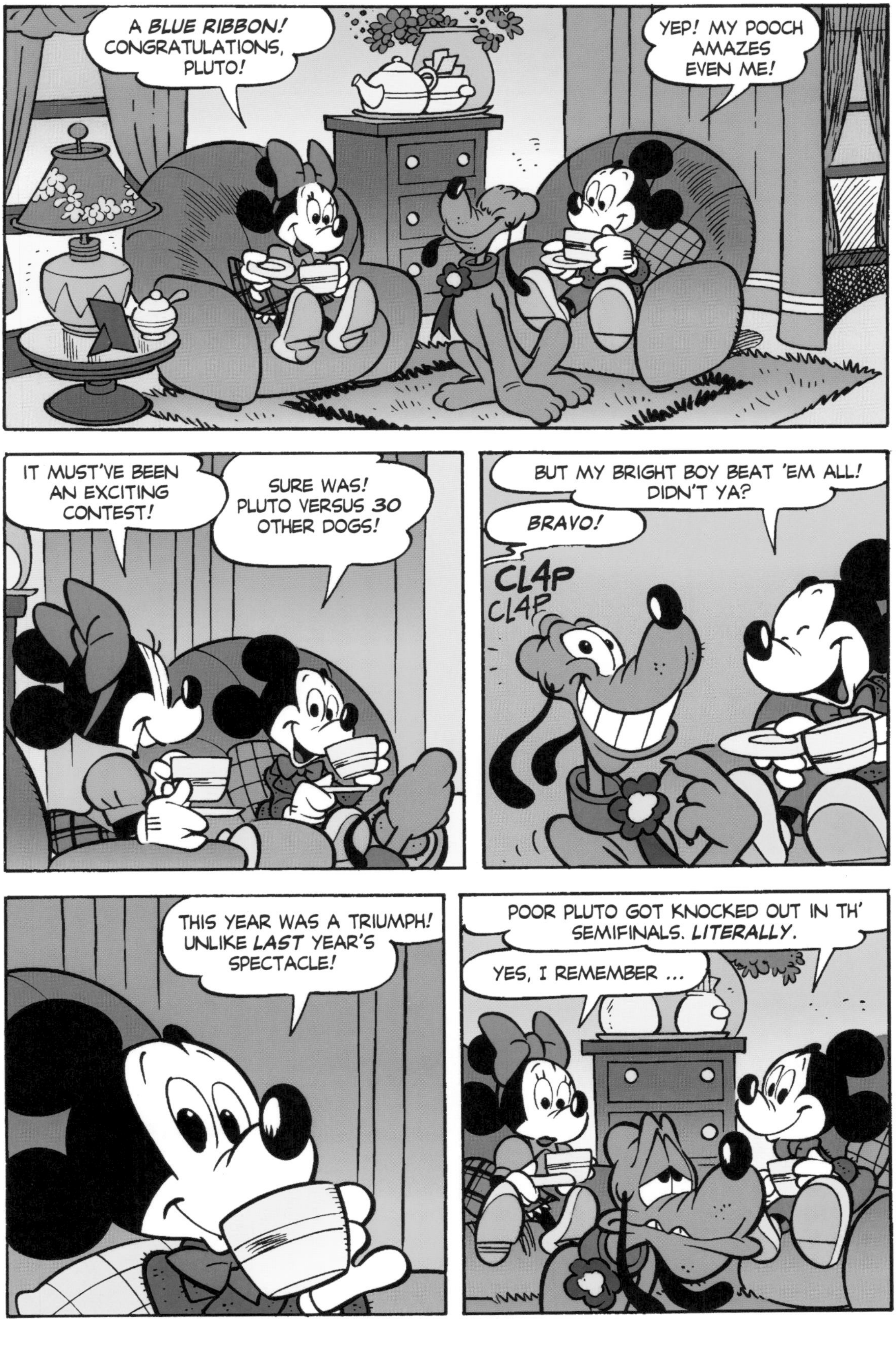
A BLUE RIBBON! CONGRATULATIONS, PLUTO!
YEP! MY POOCH AMAZES EVEN ME!
IT MUST'VE BEEN AN EXCITING CONTEST!
SURE WAS! PLUTO VERSUS 30 OTHER DOGS!
BUT MY BRIGHT BOY BEAT 'EM ALL! DIDN'T YA?
BRAVO!
CLAP
CLAP
THIS YEAR WAS A TRIUMPH! UNLIKE LAST YEAR'S SPECTACLE!
POOR PLUTO GOT KNOCKED OUT IN TH' SEMIFINALS. LITERALLY.
YES, I REMEMBER ...

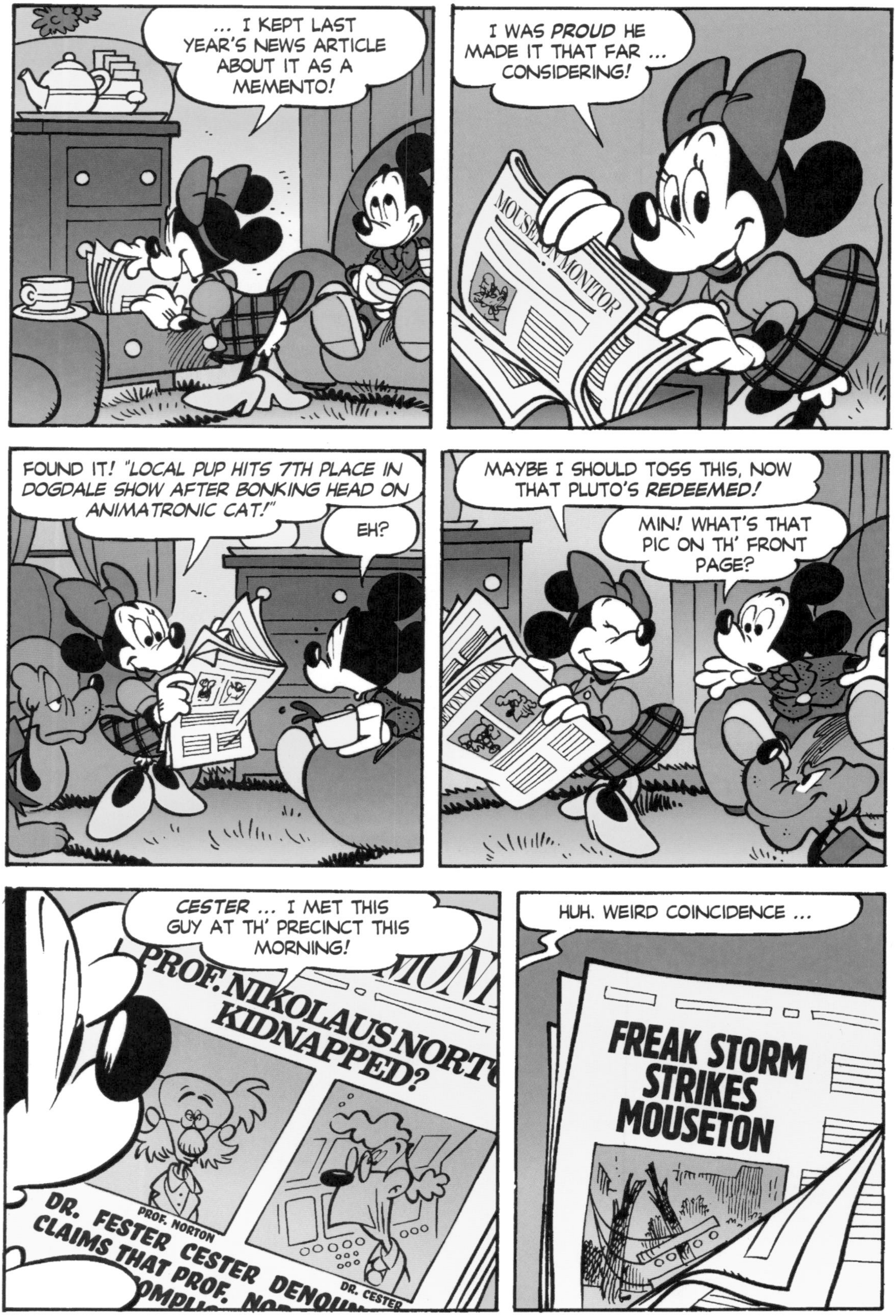
... I KEPT LAST YEAR'S NEWS ARTICLE ABOUT IT AS A MEMENTO!
I WAS PROUD HE MADE IT THAT FAR ... CONSIDERING!
MOUSETON MONITOR
FOUND IT! "LOCAL PUP HITS 7TH PLACE IN DOGDALE SHOW AFTER BONKING HEAD ON ANIMATRONIC CAT!"
EH?
MAYBE I SHOULD TOSS THIS, NOW THAT PLUTO'S REDEEMED!
MIN! WHAT'S THAT PIC ON TH' FRONT PAGE?
CESTER ... I MET THIS GUY AT TH' PRECINCT THIS MORNING!
PROF. NIKOLAUS NORTO
KIDNAPPED?
PROF. NORTON
DR. CESTER
DR. FESTER CESTER DENOU
CLAIMS THAT PROF. NO
HUH. WEIRD COINCIDENCE ...
FREAK STORM STRIKES MOUSETON

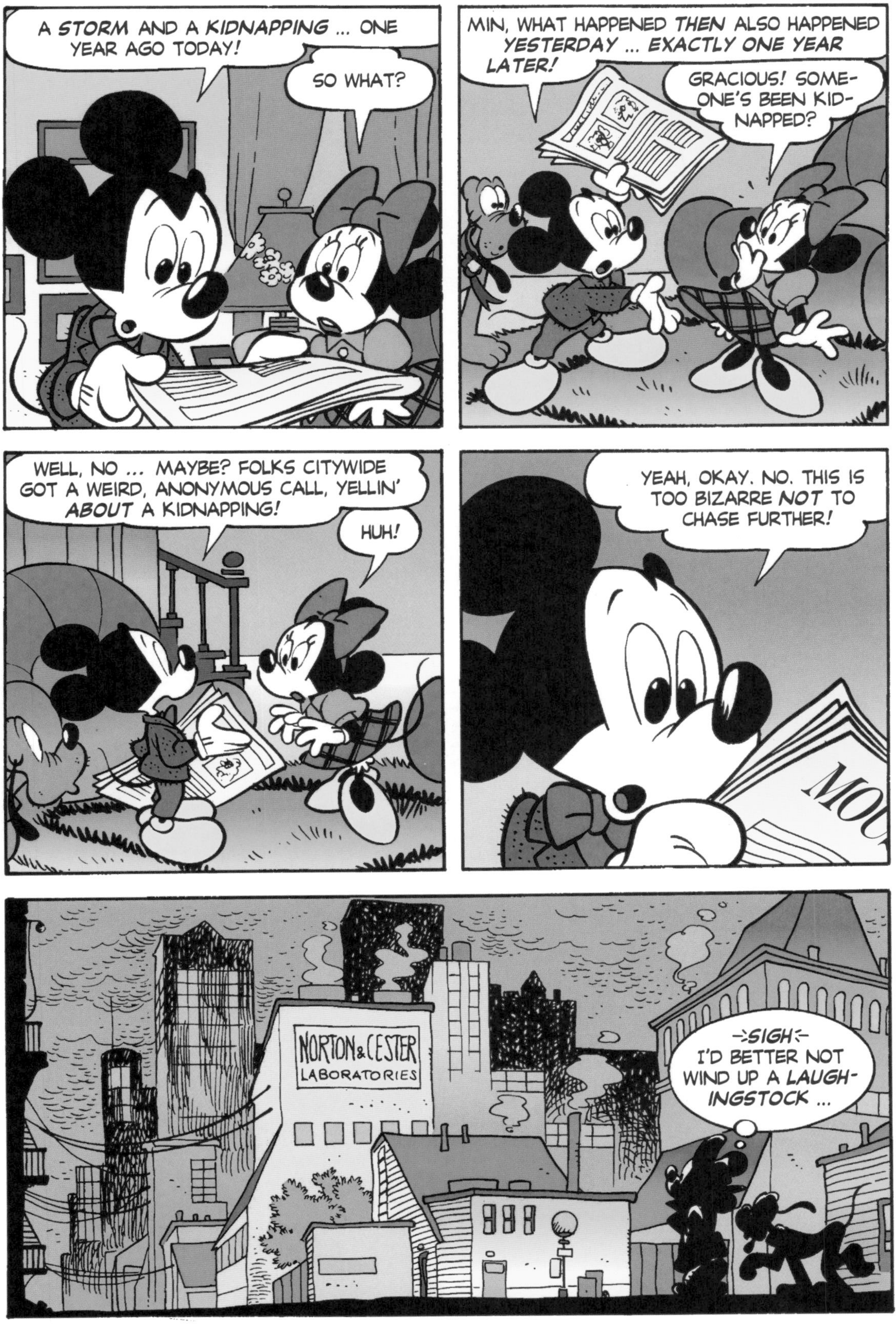
A STORM AND A KIDNAPPING ... ONE YEAR AGO TODAY!
SO WHAT?
MIN, WHAT HAPPENED THEN ALSO HAPPENED YESTERDAY ... EXACTLY ONE YEAR LATER!
GRACIOUS! SOME-ONE'S BEEN KID-NAPPED?
WELL, NO ... MAYBE? FOLKS CITYWIDE GOT A WEIRD, ANONYMOUS CALL, YELLIN' ABOUT A KIDNAPPING!
HUH!
YEAH, OKAY. NO. THIS IS TOO BIZARRE NOT TO CHASE FURTHER!
NORTON & CESTER LABORATORIES
SIGH
I'D BETTER NOT WIND UP A LAUGH-INGSTOCK ...

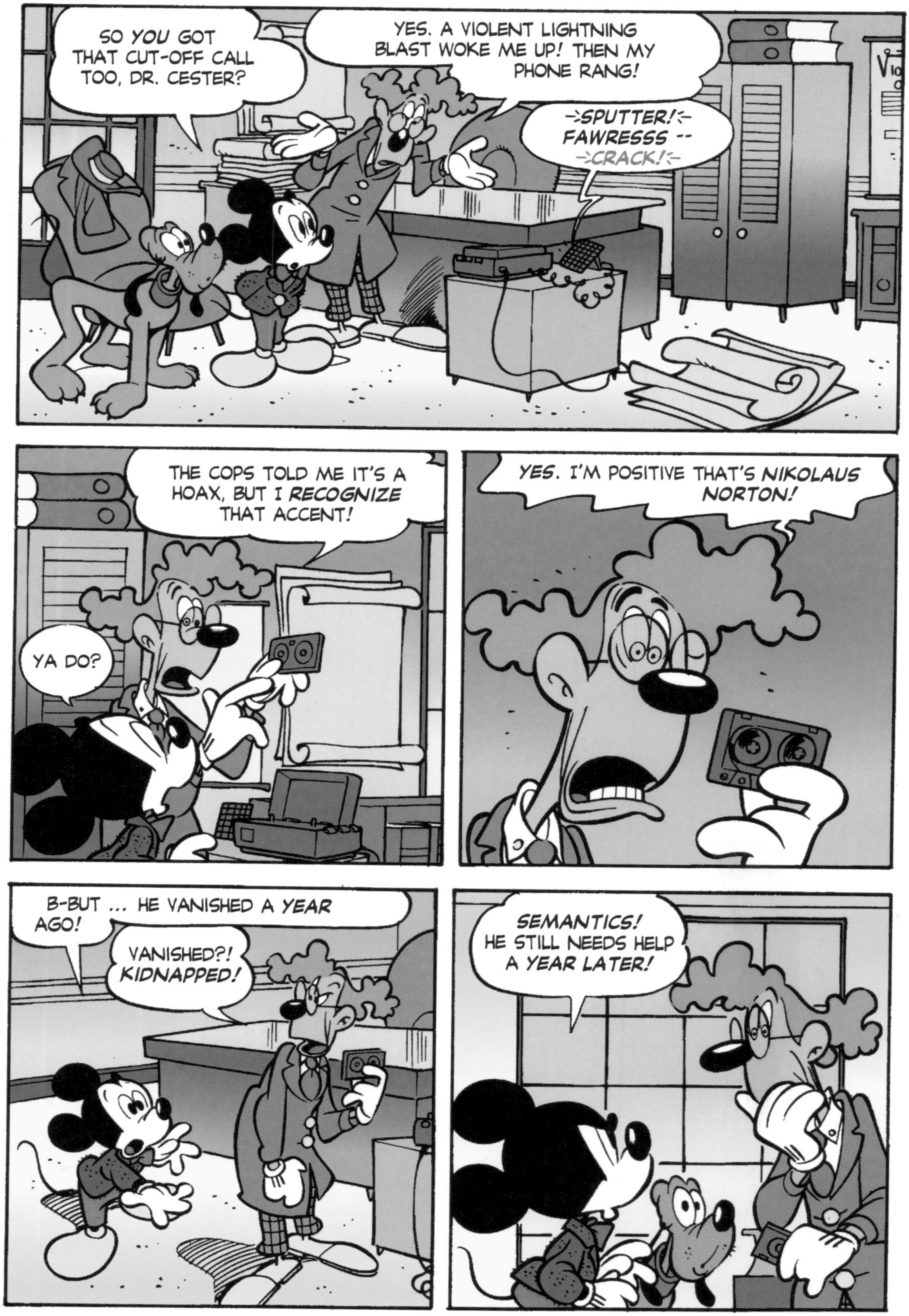
SO YOU GOT THAT CUT-OFF CALL TOO, DR. CESTER?
YES. A VIOLENT LIGHTNING BLAST WOKE ME UP! THEN MY PHONE RANG!
SPUTTER! FAWRESSS -- CRACK!
THE COPS TOLD ME IT'S A HOAX, BUT I RECOGNIZE THAT ACCENT!
YA DO?
YES. I'M POSITIVE THAT'S NIKOLAUS NORTON!
B-BUT ... HE VANISHED A YEAR AGO!
VANISHED?! KIDNAPPED!
SEMANTICS! HE STILL NEEDS HELP A YEAR LATER!

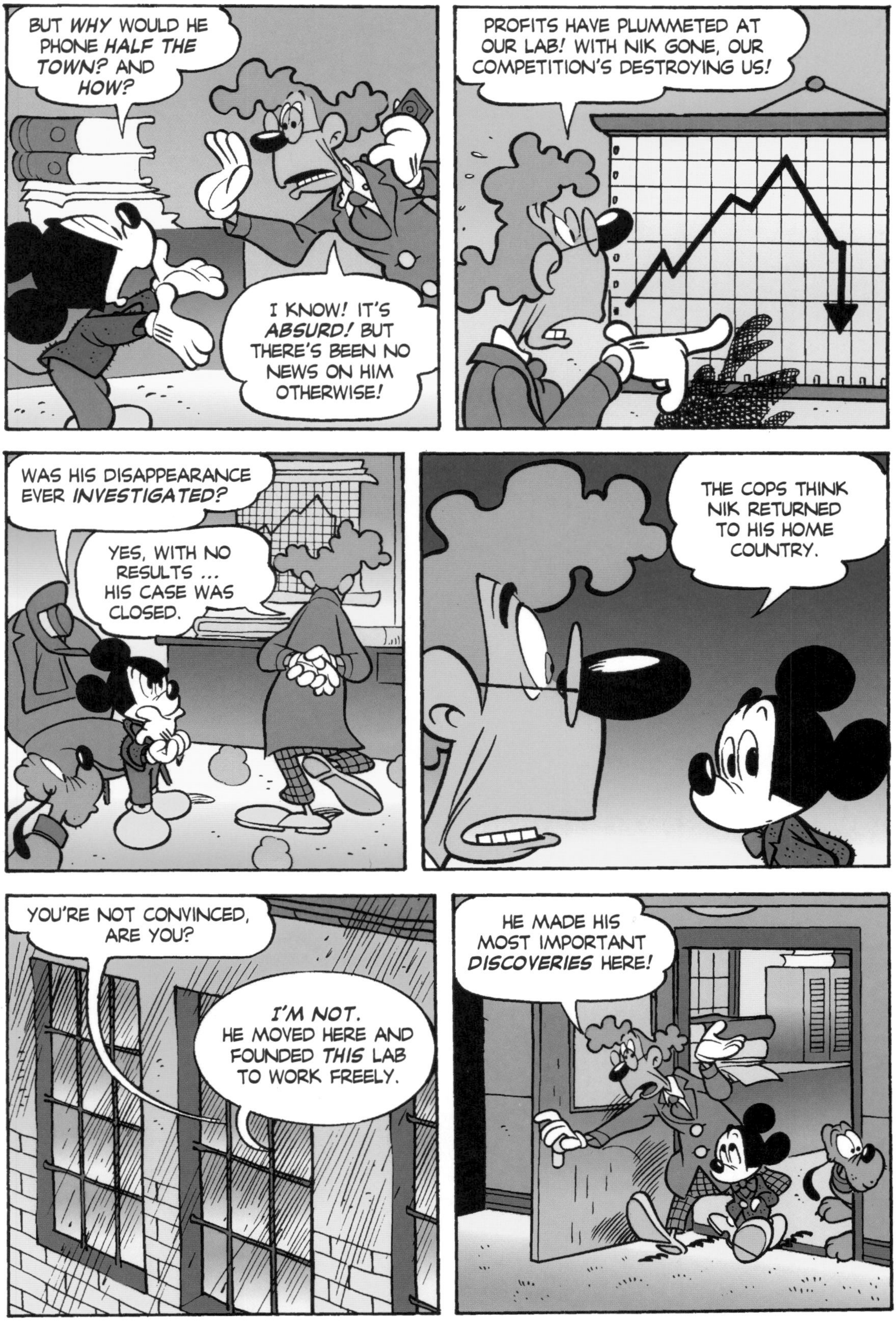
BUT WHY WOULD HE PHONE HALF THE TOWN? AND HOW?
I KNOW! IT'S ABSURD! BUT THERE'S BEEN NO NEWS ON HIM OTHERWISE!
PROFITS HAVE PLUMMETED AT OUR LAB! WITH NIK GONE, OUR COMPETITION'S DESTROYING US!
WAS HIS DISAPPEARANCE EVER INVESTIGATED?
YES, WITH NO RESULTS ... HIS CASE WAS CLOSED.
THE COPS THINK NIK RETURNED TO HIS HOME COUNTRY.
YOU'RE NOT CONVINCED, ARE YOU?
I'M NOT. HE MOVED HERE AND FOUNDED THIS LAB TO WORK FREELY.
HE MADE HIS MOST IMPORTANT DISCOVERIES HERE!

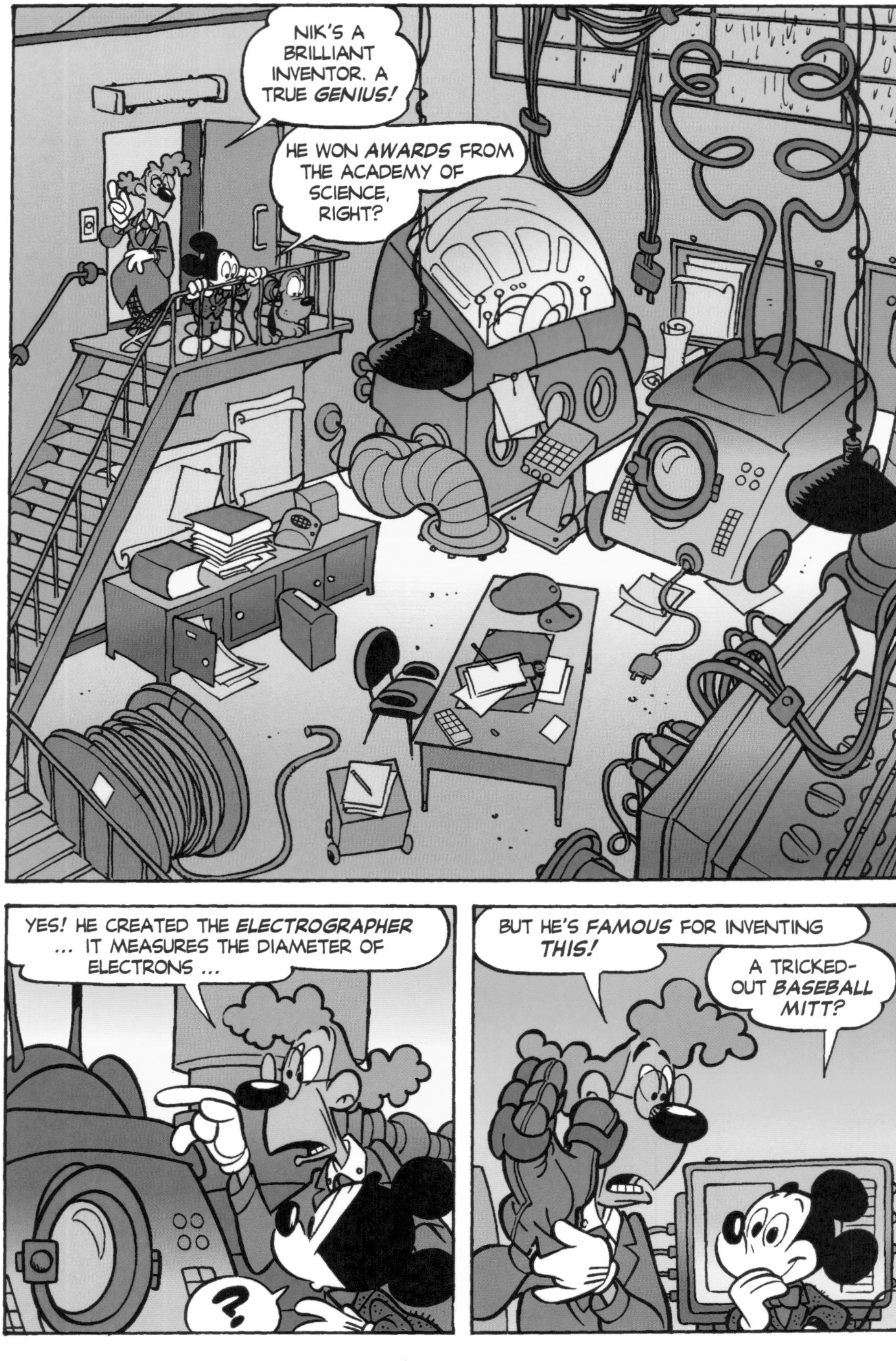
NIK'S A BRILLIANT INVENTOR. A TRUE GENIUS!
HE WON AWARDS FROM THE ACADEMY OF SCIENCE, RIGHT?
YES! HE CREATED THE ELECTROGRAPHER ... IT MEASURES THE DIAMETER OF ELECTRONS ...
?
BUT HE'S FAMOUS FOR INVENTING THIS!
A TRICKED-OUT BASEBALL MITT?

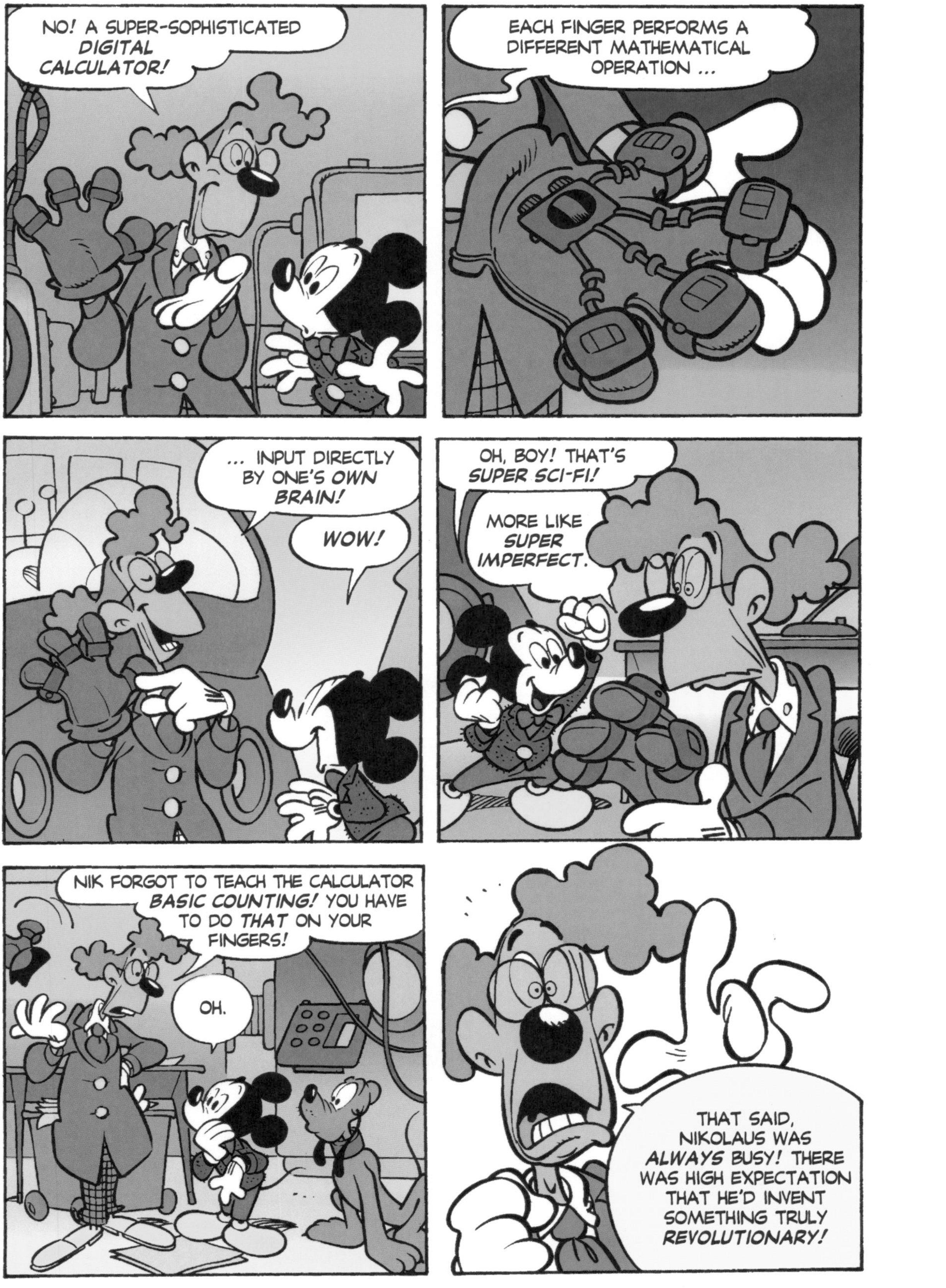

NO! A SUPER-SOPHISTICATED DIGITAL CALCULATOR!
EACH FINGER PERFORMS A DIFFERENT MATHEMATICAL OPERATION ...
... INPUT DIRECTLY BY ONE'S OWN BRAIN!
WOW!
OH, BOY! THAT'S SUPER SCI-FI!
MORE LIKE SUPER IMPERFECT.
NIK FORGOT TO TEACH THE CALCULATOR BASIC COUNTING! YOU HAVE TO DO THAT ON YOUR FINGERS!
OH.
THAT SAID, NIKOLAUS WAS ALWAYS BUSY! THERE WAS HIGH EXPECTATION THAT HE'D INVENT SOMETHING TRULY REVOLUTIONARY!

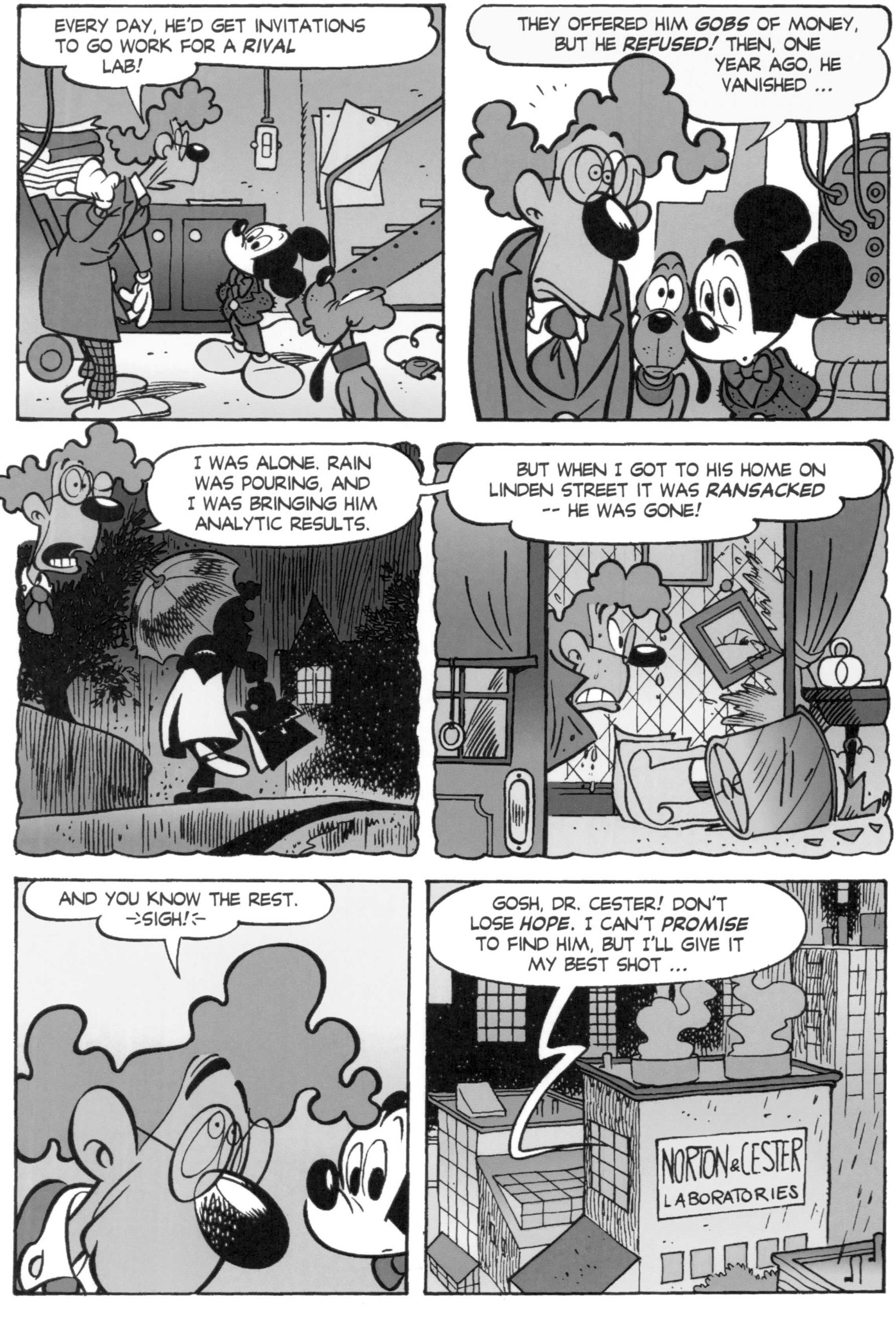

EVERY DAY, HE'D GET INVITATIONS TO GO WORK FOR A *RIVAL* LAB!
THEY OFFERED HIM *GOBS* OF MONEY, BUT HE *REFUSED!* THEN, ONE YEAR AGO, HE VANISHED ...
I WAS ALONE. RAIN WAS POURING, AND I WAS BRINGING HIM ANALYTIC RESULTS.
BUT WHEN I GOT TO HIS HOME ON LINDEN STREET IT WAS *RANSACKED* -- HE WAS GONE!
AND YOU KNOW THE REST. -SIGH!-
GOSH, DR. CESTER! DON'T LOSE *HOPE*. I CAN'T *PROMISE* TO FIND HIM, BUT I'LL GIVE IT MY BEST SHOT ...
NORTON & CESTER LABORATORIES

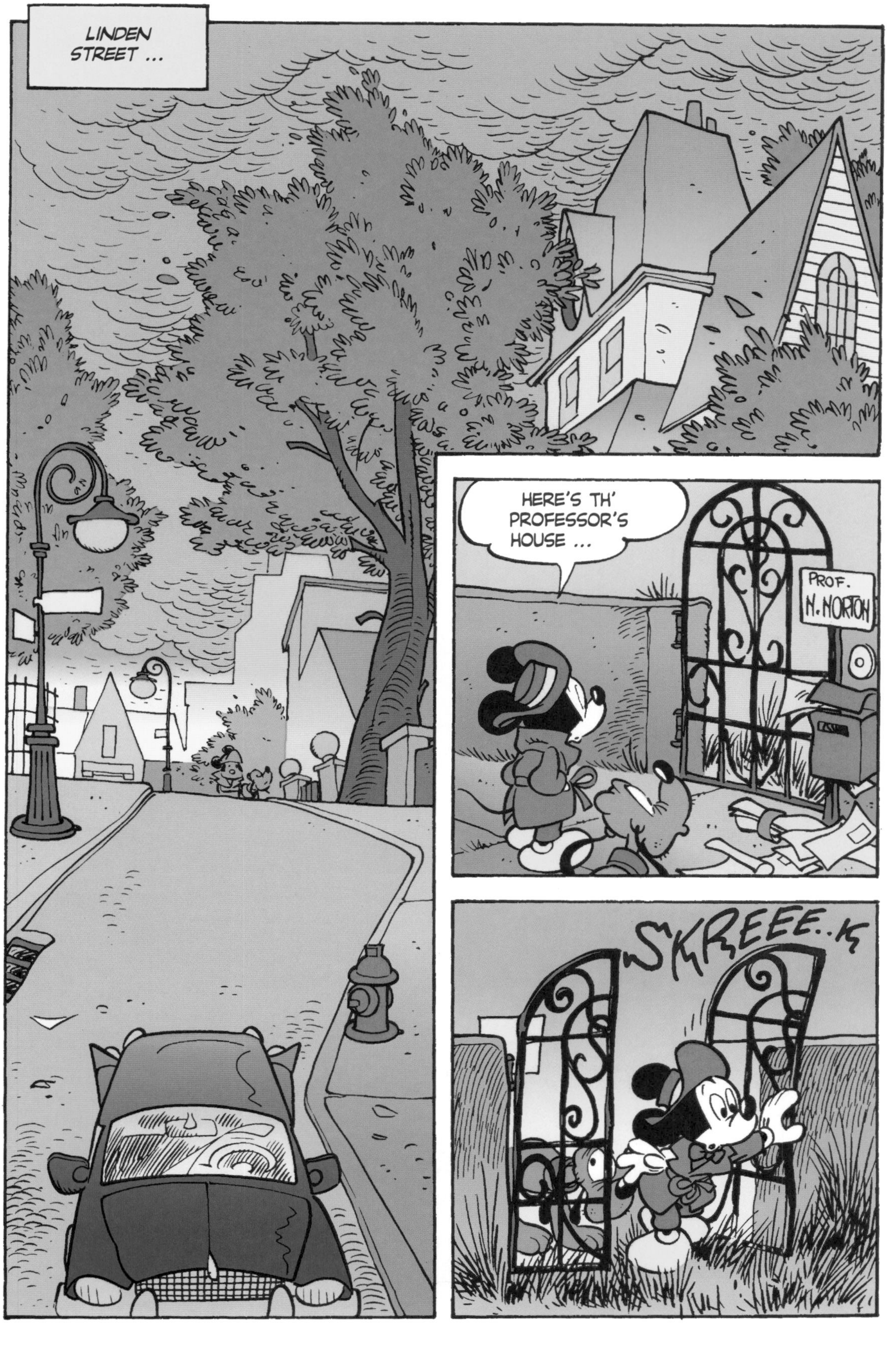
LINDEN STREET ...
HERE'S TH' PROFESSOR'S HOUSE ...
PROF. N. NORTON
SKREEE..K

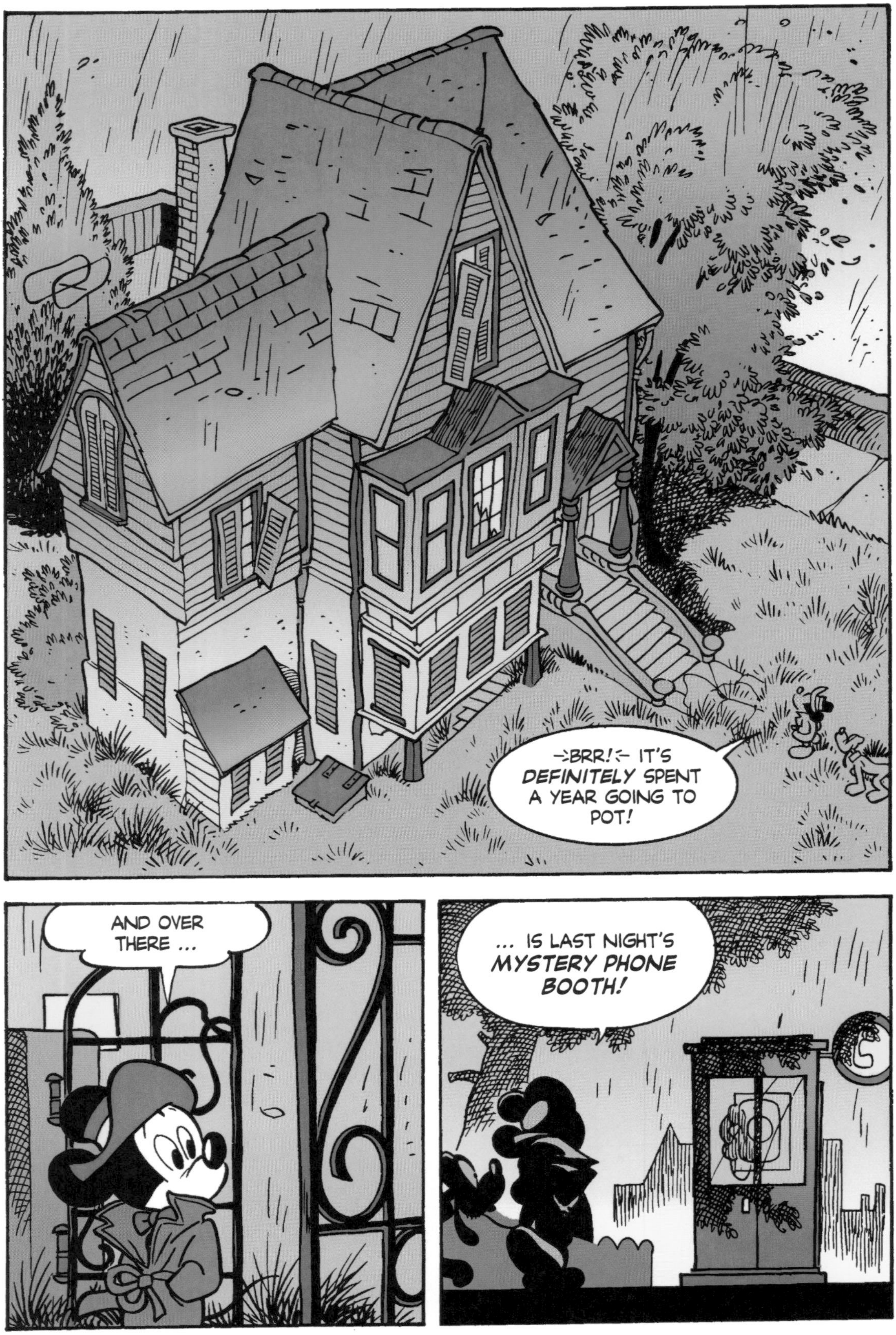
-BRR!- IT'S DEFINITELY SPENT A YEAR GOING TO POT!
AND OVER THERE ...
... IS LAST NIGHT'S MYSTERY PHONE BOOTH!

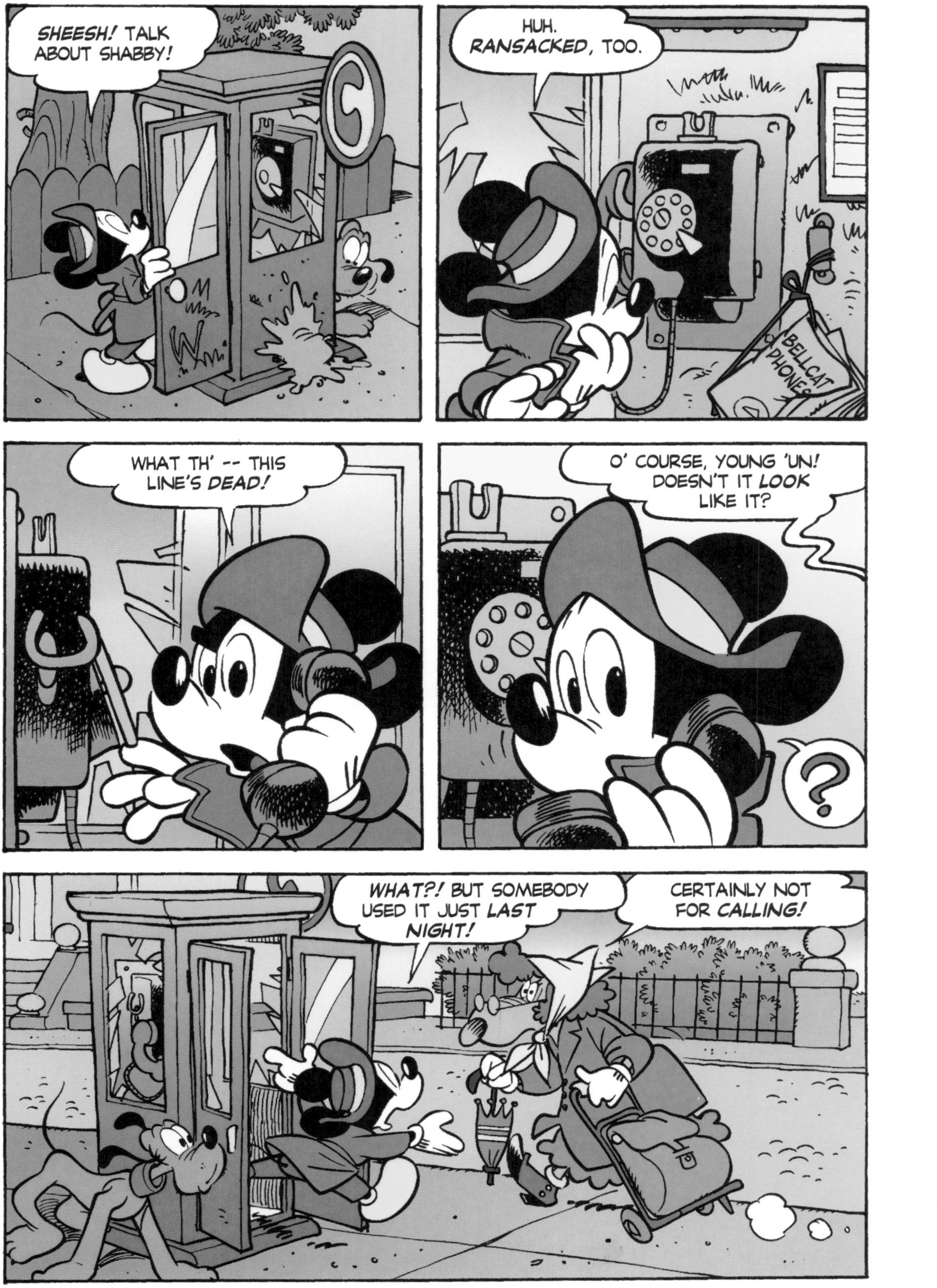

SHEESH! TALK ABOUT SHABBY!
HUH. RANSACKED, TOO.
BELLCAT PHONES
WHAT TH' -- THIS LINE'S DEAD!
O' COURSE, YOUNG 'UN! DOESN'T IT LOOK LIKE IT?
?
WHAT?! BUT SOMEBODY USED IT JUST LAST NIGHT!
CERTAINLY NOT FOR CALLING!

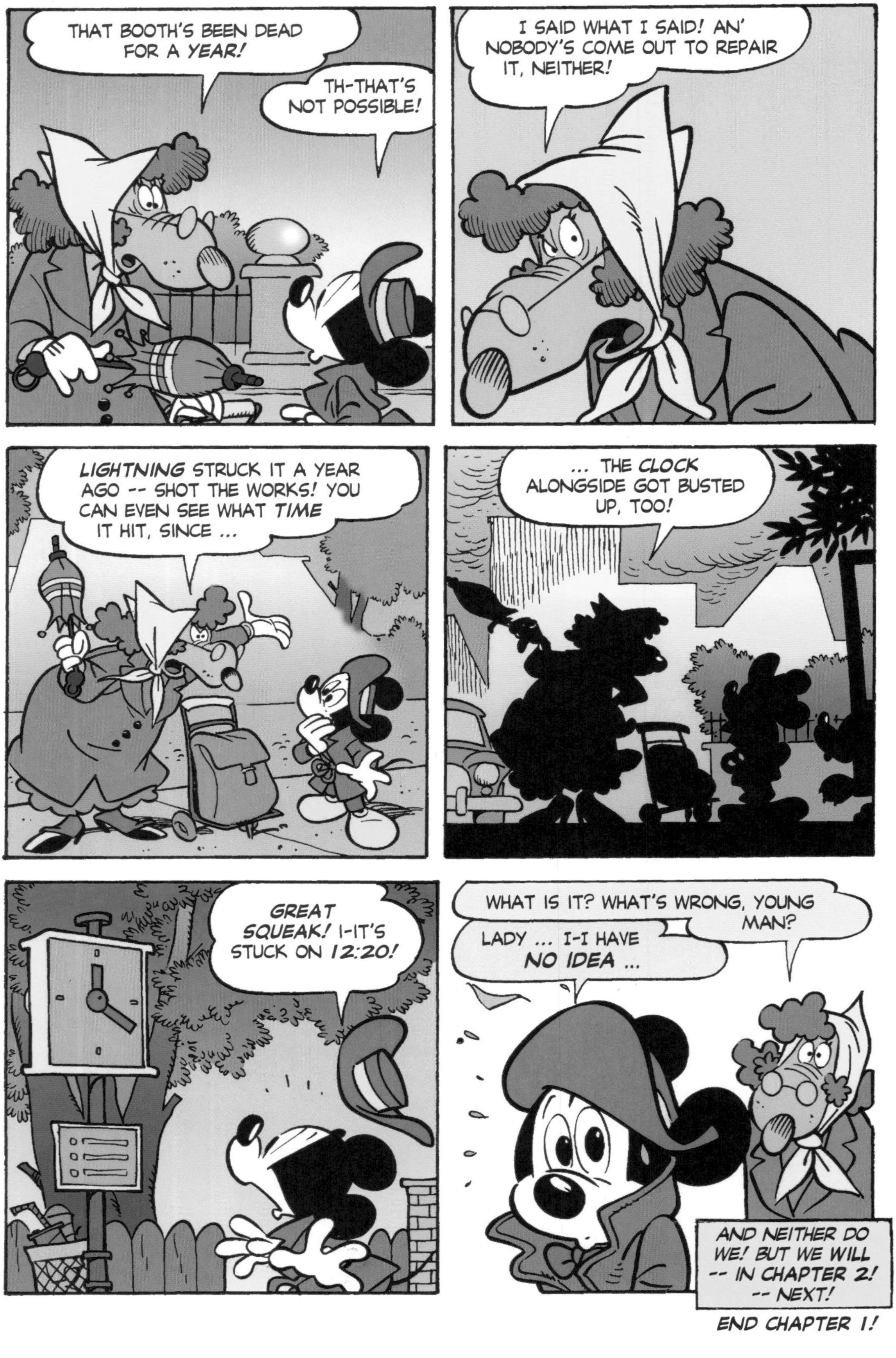

THAT BOOTH'S BEEN DEAD FOR A YEAR!
TH-THAT'S NOT POSSIBLE!
I SAID WHAT I SAID! AN' NOBODY'S COME OUT TO REPAIR IT, NEITHER!
LIGHTNING STRUCK IT A YEAR AGO -- SHOT THE WORKS! YOU CAN EVEN SEE WHAT TIME IT HIT, SINCE ...
... THE CLOCK ALONGSIDE GOT BUSTED UP, TOO!
GREAT SQUEAK! I-IT'S STUCK ON 12:20!
WHAT IS IT? WHAT'S WRONG, YOUNG MAN?
LADY ... I-I HAVE NO IDEA ...
AND NEITHER DO WE! BUT WE WILL -- IN CHAPTER 2! -- NEXT!
END CHAPTER 1!

Walt Disney

# Mickey Mouse in the Case of the Cut-Off Calls

**CHAPTER 2 OF 2:**

ON A DARK AND STORMY NIGHT, HALF OF MOUSETON'S PHONES RECEIVE THE SAME SCARY PHONE CALL -- AT EXACTLY 12:20 A.M.! SOON A LOCAL INVENTOR, DR. FESTER CESTER, RECOGNIZES THE CALLER AS PROF. NIKOLAUS NORTON ... HIS COLLEAGUE WHO VANISHED EXACTLY ONE YEAR BEFORE!
NOW, A CURIOUS MICKEY FINDS THE PHONE BOOTH WHERE THE CALL WAS MADE, ONLY TO DISCOVER THAT IT'S BEEN BROKEN FOR EXACTLY ONE YEAR! ... WHAT?!?

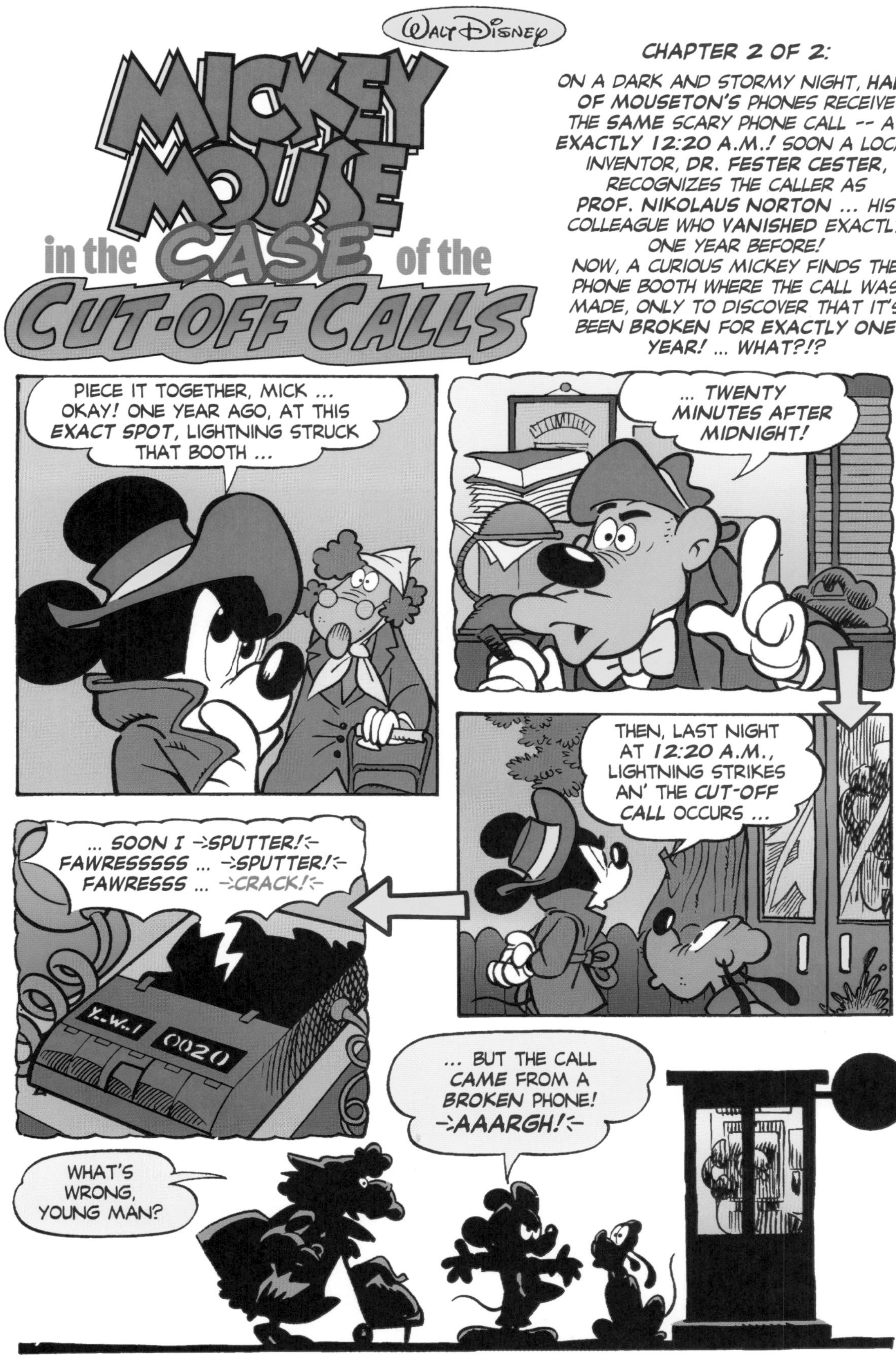
PIECE IT TOGETHER, MICK ... OKAY! ONE YEAR AGO, AT THIS EXACT SPOT, LIGHTNING STRUCK THAT BOOTH ...
... TWENTY MINUTES AFTER MIDNIGHT!
THEN, LAST NIGHT AT 12:20 A.M., LIGHTNING STRIKES AN' THE CUT-OFF CALL OCCURS ...
... SOON I -SPUTTER!- FAWRESSSSS ... -SPUTTER!- FAWRESSS ... -CRACK!-
Y..W..I
0020
... BUT THE CALL CAME FROM A BROKEN PHONE! -AAARGH!-
WHAT'S WRONG, YOUNG MAN?

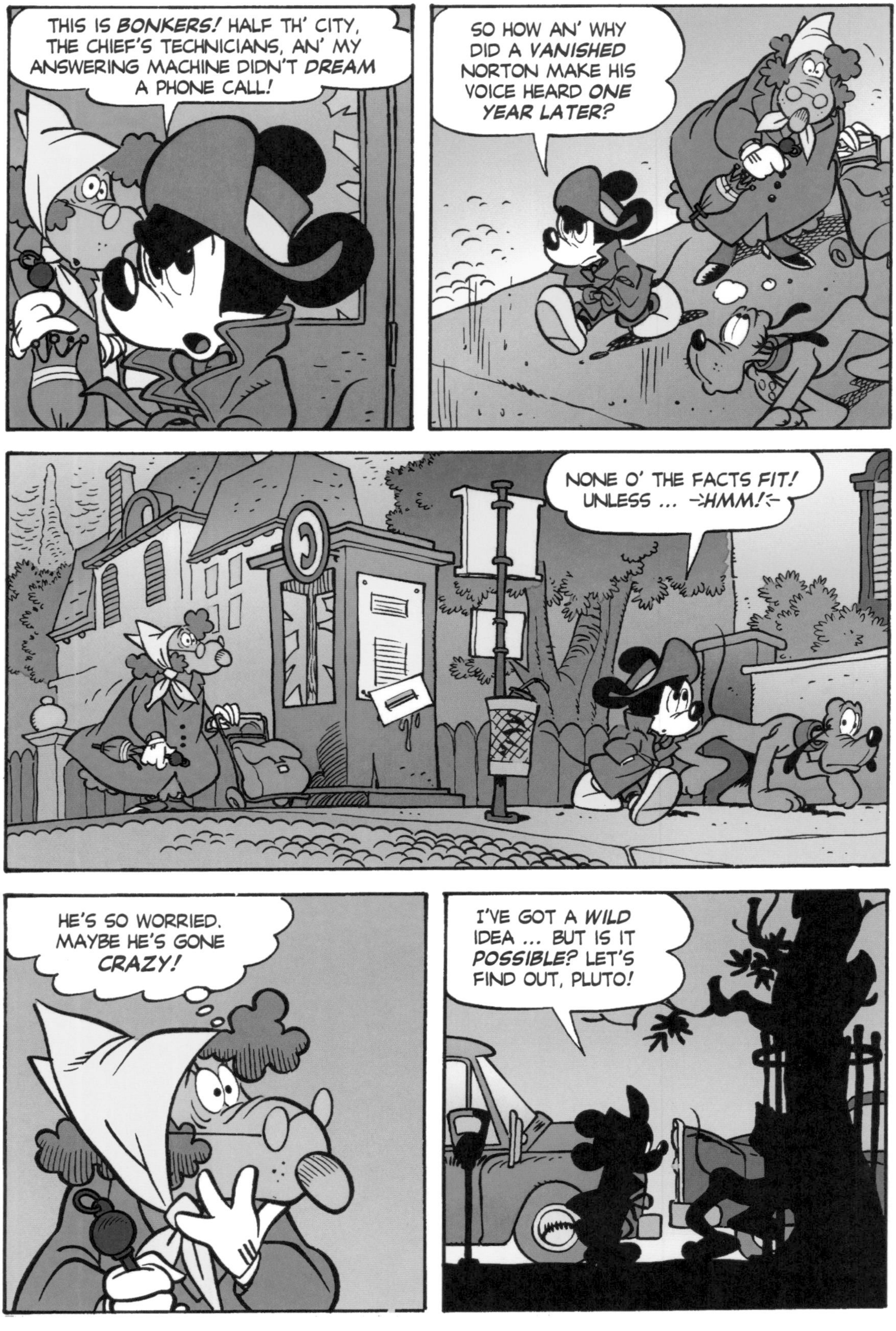
THIS IS BONKERS! HALF TH' CITY, THE CHIEF'S TECHNICIANS, AN' MY ANSWERING MACHINE DIDN'T DREAM A PHONE CALL!
SO HOW AN' WHY DID A VANISHED NORTON MAKE HIS VOICE HEARD ONE YEAR LATER?
NONE O' THE FACTS FIT! UNLESS ... HMM!
HE'S SO WORRIED. MAYBE HE'S GONE CRAZY!
I'VE GOT A WILD IDEA ... BUT IS IT POSSIBLE? LET'S FIND OUT, PLUTO!

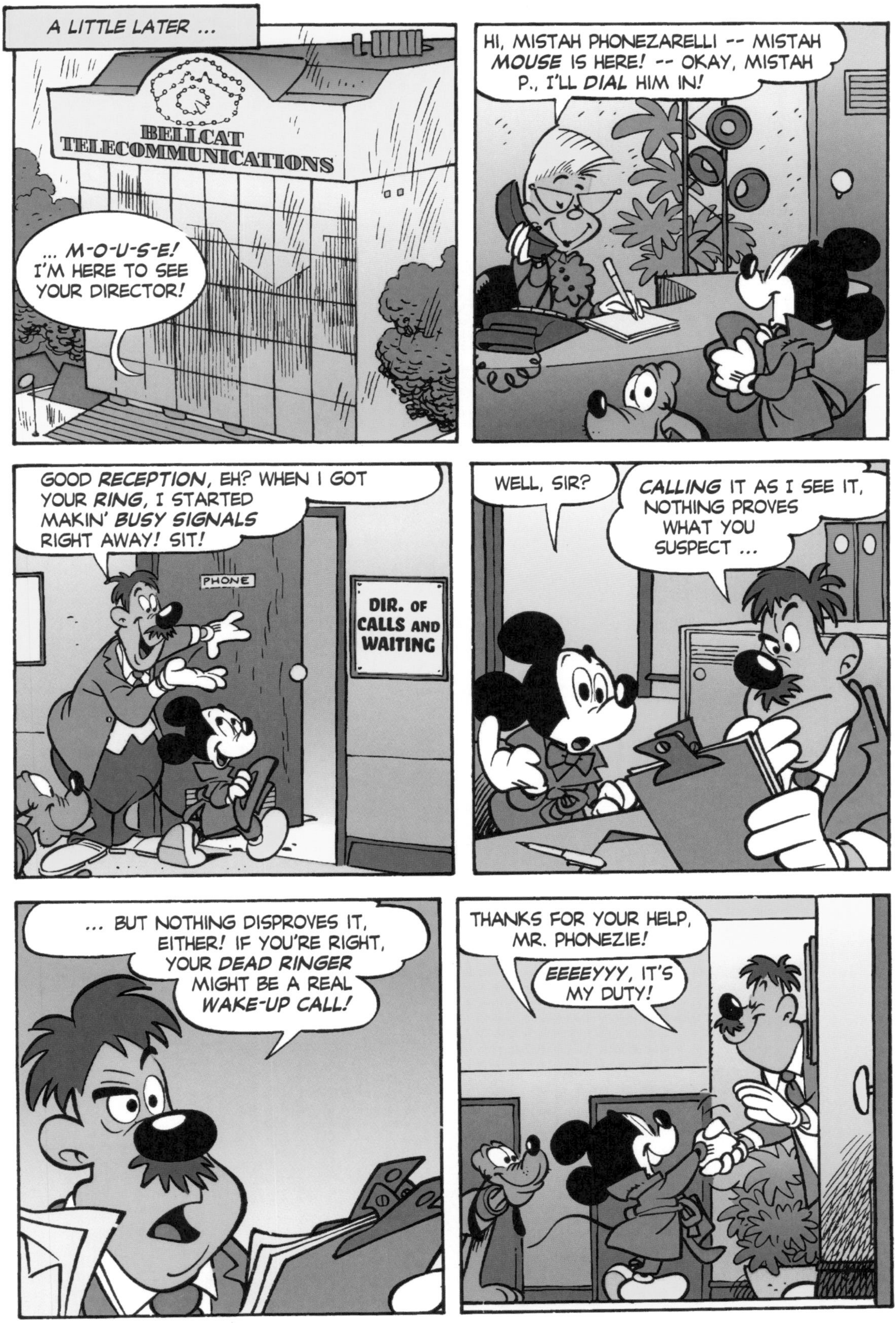
A LITTLE LATER ...
BELLCAT TELECOMMUNICATIONS
... M-O-U-S-E! I'M HERE TO SEE YOUR DIRECTOR!
HI, MISTAH PHONEZARELLI -- MISTAH MOUSE IS HERE! -- OKAY, MISTAH P., I'LL DIAL HIM IN!
GOOD RECEPTION, EH? WHEN I GOT YOUR RING, I STARTED MAKIN' BUSY SIGNALS RIGHT AWAY! SIT!
PHONE
DIR. OF CALLS AND WAITING
WELL, SIR?
CALLING IT AS I SEE IT, NOTHING PROVES WHAT YOU SUSPECT ...
... BUT NOTHING DISPROVES IT, EITHER! IF YOU'RE RIGHT, YOUR DEAD RINGER MIGHT BE A REAL WAKE-UP CALL!
THANKS FOR YOUR HELP, MR. PHONEZIE!
EEEEYYY, IT'S MY DUTY!

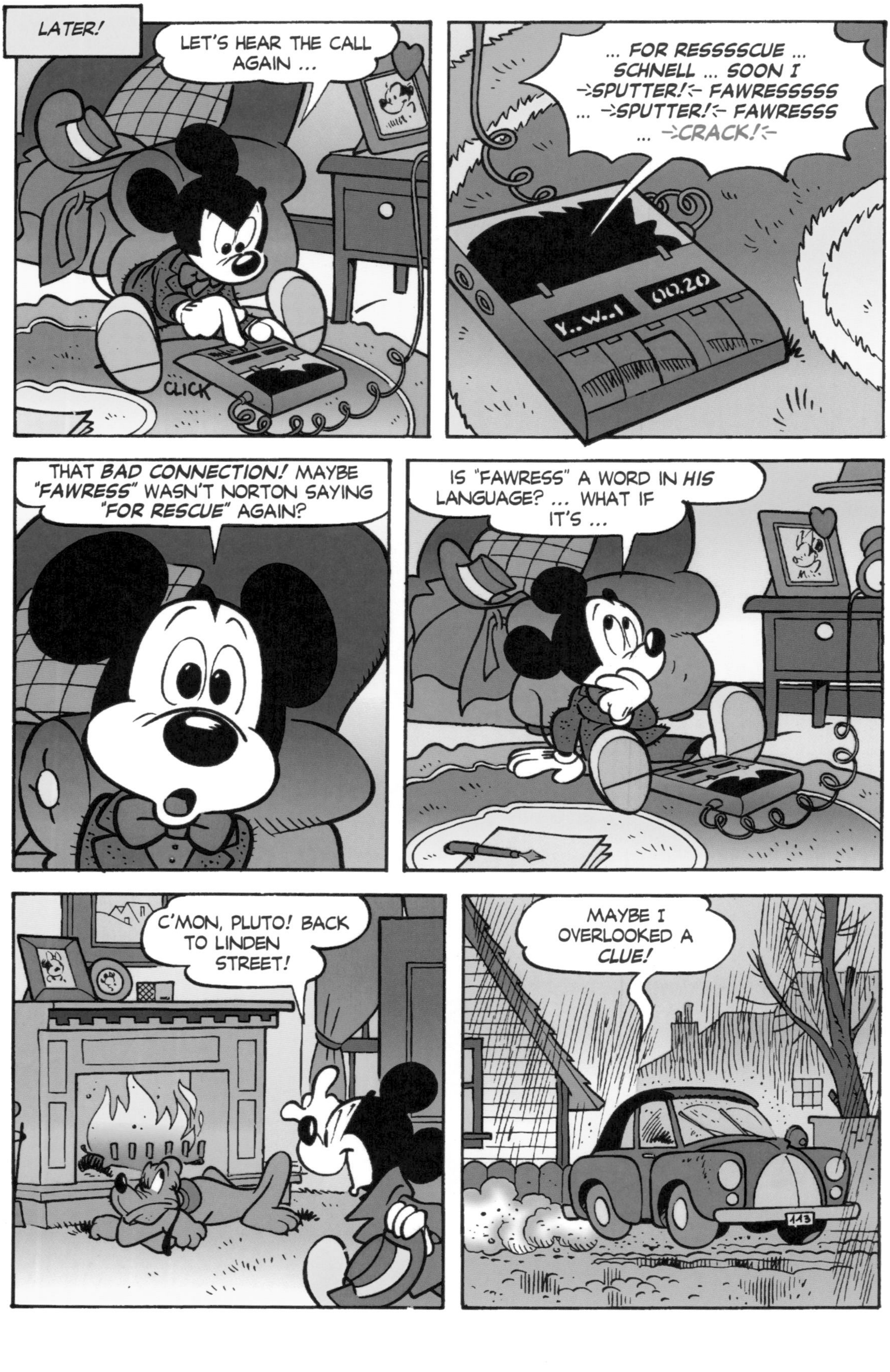
LATER!
LET'S HEAR THE CALL AGAIN ...
CLICK
... FOR RESSSSCUE ... SCHNELL ... SOON I SPUTTER! FAWRESSSSS ... SPUTTER! FAWRESSS ... CRACK!
Y..W..I
00.20
THAT BAD CONNECTION! MAYBE "FAWRESS" WASN'T NORTON SAYING "FOR RESCUE" AGAIN?
IS "FAWRESS" A WORD IN HIS LANGUAGE? ... WHAT IF IT'S ...
C'MON, PLUTO! BACK TO LINDEN STREET!
MAYBE I OVERLOOKED A CLUE!
113

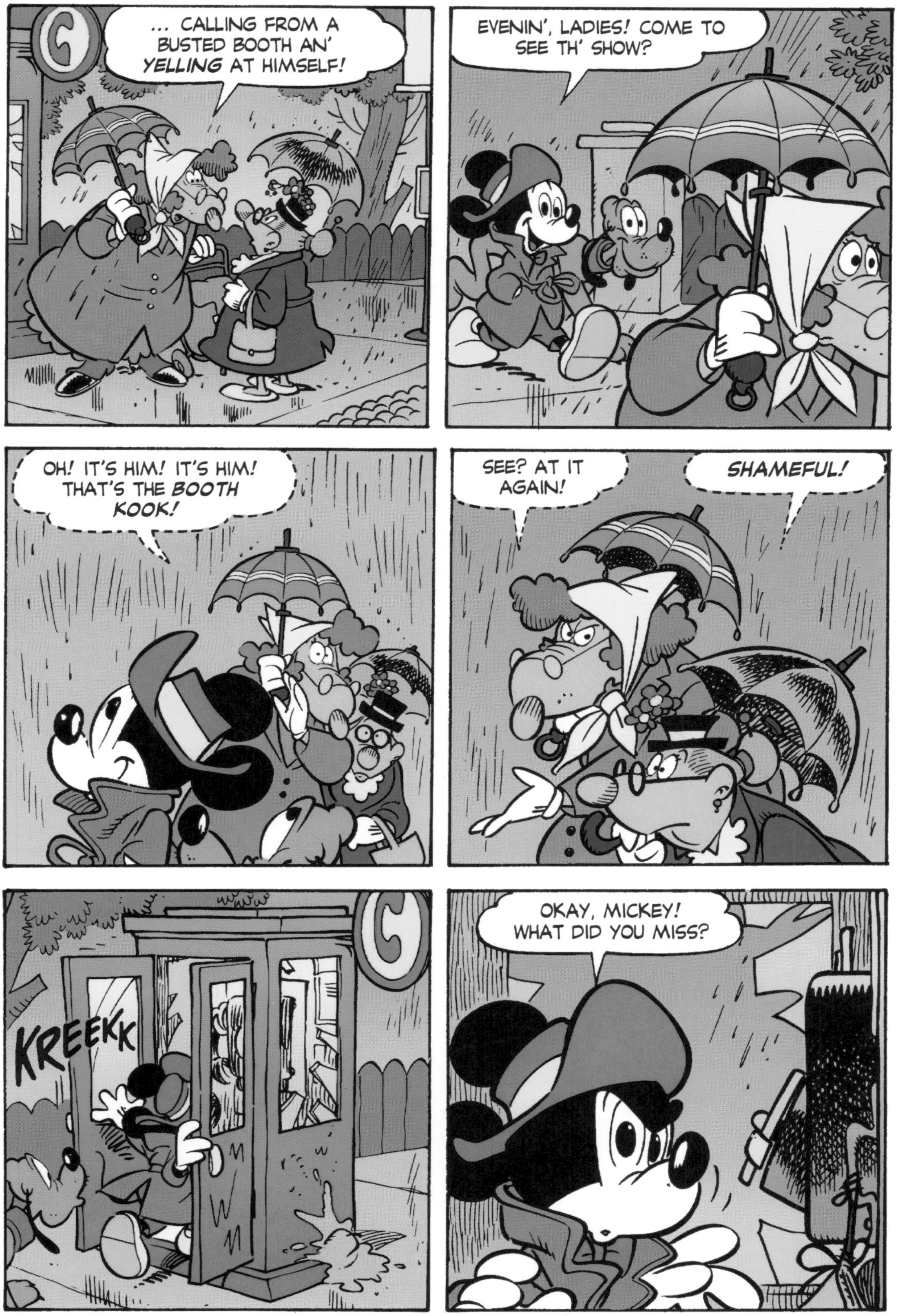
... CALLING FROM A BUSTED BOOTH AN' *YELLING* AT HIMSELF!
EVENIN', LADIES! COME TO SEE TH' SHOW?
OH! IT'S HIM! IT'S HIM! THAT'S THE *BOOTH KOOK!*
SEE? AT IT AGAIN!
*SHAMEFUL!*
KREEKK
OKAY, MICKEY! WHAT DID YOU MISS?

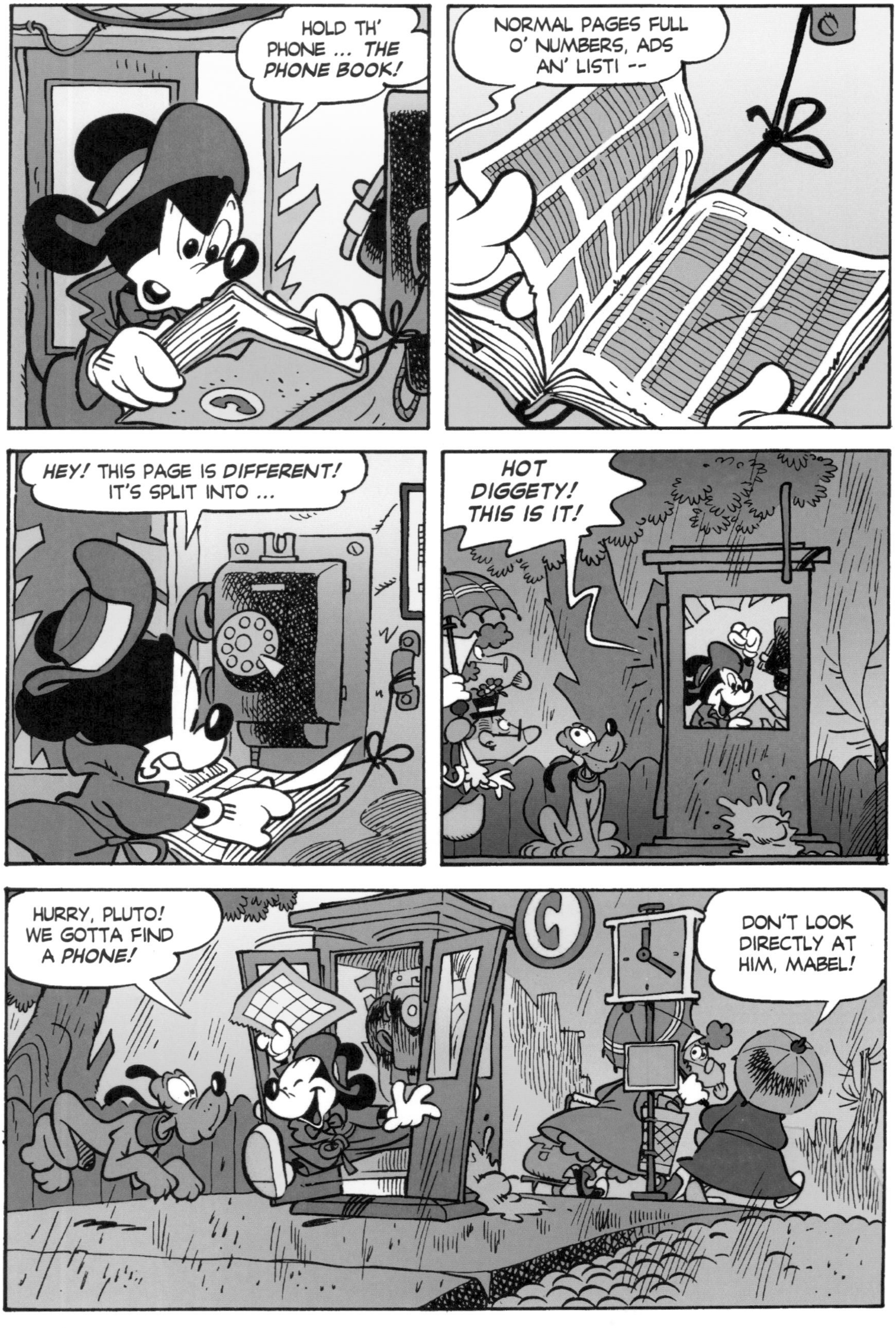
HOLD TH' PHONE ... THE PHONE BOOK!
NORMAL PAGES FULL O' NUMBERS, ADS AN' LISTI --
HEY! THIS PAGE IS DIFFERENT! IT'S SPLIT INTO ...
HOT DIGGETY! THIS IS IT!
HURRY, PLUTO! WE GOTTA FIND A PHONE!
DON'T LOOK DIRECTLY AT HIM, MABEL!

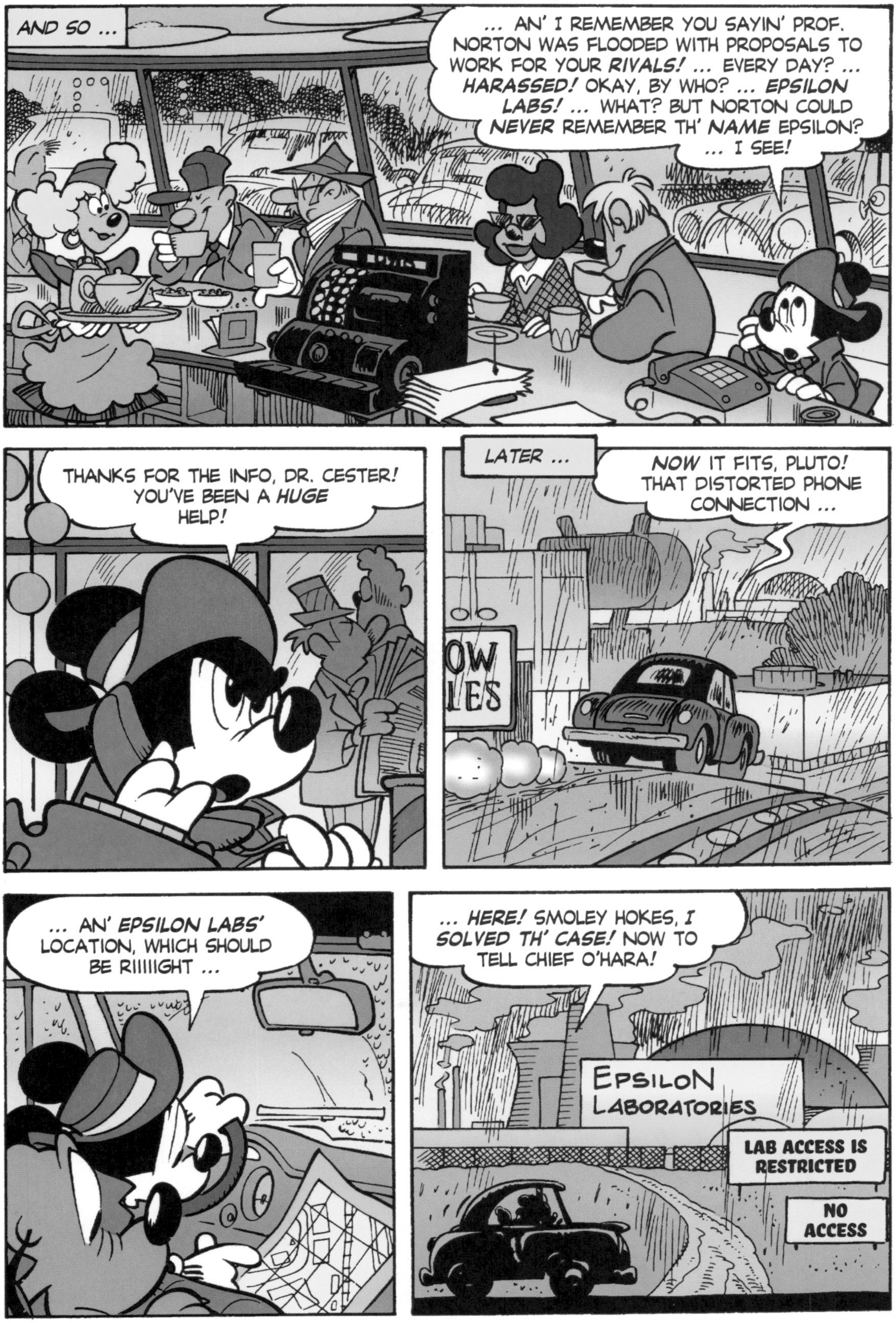
AND SO ...
... AN' I REMEMBER YOU SAYIN' PROF. NORTON WAS FLOODED WITH PROPOSALS TO WORK FOR YOUR RIVALS! ... EVERY DAY? ... HARASSED! OKAY, BY WHO? ... EPSILON LABS! ... WHAT? BUT NORTON COULD NEVER REMEMBER TH' NAME EPSILON? ... I SEE!
THANKS FOR THE INFO, DR. CESTER! YOU'VE BEEN A HUGE HELP!
LATER ...
NOW IT FITS, PLUTO! THAT DISTORTED PHONE CONNECTION ...
... AN' EPSILON LABS' LOCATION, WHICH SHOULD BE RIIIIIGHT ...
... HERE! SMOLEY HOKES, I SOLVED TH' CASE! NOW TO TELL CHIEF O'HARA!
EPSILON LABORATORIES
LAB ACCESS IS RESTRICTED
NO ACCESS

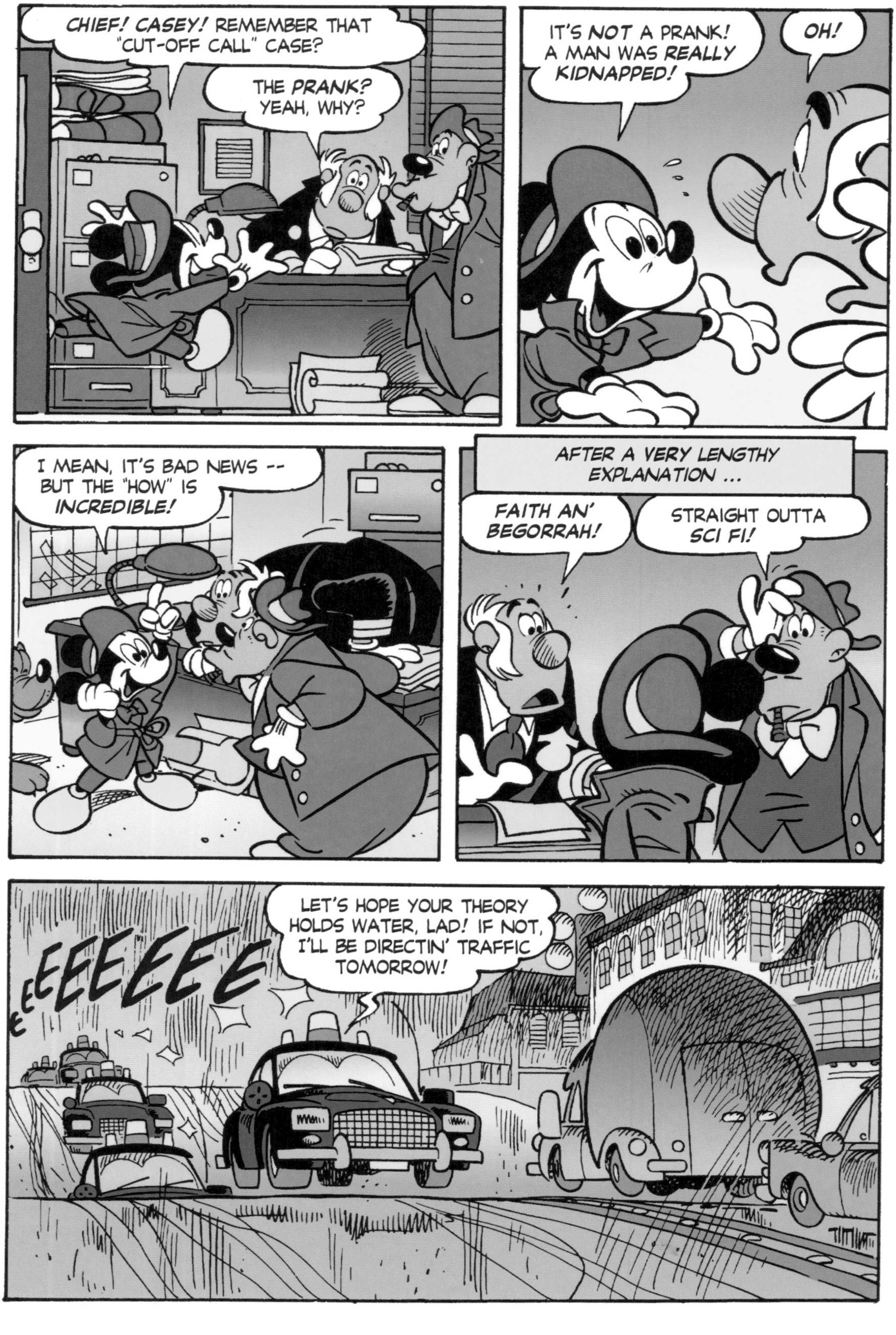
CHIEF! CASEY! REMEMBER THAT "CUT-OFF CALL" CASE?
THE PRANK? YEAH, WHY?
IT'S NOT A PRANK! A MAN WAS REALLY KIDNAPPED!
OH!
I MEAN, IT'S BAD NEWS -- BUT THE "HOW" IS INCREDIBLE!
AFTER A VERY LENGTHY EXPLANATION ...
FAITH AN' BEGORRAH!
STRAIGHT OUTTA SCI FI!
EEEEEEEE
LET'S HOPE YOUR THEORY HOLDS WATER, LAD! IF NOT, I'LL BE DIRECTIN' TRAFFIC TOMORROW!

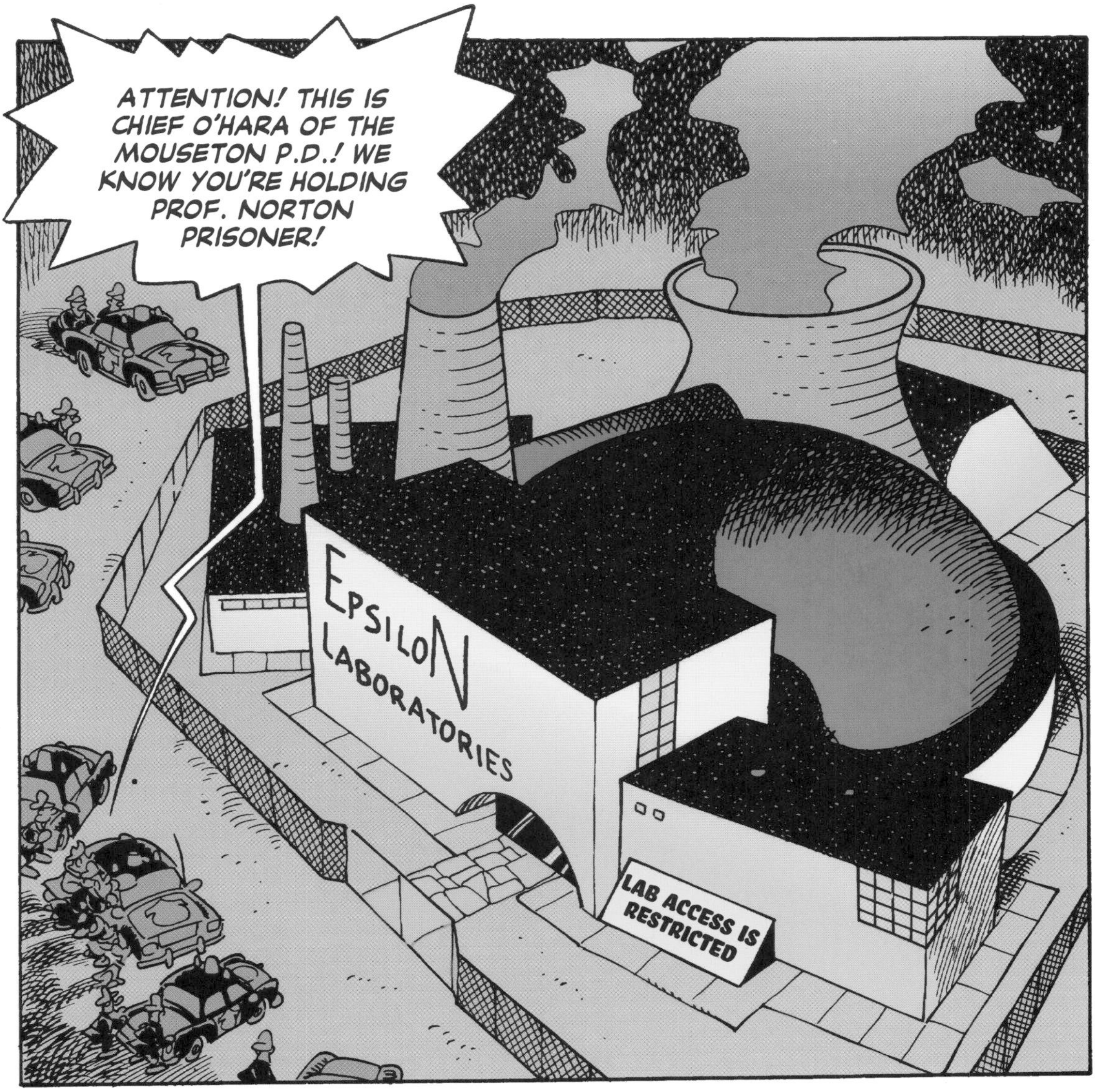
ATTENTION! THIS IS CHIEF O'HARA OF THE MOUSETON P.D.! WE KNOW YOU'RE HOLDING PROF. NORTON PRISONER!
EPSILON LABORATORIES
LAB ACCESS IS RESTRICTED

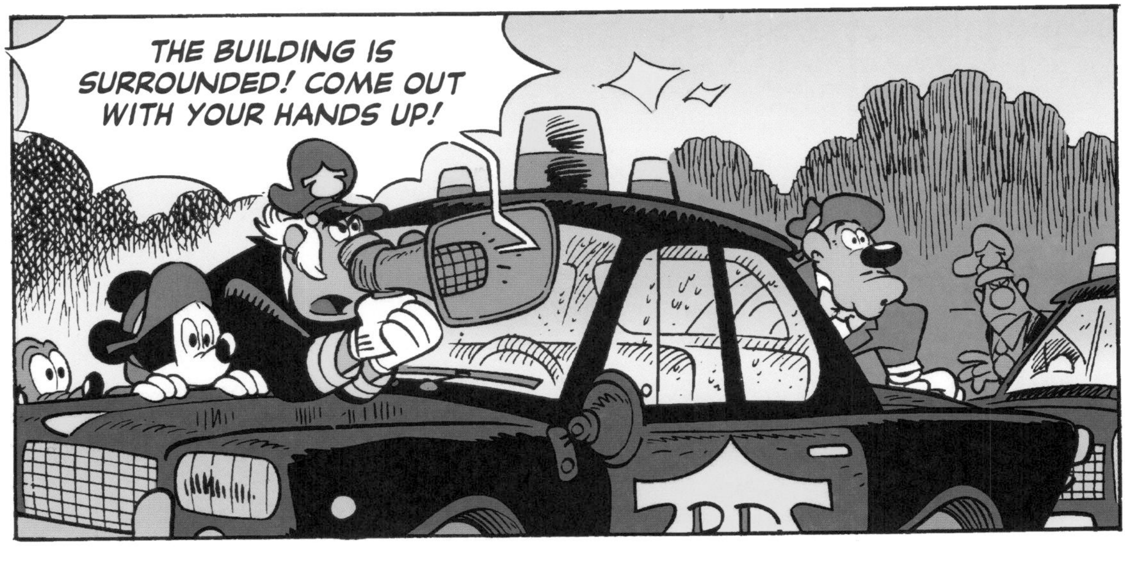
THE BUILDING IS SURROUNDED! COME OUT WITH YOUR HANDS UP!

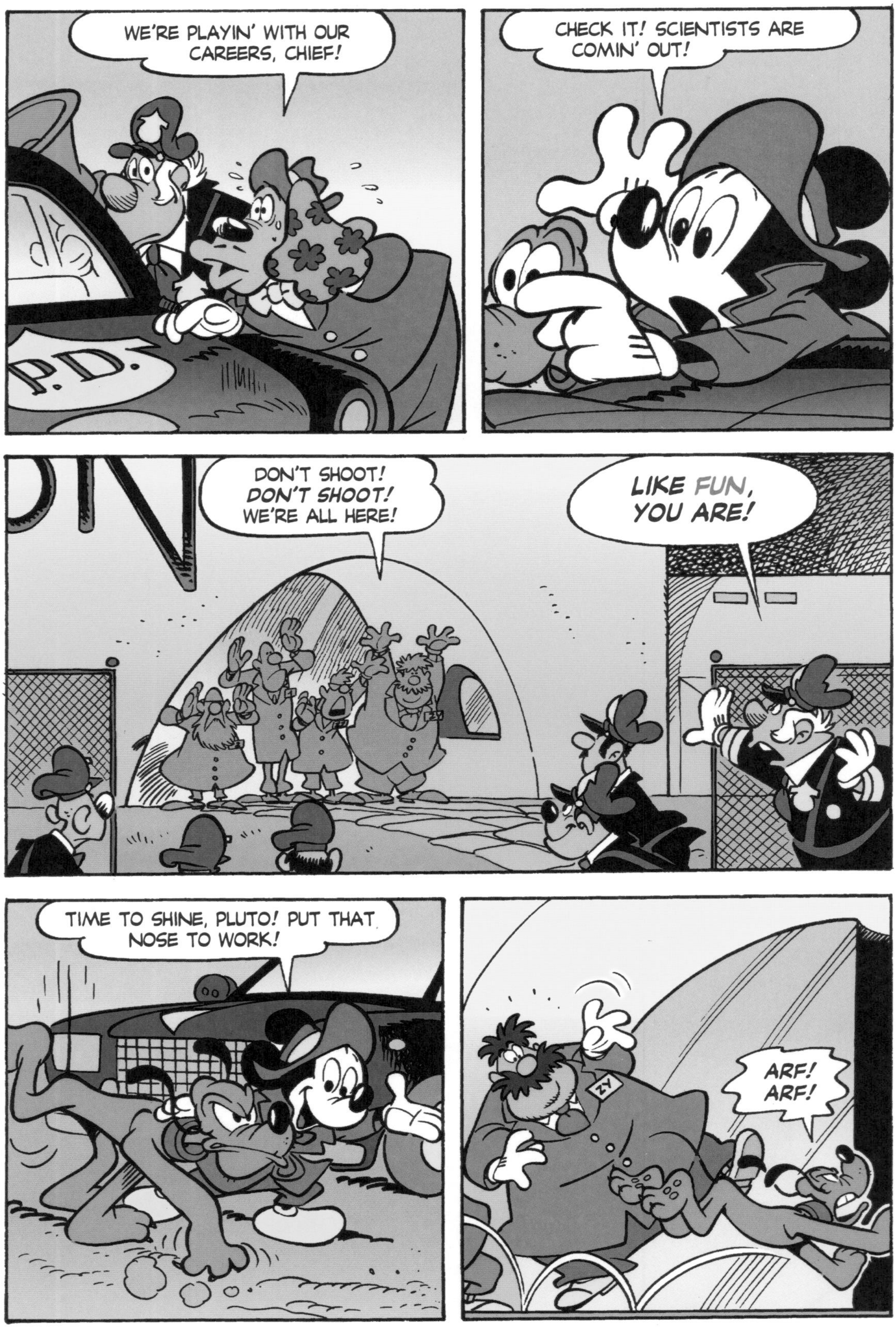
WE'RE PLAYIN' WITH OUR CAREERS, CHIEF!
CHECK IT! SCIENTISTS ARE COMIN' OUT!
DON'T SHOOT! DON'T SHOOT! WE'RE ALL HERE!
LIKE FUN, YOU ARE!
TIME TO SHINE, PLUTO! PUT THAT NOSE TO WORK!
ARF! ARF!

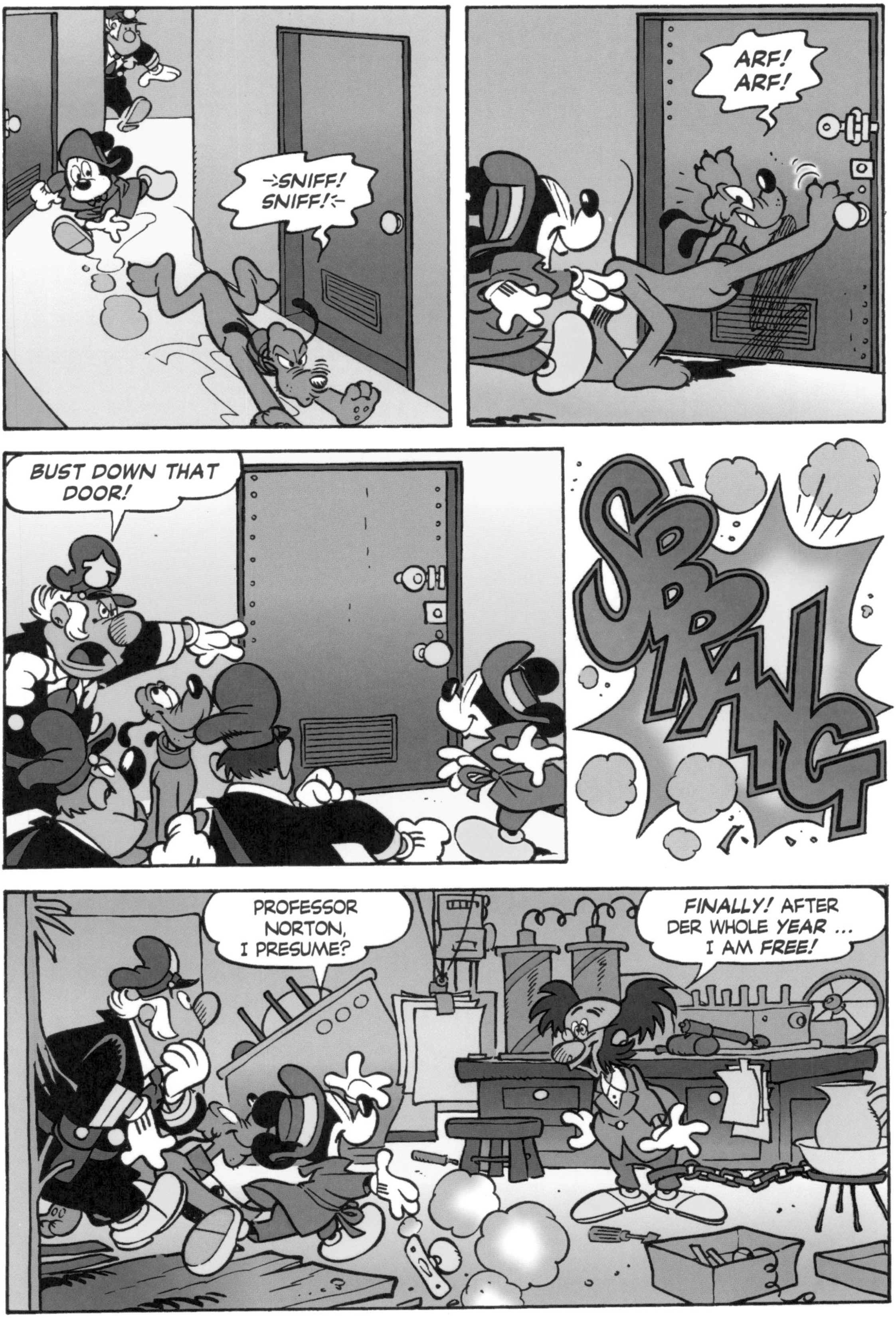

-SNIFF! SNIFF!-
ARF! ARF!
BUST DOWN THAT DOOR!
SBRANG
PROFESSOR NORTON, I PRESUME?
FINALLY! AFTER DER WHOLE YEAR ... I AM FREE!

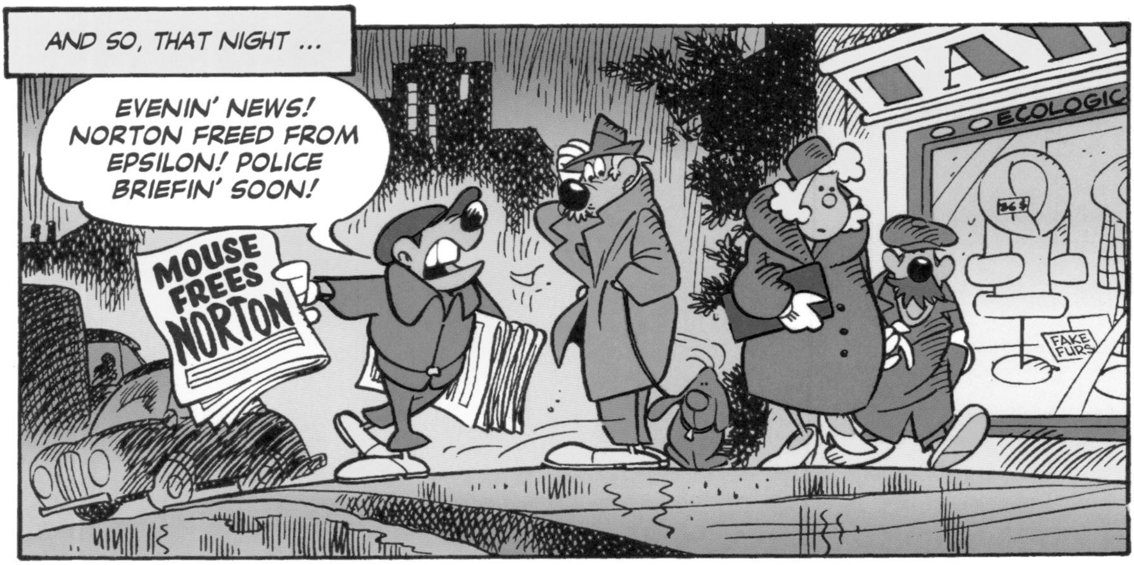
AND SO, THAT NIGHT ...
EVENIN' NEWS! NORTON FREED FROM EPSILON! POLICE BRIEFIN' SOON!
MOUSE FREES NORTON
ECOLOGIC
FAKE FURS

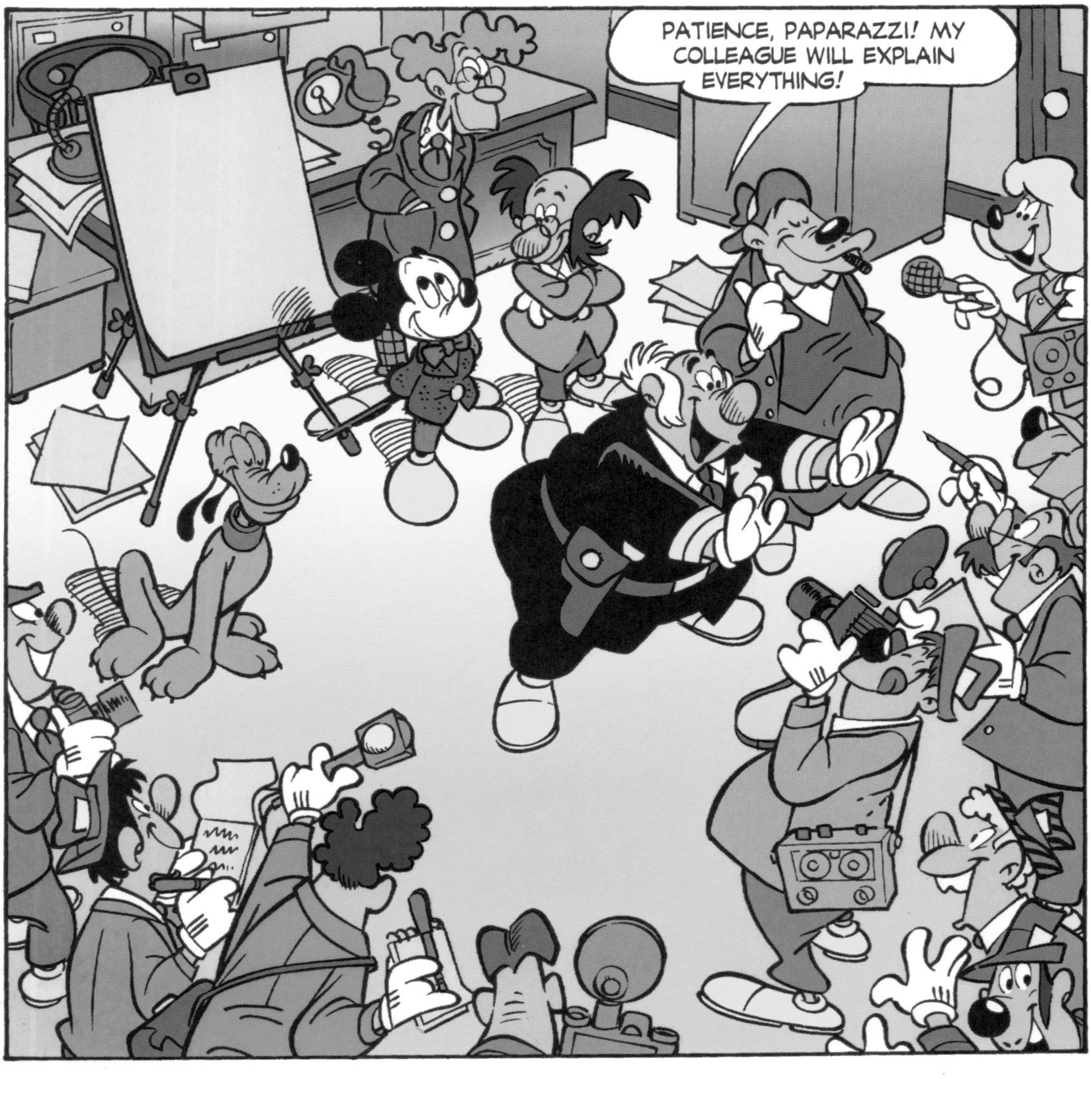
PATIENCE, PAPARAZZI! MY COLLEAGUE WILL EXPLAIN EVERYTHING!

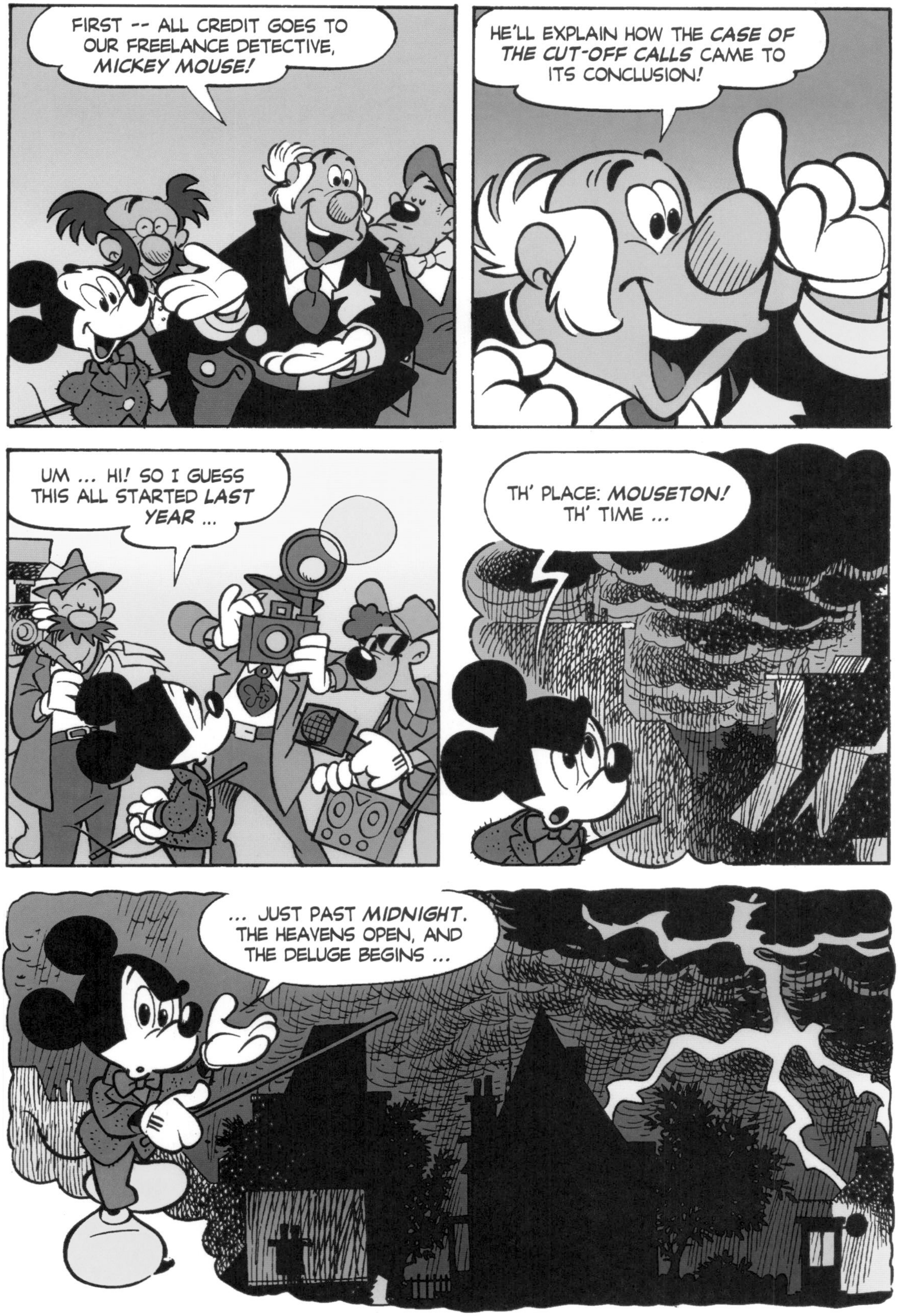
FIRST -- ALL CREDIT GOES TO OUR FREELANCE DETECTIVE, MICKEY MOUSE!
HE'LL EXPLAIN HOW THE CASE OF THE CUT-OFF CALLS CAME TO ITS CONCLUSION!
UM ... HI! SO I GUESS THIS ALL STARTED LAST YEAR ...
TH' PLACE: MOUSETON! TH' TIME ...
... JUST PAST MIDNIGHT. THE HEAVENS OPEN, AND THE DELUGE BEGINS ...

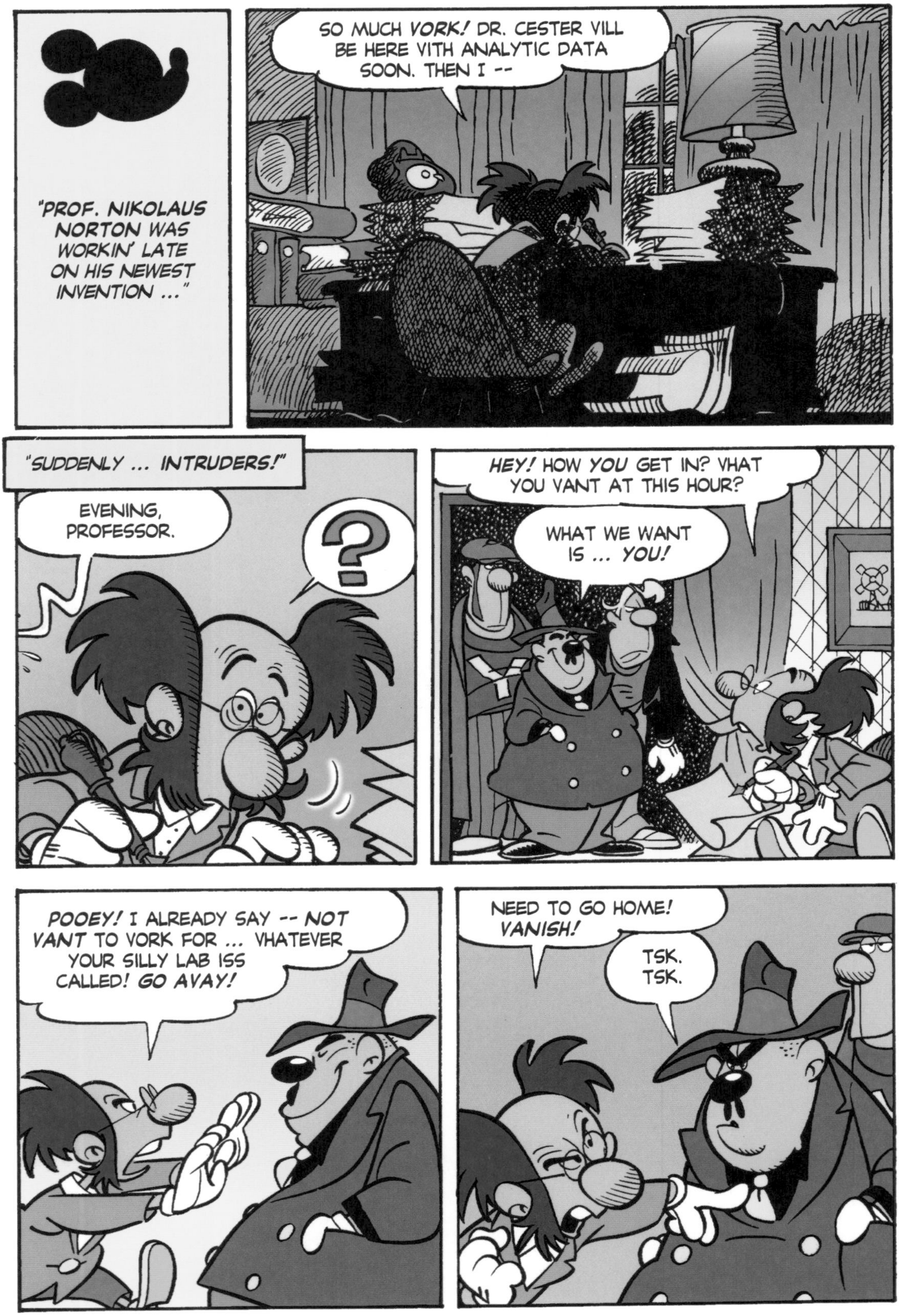
"PROF. NIKOLAUS NORTON WAS WORKIN' LATE ON HIS NEWEST INVENTION ..."
SO MUCH VORK! DR. CESTER VILL BE HERE VITH ANALYTIC DATA SOON. THEN I --
"SUDDENLY ... INTRUDERS!"
EVENING, PROFESSOR.
?
HEY! HOW YOU GET IN? VHAT YOU VANT AT THIS HOUR?
WHAT WE WANT IS ... YOU!
POOEY! I ALREADY SAY -- NOT VANT TO VORK FOR ... VHATEVER YOUR SILLY LAB ISS CALLED! GO AVAY!
NEED TO GO HOME! VANISH!
TSK. TSK.

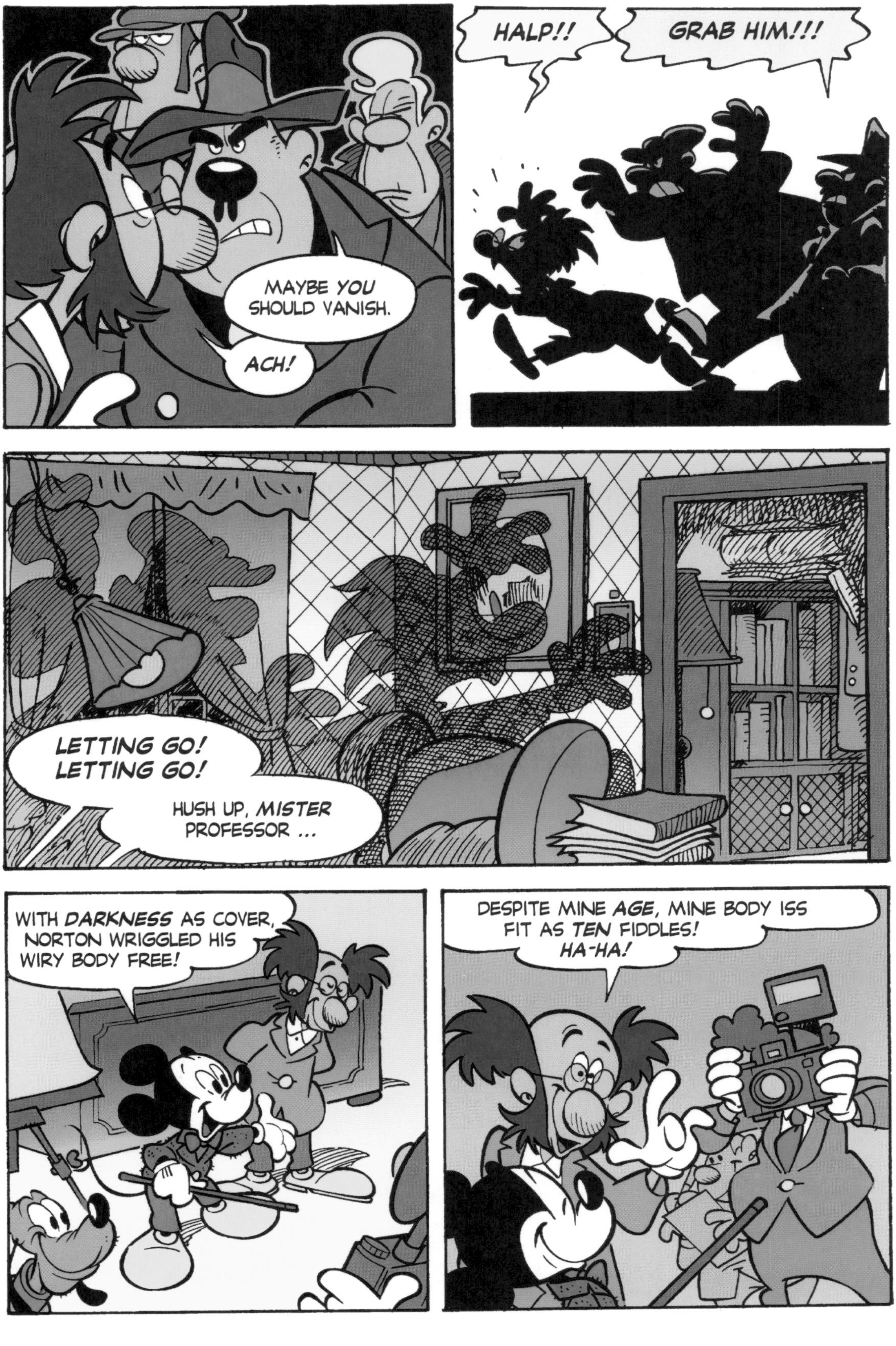
MAYBE YOU SHOULD VANISH.
ACH!
HALP!!
GRAB HIM!!!
LETTING GO! LETTING GO!
HUSH UP, MISTER PROFESSOR ...
WITH DARKNESS AS COVER, NORTON WRIGGLED HIS WIRY BODY FREE!
DESPITE MINE AGE, MINE BODY ISS FIT AS TEN FIDDLES! HA-HA!

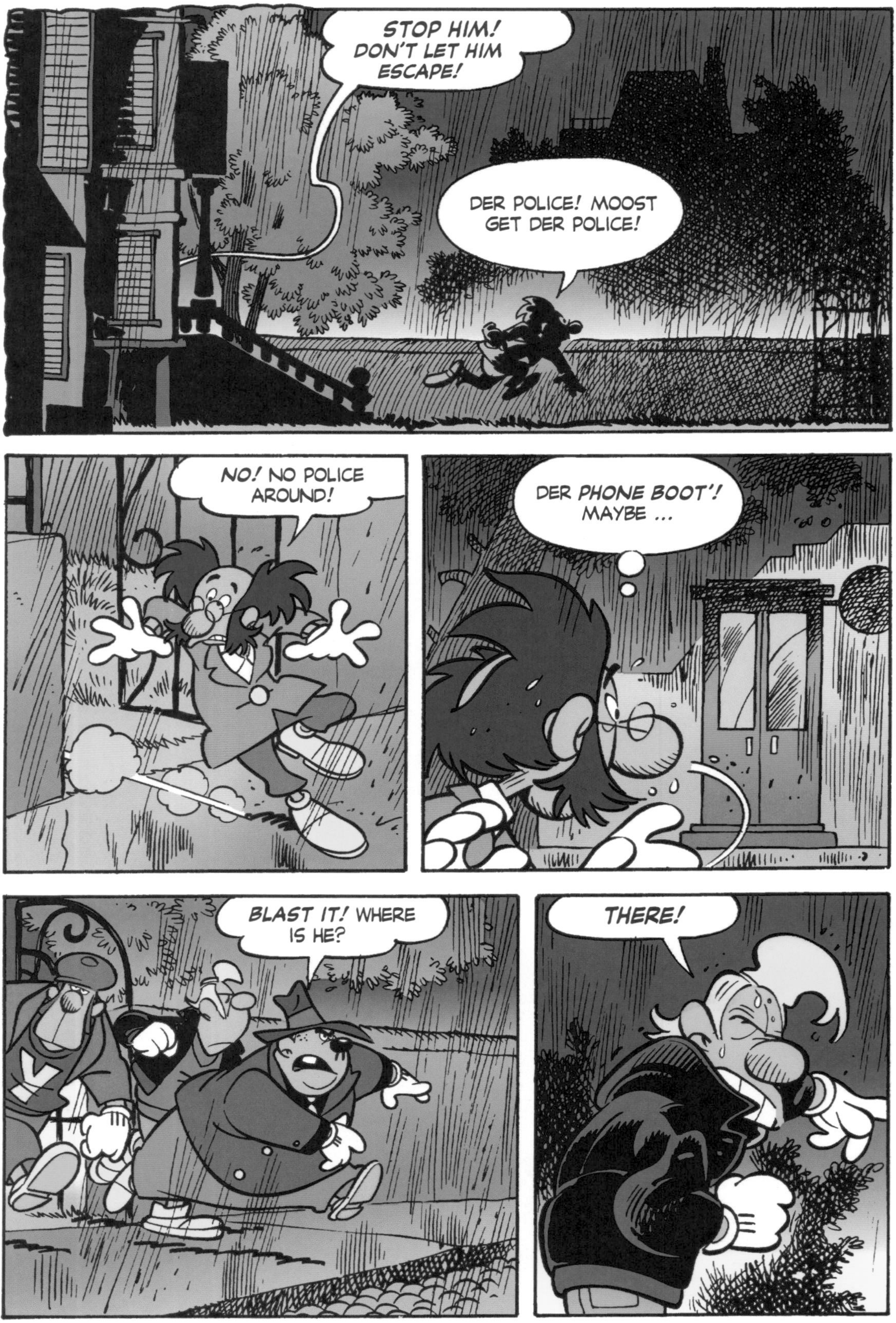
STOP HIM! DON'T LET HIM ESCAPE!
DER POLICE! MOOST GET DER POLICE!
NO! NO POLICE AROUND!
DER PHONE BOOT'! MAYBE ...
BLAST IT! WHERE IS HE?
THERE!

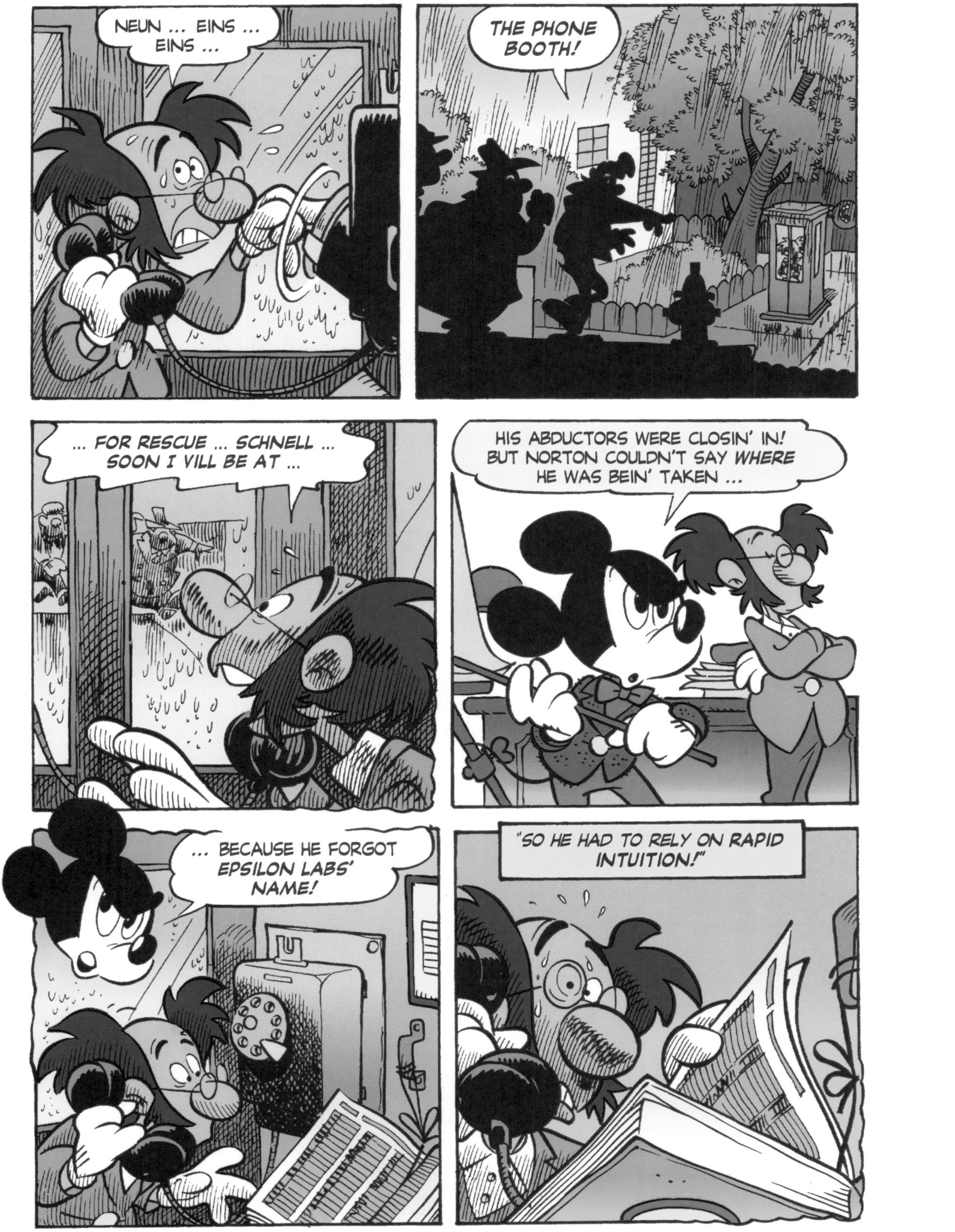
NEUN ... EINS ... EINS ...
THE PHONE BOOTH!
... FOR RESCUE ... SCHNELL ... SOON I VILL BE AT ...
HIS ABDUCTORS WERE CLOSIN' IN! BUT NORTON COULDN'T SAY WHERE HE WAS BEIN' TAKEN ...
... BECAUSE HE FORGOT EPSILON LABS' NAME!
"SO HE HAD TO RELY ON RAPID INTUITION!"

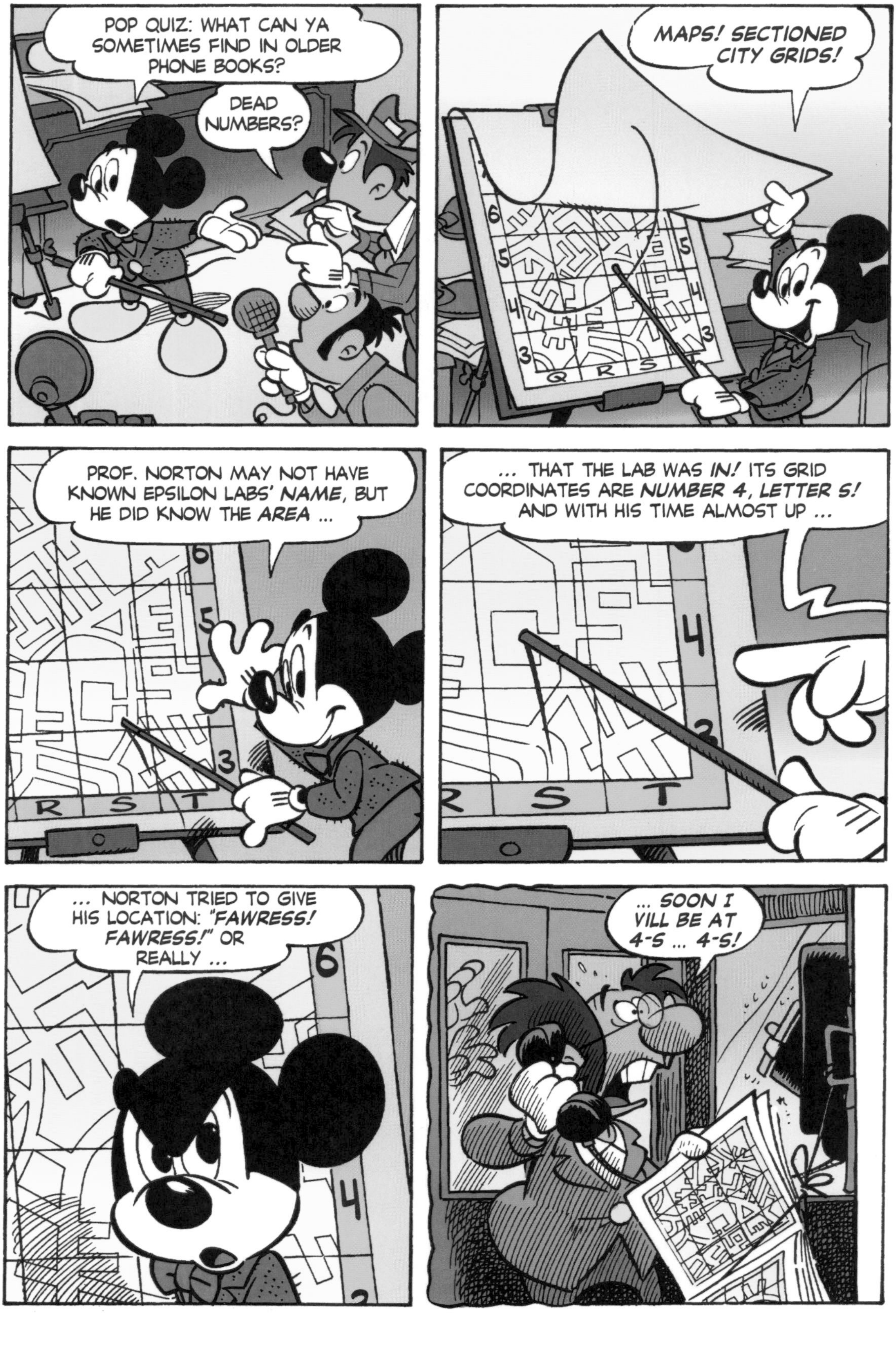
POP QUIZ: WHAT CAN YA SOMETIMES FIND IN OLDER PHONE BOOKS?
DEAD NUMBERS?
MAPS! SECTIONED CITY GRIDS!
PROF. NORTON MAY NOT HAVE KNOWN EPSILON LABS' NAME, BUT HE DID KNOW THE AREA ...
... THAT THE LAB WAS IN! ITS GRID COORDINATES ARE NUMBER 4, LETTER S! AND WITH HIS TIME ALMOST UP ...
... NORTON TRIED TO GIVE HIS LOCATION: "FAWRESS! FAWRESS!" OR REALLY ...
... SOON I VILL BE AT 4-S ... 4-S!

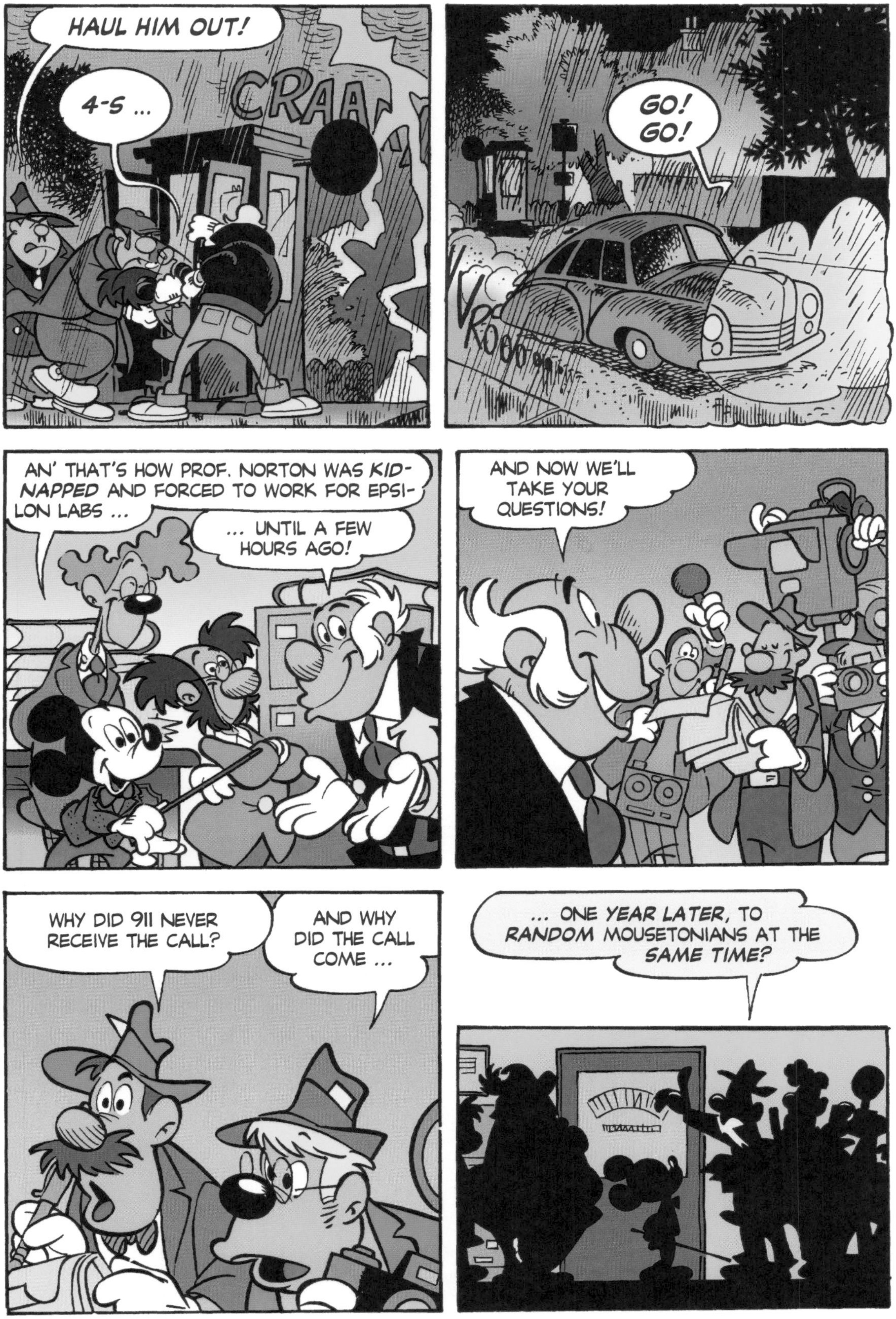
HAUL HIM OUT!
4-S ...
CRAA
GO! GO!
AN' THAT'S HOW PROF. NORTON WAS KID-NAPPED AND FORCED TO WORK FOR EPSILON LABS ...
... UNTIL A FEW HOURS AGO!
AND NOW WE'LL TAKE YOUR QUESTIONS!
WHY DID 911 NEVER RECEIVE THE CALL?
AND WHY DID THE CALL COME ...
... ONE YEAR LATER, TO RANDOM MOUSETONIANS AT THE SAME TIME?

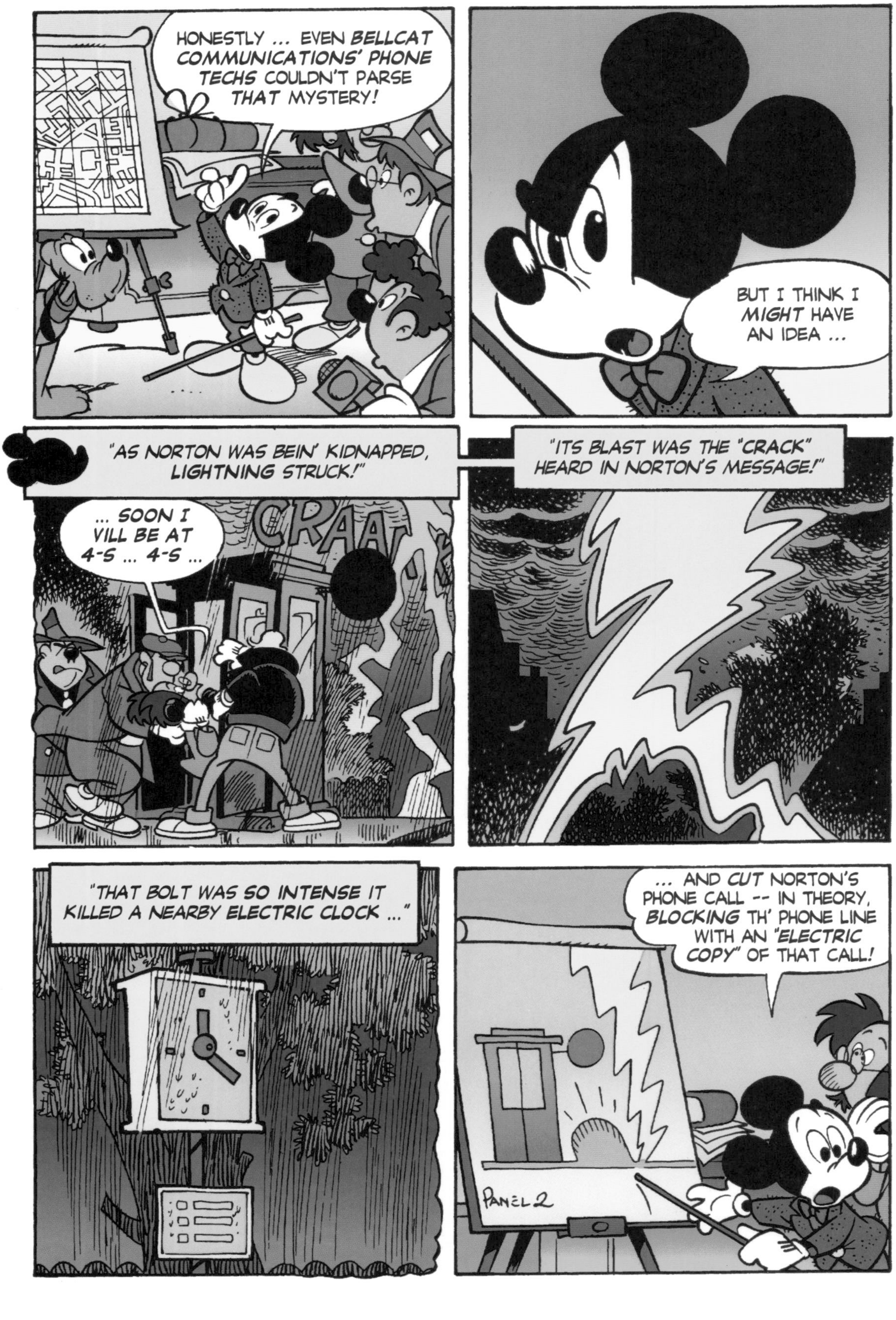
HONESTLY ... EVEN BELLCAT COMMUNICATIONS' PHONE TECHS COULDN'T PARSE THAT MYSTERY!
BUT I THINK I MIGHT HAVE AN IDEA ...
"AS NORTON WAS BEIN' KIDNAPPED, LIGHTNING STRUCK!"
... SOON I VILL BE AT 4-S ... 4-S ...
CRAA
"ITS BLAST WAS THE "CRACK" HEARD IN NORTON'S MESSAGE!"
"THAT BOLT WAS SO INTENSE IT KILLED A NEARBY ELECTRIC CLOCK ..."
... AND CUT NORTON'S PHONE CALL -- IN THEORY, BLOCKING TH' PHONE LINE WITH AN "ELECTRIC COPY" OF THAT CALL!
PANEL 2

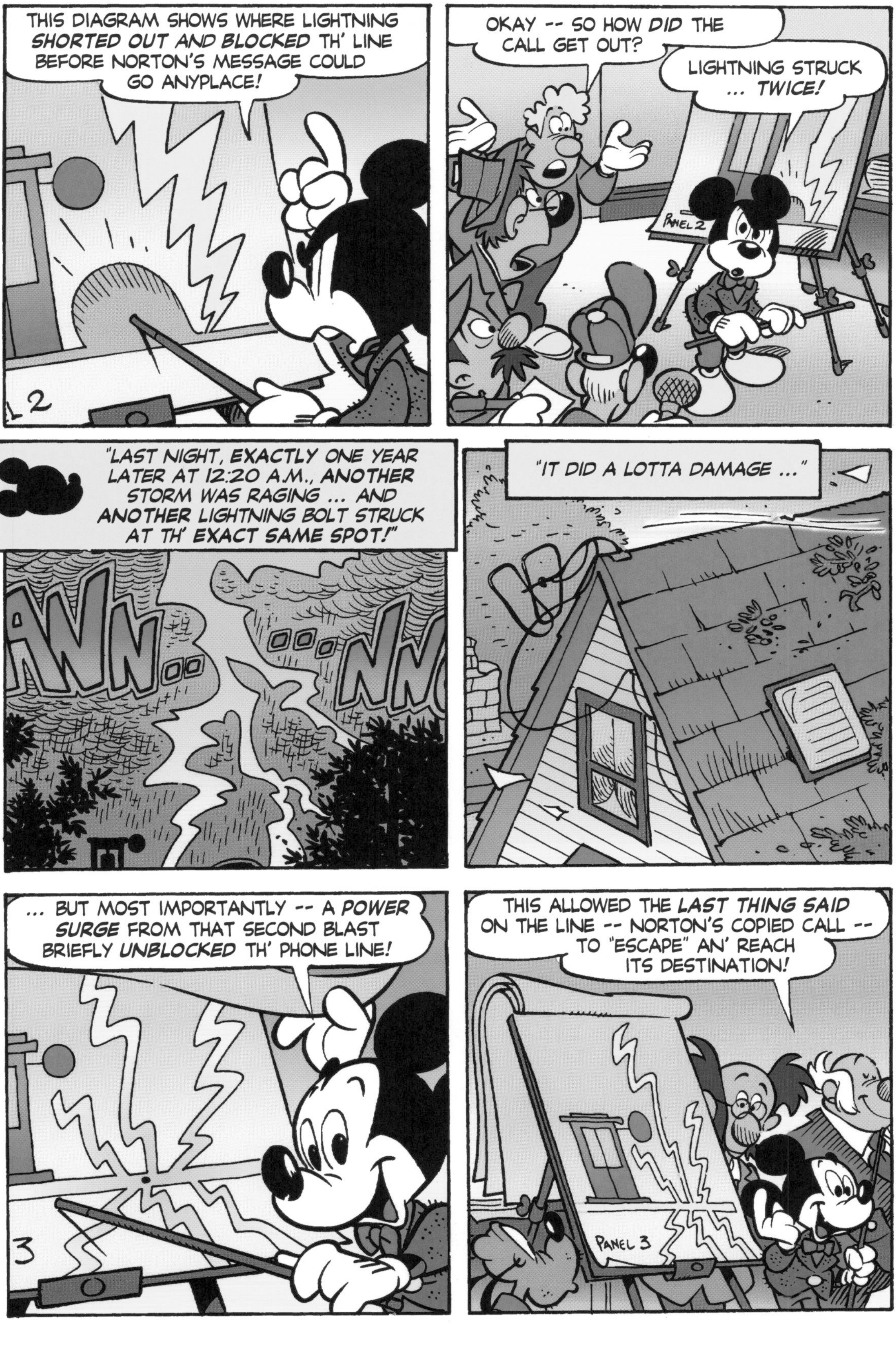

THIS DIAGRAM SHOWS WHERE LIGHTNING SHORTED OUT AND BLOCKED TH' LINE BEFORE NORTON'S MESSAGE COULD GO ANYPLACE!
2
OKAY -- SO HOW DID THE CALL GET OUT?
LIGHTNING STRUCK ... TWICE!
PANEL 2
"LAST NIGHT, EXACTLY ONE YEAR LATER AT 12:20 A.M., ANOTHER STORM WAS RAGING ... AND ANOTHER LIGHTNING BOLT STRUCK AT TH' EXACT SAME SPOT!"
AWN..
OO..NNO
"IT DID A LOTTA DAMAGE ..."
... BUT MOST IMPORTANTLY -- A POWER SURGE FROM THAT SECOND BLAST BRIEFLY UNBLOCKED TH' PHONE LINE!
3
THIS ALLOWED THE LAST THING SAID ON THE LINE -- NORTON'S COPIED CALL -- TO "ESCAPE" AN' REACH ITS DESTINATION!
PANEL 3

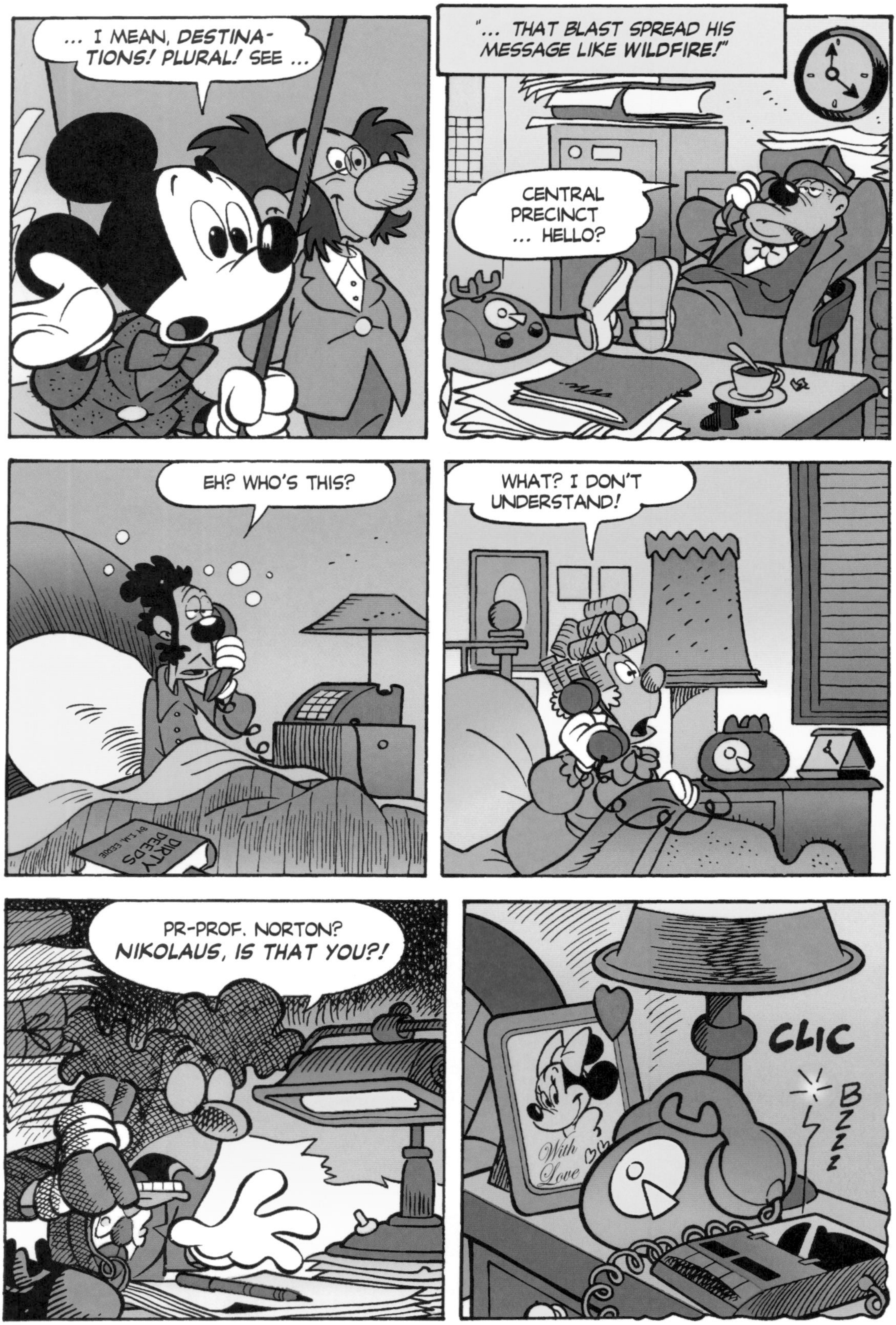

... I MEAN, DESTINATIONS! PLURAL! SEE ...
"... THAT BLAST SPREAD HIS MESSAGE LIKE WILDFIRE!"
CENTRAL PRECINCT ... HELLO?
EH? WHO'S THIS?
DIRTY DEEDS BY T.H. EERIE
WHAT? I DON'T UNDERSTAND!
PR-PROF. NORTON? NIKOLAUS, IS THAT YOU?!
With Love
CLIC
BZZZ

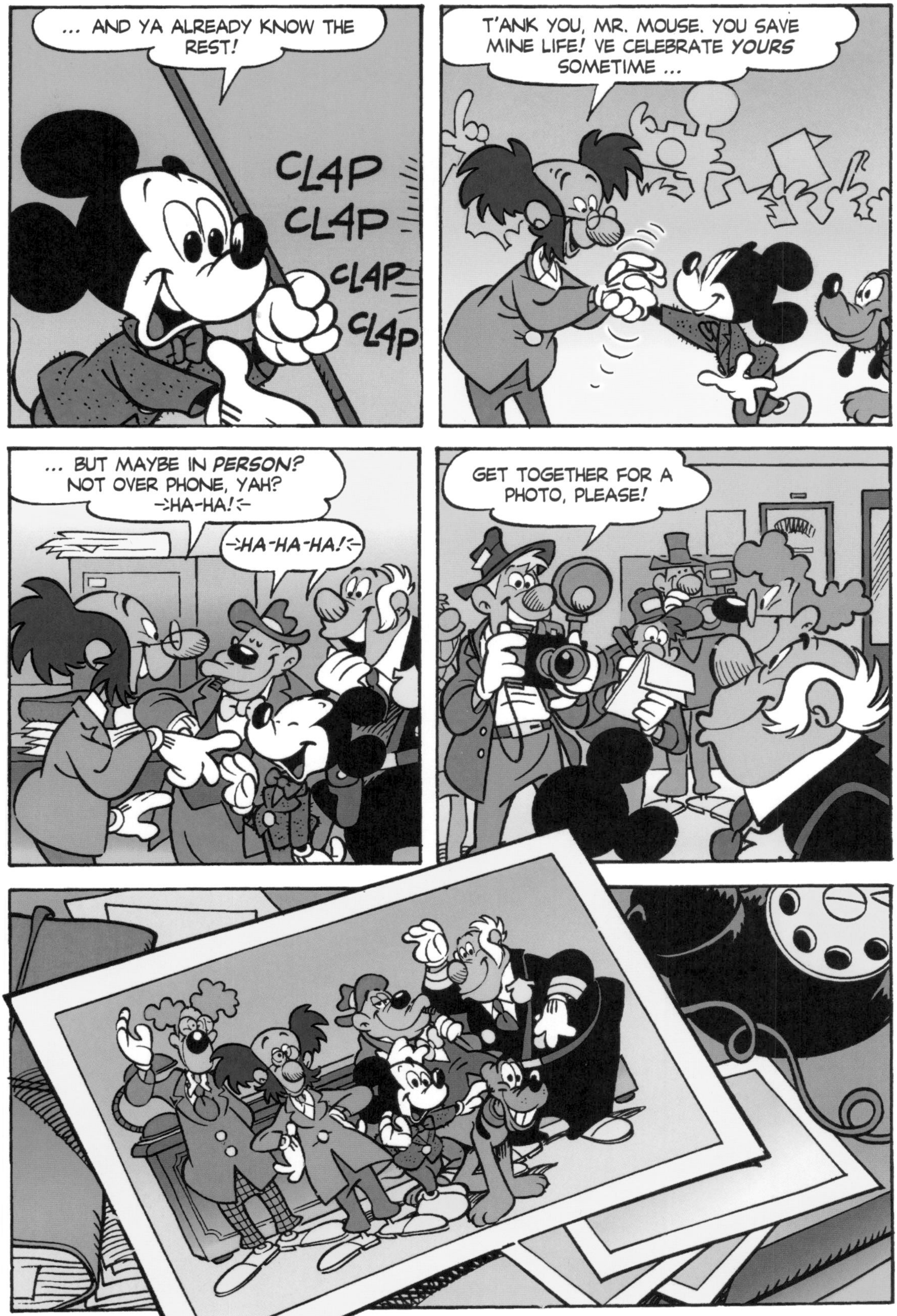
... AND YA ALREADY KNOW THE REST!
CLAP CLAP CLAP CLAP
T'ANK YOU, MR. MOUSE. YOU SAVE MINE LIFE! VE CELEBRATE YOURS SOMETIME ...
... BUT MAYBE IN PERSON? NOT OVER PHONE, YAH? -HA-HA!-
-HA-HA-HA!-
GET TOGETHER FOR A PHOTO, PLEASE!

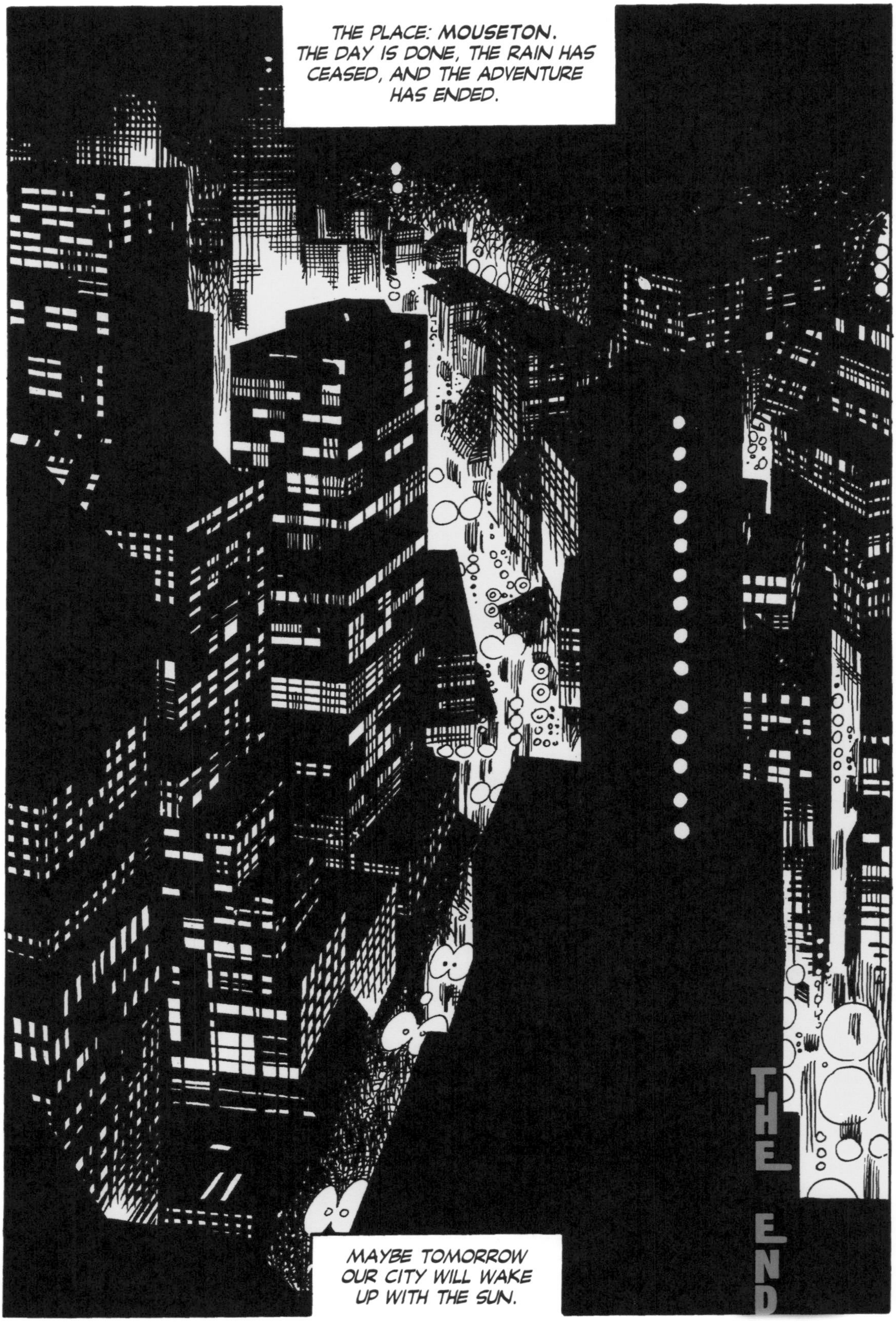
THE PLACE: MOUSETON.
THE DAY IS DONE, THE RAIN HAS CEASED, AND THE ADVENTURE HAS ENDED.
MAYBE TOMORROW OUR CITY WILL WAKE UP WITH THE SUN.
THE END

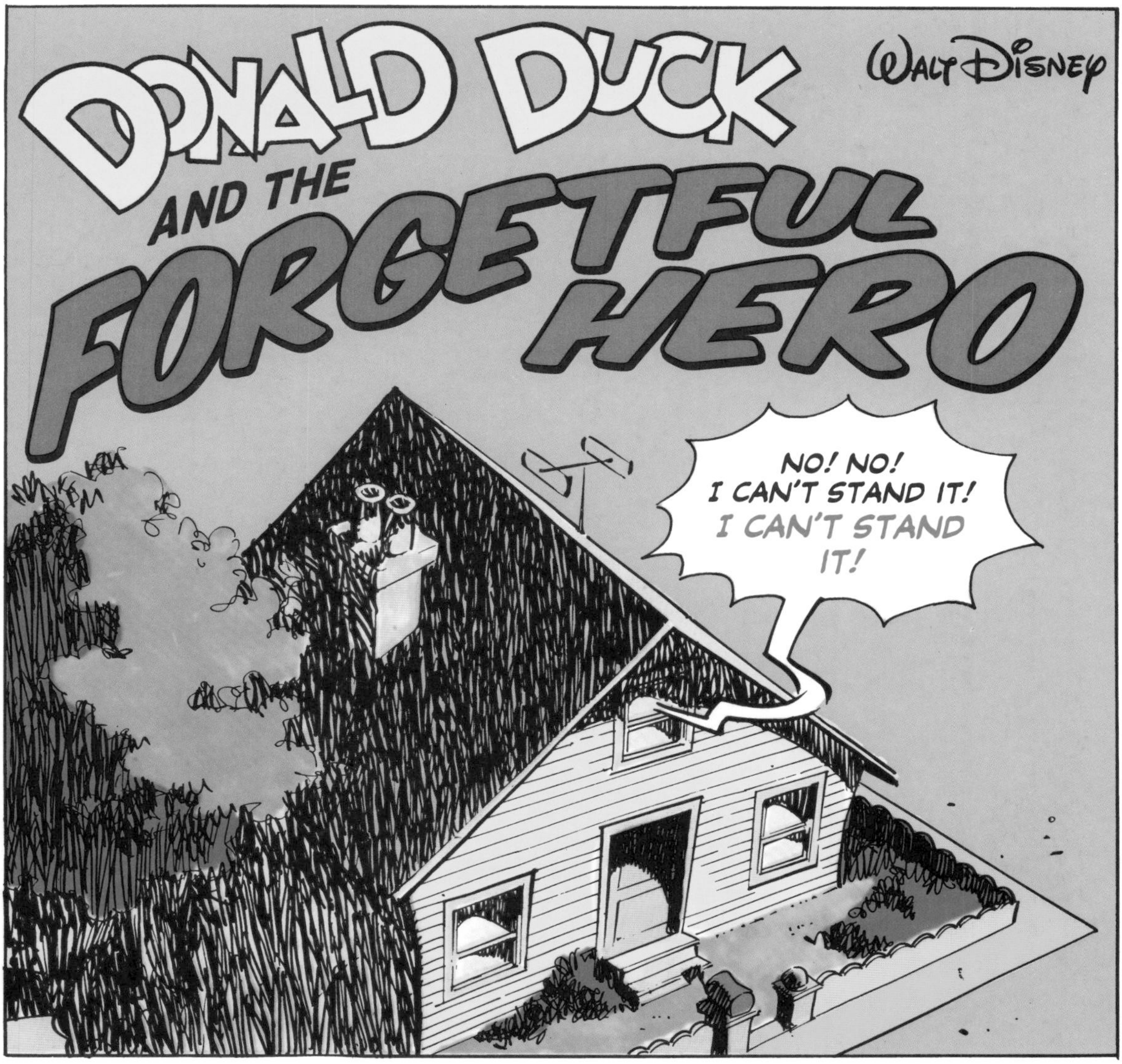
DONALD DUCK
WALT DISNEY
AND THE
FORGETFUL HERO
NO! NO! I CAN'T STAND IT! I CAN'T STAND IT!

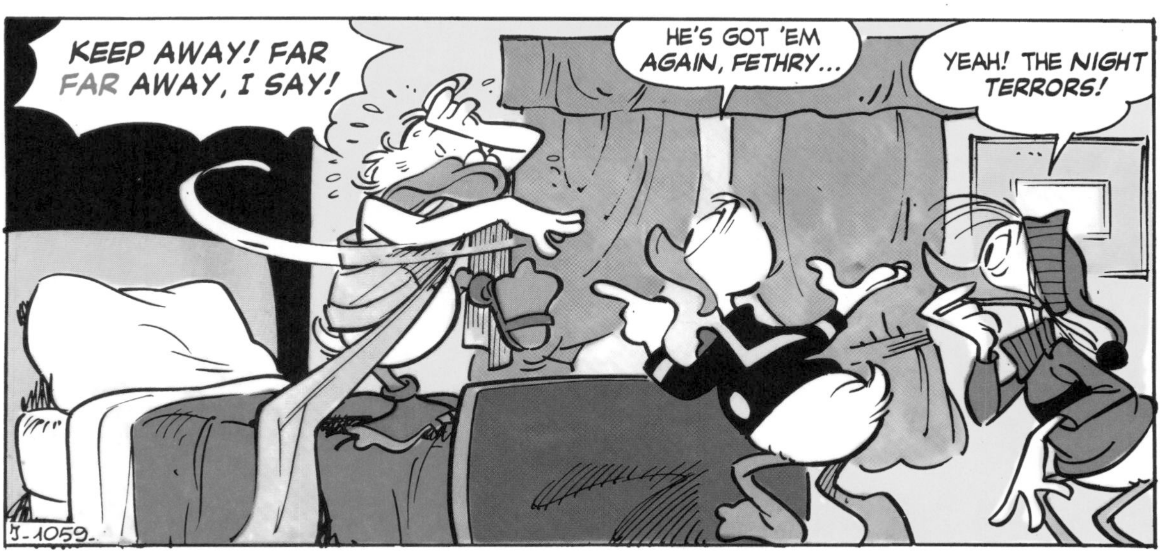
KEEP AWAY! FAR FAR AWAY, I SAY!
HE'S GOT 'EM AGAIN, FETHRY...
YEAH! THE NIGHT TERRORS!
J-1059

STORY BY GIORGIO PEZZIN • ART BY GIORGIO CAVAZZANO • TRANSLATION AND DIALOGUE BY THAD KOMOROWSKI • EDITING BY J. MICHAEL CATRON AND DAVID GERSTEIN

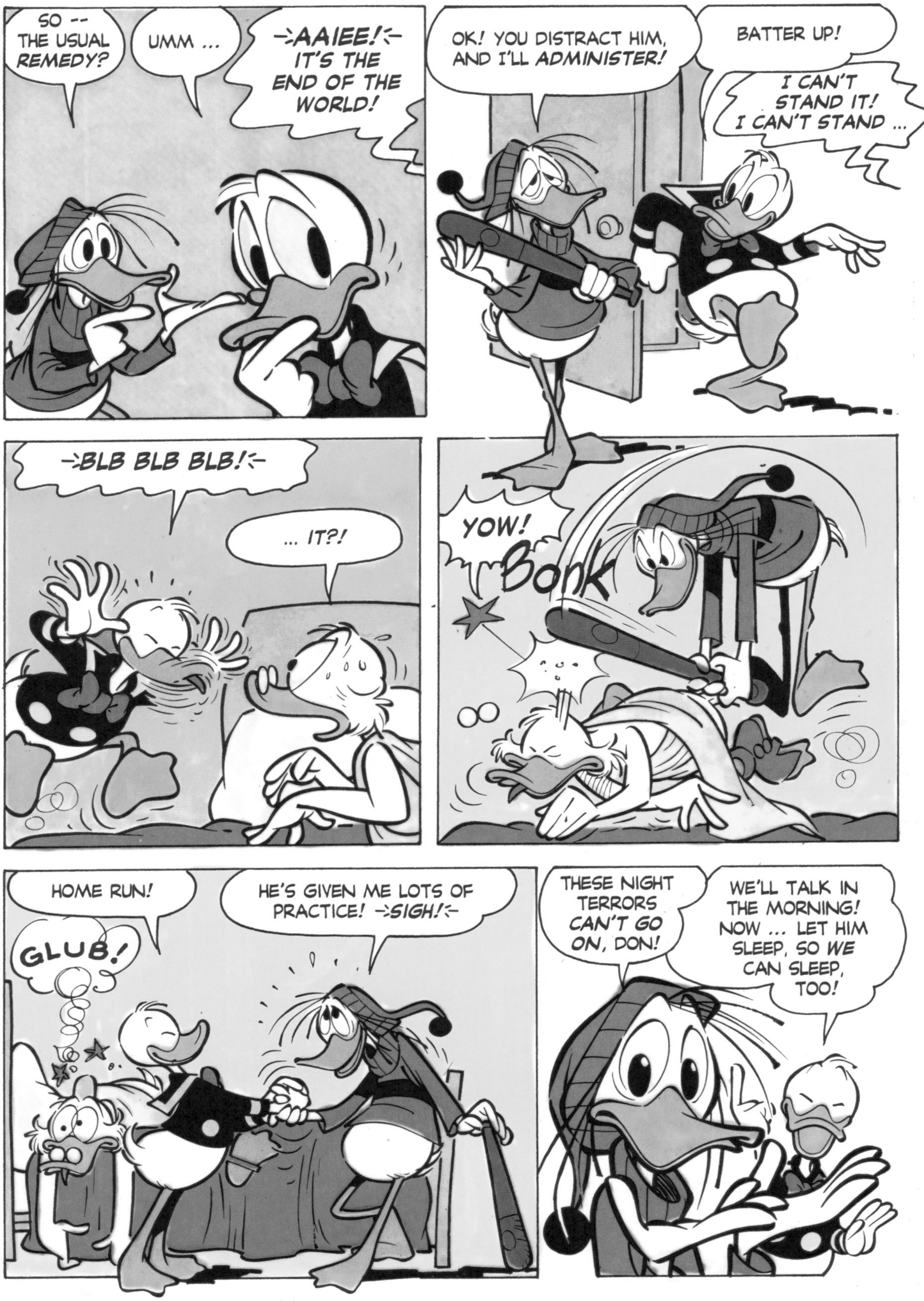
SO -- THE USUAL REMEDY?
UMM ...
AAIEE! IT'S THE END OF THE WORLD!
OK! YOU DISTRACT HIM, AND I'LL ADMINISTER!
BATTER UP!
I CAN'T STAND IT! I CAN'T STAND ...
BLB BLB BLB!
... IT?!
YOW!
Bonk
HOME RUN!
GLUB!
HE'S GIVEN ME LOTS OF PRACTICE! SIGH!
THESE NIGHT TERRORS CAN'T GO ON, DON!
WE'LL TALK IN THE MORNING! NOW ... LET HIM SLEEP, SO WE CAN SLEEP, TOO!

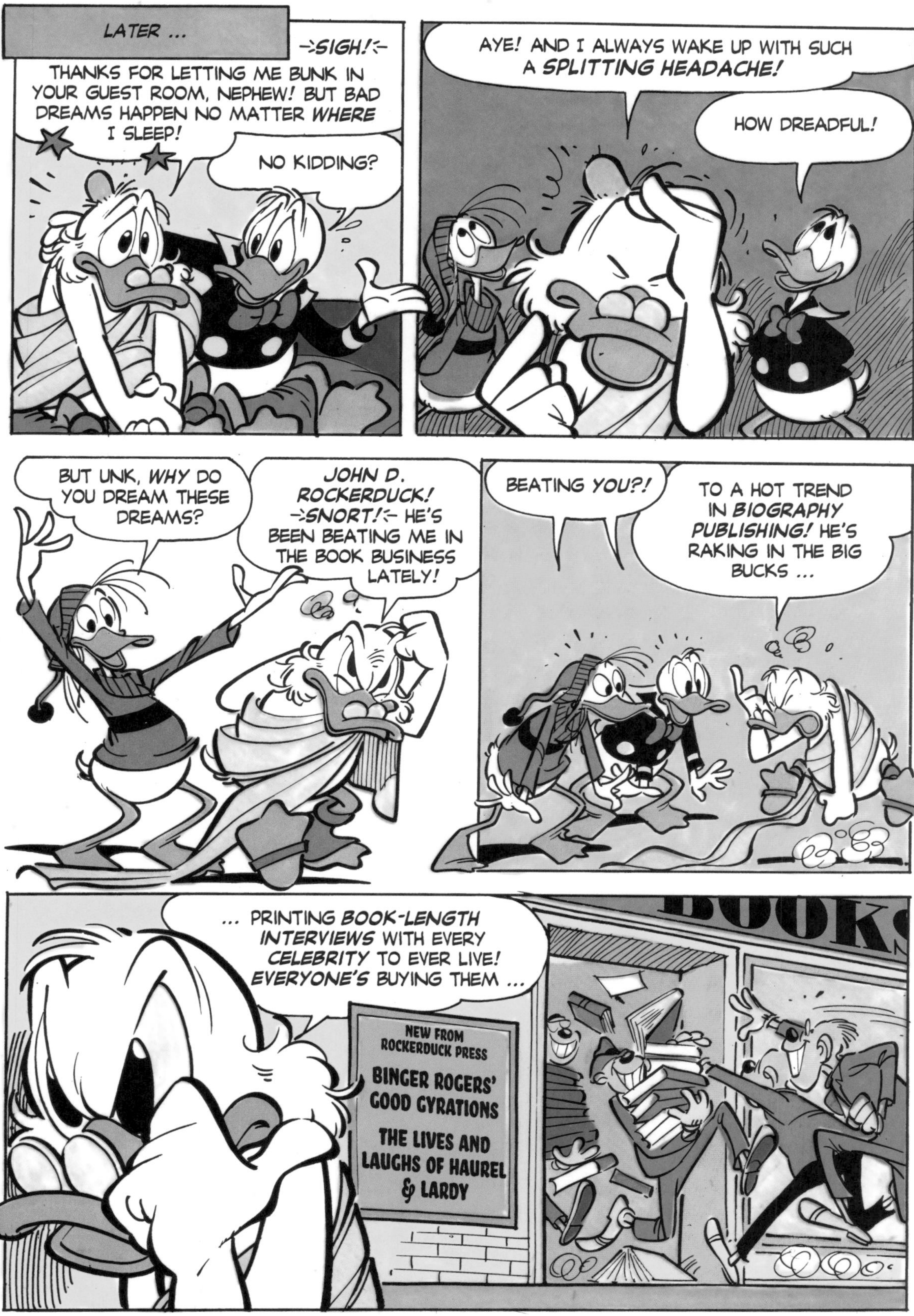
LATER ...
-SIGH!-
THANKS FOR LETTING ME BUNK IN YOUR GUEST ROOM, NEPHEW! BUT BAD DREAMS HAPPEN NO MATTER WHERE I SLEEP!
NO KIDDING?
AYE! AND I ALWAYS WAKE UP WITH SUCH A SPLITTING HEADACHE!
HOW DREADFUL!
BUT UNK, WHY DO YOU DREAM THESE DREAMS?
JOHN D. ROCKERDUCK! -SNORT!- HE'S BEEN BEATING ME IN THE BOOK BUSINESS LATELY!
BEATING YOU?!
TO A HOT TREND IN BIOGRAPHY PUBLISHING! HE'S RAKING IN THE BIG BUCKS ...
... PRINTING BOOK-LENGTH INTERVIEWS WITH EVERY CELEBRITY TO EVER LIVE! EVERYONE'S BUYING THEM ...
BOOKS
NEW FROM ROCKERDUCK PRESS
BINGER ROGERS' GOOD GYRATIONS
THE LIVES AND LAUGHS OF HAUREL & LARDY

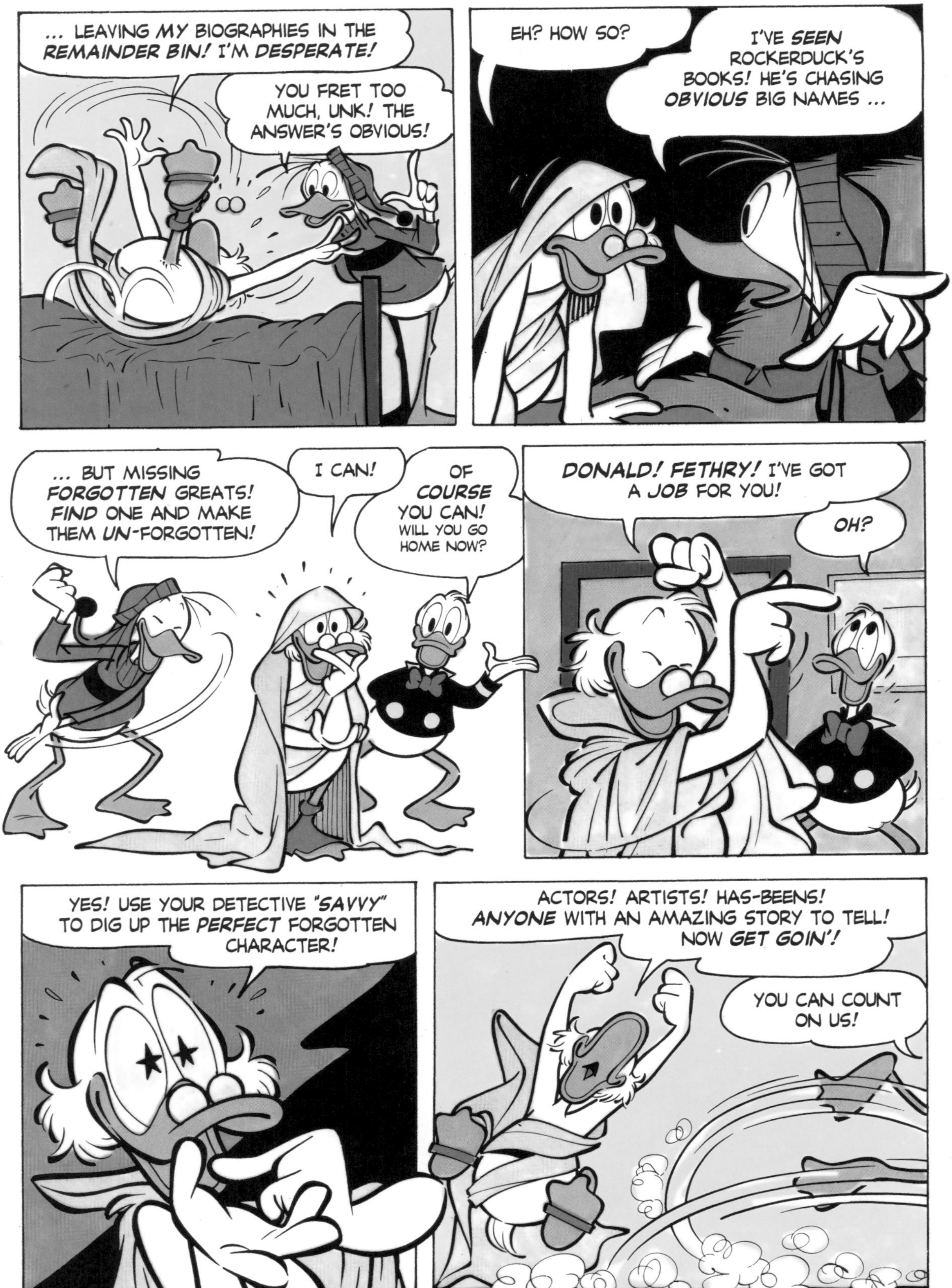
... LEAVING MY BIOGRAPHIES IN THE REMAINDER BIN! I'M DESPERATE!
YOU FRET TOO MUCH, UNK! THE ANSWER'S OBVIOUS!
EH? HOW SO?
I'VE SEEN ROCKERDUCK'S BOOKS! HE'S CHASING OBVIOUS BIG NAMES ...
... BUT MISSING FORGOTTEN GREATS! FIND ONE AND MAKE THEM UN-FORGOTTEN!
I CAN!
OF COURSE YOU CAN! WILL YOU GO HOME NOW?
DONALD! FETHRY! I'VE GOT A JOB FOR YOU!
OH?
YES! USE YOUR DETECTIVE "SAVVY" TO DIG UP THE PERFECT FORGOTTEN CHARACTER!
ACTORS! ARTISTS! HAS-BEENS! ANYONE WITH AN AMAZING STORY TO TELL! NOW GET GOIN'!
YOU CAN COUNT ON US!

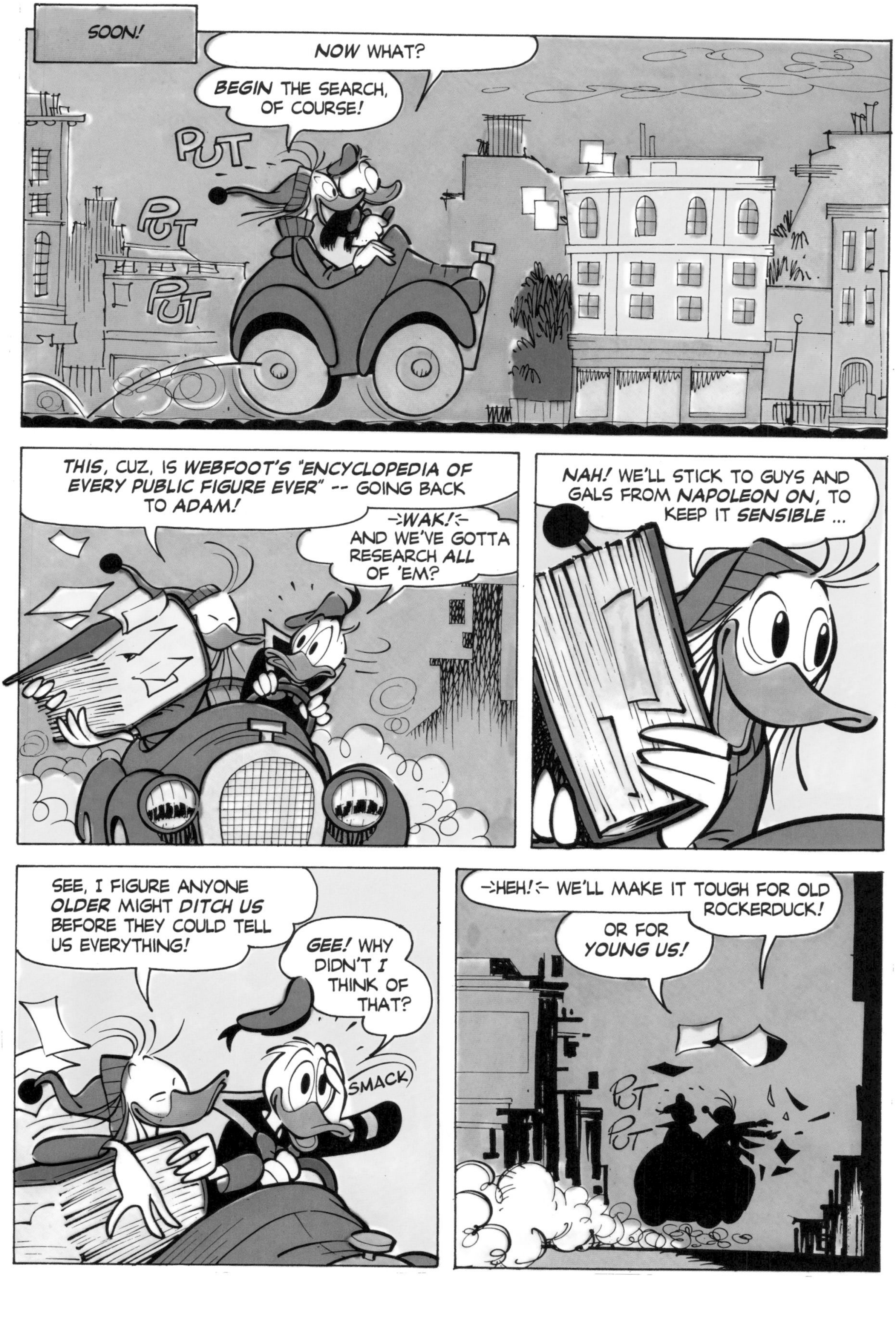

SOON!
NOW WHAT?
BEGIN THE SEARCH, OF COURSE!
PUT
PUT
PUT
THIS, CUZ, IS WEBFOOT'S "ENCYCLOPEDIA OF EVERY PUBLIC FIGURE EVER" -- GOING BACK TO ADAM!
-WAK!- AND WE'VE GOTTA RESEARCH ALL OF 'EM?
NAH! WE'LL STICK TO GUYS AND GALS FROM NAPOLEON ON, TO KEEP IT SENSIBLE ...
SEE, I FIGURE ANYONE OLDER MIGHT DITCH US BEFORE THEY COULD TELL US EVERYTHING!
GEE! WHY DIDN'T I THINK OF THAT?
SMACK
-HEH!- WE'LL MAKE IT TOUGH FOR OLD ROCKERDUCK!
OR FOR YOUNG US!
PUT
PUT

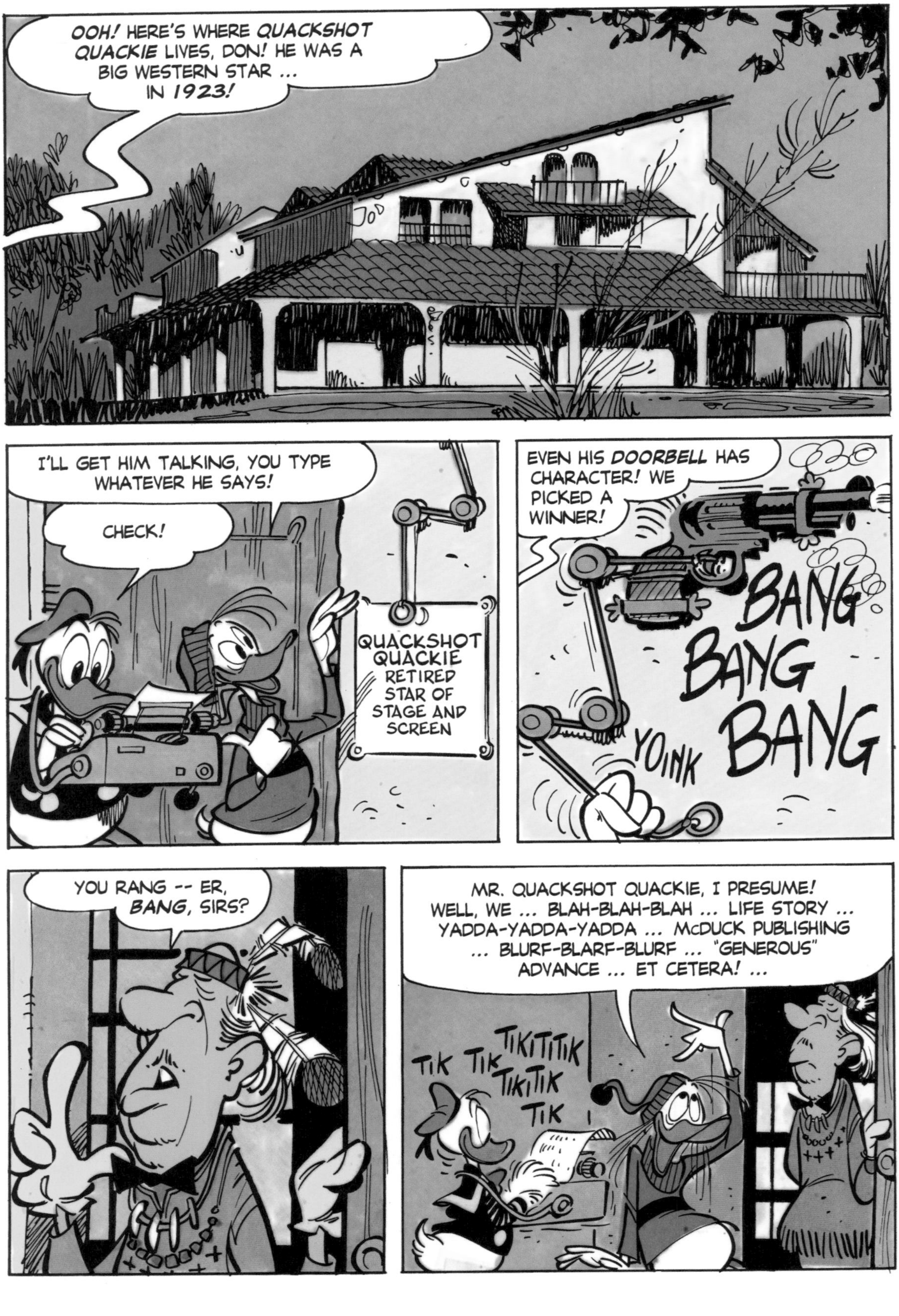
OOH! HERE'S WHERE QUACKSHOT QUACKIE LIVES, DON! HE WAS A BIG WESTERN STAR ... IN 1923!
I'LL GET HIM TALKING, YOU TYPE WHATEVER HE SAYS!
CHECK!
QUACKSHOT QUACKIE RETIRED STAR OF STAGE AND SCREEN
EVEN HIS DOORBELL HAS CHARACTER! WE PICKED A WINNER!
BANG
BANG
BANG
YOINK
YOU RANG -- ER, BANG, SIRS?
MR. QUACKSHOT QUACKIE, I PRESUME! WELL, WE ... BLAH-BLAH-BLAH ... LIFE STORY ... YADDA-YADDA-YADDA ... McDUCK PUBLISHING ... BLURF-BLARF-BLURF ... "GENEROUS" ADVANCE ... ET CETERA! ...
TIK TIK TIKITITIK TIKITIK TIK

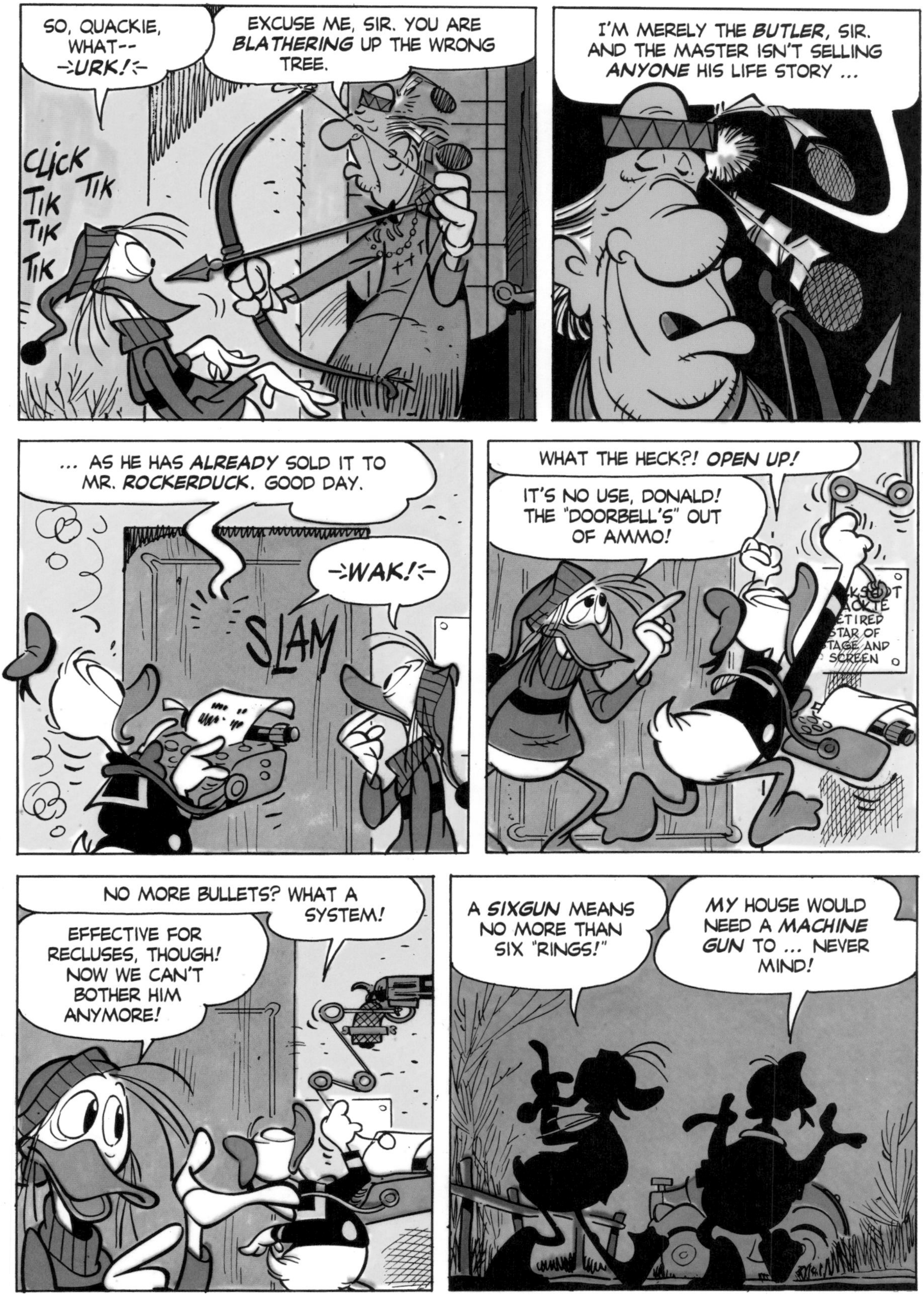
SO, QUACKIE, WHAT-- -URK!-
EXCUSE ME, SIR. YOU ARE BLATHERING UP THE WRONG TREE.
CLICK
TIK
TIK
TIK
TIK
I'M MERELY THE BUTLER, SIR. AND THE MASTER ISN'T SELLING ANYONE HIS LIFE STORY ...
... AS HE HAS ALREADY SOLD IT TO MR. ROCKERDUCK. GOOD DAY.
SLAM
-WAK!-
WHAT THE HECK?! OPEN UP!
IT'S NO USE, DONALD! THE "DOORBELL'S" OUT OF AMMO!
NO MORE BULLETS? WHAT A SYSTEM!
EFFECTIVE FOR RECLUSES, THOUGH! NOW WE CAN'T BOTHER HIM ANYMORE!
A SIXGUN MEANS NO MORE THAN SIX "RINGS!"
MY HOUSE WOULD NEED A MACHINE GUN TO ... NEVER MIND!

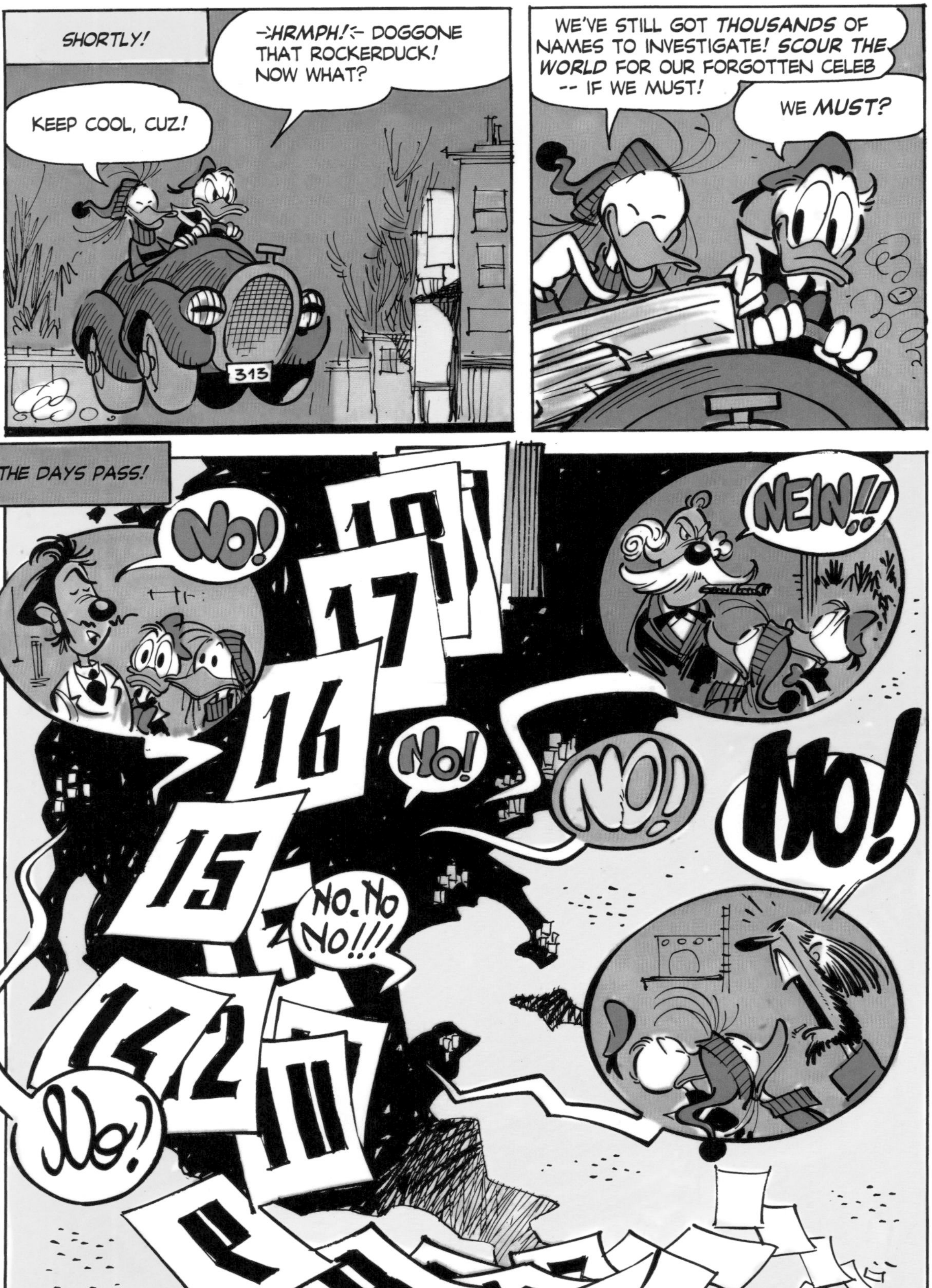
SHORTLY!
–HRMPH!– DOGGONE THAT ROCKERDUCK! NOW WHAT?
KEEP COOL, CUZ!
313
WE'VE STILL GOT *THOUSANDS* OF NAMES TO INVESTIGATE! *SCOUR THE WORLD* FOR OUR FORGOTTEN CELEB -- IF WE MUST!
WE *MUST?*
THE DAYS PASS!
NO!
NEIN!!
17
16
NO!
15
NO!
NO!
NO. NO NO!!!
14
NO!

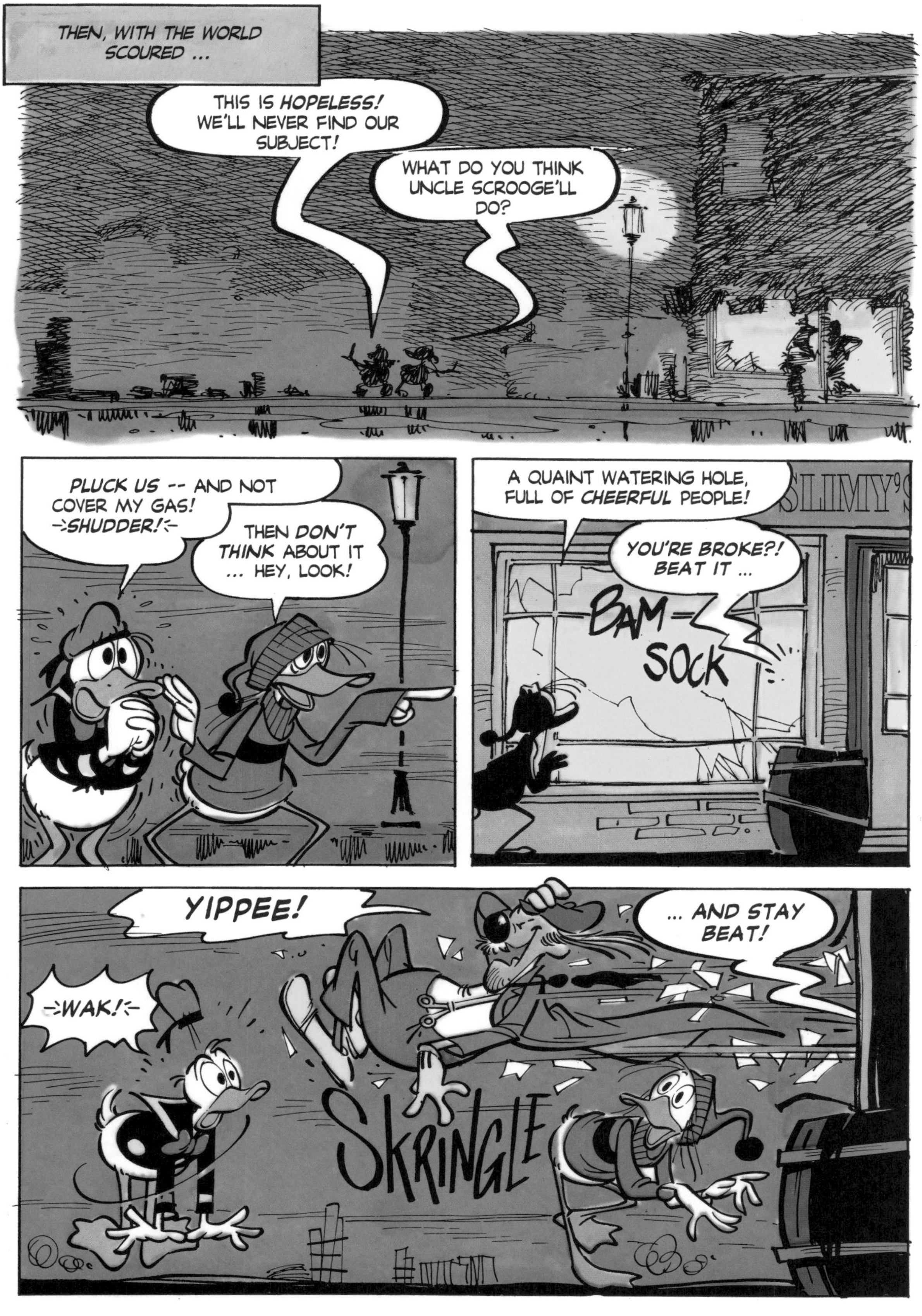
THEN, WITH THE WORLD SCOURED ...
THIS IS HOPELESS! WE'LL NEVER FIND OUR SUBJECT!
WHAT DO YOU THINK UNCLE SCROOGE'LL DO?
PLUCK US -- AND NOT COVER MY GAS! -SHUDDER!-
THEN DON'T THINK ABOUT IT ... HEY, LOOK!
A QUAINT WATERING HOLE, FULL OF CHEERFUL PEOPLE!
SLIMY'S
YOU'RE BROKE?! BEAT IT ...
BAM
SOCK
YIPPEE!
... AND STAY BEAT!
-WAK!-
SKRINGLE

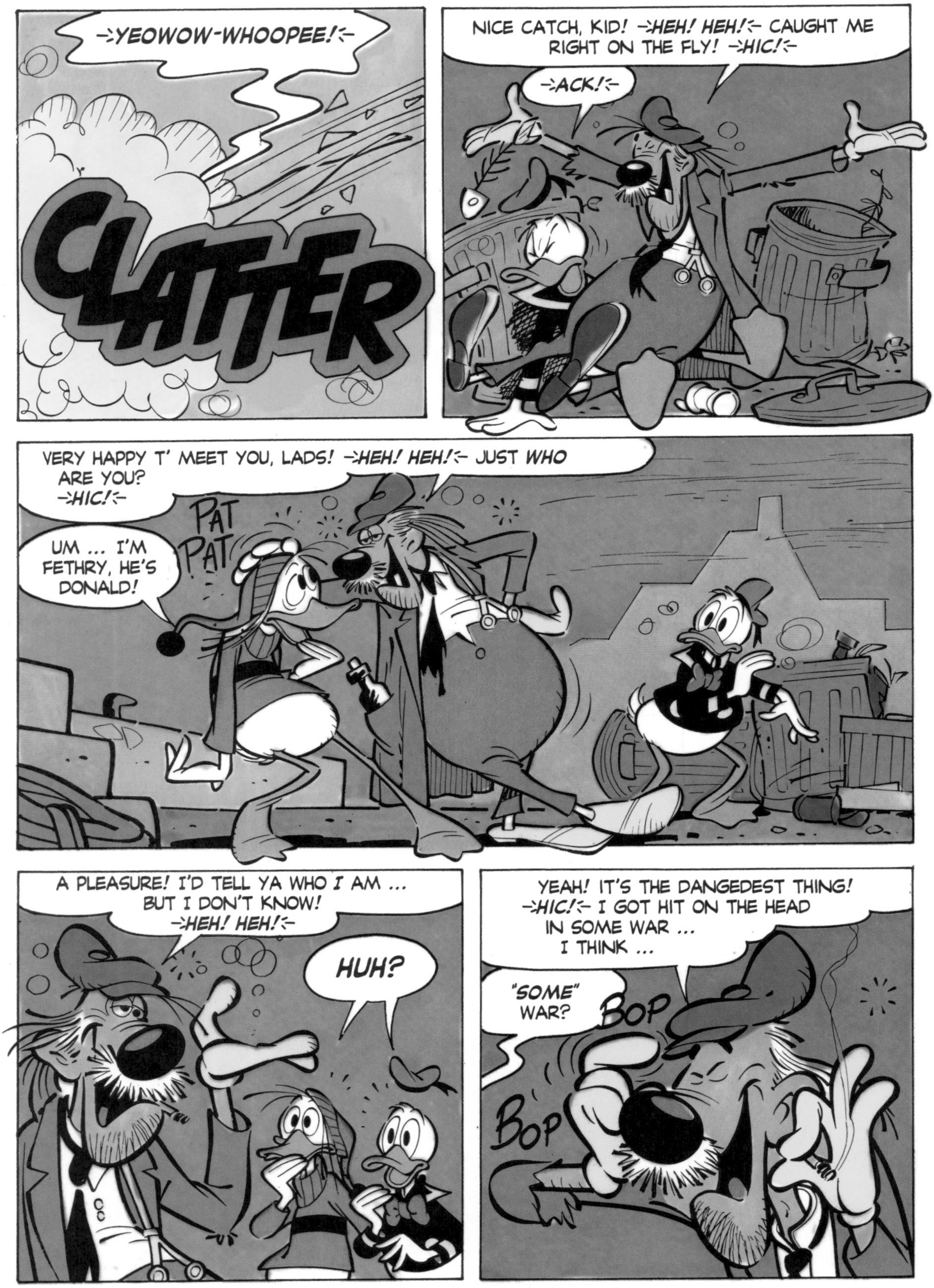
-YEOWOW-WHOOPEE!-
CLATTER
NICE CATCH, KID! -HEH! HEH!- CAUGHT ME RIGHT ON THE FLY! -HIC!-
-ACK!-
VERY HAPPY T' MEET YOU, LADS! -HEH! HEH!- JUST WHO ARE YOU? -HIC!-
PAT PAT
UM ... I'M FETHRY, HE'S DONALD!
A PLEASURE! I'D TELL YA WHO I AM ... BUT I DON'T KNOW! -HEH! HEH!-
HUH?
YEAH! IT'S THE DANGEDEST THING! -HIC!- I GOT HIT ON THE HEAD IN SOME WAR ... I THINK ...
"SOME" WAR?
BOP
BOP

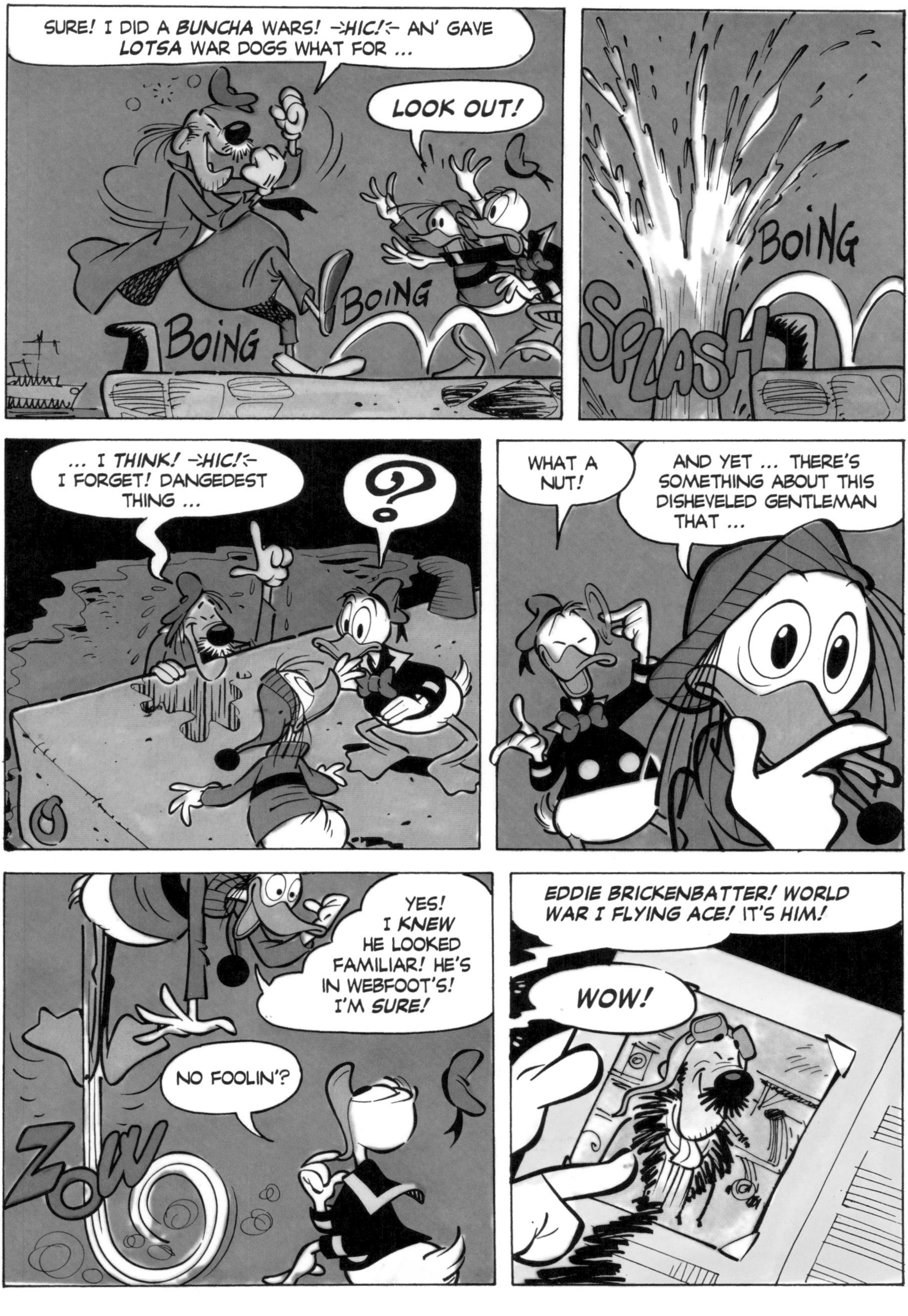

SURE! I DID A BUNCHA WARS! -HIC!- AN' GAVE LOTSA WAR DOGS WHAT FOR ...
LOOK OUT!
BOING
BOING
BOING
SPLASH
... I THINK! -HIC!- I FORGET! DANGEDEST THING ...
?
WHAT A NUT!
AND YET ... THERE'S SOMETHING ABOUT THIS DISHEVELED GENTLEMAN THAT ...
YES! I KNEW HE LOOKED FAMILIAR! HE'S IN WEBFOOT'S! I'M SURE!
NO FOOLIN'?
ZOW
EDDIE BRICKENBATTER! WORLD WAR I FLYING ACE! IT'S HIM!
WOW!

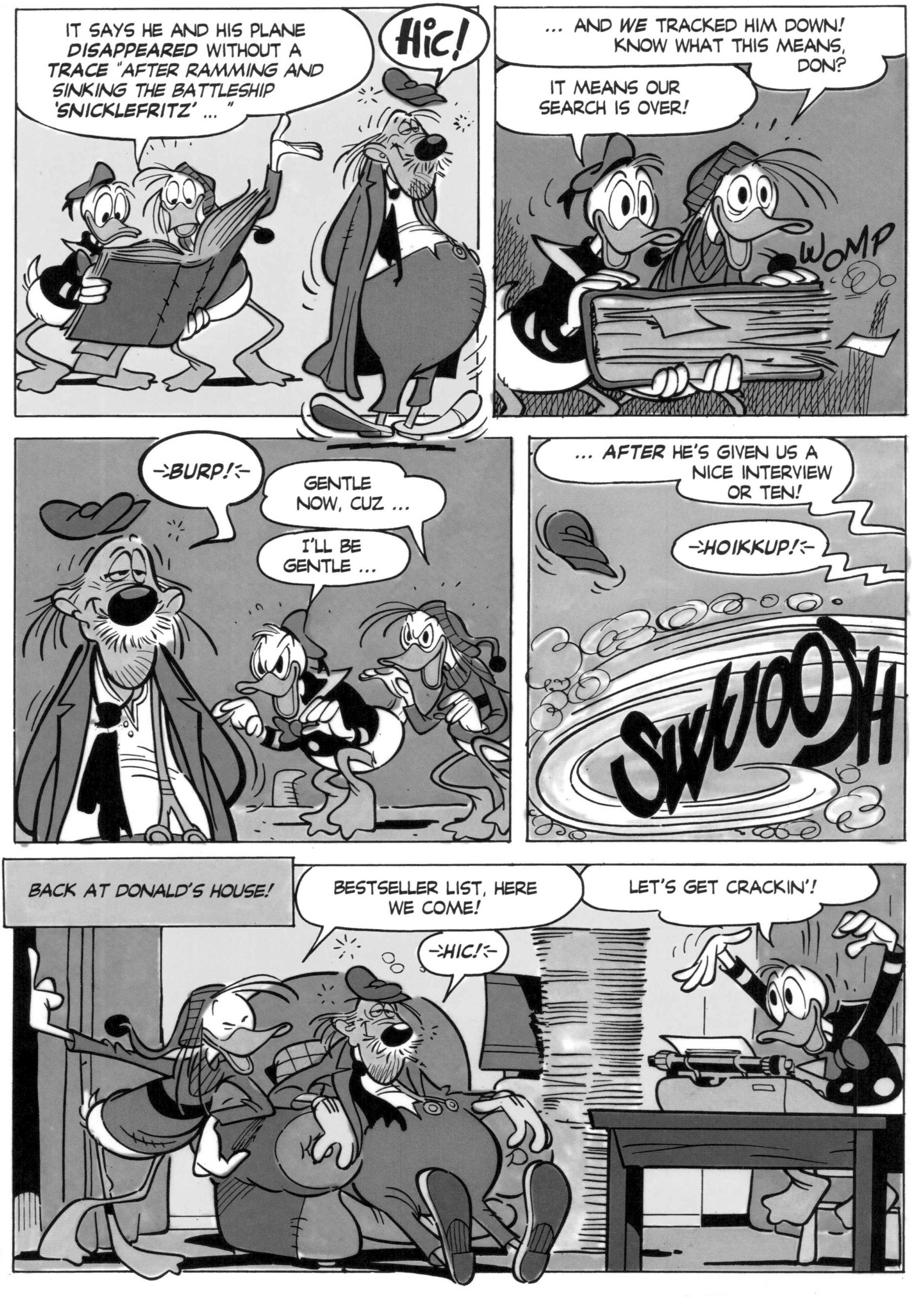
IT SAYS HE AND HIS PLANE DISAPPEARED WITHOUT A TRACE "AFTER RAMMING AND SINKING THE BATTLESHIP 'SNICKLEFRITZ' ... "
Hic!
... AND WE TRACKED HIM DOWN! KNOW WHAT THIS MEANS, DON?
IT MEANS OUR SEARCH IS OVER!
WOMP
-BURP!-
GENTLE NOW, CUZ ...
I'LL BE GENTLE ...
... AFTER HE'S GIVEN US A NICE INTERVIEW OR TEN!
-HOIKKUP!-
SWWOOSH
BACK AT DONALD'S HOUSE!
BESTSELLER LIST, HERE WE COME!
LET'S GET CRACKIN'!
-HIC!-

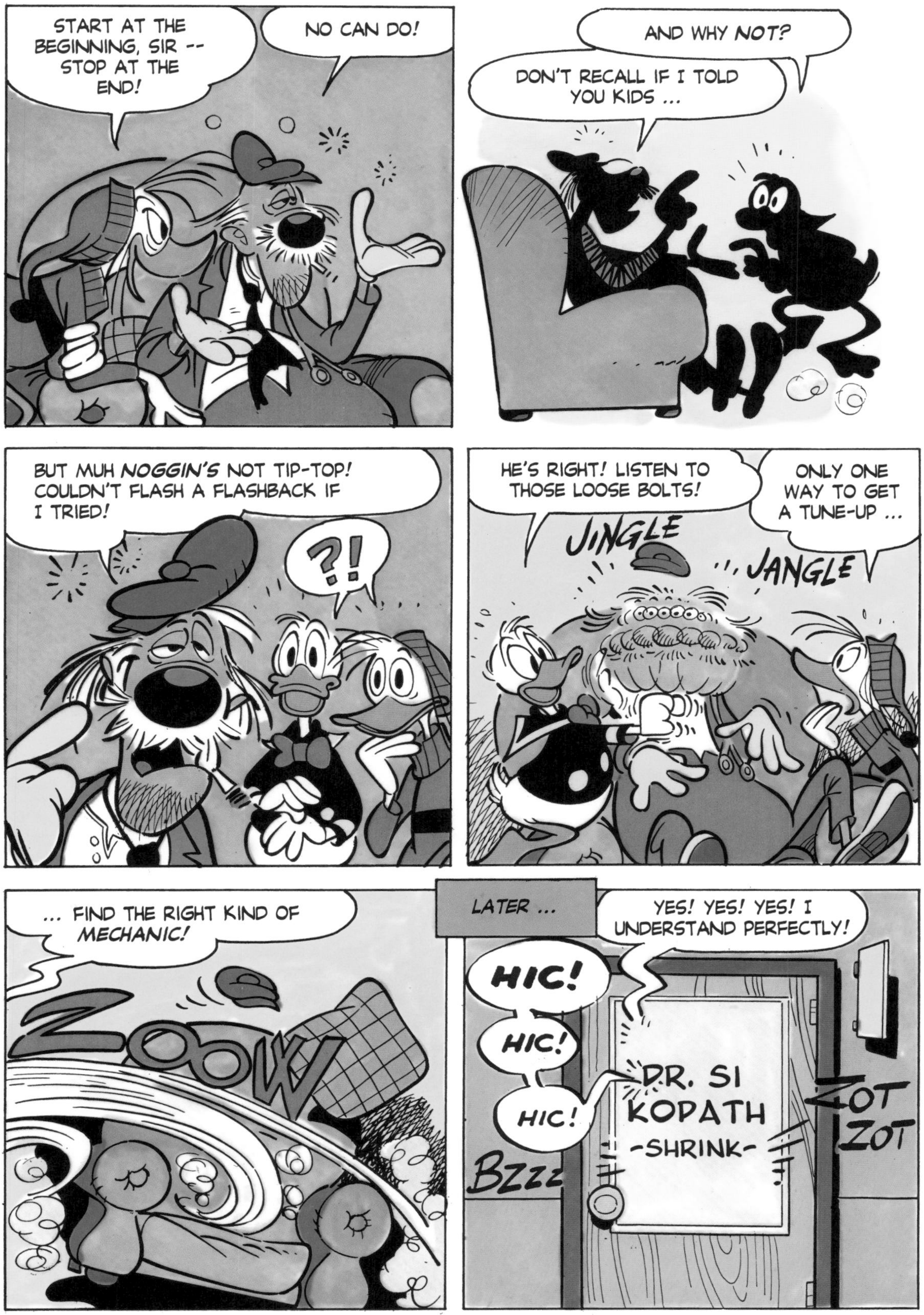

START AT THE BEGINNING, SIR -- STOP AT THE END!
NO CAN DO!
AND WHY NOT?
DON'T RECALL IF I TOLD YOU KIDS ...
BUT MUH NOGGIN'S NOT TIP-TOP! COULDN'T FLASH A FLASHBACK IF I TRIED!
?!
HE'S RIGHT! LISTEN TO THOSE LOOSE BOLTS!
ONLY ONE WAY TO GET A TUNE-UP ...
JINGLE
JANGLE
... FIND THE RIGHT KIND OF MECHANIC!
ZOOOW
LATER ...
YES! YES! YES! I UNDERSTAND PERFECTLY!
HIC!
HIC!
HIC!
DR. SI KOPATH -SHRINK-
ZOT ZOT
BZZZ

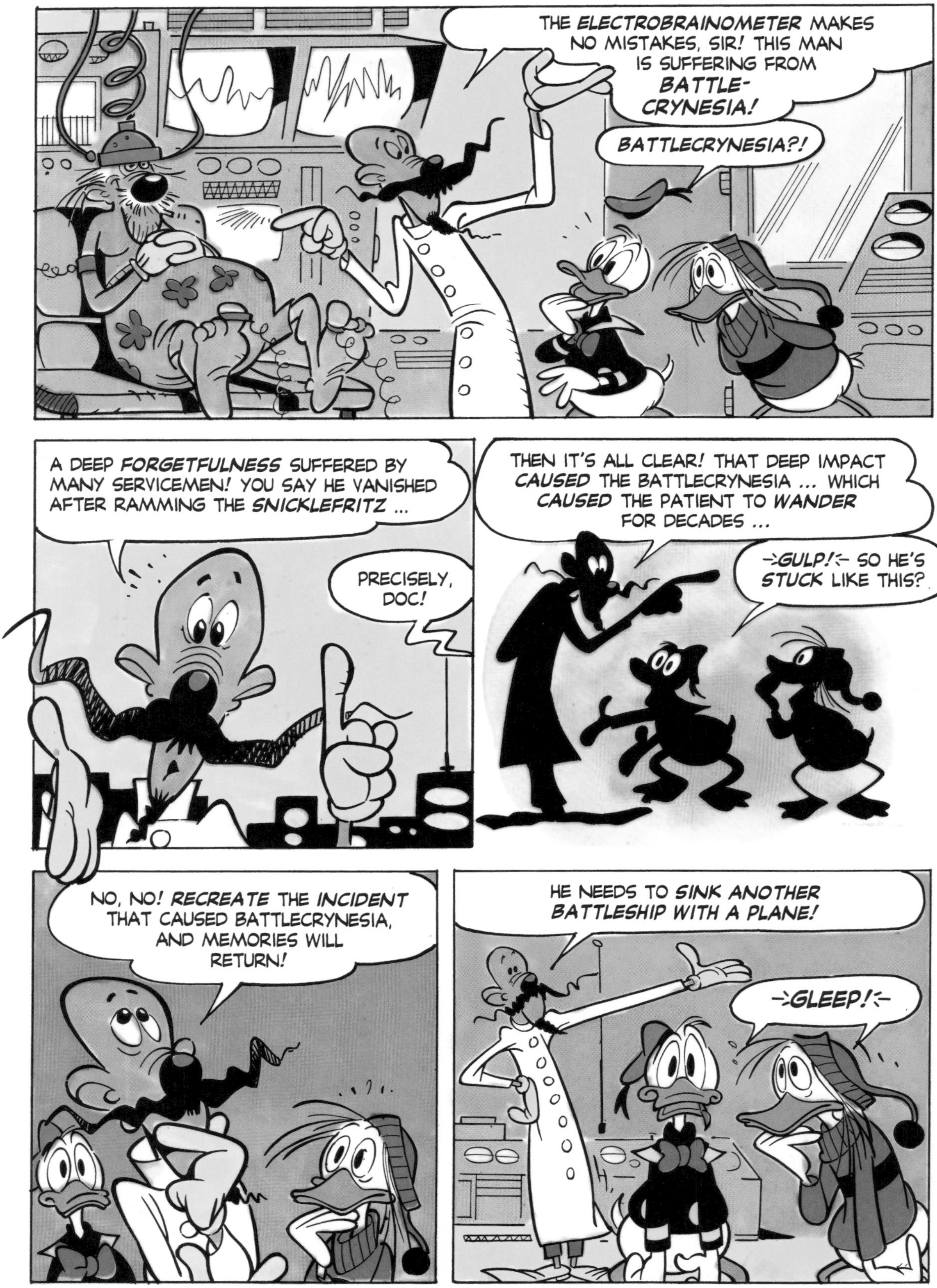
THE ELECTROBRAINOMETER MAKES NO MISTAKES, SIR! THIS MAN IS SUFFERING FROM BATTLE-CRYNESIA!
BATTLECRYNESIA?!
A DEEP FORGETFULNESS SUFFERED BY MANY SERVICEMEN! YOU SAY HE VANISHED AFTER RAMMING THE SNICKLEFRITZ ...
PRECISELY, DOC!
THEN IT'S ALL CLEAR! THAT DEEP IMPACT CAUSED THE BATTLECRYNESIA ... WHICH CAUSED THE PATIENT TO WANDER FOR DECADES ...
GULP! SO HE'S STUCK LIKE THIS?
NO, NO! RECREATE THE INCIDENT THAT CAUSED BATTLECRYNESIA, AND MEMORIES WILL RETURN!
HE NEEDS TO SINK ANOTHER BATTLESHIP WITH A PLANE!
GLEEP!

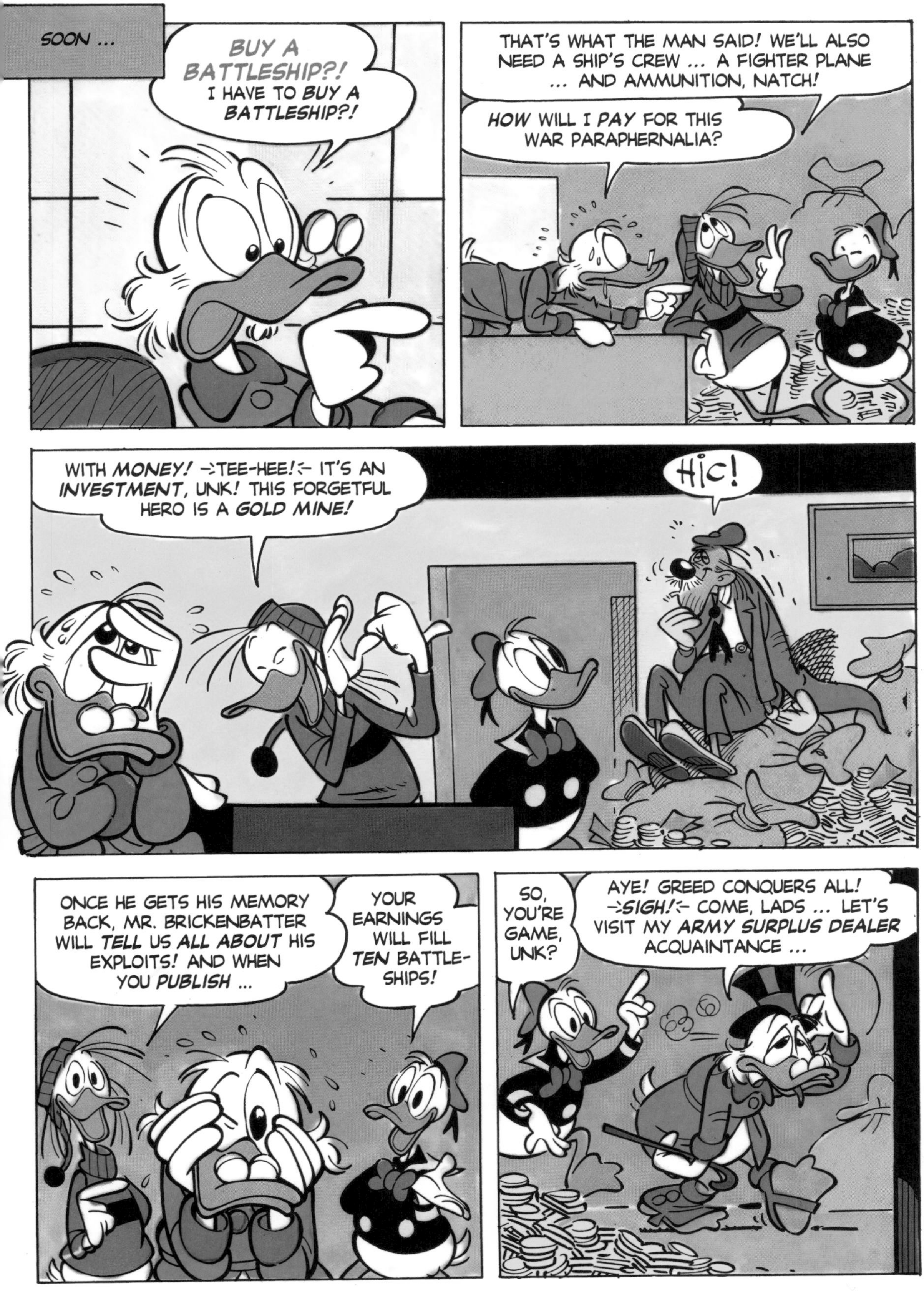
SOON ...
BUY A BATTLESHIP?! I HAVE TO BUY A BATTLESHIP?!
THAT'S WHAT THE MAN SAID! WE'LL ALSO NEED A SHIP'S CREW ... A FIGHTER PLANE ... AND AMMUNITION, NATCH!
HOW WILL I PAY FOR THIS WAR PARAPHERNALIA?
WITH MONEY! →TEE-HEE!← IT'S AN INVESTMENT, UNK! THIS FORGETFUL HERO IS A GOLD MINE!
HIC!
ONCE HE GETS HIS MEMORY BACK, MR. BRICKENBATTER WILL TELL US ALL ABOUT HIS EXPLOITS! AND WHEN YOU PUBLISH ...
YOUR EARNINGS WILL FILL TEN BATTLE-SHIPS!
SO, YOU'RE GAME, UNK?
AYE! GREED CONQUERS ALL! →SIGH!← COME, LADS ... LET'S VISIT MY ARMY SURPLUS DEALER ACQUAINTANCE ...

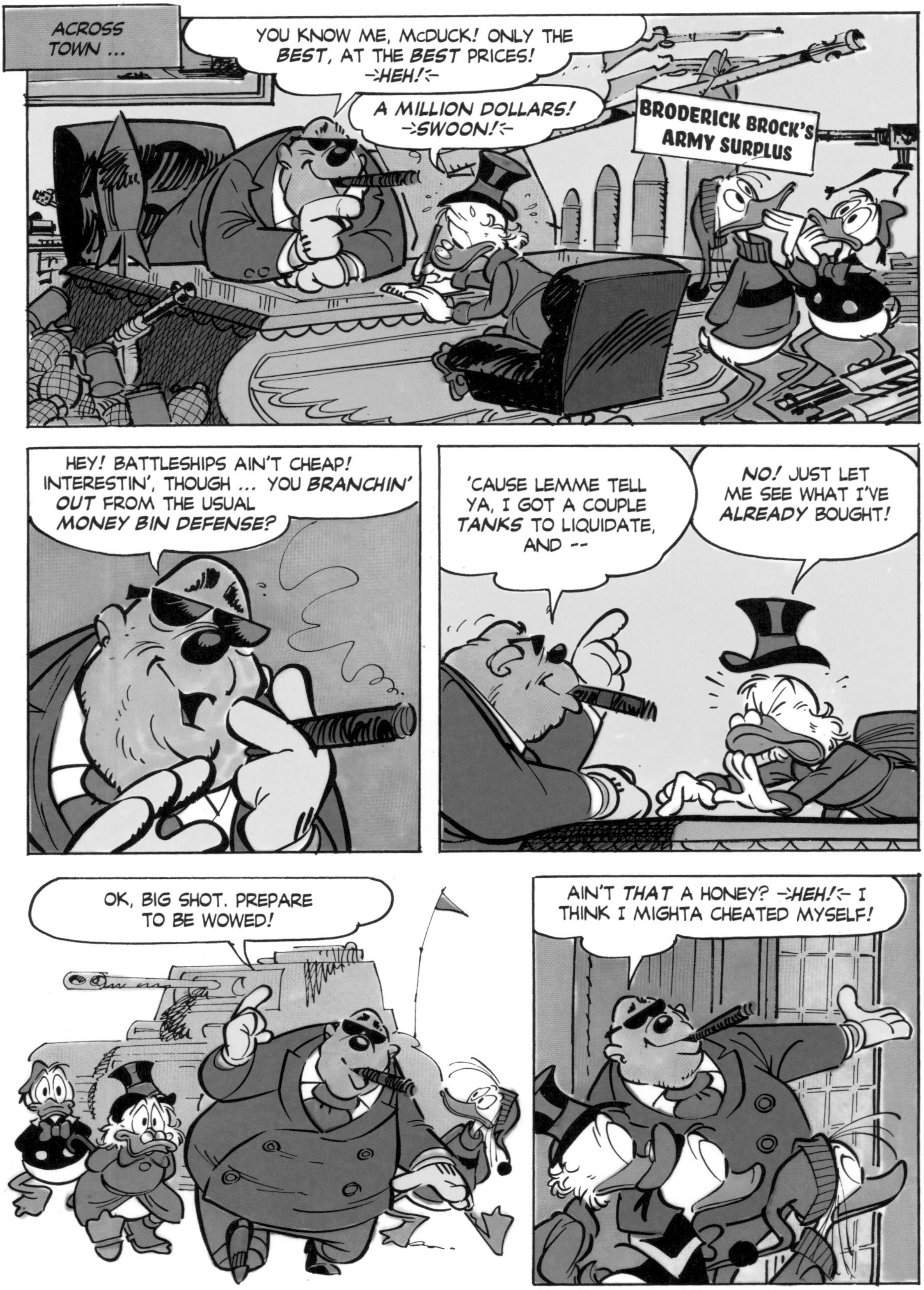
ACROSS TOWN ...
YOU KNOW ME, McDUCK! ONLY THE BEST, AT THE BEST PRICES! -HEH!-
A MILLION DOLLARS! -SWOON!-
BRODERICK BROCK'S ARMY SURPLUS
HEY! BATTLESHIPS AIN'T CHEAP! INTERESTIN', THOUGH ... YOU BRANCHIN' OUT FROM THE USUAL MONEY BIN DEFENSE?
'CAUSE LEMME TELL YA, I GOT A COUPLE TANKS TO LIQUIDATE, AND --
NO! JUST LET ME SEE WHAT I'VE ALREADY BOUGHT!
OK, BIG SHOT. PREPARE TO BE WOWED!
AIN'T THAT A HONEY? -HEH!- I THINK I MIGHTA CHEATED MYSELF!

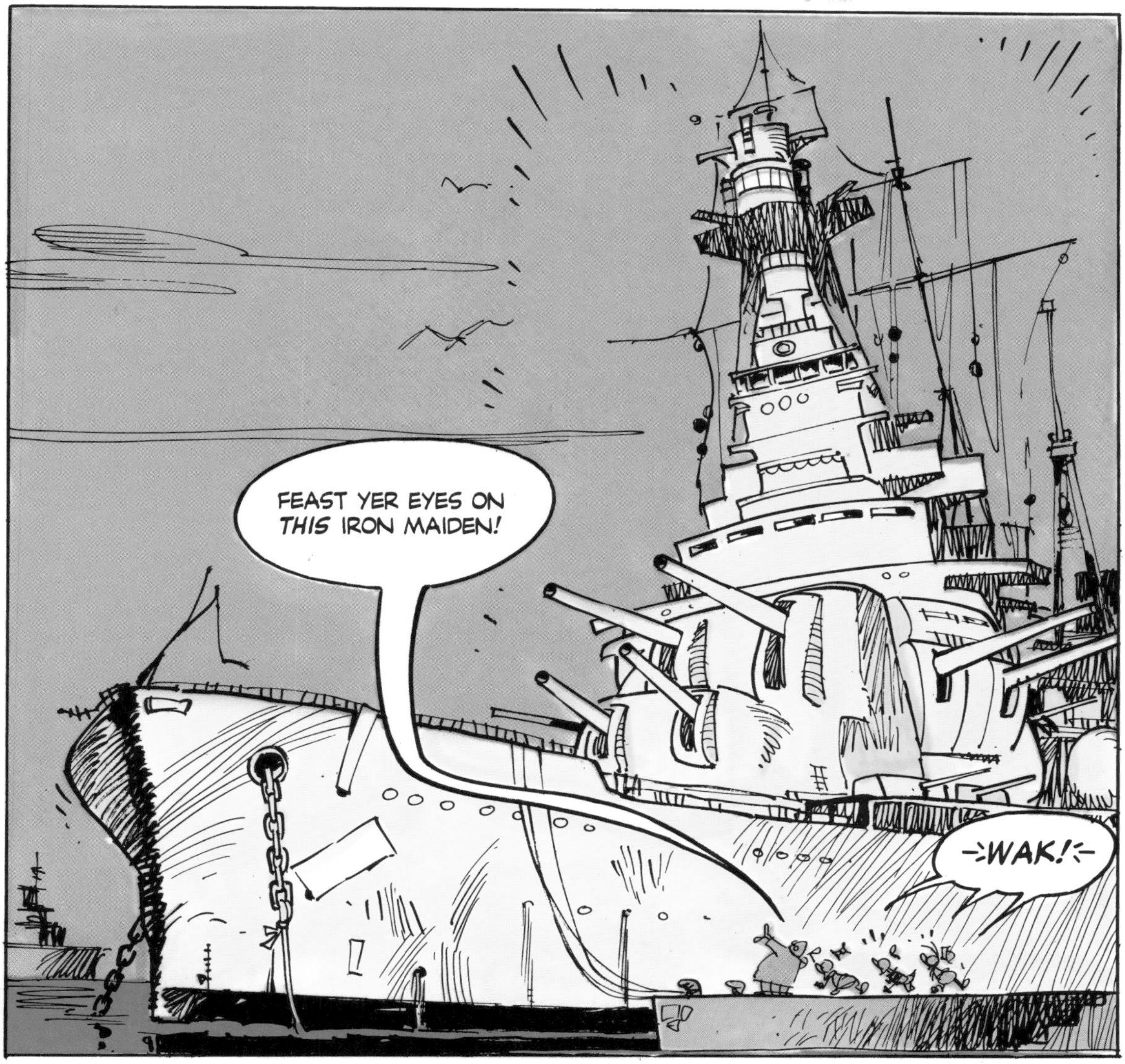
FEAST YER EYES ON *THIS* IRON MAIDEN!
WAK!

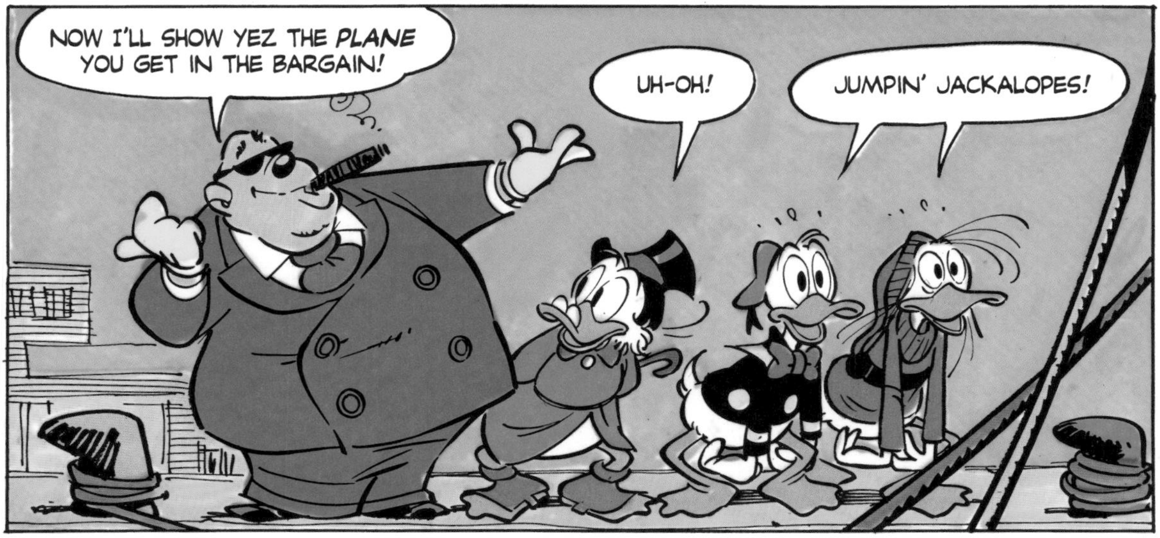
NOW I'LL SHOW YEZ THE *PLANE* YOU GET IN THE BARGAIN!
UH-OH!
JUMPIN' JACKALOPES!

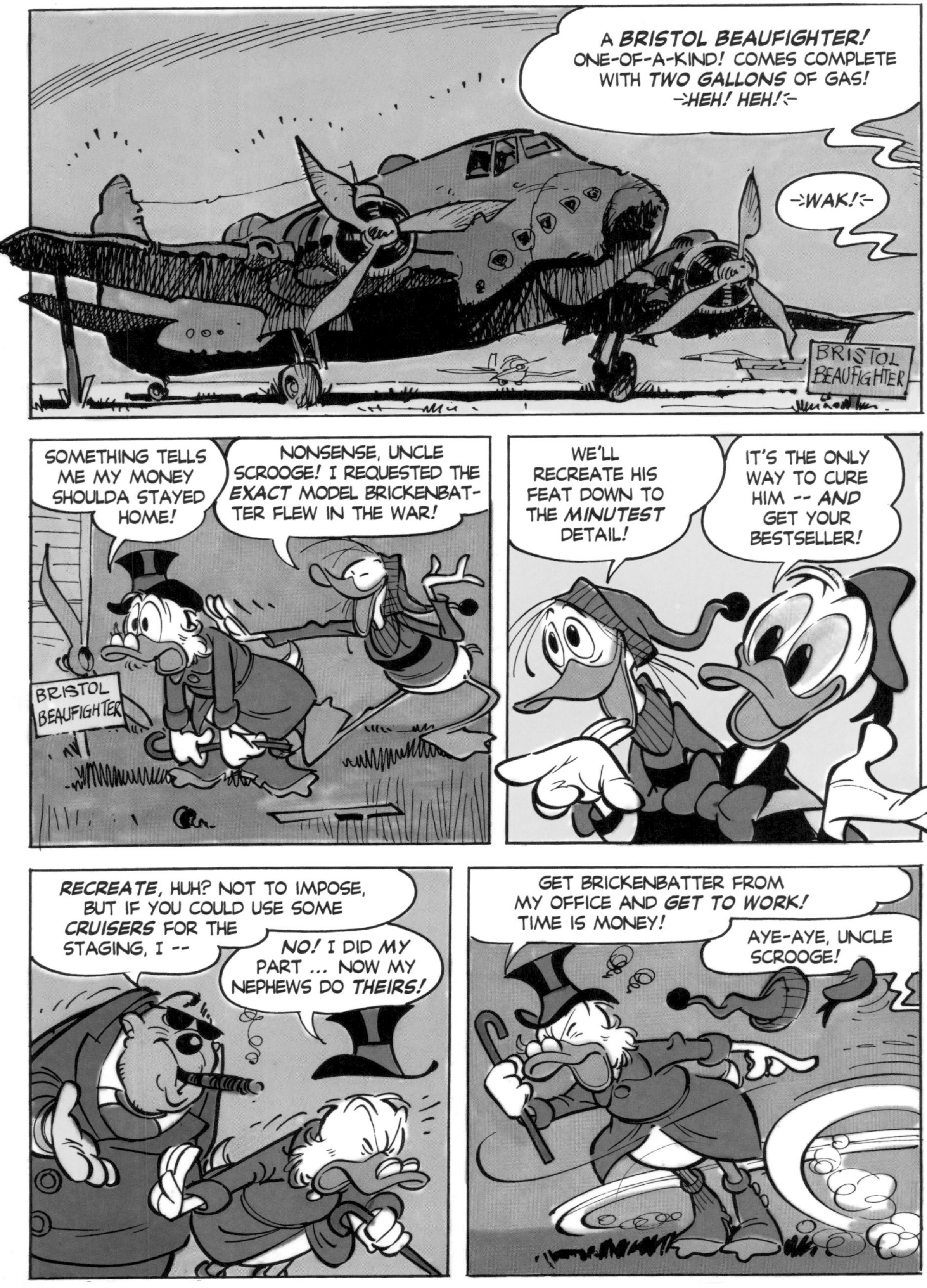
A BRISTOL BEAUFIGHTER! ONE-OF-A-KIND! COMES COMPLETE WITH TWO GALLONS OF GAS! HEH! HEH!
WAK!
BRISTOL BEAUFIGHTER
SOMETHING TELLS ME MY MONEY SHOULDA STAYED HOME!
NONSENSE, UNCLE SCROOGE! I REQUESTED THE EXACT MODEL BRICKENBATTER FLEW IN THE WAR!
BRISTOL BEAUFIGHTER
WE'LL RECREATE HIS FEAT DOWN TO THE MINUTEST DETAIL!
IT'S THE ONLY WAY TO CURE HIM -- AND GET YOUR BESTSELLER!
RECREATE, HUH? NOT TO IMPOSE, BUT IF YOU COULD USE SOME CRUISERS FOR THE STAGING, I --
NO! I DID MY PART ... NOW MY NEPHEWS DO THEIRS!
GET BRICKENBATTER FROM MY OFFICE AND GET TO WORK! TIME IS MONEY!
AYE-AYE, UNCLE SCROOGE!

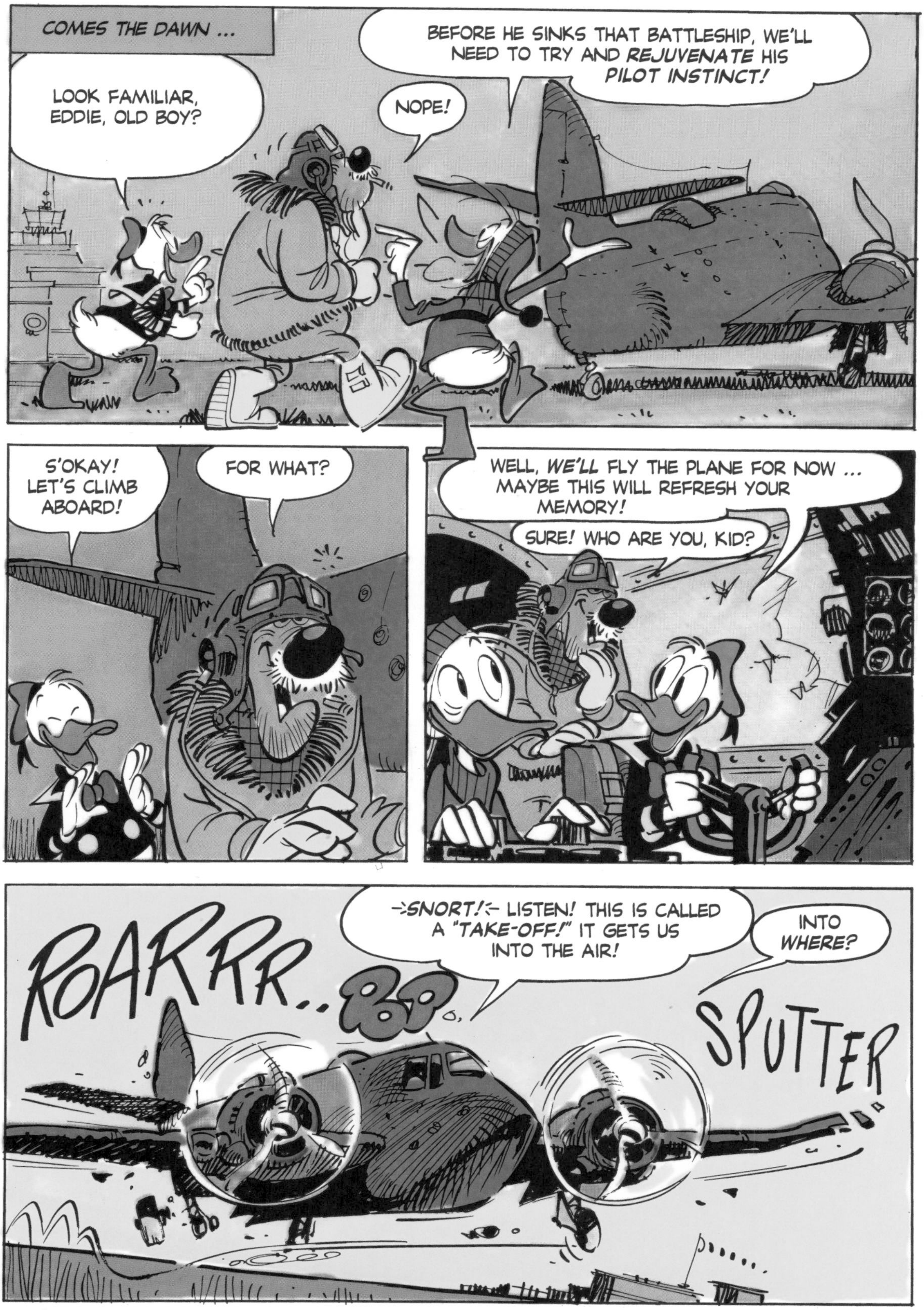
COMES THE DAWN ...
LOOK FAMILIAR, EDDIE, OLD BOY?
NOPE!
BEFORE HE SINKS THAT BATTLESHIP, WE'LL NEED TO TRY AND *REJUVENATE* HIS *PILOT INSTINCT!*
S'OKAY! LET'S CLIMB ABOARD!
FOR WHAT?
WELL, *WE'LL* FLY THE PLANE FOR NOW ... MAYBE THIS WILL REFRESH YOUR MEMORY!
SURE! WHO ARE YOU, KID?
ROARRR...
*SNORT!* LISTEN! THIS IS CALLED A "*TAKE-OFF!*" IT GETS US INTO THE AIR!
INTO *WHERE?*
SPUTTER

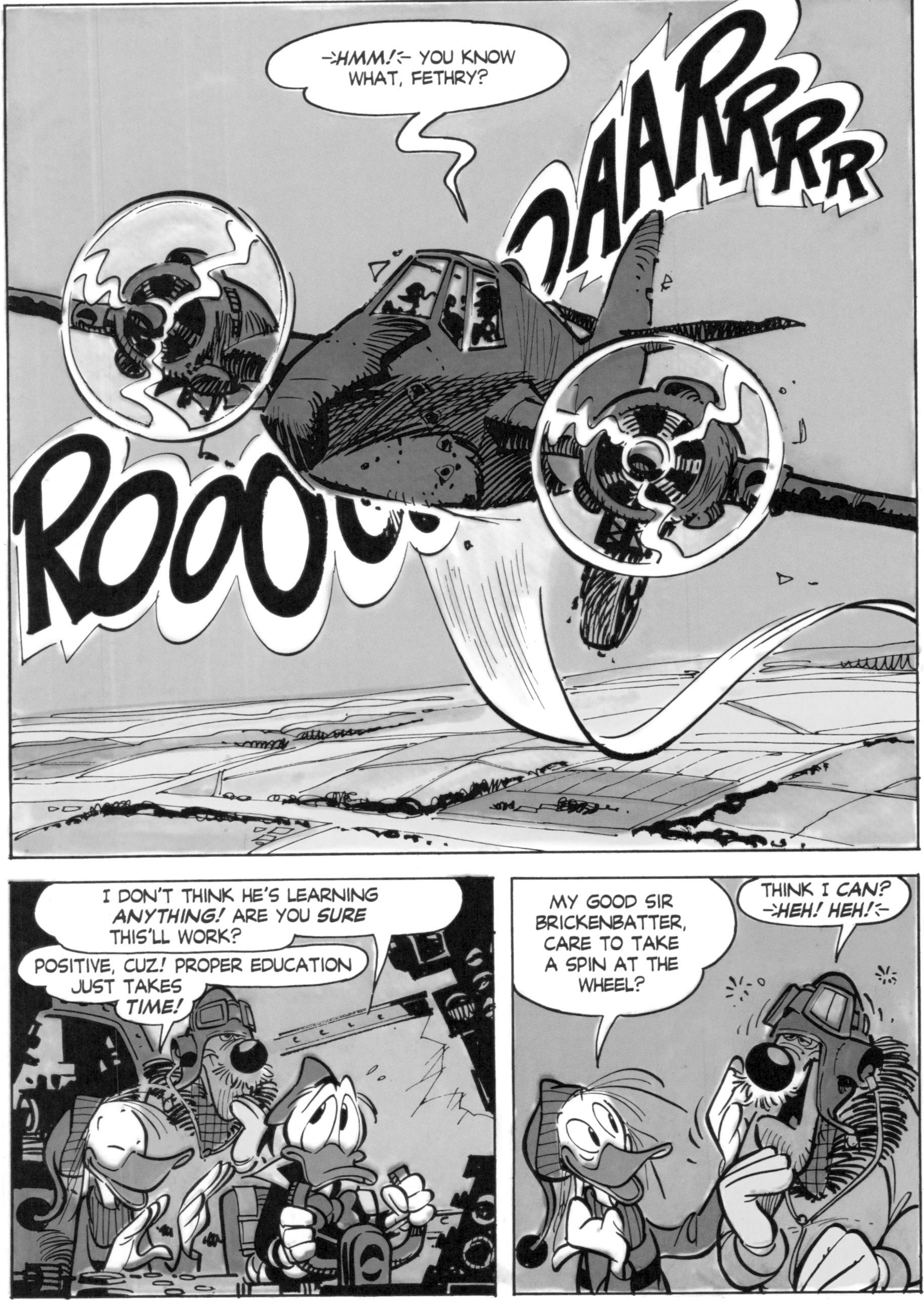

–HMM!– YOU KNOW WHAT, FETHRY?
ROOO
AARRRRR
I DON'T THINK HE'S LEARNING ANYTHING! ARE YOU SURE THIS'LL WORK?
POSITIVE, CUZ! PROPER EDUCATION JUST TAKES TIME!
MY GOOD SIR BRICKENBATTER, CARE TO TAKE A SPIN AT THE WHEEL?
THINK I CAN? –HEH! HEH!–

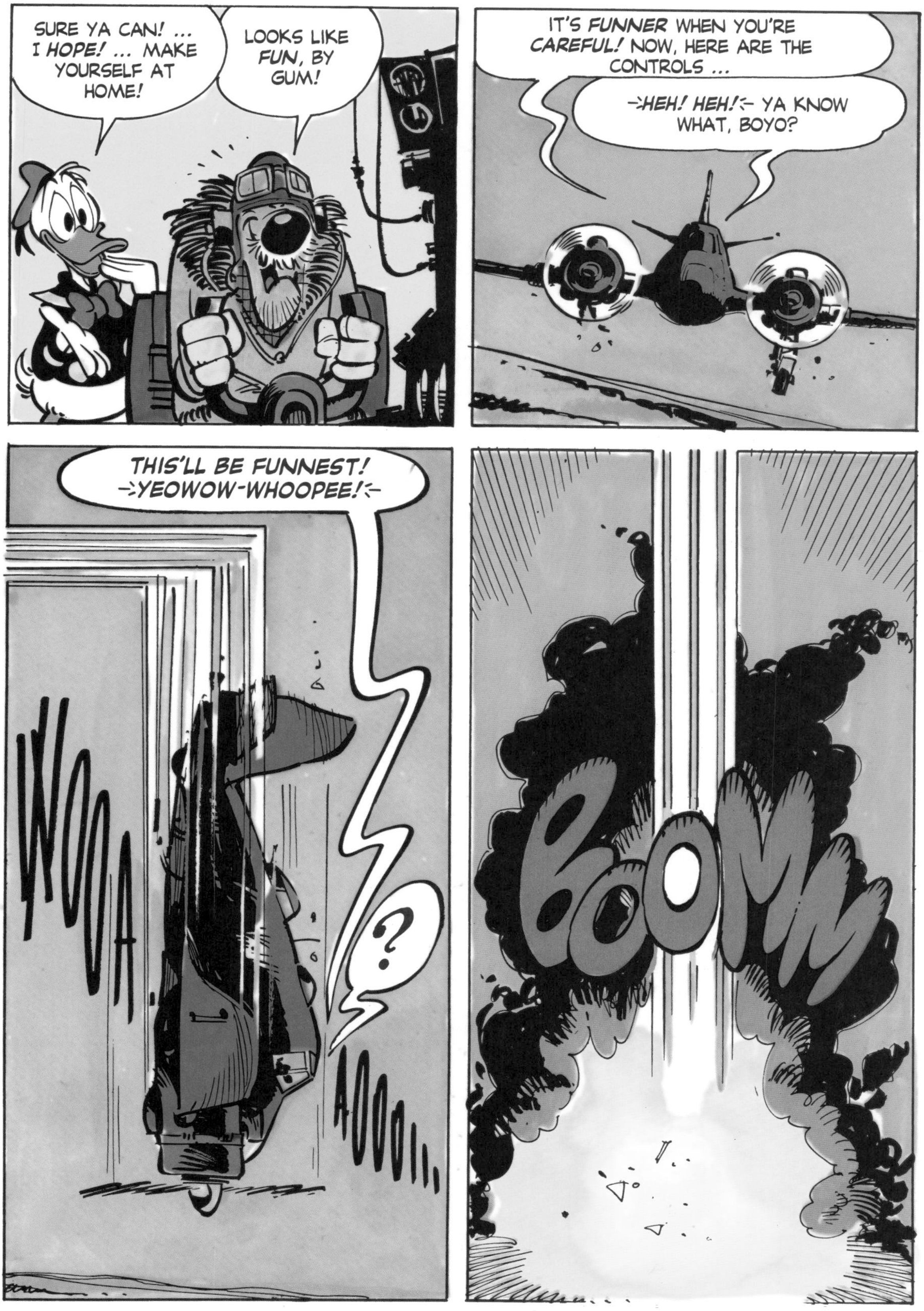
SURE YA CAN! ... I HOPE! ... MAKE YOURSELF AT HOME!
LOOKS LIKE FUN, BY GUM!
IT'S FUNNER WHEN YOU'RE CAREFUL! NOW, HERE ARE THE CONTROLS ...
HEH! HEH! YA KNOW WHAT, BOYO?
THIS'LL BE FUNNEST! YEOWOW-WHOOPEE!
WOOOA
AOOO
?
BOOMM

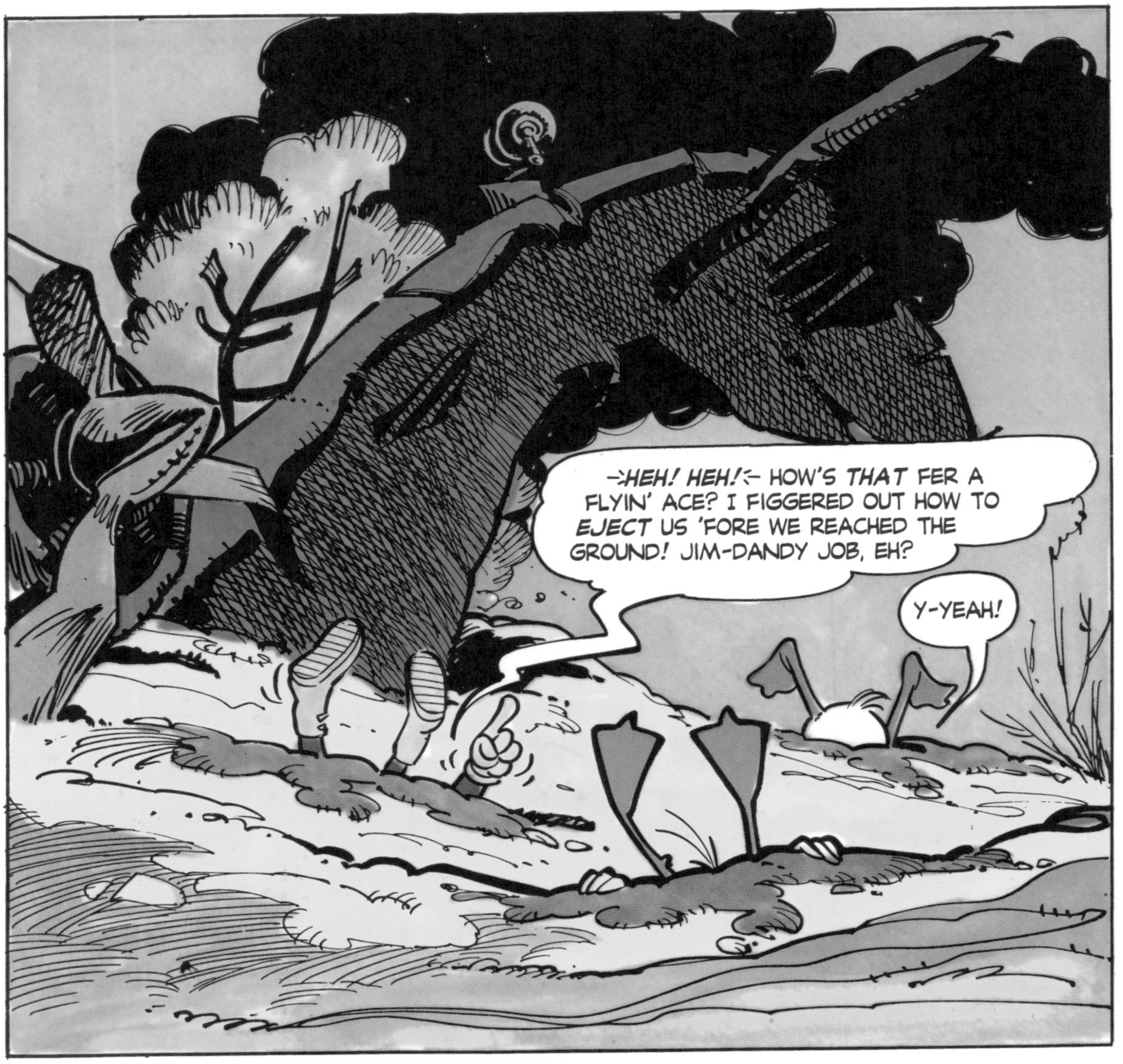

-HEH! HEH!- HOW'S THAT FER A FLYIN' ACE? I FIGGERED OUT HOW TO EJECT US 'FORE WE REACHED THE GROUND! JIM-DANDY JOB, EH?
Y-YEAH!


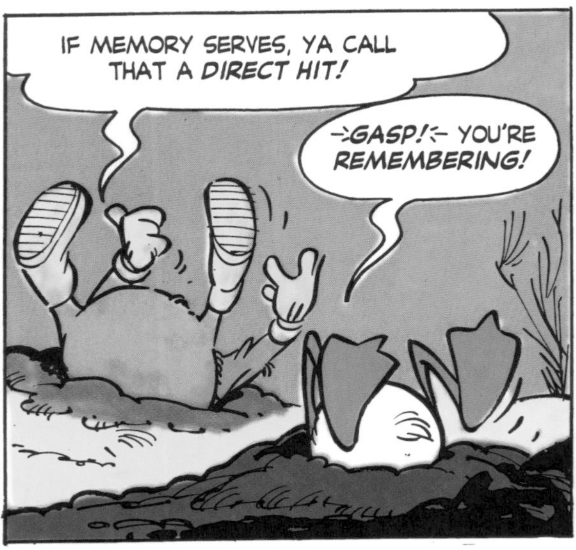

IF MEMORY SERVES, YA CALL THAT A DIRECT HIT!
-GASP!- YOU'RE REMEMBERING!


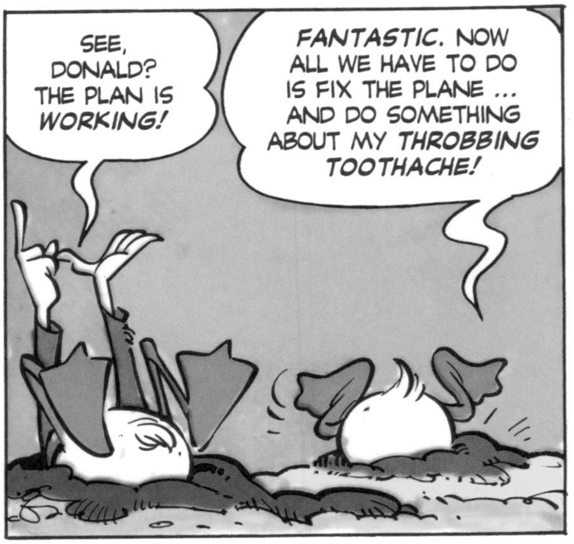

SEE, DONALD? THE PLAN IS WORKING!
FANTASTIC. NOW ALL WE HAVE TO DO IS FIX THE PLANE ... AND DO SOMETHING ABOUT MY THROBBING TOOTHACHE!

MANY HOURS LATER ...

THE BEAUFIGHTER'S GOOD AS NEW! NOW, MR. BRICKENBATTER, A REFRESHER ...

POP GRINGLE

ROAROAR

AAARR...POP

YOU REMEMBER WHAT *"TAKEOFF"* MEANS ... RIGHT?

SURE DO, FREDDERY! ->HEH! HEH!<-

I'LL BE AN ACE AGAIN IN NO TIME! YE GRAB ONTO THESE ... EH, "HANDLE-BARS"...

GRIND

BROOOOOOOOAARRR

AND JUST PULL, MAN, *PULL!*

NO, NO! THAT'S THE WRONG WA--

BOOMM

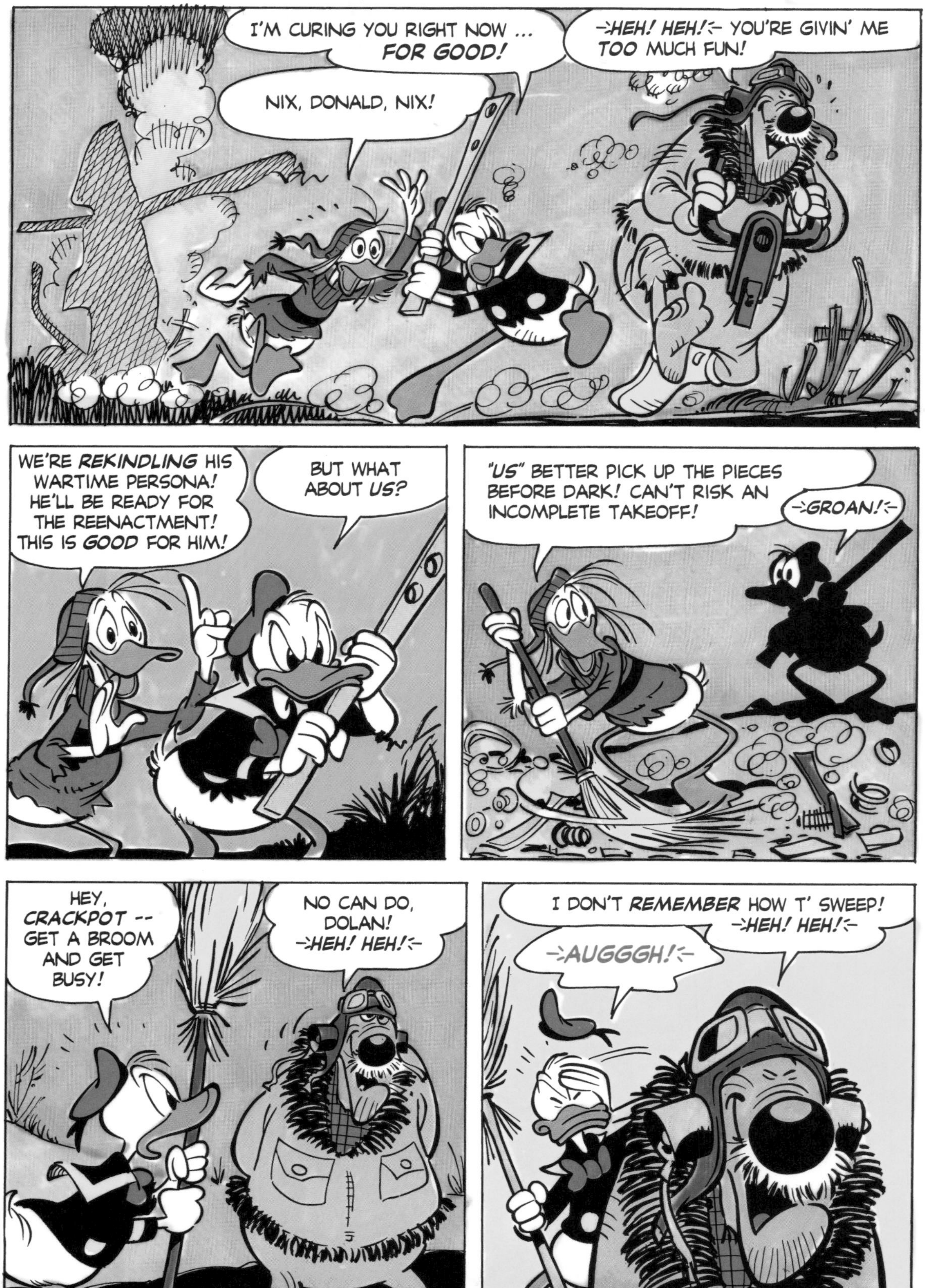
I'M CURING YOU RIGHT NOW ... FOR GOOD!
NIX, DONALD, NIX!
-HEH! HEH!- YOU'RE GIVIN' ME TOO MUCH FUN!
WE'RE REKINDLING HIS WARTIME PERSONA! HE'LL BE READY FOR THE REENACTMENT! THIS IS GOOD FOR HIM!
BUT WHAT ABOUT US?
"US" BETTER PICK UP THE PIECES BEFORE DARK! CAN'T RISK AN INCOMPLETE TAKEOFF!
-GROAN!-
HEY, CRACKPOT -- GET A BROOM AND GET BUSY!
NO CAN DO, DOLAN! -HEH! HEH!-
I DON'T REMEMBER HOW T' SWEEP! -HEH! HEH!-
-AUGGGH!-

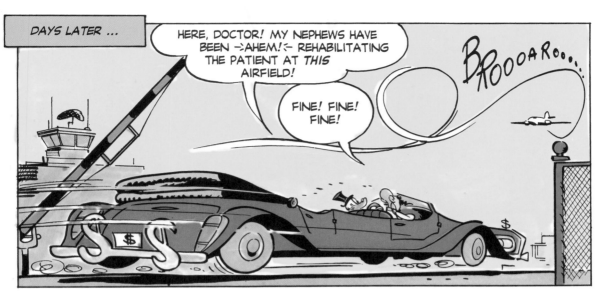

DAYS LATER ...

HERE, DOCTOR! MY NEPHEWS HAVE BEEN →AHEM!← REHABILITATING THE PATIENT AT *THIS* AIRFIELD!

FINE! FINE! FINE!

BROOOAROO....

I THOUGHT YOU MIGHT BE ABLE TO EXAMINE MR. BRICKENBATTER'S CURRENT CONDITION ...

YES! YES!

... AND →*KOFF!*← PRESCRIBE A *CHEAPER* ALTERNATIVE THAN REENACTING--

NO! NO! NO! SINKING A BATTLESHIP IS THE ONLY *SURE CURE!*

WOOOAAAAAA

BUT ... WHAT IS THAT *NOISE*, PRAY TELL?

AN INCOMING BRISTOL BEAUFIGHTER!

WOOOOAAAAA

→AHEM!← LET'S SEE IF OUR FORGETFUL HERO REMEMBERS HOW TO LAND!

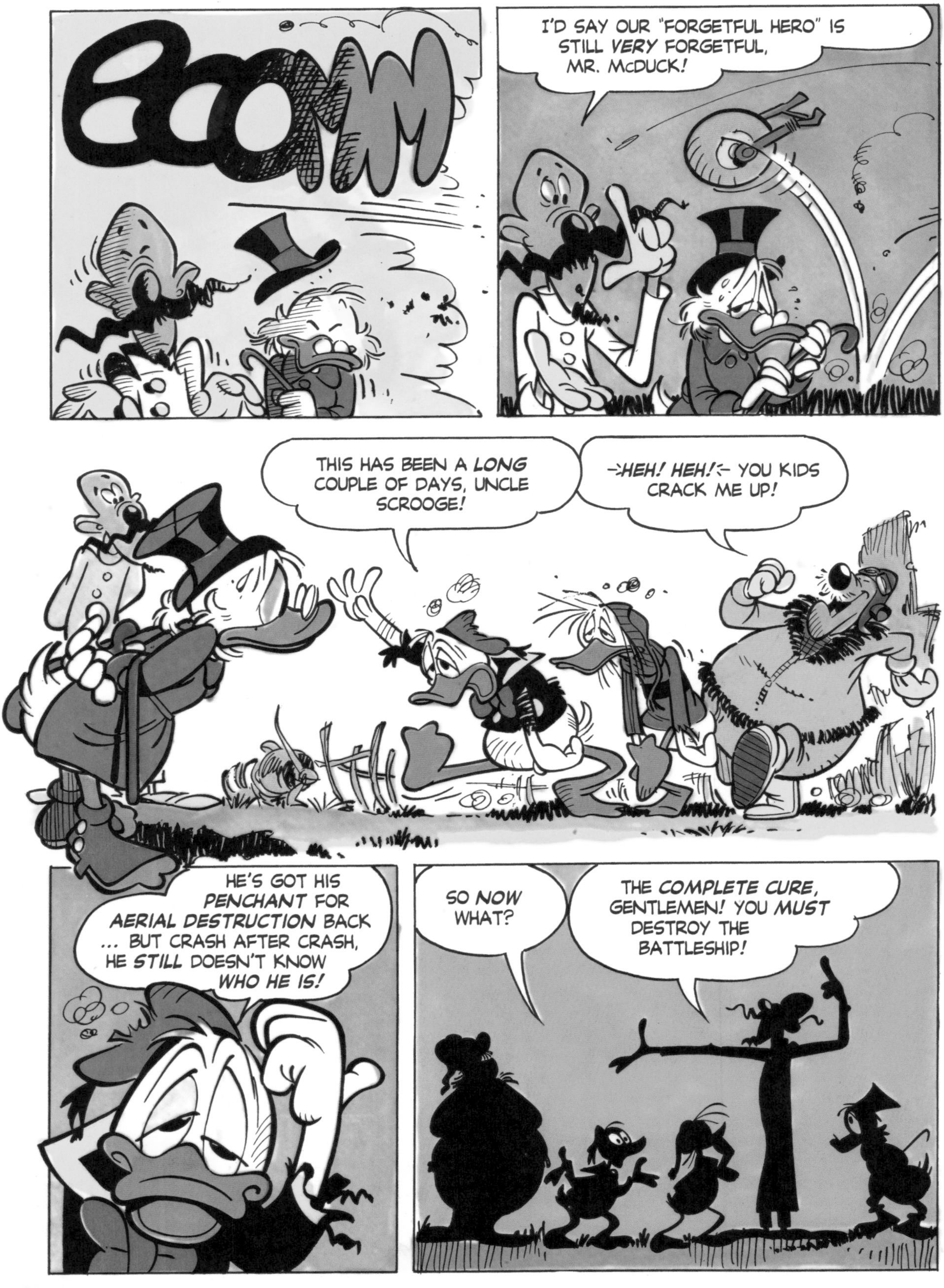
BOOM
I'D SAY OUR "FORGETFUL HERO" IS STILL VERY FORGETFUL, MR. McDUCK!
THIS HAS BEEN A LONG COUPLE OF DAYS, UNCLE SCROOGE!
HEH! HEH! YOU KIDS CRACK ME UP!
HE'S GOT HIS PENCHANT FOR AERIAL DESTRUCTION BACK ... BUT CRASH AFTER CRASH, HE STILL DOESN'T KNOW WHO HE IS!
SO NOW WHAT?
THE COMPLETE CURE, GENTLEMEN! YOU MUST DESTROY THE BATTLESHIP!

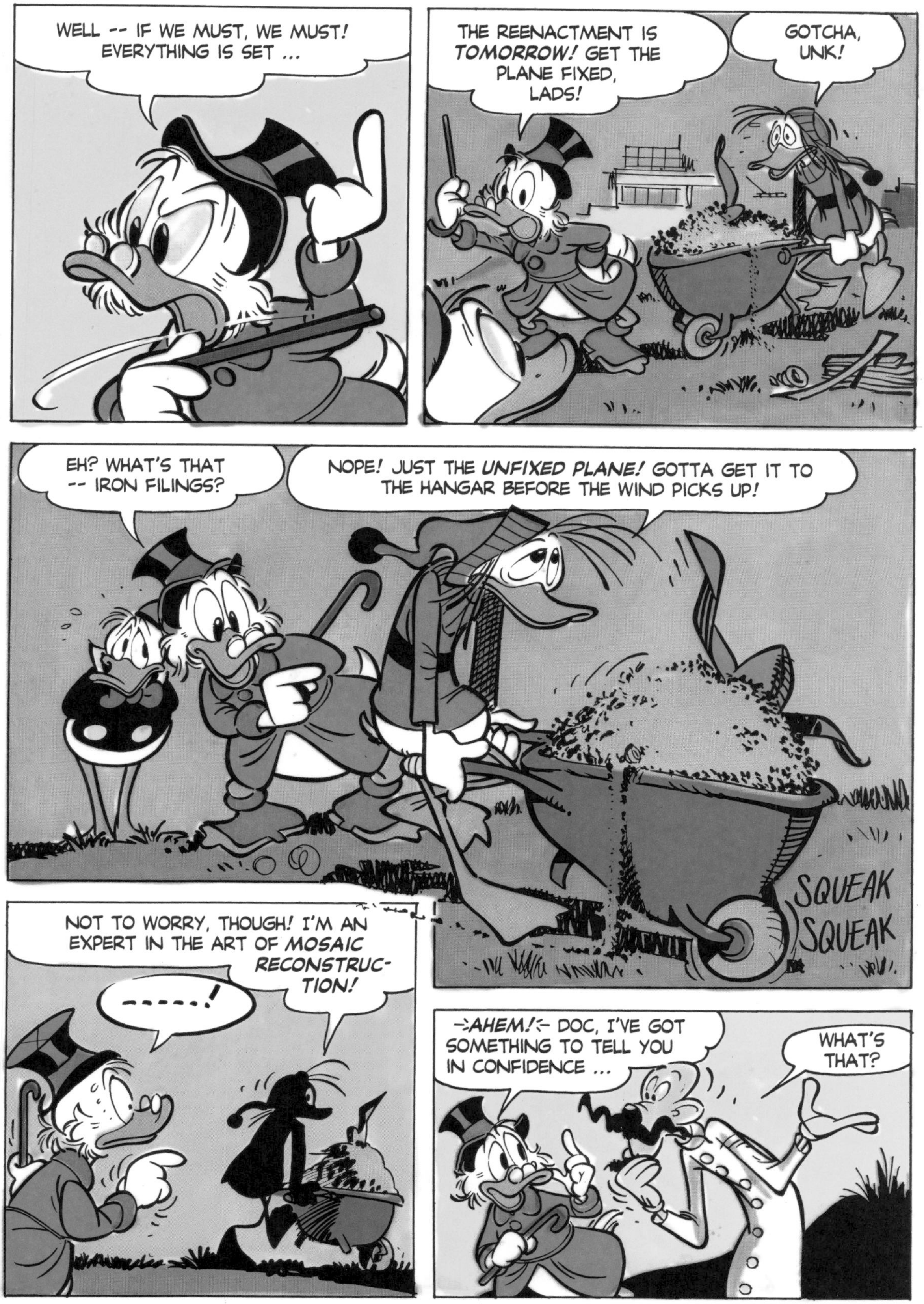
WELL -- IF WE MUST, WE MUST! EVERYTHING IS SET ...
THE REENACTMENT IS *TOMORROW!* GET THE PLANE FIXED, LADS!
GOTCHA, UNK!
EH? WHAT'S THAT -- IRON FILINGS?
NOPE! JUST THE *UNFIXED PLANE!* GOTTA GET IT TO THE HANGAR BEFORE THE WIND PICKS UP!
SQUEAK SQUEAK
NOT TO WORRY, THOUGH! I'M AN EXPERT IN THE ART OF *MOSAIC RECONSTRUC-TION!*
-----!
-*AHEM!*- DOC, I'VE GOT SOMETHING TO TELL YOU IN CONFIDENCE ...
WHAT'S THAT?

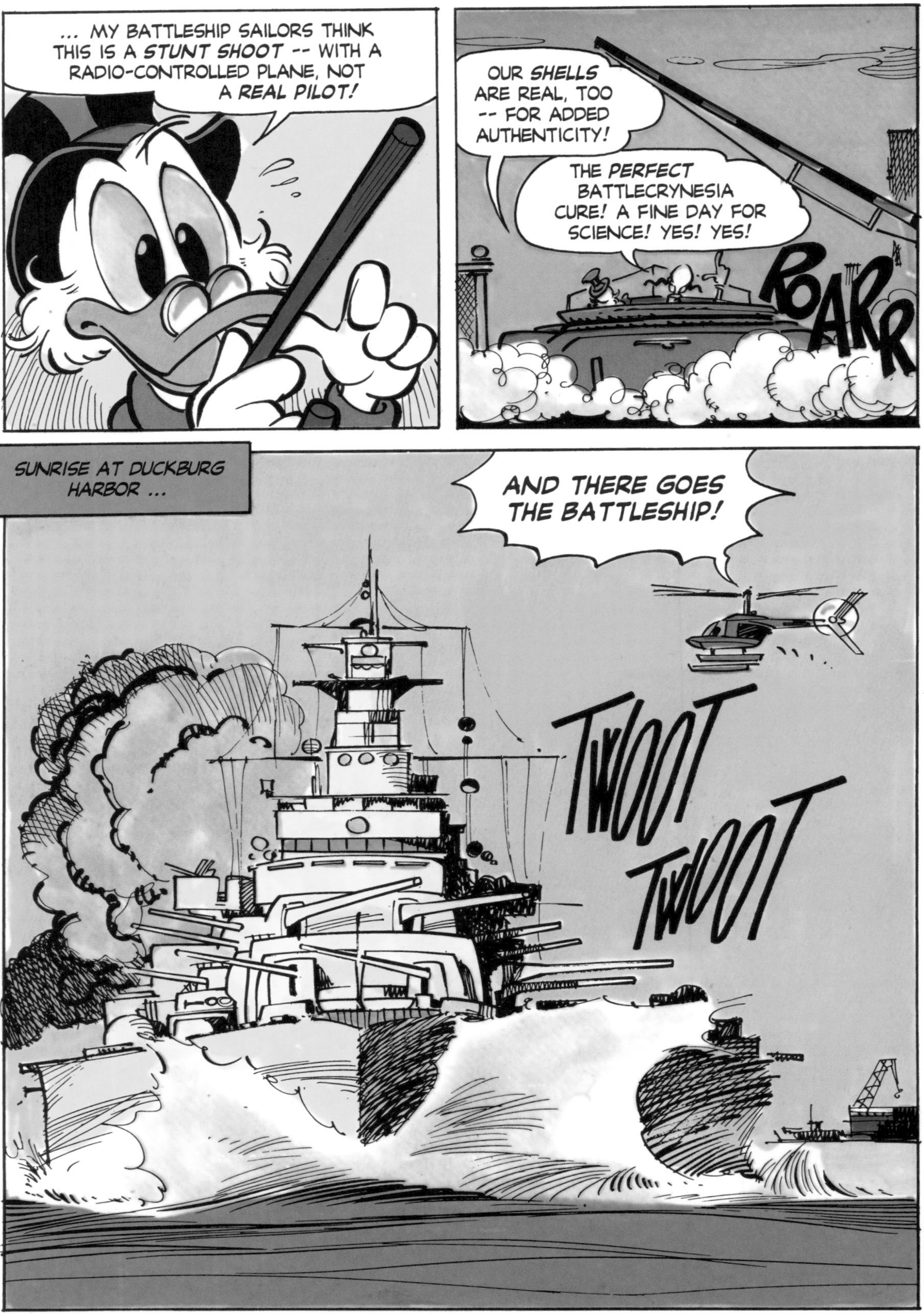
... MY BATTLESHIP SAILORS THINK THIS IS A STUNT SHOOT -- WITH A RADIO-CONTROLLED PLANE, NOT A REAL PILOT!
OUR SHELLS ARE REAL, TOO -- FOR ADDED AUTHENTICITY!
THE PERFECT BATTLECRYNESIA CURE! A FINE DAY FOR SCIENCE! YES! YES!
ROARR
SUNRISE AT DUCKBURG HARBOR ...
AND THERE GOES THE BATTLESHIP!
TWOOT
TWOOT

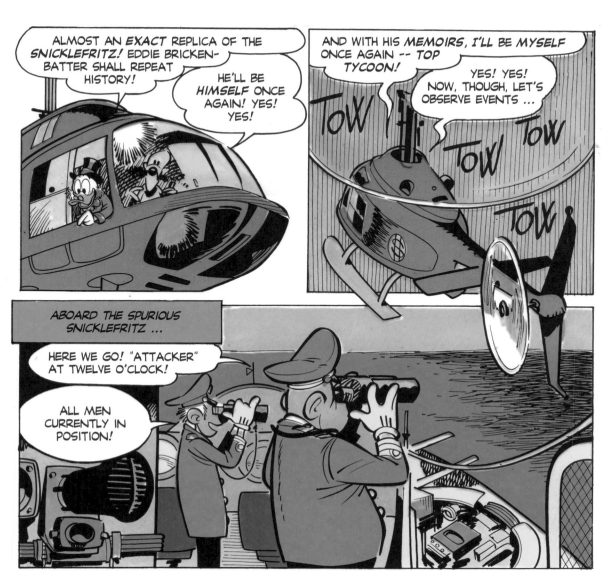

ALMOST AN *EXACT* REPLICA OF THE *SNICKLEFRITZ!* EDDIE BRICKEN-BATTER SHALL REPEAT HISTORY!

HE'LL BE *HIMSELF* ONCE AGAIN! YES! YES!

AND WITH HIS *MEMOIRS*, I'LL BE MYSELF ONCE AGAIN -- *TOP TYCOON!*

YES! YES! NOW, THOUGH, LET'S OBSERVE EVENTS ...

TOW TOW TOW TOW

ABOARD THE SPURIOUS SNICKLEFRITZ ...

HERE WE GO! "ATTACKER" AT TWELVE O'CLOCK!

ALL MEN CURRENTLY IN POSITION!

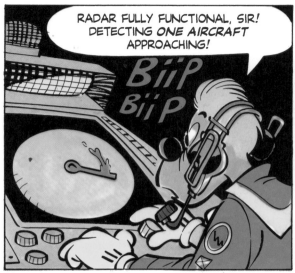

RADAR FULLY FUNCTIONAL, SIR! DETECTING *ONE AIRCRAFT* APPROACHING!

BïïP BïïP

STRANGE! THE PLANE'S AT A *VERY LOW* ALTITUDE ... AS IF IT'S *UNDERWATER!*

181

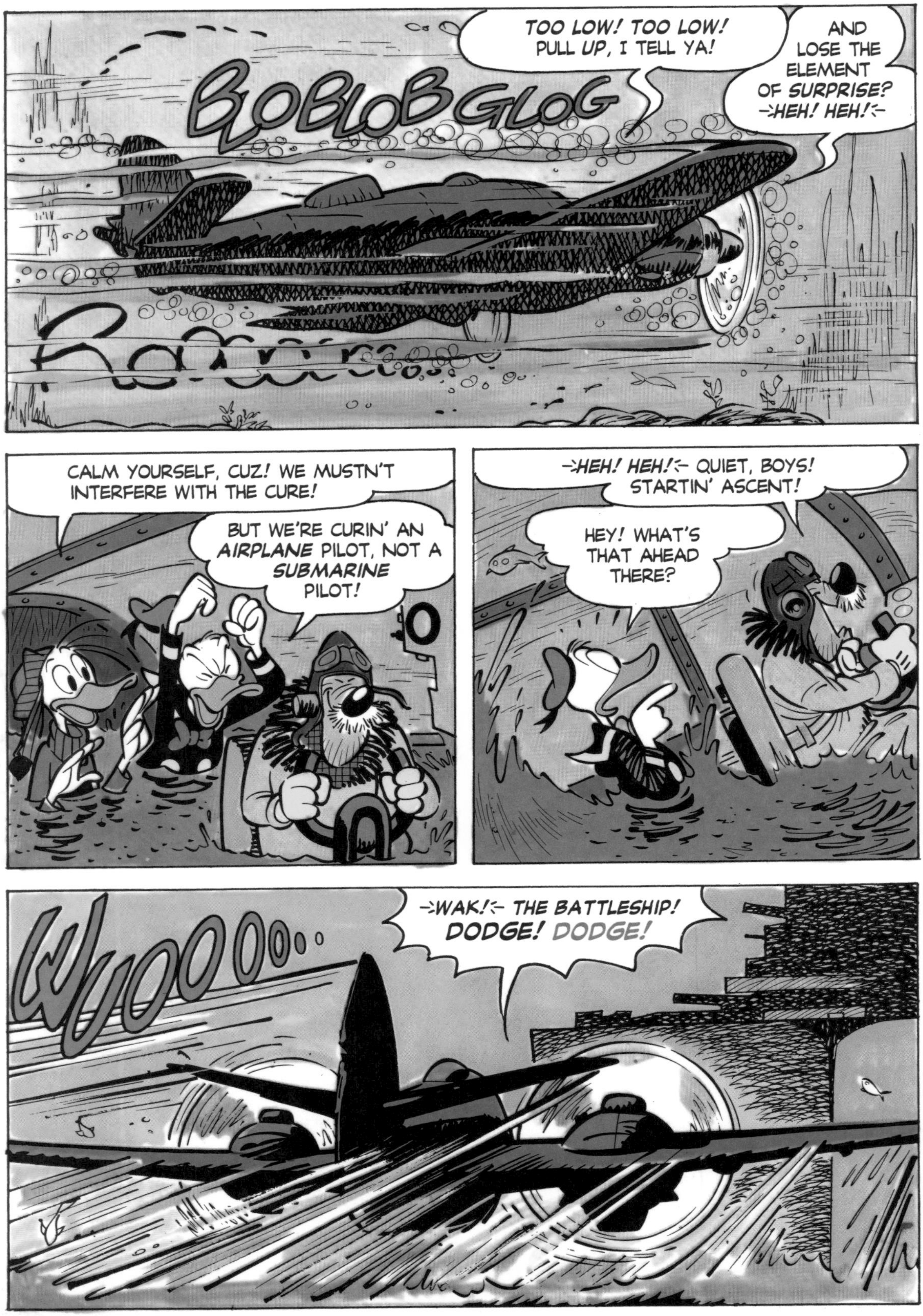
BLOBLOBGLOG
TOO LOW! TOO LOW! PULL UP, I TELL YA!
AND LOSE THE ELEMENT OF SURPRISE? ~HEH! HEH!~
CALM YOURSELF, CUZ! WE MUSTN'T INTERFERE WITH THE CURE!
BUT WE'RE CURIN' AN AIRPLANE PILOT, NOT A SUBMARINE PILOT!
~HEH! HEH!~ QUIET, BOYS! STARTIN' ASCENT!
HEY! WHAT'S THAT AHEAD THERE?
~WAK!~ THE BATTLESHIP! DODGE! DODGE!

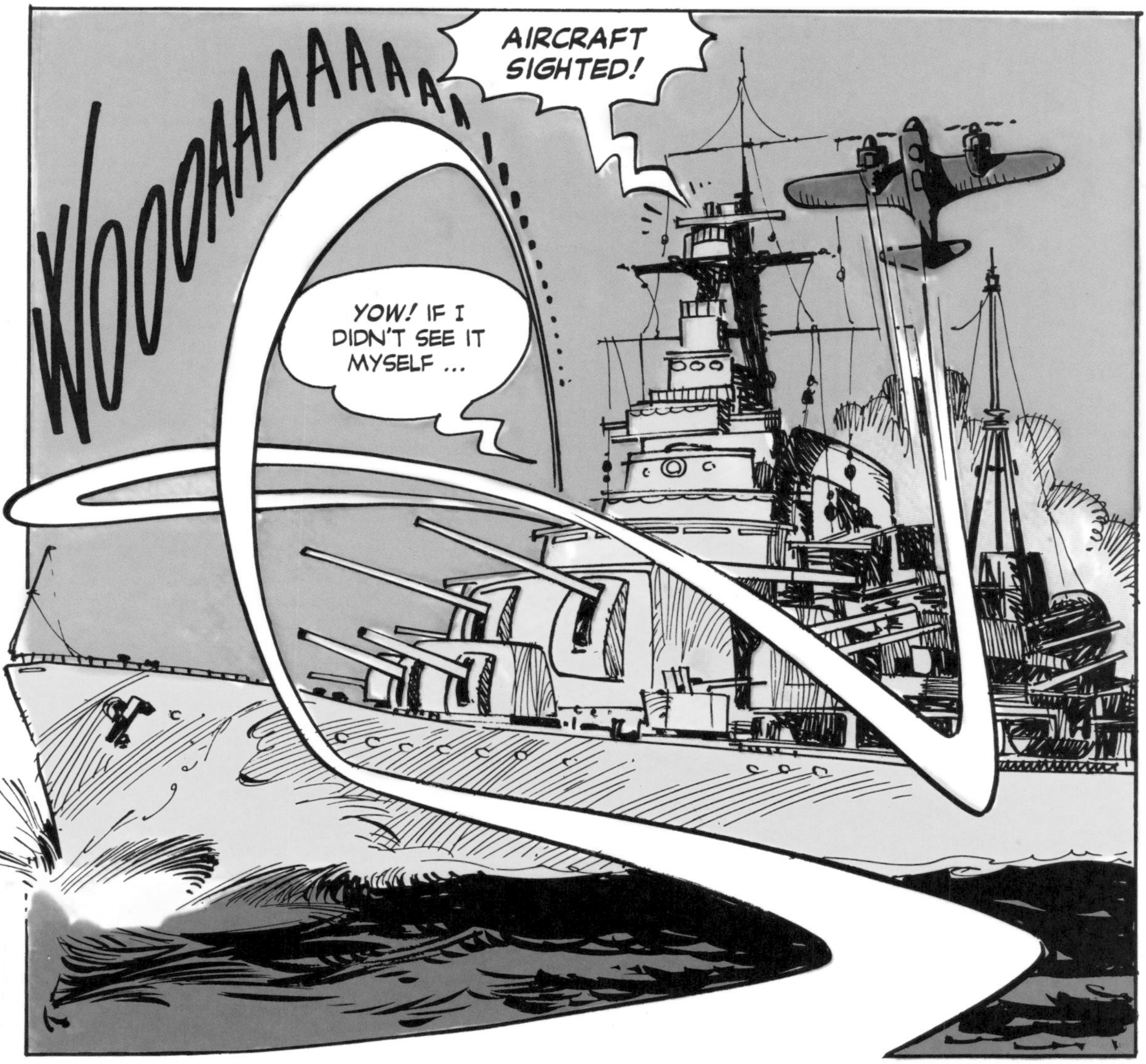
AIRCRAFT SIGHTED!
WOOOAAAAAAAA
YOW! IF I DIDN'T SEE IT MYSELF ...

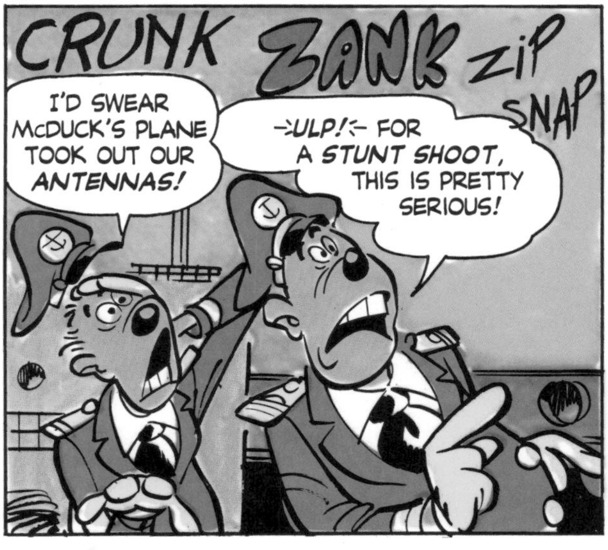
CRUNK ZANK ZIP SNAP
I'D SWEAR McDUCK'S PLANE TOOK OUT OUR ANTENNAS!
–ULP!– FOR A STUNT SHOOT, THIS IS PRETTY SERIOUS!

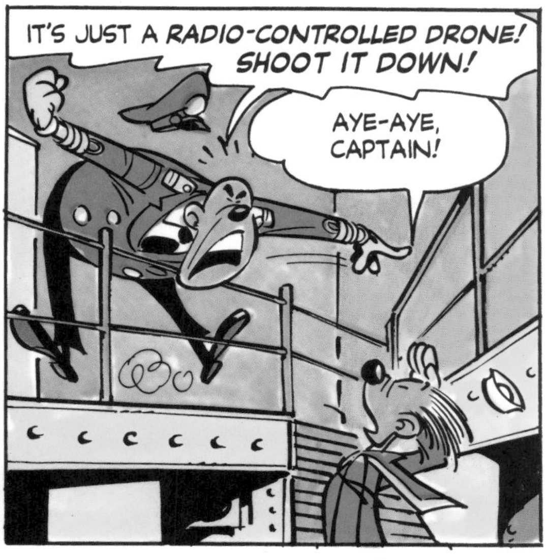
IT'S JUST A RADIO-CONTROLLED DRONE! SHOOT IT DOWN!
AYE-AYE, CAPTAIN!

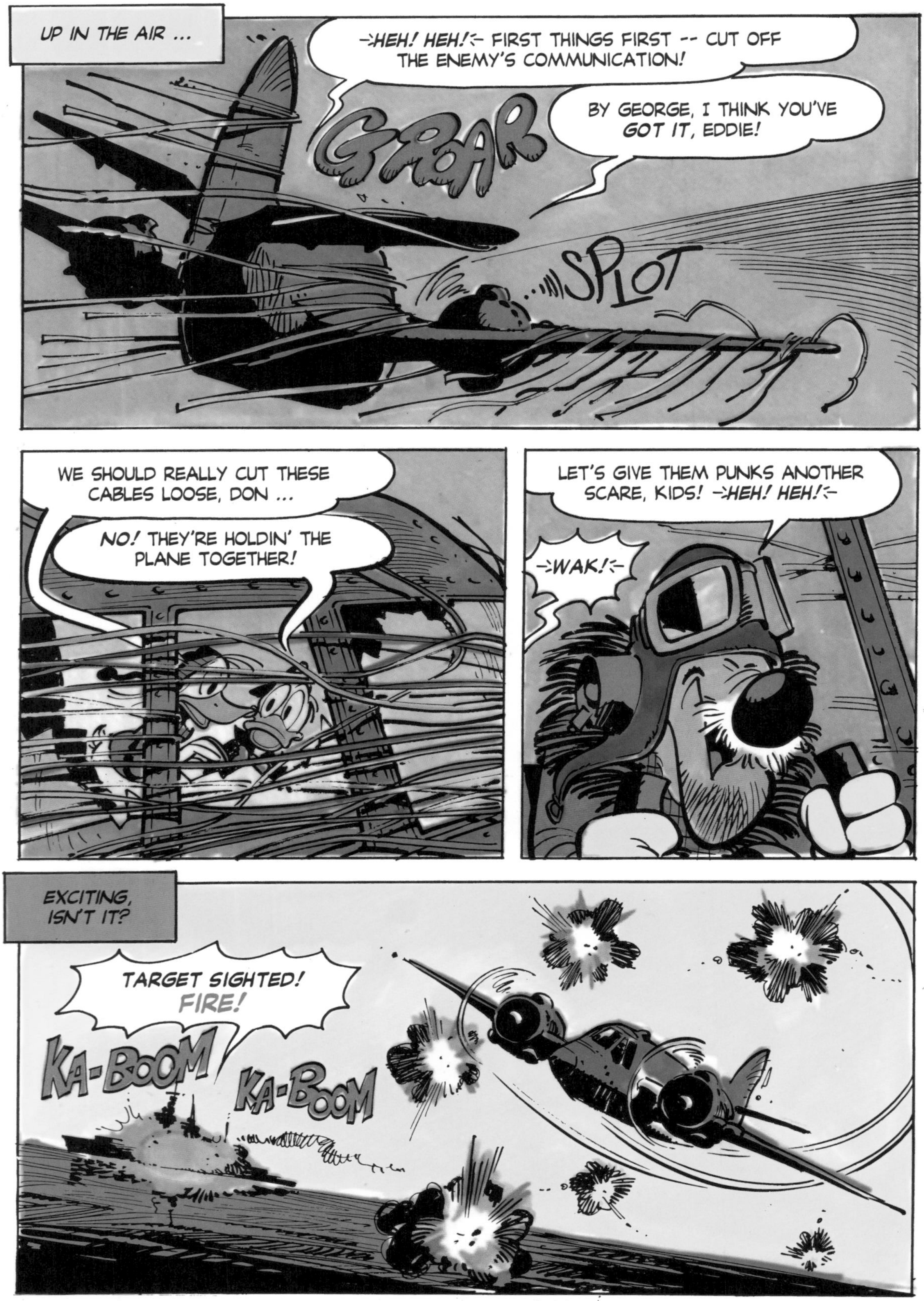
UP IN THE AIR ...
-HEH! HEH!- FIRST THINGS FIRST -- CUT OFF THE ENEMY'S COMMUNICATION!
GROAR
BY GEORGE, I THINK YOU'VE GOT IT, EDDIE!
SPLOT
WE SHOULD REALLY CUT THESE CABLES LOOSE, DON ...
NO! THEY'RE HOLDIN' THE PLANE TOGETHER!
LET'S GIVE THEM PUNKS ANOTHER SCARE, KIDS! -HEH! HEH!-
-WAK!-
EXCITING, ISN'T IT?
TARGET SIGHTED! FIRE!
KA-BOOM
KA-BOOM

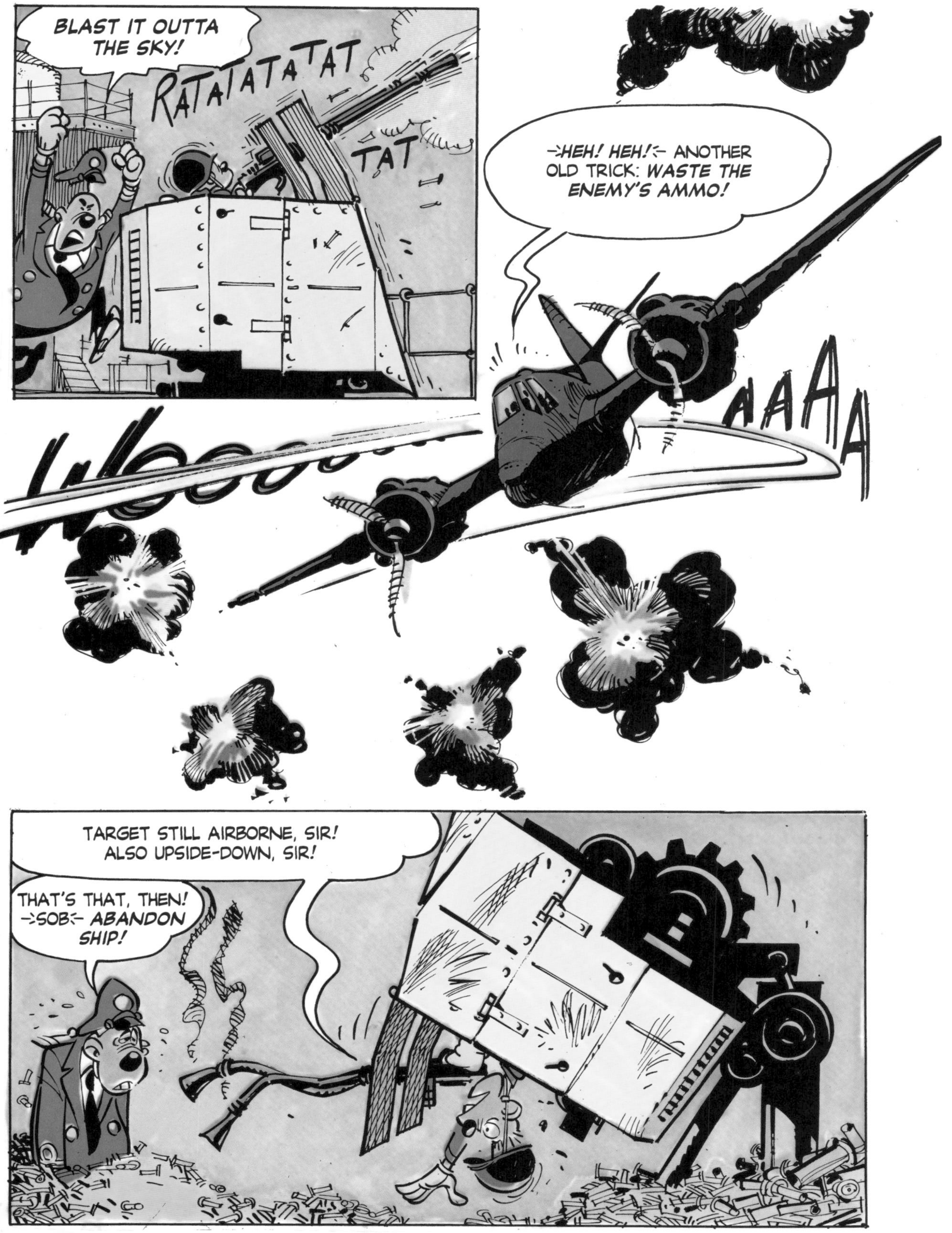
BLAST IT OUTTA THE SKY!
RATATATATAT
TAT
–HEH! HEH!– ANOTHER OLD TRICK: WASTE THE ENEMY'S AMMO!
TARGET STILL AIRBORNE, SIR! ALSO UPSIDE-DOWN, SIR!
THAT'S THAT, THEN! –SOB– ABANDON SHIP!

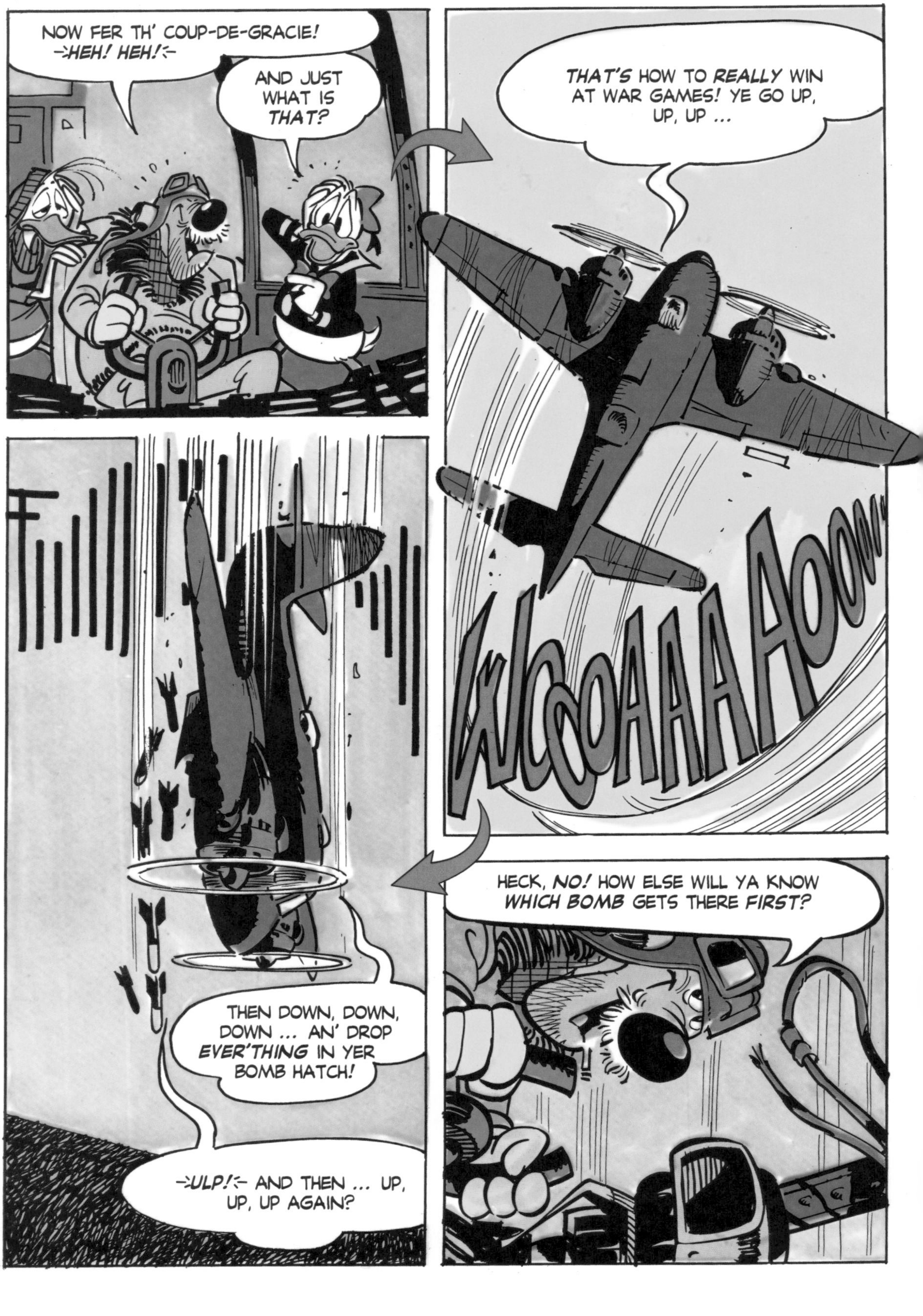
NOW FER TH' COUP-DE-GRACIE! —HEH! HEH!—
AND JUST WHAT IS THAT?
THAT'S HOW TO REALLY WIN AT WAR GAMES! YE GO UP, UP, UP ...
WOOAAAAAOOO
THEN DOWN, DOWN, DOWN ... AN' DROP EVER'THING IN YER BOMB HATCH!
—ULP!— AND THEN ... UP, UP, UP AGAIN?
HECK, NO! HOW ELSE WILL YA KNOW WHICH BOMB GETS THERE FIRST?

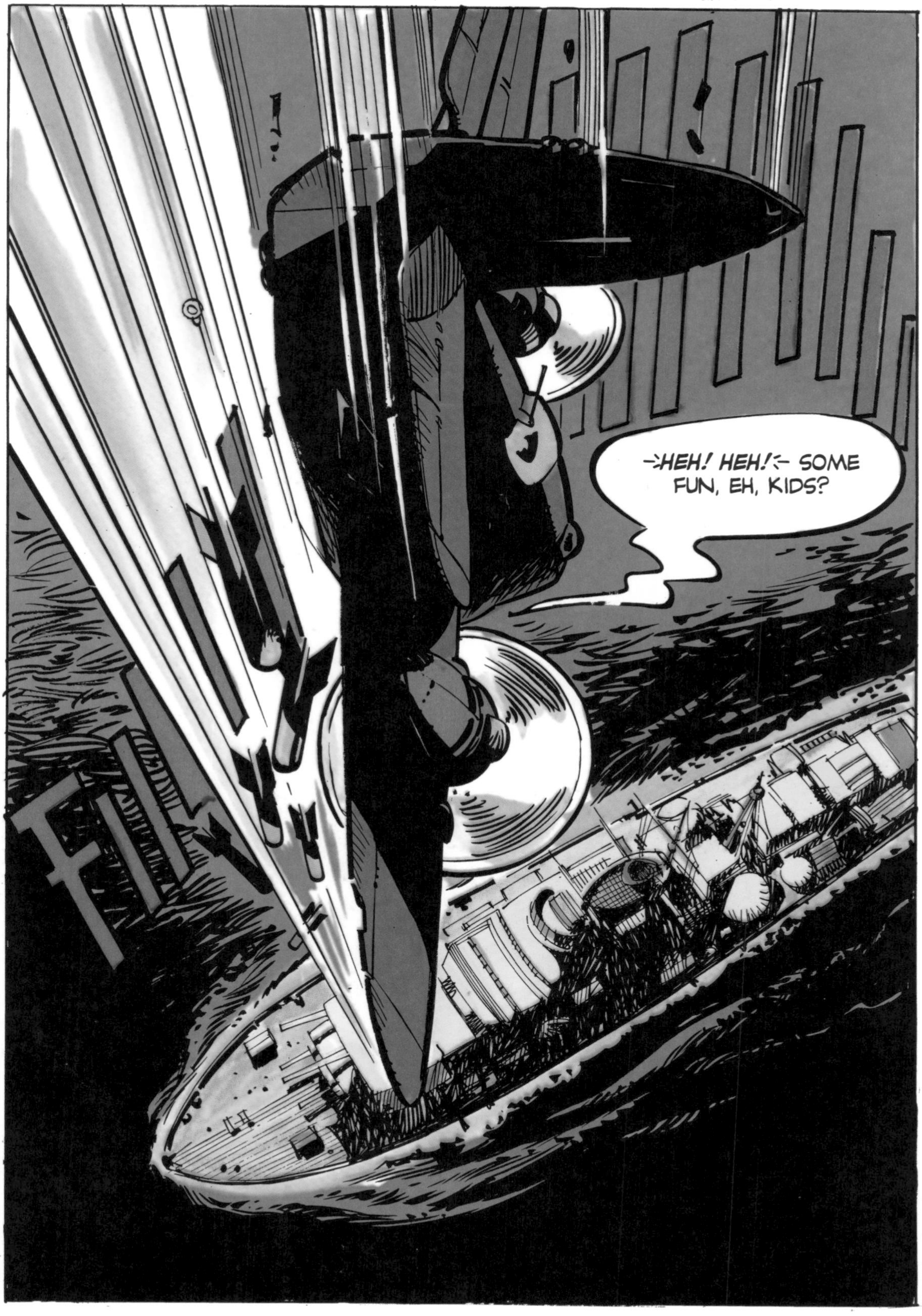

-HEH! HEH!- SOME FUN, EH, KIDS?

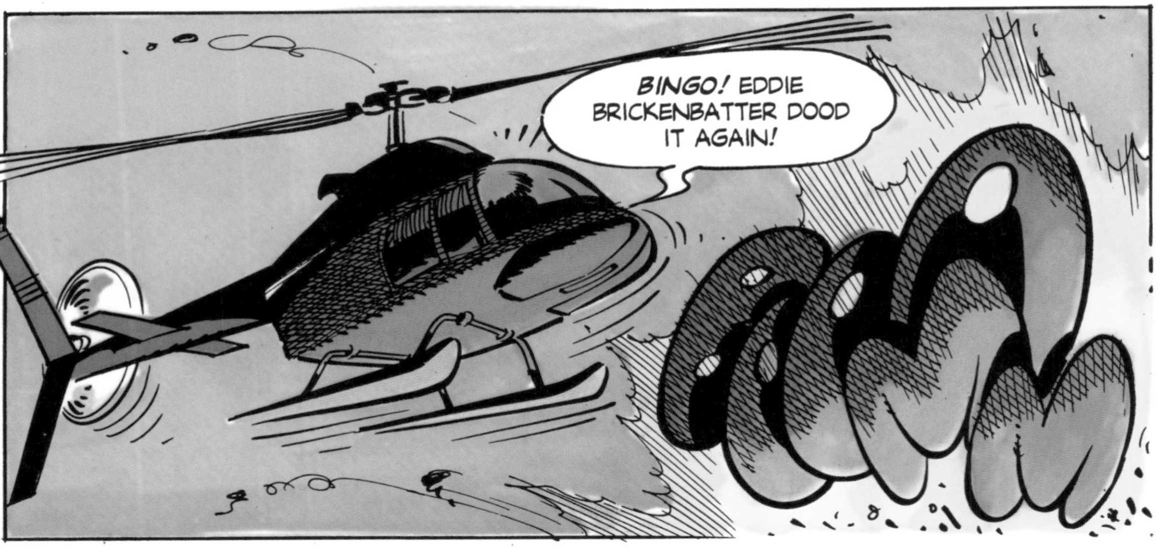
BINGO! EDDIE BRICKENBATTER DOOD IT AGAIN!
BAM

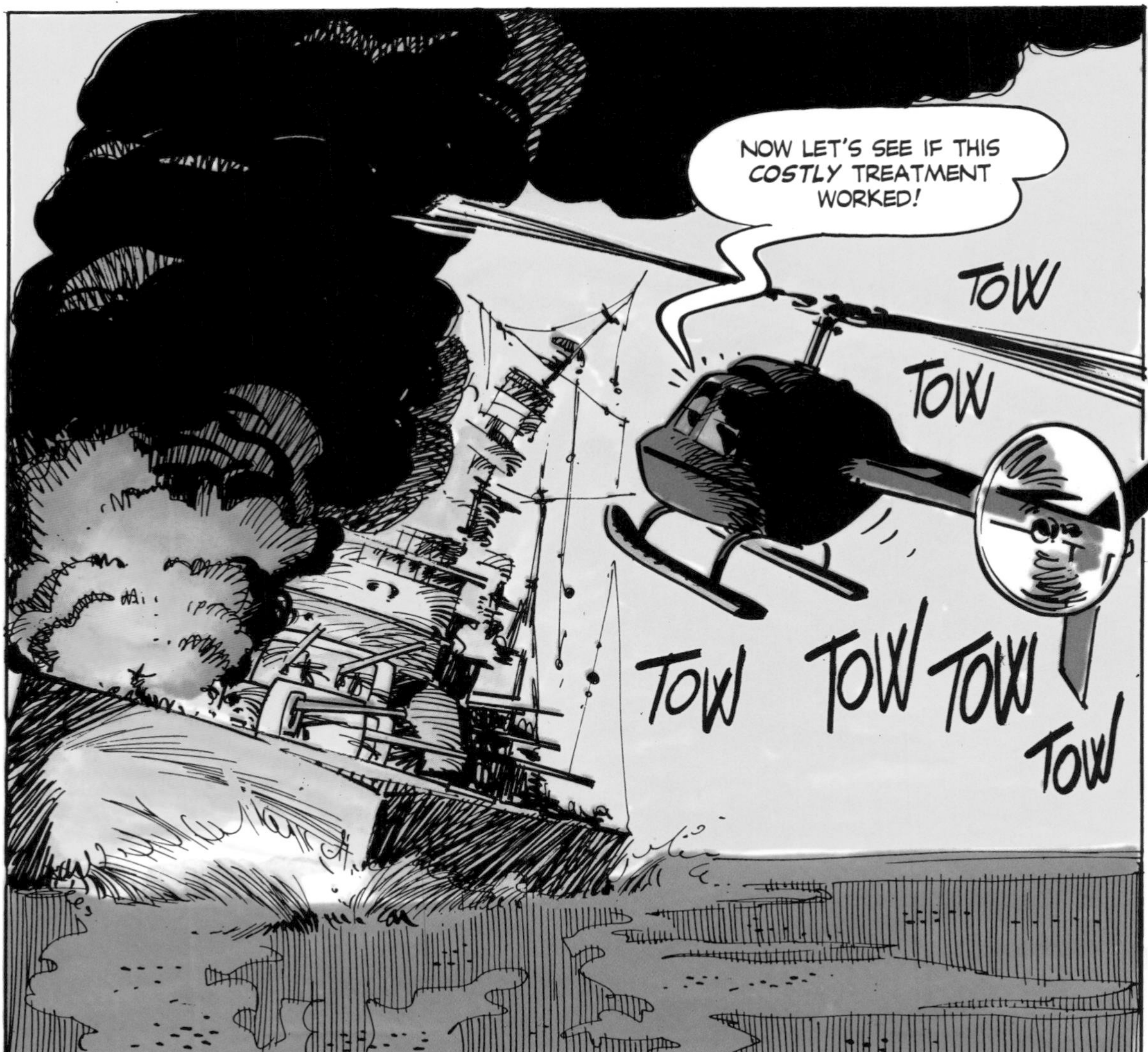
NOW LET'S SEE IF THIS COSTLY TREATMENT WORKED!
TOW
TOW
TOW TOW TOW
TOW

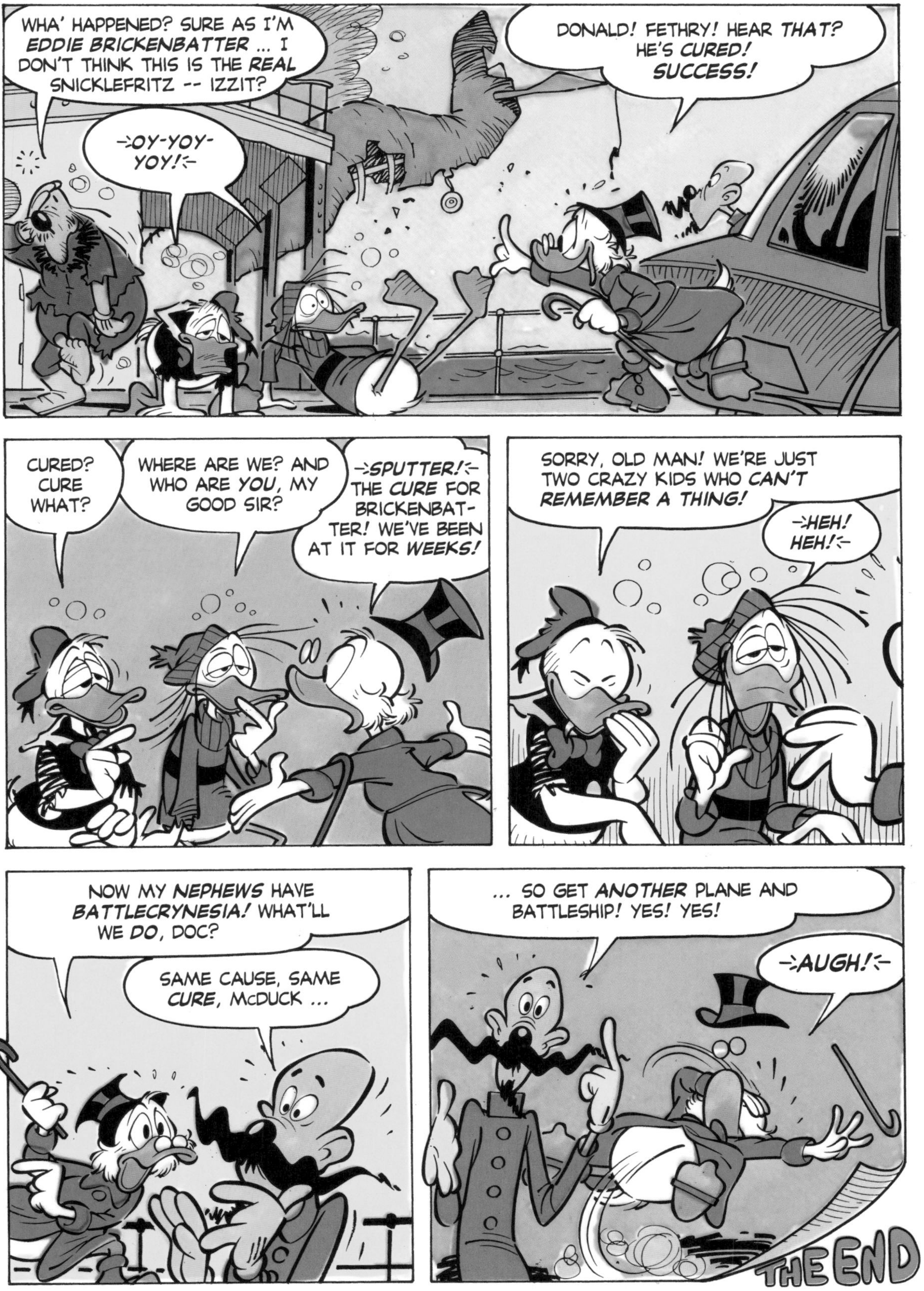
WHA' HAPPENED? SURE AS I'M EDDIE BRICKENBATTER ... I DON'T THINK THIS IS THE REAL SNICKLEFRITZ -- IZZIT?
-OY-YOY-YOY!-
DONALD! FETHRY! HEAR THAT? HE'S CURED! SUCCESS!
CURED? CURE WHAT?
WHERE ARE WE? AND WHO ARE YOU, MY GOOD SIR?
-SPUTTER!- THE CURE FOR BRICKENBATTER! WE'VE BEEN AT IT FOR WEEKS!
SORRY, OLD MAN! WE'RE JUST TWO CRAZY KIDS WHO CAN'T REMEMBER A THING!
-HEH! HEH!-
NOW MY NEPHEWS HAVE BATTLECRYNESIA! WHAT'LL WE DO, DOC?
SAME CAUSE, SAME CURE, McDUCK ...
... SO GET ANOTHER PLANE AND BATTLESHIP! YES! YES!
-AUGH!-
THE END

# GIORGIO CAVAZZANO

### *by* SOLVEIG THIME AND DAVID GERSTEIN

BORN IN VENICE, ITALY, in 1947, Giorgio Cavazzano's interest in art started in childhood when he began working in the studio of his cousin, Luciano Capitano — himself a famous Italian Disney comics artist in the late 1950s. But in 1961, a lucky break afforded the teenage Cavazzano the opportunity to work with an even more significant Italian Disney master: Romano Scarpa (1927–2005), creator of numerous watershed Mickey Mouse and Uncle Scrooge adventures (see Volumes 1, 5, and 8 in this series).

Cavazzano inked a large number of stories for Scarpa and others, making his Disney debut as inker on a Scarpa Donald Duck story, "Secret Agent Man" (*Topolino* #370, 1962). The first story Cavazzano drew entirely on his own, "Donald Duck and the Sledgehammer Hiccups" (*Topolino*

Giorgio Cavazzano, in a 1990s Disney publicity photo. Image courtesy The Walt Disney Company Italia.

#611), was published in 1967. Over time, Cavazzano would become a trendsetting, internationally celebrated creator of Duck tales rivaling Scarpa himself.

Like Scarpa, Cavazzano made his name designing new recurring characters. Queen Reginella, ruler of a "Kingdom Under the Sea" (*Topolino* #873, 1972) and Donald's secret crush, arrived first, in a story scripted by Rodolfo Cimino. Then, with writer Guido Martina, Cavazzano created Daisy Duck's heroic alter ego, "The Dazzling Duck She-Venger" (p. 57), in

an effort to give Duckburg's womenfolk a champion and some relief from the sexism of earlier times. Cavazzano later teamed up with writer Carlo Chendi to design O.K. Quack, the naïve ducklike alien from planet Anatidae, and Humphrey Gokart, a hardboiled duck detective who would most frequently team up with Donald's fad-chasing cousin, Fethry.

Cavazzano's success soon grew beyond Ducks. In the 1970s and 1980s, working with scriptwriter Giorgio Pezzin (b. 1949), Cavazzano began drawing comics features for non-Disney Italian magazines: the bears "Oscar and Tango" for *Il Messaggero dei Ragazzi*, detectives "Walkie and Talkie" for *Il Corriere dei Piccoli*, the con artists "Smalto and Johnny" for *Il Mago*, and — with coauthor Romano Garofalo — the scruffy detective Slim Norton. In addition to those comedic features, Cavazzano also drew serious science fiction comics for the magazine *Alter* in a realistic style quite unlike his other work.

This is not, however, to say that Cavazzano's more typical comedies were drawn in a traditional Disney style — or even a traditional funny animal style. In his formative years, Cavazzano was most heavily inspired not by Carl Barks, but by the Franco-Belgian school of cartooning, encompassing comics

I DON'T S'POSE YOU FILED YOUR INCOME TAX IN APRIL?
...GOT AN EXTENSION...
OH! POSTPONIN' TH' HASSLE, EH? TH' B&B CELLBLOCK TAX PREPARATION CO. IS HERE TO HELP!
?
SQUEEK!
TAKE THIS DOWN, 176-21! BUSINESS INCOME...$1,500,000! CAPITAL GAINS... $2,000,000! FARM INCOME...$25,000 AND ONE COW!
WAK! 1040...FORM 1040!

"The Fifty Money Bins Caper" (*Almanacco Topolino* #118, 1966; American version from *Uncle Scrooge* #404, June 2011), written by Michele Gazzarri, was an early example of a Scarpa story Cavazzano inked — whose influence was evident in these wide-bottomed Donald and Beagle Boys designs. Translation by David Gerstein.

such as René Goscinny and Albert Uderzo's *Asterix* and André Franquin's *Spirou.*[1] From the start of his career, Cavazzano brought the bounce and exaggeration of these influences into his Disney work. Then in the 1970s, Cavazzano entered his "techno phase," in which he intermingled his bouncy characters with strikingly realistic machinery and hi-tech gadgets. Many "techno" stories were scripted for Cavazzano by his friend and colleague, Giorgio Pezzin. This volume's title story, "The Forgetful Hero" (p. 153) is an especially beloved example. While its "Bristol Beaufighter" plane looks realistic at first, things get hilariously surreal as Donald and Fethry are asked to reenact a famous crash again and again — and somehow rebuild the wrecked plane themselves after each collision.

Cavazzano's "techno" style entered his non-Disney work as well. Between 1975 and 1986, with writer Tiziano Sclavi (b. 1953), he produced the detective comic *Altai & Johnson*, characterized by that same stylized look. In 1979, for a German publisher, Cavazzano and Sclavi created a second comics feature, *Peter O'Pencil*, focusing on a greenhorn reporter in the Wild West.

Ironically, while Cavazzano drew a lot of non-Disney detective stories and Westerns, the 1960s and 1970s saw him rarely inclined to work with Mickey Mouse, the Disney character most often cast in such stories. As Cavazzano later explained, he enjoyed the early Mickey work of Floyd Gottfredson, but found the then-current Mouse comics less inspiring.[2] In the 1980s, however, a journalist friend suggested that Cavazzano create a Mickey story spoofing the classic film *Casablanca* (1942), and Cavazzano decided to try using Gottfredson-inspired character designs and poses. The thrill of creating this story, and the success of the result, led to another movie parody — director

1 Frank Stajano, "Giorgio Cavazzano," in *Walt Disney's World of the Dragonlords* (Gemstone Publishing, 2005), p. 183.

2 Giorgio Cavazzano, "From Mouseton to Casablanca," in *Walt Disney's Mickey Mouse Volume 8: "The Tomorrow Wars"* (Fantagraphics Books, 2015), p. 12.

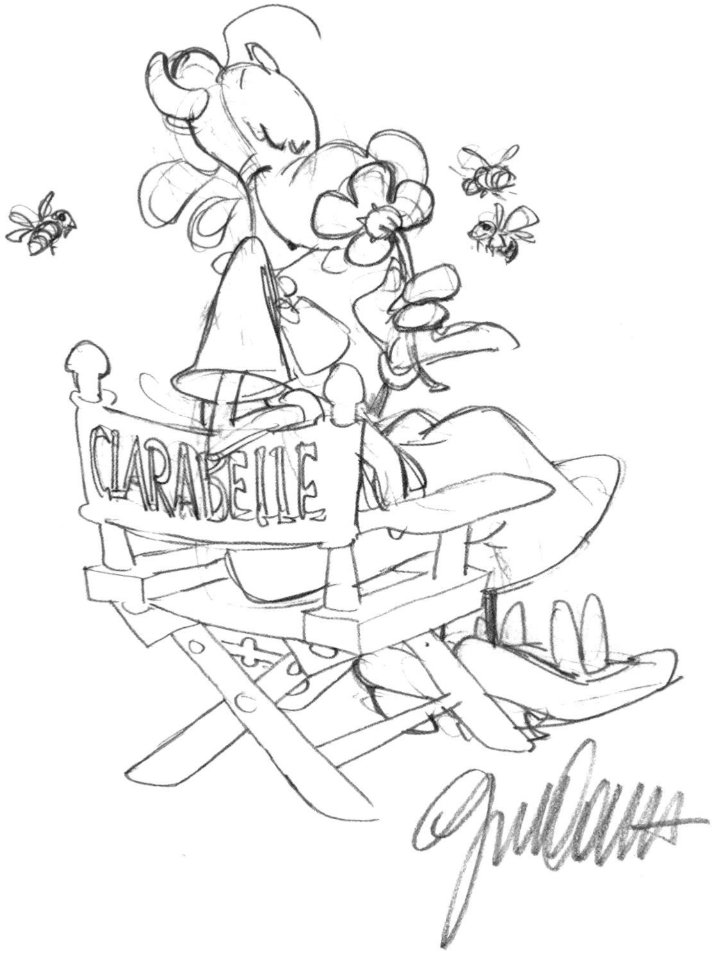
CLARABELLE

Clarabelle Cow found new stardom in Cavazzano's "Roaring '20s" series. Sketch courtesy The Walt Disney Company Italia.

Federico Fellini personally asked Cavazzano for a Mickey pastiche of his own *La Strada* (1954). The end product, acclaimed by Fellini himself, was another deeply felt personal triumph for Cavazzano — who, inspired by the experience, would thereafter draw as many Mickey stories as Duck tales. In the late 1990s, a poll of *Topolino* readers found that the most popular story of the decade, "The Case of the Cut-Off Calls" (p. 101), was a Cavazzano-drawn Mickey.

Over time, Cavazzano began to draw for publishers outside of Italy. His work on the classic French comic characters *Spiff and Hercules* — a bourgeois dog and chiseling cat — was followed by French Disney stories drawn for Hachette, publishers of the long-lived weekly *Le Journal De Mickey*. In 1988, Cavazzano began his best-known Hachette series: "Clarabelle's Roaring '20s", costume-drama tales with Mickey's gossipy cow pal as a Jazz Age roving reporter. Then, with Journal de Mickey writer Francois Corteggiani, Cavazzano created another popular non-Disney comics character, *Timothée Titan*.

The 21st century has found Cavazzano crafting Disney and non-Disney comics for all kinds of international venues. For Nordic comics production house Egmont, Cavazzano drew "World of the Dragonlords" (German *Donald Duck Sonderheft* #189–200, 2003–2004), a Duck family sword-and-sorcery miniseries written by Gladstone Publishing veteran Byron Erickson. For The Walt Disney Company Italia, Cavazzano once again visually designed popular new characters: Mickey's wild explorer pal, Eurasia Toft, and Detective Casey's tough-cop partner, Brick Boulder, co-created by writers Andrea "Casty" Castellan and Tito Faraci, respectively.

Cavazzano drew "The Persistence of Mickey" (*Topolino* #2861, 2010), the official tie-in story to the Disney/Salvador Dali team-up film *Destino* (2003). And Cavazzano turns up today as guest artist for all manner of non-Disney European comics series, from Alfredo Castelli's *Martin Mystery* to Angela and Luciana Giussani's *Diabolik*.

Giorgio Cavazzano's vital, adventurous versions of Donald, Mickey, Clarabelle, and the gang have inspired two generations of Disney pros and aficionados in Europe and around the world.

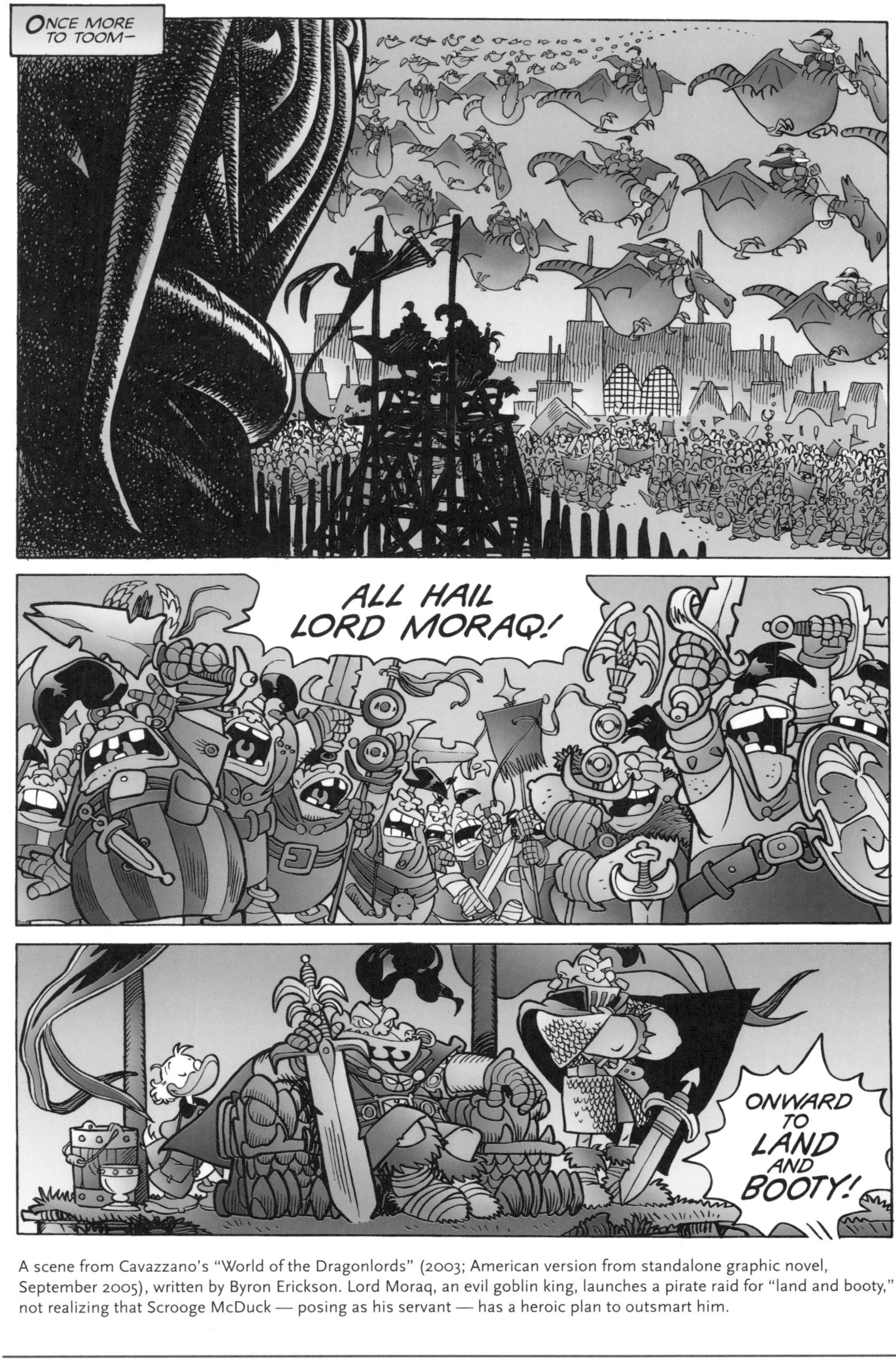
ONCE MORE TO TOOM—
ALL HAIL LORD MORAQ!
ONWARD TO LAND AND BOOTY!

A scene from Cavazzano's "World of the Dragonlords" (2003; American version from standalone graphic novel, September 2005), written by Byron Erickson. Lord Moraq, an evil goblin king, launches a pirate raid for "land and booty," not realizing that Scrooge McDuck — posing as his servant — has a heroic plan to outsmart him.

# DISNEY MASTERS

**ROMANO SCARPA**
Volume 8

**MASSIMO DE VITA**
Volume 9

**MAU AND BAS HEYMANS**
Volume 10

**MASSIMO DE VITA**
Volume 11

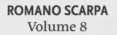

*Plus...*

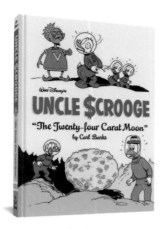

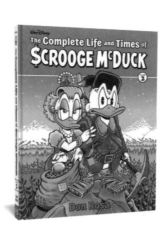

**CARL BARKS**

**DON ROSA**

**FLOYD GOTTFREDSON**